Her Dark

SALVATION

Her Dark SALVATION

KATELYN BREHM

To MIT

Author's Note

I chose not to italicize the Italian words and phrases throughout this book. I wanted the characters' speech to flow seamlessly between American English and Italian given they are first-generation Italian-Americans. In addition to Italian, I used Italian-American slang (e.g. capisce, goomar, stunad, etc.) to lend authenticity to the regional Italian-American experience. Any mistakes in the application of Italian or Italian-American slang are entirely my own, but the sins were committed despite my best intentions as well as the heroic efforts of my two Italian-language reviewers, Giulia and Sara, who were incredibly patient with my misapplication of mia and mio and my rampant use of the word capisce.

Chapter One

Marco

Boston, Massachusetts, December 1965

The whine of an approaching streetcar tore through the quiet twilight and consumed all other sound. Even the heavy breathing and soft moans of the woman whose warm blood coated my tongue.

From the shadowed alcove between buildings, I lifted my gaze. The vehicle lumbered toward us, swaying on its tracks under the erratic glow of a single flickering streetlamp.

Tony'd be on that train. Right on time for dinner with my family. And for me to drop the bomb that had been ticking away in my head for weeks.

Renee shifted, pressing herself close. I tugged on her hair to expose more of her neck and took a sinfully deep drink. Steam rose from where my fangs sank into her flesh. She groaned and dug her fingers into my forearm, her body pliant and given over to sensation.

The rattle and shriek of the streetcar persisted, demanding an answer. I drew in a final mouthful of blood. The force of my pull injected more of my venom into her veins, enough to push her over the edge, and she shook through a feeding-induced release.

I freed her from my bite. Two drops of blood trailed down the pale length of her neck from holes that stared back at me like my own red eyes. I licked the wounds to staunch the bleeding, and she shivered through an aftershock.

I eased her out of my arms until she stood under her own weight. She leaned against the side of the building, and her head fell back to rest on the brick.

Eyes dilated and cheeks flushed, her lips pulled up at the corners. "Marco," she said with a breathy sigh. "That was…"

Filling? Energizing?

The streetcar screeched to a stop. Perfect timing. I licked my lips and stepped out of the alcove, satisfied, but not in the same way as Renee.

She was a nice enough girl even if too attached to feeding. Not that I was complaining. I'd used her before. So had others. No shame in sharing willing Sources. But I didn't want any complications, and Renee would've liked nothing better than to engage in complications.

I grabbed her hand, turned it over, and placed four dollars in her palm. "Get yourself home, Renee."

She closed her fingers around the cash and shoved it in her pocket. "Why don't you come with me?" Husky need laced her invitation, and she pushed off the wall, stepping toward me with hooded eyes. A provocative smile danced on her lips, and she trailed a gloved fingertip down the buttons of my waistcoat and hooked it around the inside of my belt buckle.

I jerked her hand away from my body. She winced but needed the reminder; my answer to her come-ons would never change.

Seduction transformed into amusement, and the pouty shape of her lips arched into a sly grin. "You'll ring me next time?"

"Your blood's as good as anyone's," I muttered and released her wrist.

She straightened her scarf, smoothed the loose strands of hair peeking out from beneath her hat, and stepped onto the platform. The sway of her hips turned heads, drawing both leers and reproach.

I swiped a hand down my face; I needed to find a new Source.

Renee'd grown tiresome. She wanted more than my teeth in her neck. She wanted my cock in her cunt, but that was never going to happen. I didn't fuck where I fed, and Renee was a pleasure junkie who wanted sex as badly as she wanted a feeding. No doubt at the same time if she could manage it. Wouldn't be hard. There were plenty of blood demons who fed for more than necessity, even more who didn't have my hang-ups about feeding and sex.

Passengers disembarked and walked with fast-paced determination away from the train, weaving paths between those clambering to get on. They shoved their hands into their pockets and turned their collars up against the early December wind. Tony's imposing frame stepped off the last car, and his long legs quickly carried him across the platform. He adjusted the brim of his fedora, pulling it low to mask his eyes. I did the same, and when he reached the alcove where I waited, I fell in step alongside him.

We crossed the tracks and headed north toward the Italian end of the city, our turf and our safety. We walked in silence until the cars, pedestrians, and noise of the Haymarket drowned out our conversation.

"I want out," I said.

He eyed me sideways, and his surprise and concern drilled into my skull. I'd expected backlash—loud words announcing my stupidity followed by a string of Italian profanities. Instead, the soles of our leather Oxfords clapped the pavement, the sound deafening against the strained silence.

"Not easy," he said. "Not impossible. But not easy."

The dangerous urge to trust his reaction thrashed against my skepticism and the cold reality of my life. Antonio Moretti was my best friend, my brother-in-arms if not in blood, and I trusted him, but not as much as I trusted his loyalty to Cosa Nostra.

"Remember when we were kids?" he asked. "And the Gallo twins jumped me outside Salvatore's?"

I grunted. How could I forget?

"The old man didn't bat an eye. Kept slicing prosciutto and singing to himself over that damned radio of his while they pulled me into the alley."

"He had a terrible voice."

"The worst."

Tony stopped me with a hand on my arm. "You came outta nowhere—arms swinging, fists flying, even though they were twice our size."

I remembered. I remembered the rags hanging off Tony's starved body. They'd been in even worse shape than my own sorry excuse for clothing. I remembered how the red glow of his eyes had dimmed amid the streaks of dirt and blood covering his face, his strength waning with each starved attempt to fight back. And I remembered those idiot Gallo bullies shaking down a street kid with nothing left. That had been the first time we met.

"My life changed that day, and I'll never forget who changed it. Sei mio fratello, Marco." The conviction in his voice and the sincerity in his dark eyes told me he meant every word.

I clenched my teeth and gave him a short nod. We'd come a long way since those early days, and we'd done it together. I should've known that would be enough.

We resumed our march and crossed the border into the North End.

"Can't be the money's turning you off," Tony said dryly.

I snorted. "I like money, and you know what I'm willing to do to get it." Illegal fights and gambling. Loans and protection. Extortion and armed robbery. I'd been at the game for twenty-three years. "But Vinnie's invested in the narcotics racket, and Big Frankie isn't stopping him. That's where I draw the line. I want out."

Big Frankie Valenzano had given me a chance to pull my family out of squalor, turn the DeVita name into one people respected. I'd taken it. No regrets. But Big Frankie was human. He wouldn't be around forever, and Vinnie was set to take over as boss of the Valenzano crime family. I wanted out before a federal indictment was pointed at my head like a loaded gun. One of the New York capos had already been pinched by the feds. Was doing fifteen-to-twenty on narcotics charges. I couldn't provide for my family if I was in jail. Or dead. Human jails weren't staffed with Sources.

Not to mention the damage inflicted by that drug shit.

That was the difference between made men like me and Tony and an underboss like Vinnie. Tony and I came up from nothing. Hell, Tony was an orphan, a street rat before he started working for the Valenzanos. But Vinnie'd been born into privilege. Grew up with a silver spoon, however tarnished. He hadn't lived what we'd lived or seen what we'd seen on the streets. Starvation from lack of food or blood or drugs, it didn't matter. It was real, and it was ugly. And I wanted nothing to do with creating that kind of pain.

"Fuck, Tony, you know what it's like to need something. Big Frankie's Source racket makes money for a reason. We don't have a choice. We need blood. But drugs?" I shot him a hard look. "That shit's inflicted. That addiction doesn't need to exist." My jaw tightened. "I won't be a part of it."

"We all have our limits, Marco. Sounds like you found yours."

I'd taken several steps before I realized he'd stopped. I pivoted to face him. The streetlamps lining Hanover Street cast a soft glow through the twilight. They illuminated the steam rising from the sewers and the serious expression on Tony's face.

"But I haven't found mine yet," he finished.

Cars rumbled and clanked atop the century-old cobbles. Pedestrians sped down the sidewalk and across the street. Diners hurried into restaurants, escaping icy snaps of wind. Amid the commotion, two brothers stood at a crossroads.

"Our relationship will change," he said. "Once you're out."

My body tensed. "I know."

He stepped forward and clasped my arm. "But we'll always be brothers."

I clapped my hand over his. "Grazie."

The remaining twilight had waned while we'd discussed my future, a silent reminder we were late. We darted between cars and turned down one of the narrow cross streets. Unending walls of red brick rose on either side of us, fragmented by the soft light emanating from first-story windows and the occasional front-door lamp. A few neighborhood kids ran by. The leader shouted over his shoulder for his followers to hurry up. Muted voices and the clang of pots and pans accompanied the faint aroma of pasta and garlic. My stomach rumbled.

"When you gonna tell Big Frankie?" Tony asked.

"Tomorrow."

"So soon?"

I shrugged. "I've been thinking about this for weeks."

"What's your plan?"

"Not sure." I didn't want to divulge too much. I couldn't.

Not with this new relationship. "I have a lead on some real estate near the Commons. Always preferred that end of the business."

He arched an eyebrow and gave me a knowing grin. Yeah. Things had already changed.

A soft light illuminated the short set of stairs that led up to the front door of my family home. My sister stood at the top of the steps and hugged her shawl close around her shoulders. She folded her arms when she saw us and glared.

"Marco. Antonio. Era ora. You're late."

I stood on the bottom step, and with my height, met her eye to eye. "Gina, la mia cara sorella." I kissed her on either side of her stern mouth. "We were busy with work." I opened my eyes wide with innocence and penance.

She bit the inside of her cheek, trying not to smile, but then I delivered my killing blow. I winked. She huffed out a laugh and punched me in the shoulder. "Fine. You deal with Mamma. You know how she gets if her sauce gets cold." She opened the door and waved us up the stairs.

Warmth, light, and the smell of Mamma's cooking mingled with the crisp winter wind.

Tony groaned and pushed past me. "Braciole! Ottimo!" He stopped when he reached Gina and greeted her with kisses before he removed his hat and stepped inside.

"Antonio!" Mamma called from the kitchen. "Finalmente! It's getting cold!"

I chuckled.

My sister arched an eyebrow. "You better get in there."

"Go. Tell Mamma to start. I need a minute."

She narrowed her eyes.

I gave her arm a reassuring squeeze. "I'm fine. Just need to clear my head."

She hesitated, but patted my hand and went inside, shutting the door behind her.

I leaned against the inside of the stairwell and faced the cold Boston night. I pulled out half a Cuban cigar I'd cut earlier in the day and considered how something so simple could change so much.

The flick of the match crackled through the quiet, and I puffed, each drag longer than the last until the cigar was lit. I pulled the thick, fragrant smoke into my mouth and held it there, letting the flavors swirl on my tongue and sting the back of my throat. The conflict of sensation calmed my nerves, and ease spread across my shoulders.

Twenty-three years. I'd worked for the Valenzano crime family for twenty-three years.

The red end of the stolen cigar burned hot and intense. Like my life. So easily snuffed out.

We'd lifted the illegal Cubans from a truck bound for New York three years ago, one of the last shipments that made it into the States before Kennedy's embargo. I'd kept an eye on the specialty importer, knew when cargo was set to leave the docks. The Valenzanos were connected with the New England Teamsters. The drivers handed me tips, and I gave them a cut. They were smart enough to know a planned hijack was better for their health.

Me and Tony made a shitload off that haul. So did Big Frankie. It was the job that tipped the scales. Six months later, we were made men.

Smoke swirled through the night, and guilt churned in my stomach. The Valenzanos had saved me and Tony, and the weight of that debt wasn't something I could easily shake. We were family, brothers, bonded by the demon blood that ran through our veins and the oaths we'd taken to Cosa Nostra, and I was about to sever one of those bonds.

I stepped into the street and looked back at the row house I'd bought for my family as soon as I'd earned enough to get us out of the rat-infested shithole we used to call home. Through the gap between the curtains, Gina threw her head back in laughter. Tony stepped into view, and she grabbed his arm, covering her heart as she laughed. Tony continued his story, his face relaxed and amused.

I turned back to the street—cold, dirty, unforgiving—a stark contrast to our bright and inviting home.

I'd done what I'd needed to do to protect my family, to make sure we didn't go hungry. So had Mamma.

A memory flashed, a scene from a movie I'd tried to forget. I pushed it away, disgusted. I didn't want to think about what Mamma had sacrificed to put food on our table. The blood that stained my hands was for her. To make sure she never had to sell her blood again. To make sure Gina was never faced with that decision.

But I couldn't protect them if I starved to death in a federal penitentiary doing hard time for narcotics. It didn't matter how much I owed Big Frankie. The DeVitas came first.

A sharp blast of wind struck my face. I chewed the bitter end of my cigar and popped my collar against its brutality.

The front door opened and shut with a click, and my sister stepped up next to me, her sweet perfume cutting through the earthy smoke. "She's grumbling about ungrateful sons who no longer appreciate their mamma's cooking."

I chuckled and tossed the butt of my cigar onto the pavement, snuffing out the final smoldering ember with the toe of my shoe. Gina shivered beneath her shawl and rubbed her arms. I placed a hand on her shoulder and led us inside.

The light and warmth of home wrapped its comforting arms around me, and I paused to take in the familiar scene. Gina walked into the kitchen and sat next to Tony. They picked up their animated conversation, loud and fast Italian interrupted with bouts of my sister's infectious laughter. The scrape of cutlery on china and the trickle of wine into crystal. Mamma served up thick slices of steaming braciole, and Papà poured wine while getting a lecture, "Not too much!" Garlic, tomato, and parmesan beckoned.

We'd come a long way since my childhood. No more haggard faces huddled over thin soup and stale bread in a one-room, basement apartment.

Mamma threw me a pointed look. I took off my hat, shrugged out of my coat, and hung both next to the door before taking my seat at the head of the table.

The four people I cherished most in the world ate, drank, and laughed. For two decades, I'd been secure in the knowledge I could provide for them and keep them safe with the power of the Valenzanos at my back. Tomorrow, I'd talk to Big Frankie and all responsibility would fall on my shoulders and my shoulders alone.

Determination steeled my resolve. I'd sacrifice anything to provide for each person at that table, to protect blood demons and immigrants, anyone in our community who couldn't protect themselves. But I'd do it my way, without Vinnie or his drug money.

Back to basics. Bribes, extortion, gambling. These were the rackets I knew, the rackets that got me made. Back to my roots. Even if it meant building my own empire.

Chapter Two

Anna

Cambridge, Massachusetts, January 2024

Students had returned from the holiday break, and their presence was suffocating. Another reminder that the first day of second semester was fast approaching. Its imminent arrival tightened beneath my chin like a noose, cutting off my air and threatening to snap my neck.

They packed the length of the Infinite Corridor, MIT's main thoroughfare, and I darted between them as if they were obstacles on a course, speed-walking toward the east-end of campus and my meeting with the dean. Excitement propelled my legs as much as nerves, my mind's singular focus on securing my escape.

And the fact that I considered going on sabbatical an escape reinforced just how badly I needed a change.

MIT's campus was a maze of interconnected buildings, its tunnels and corridors an afterthought resulting in a confusing web of disjointed parts. I'd been so lost the first time I'd navigated the labyrinth twenty years ago, a new doctoral candidate in Corporate Finance, trying to make sense of all the nameless schools and offices with only numbers as my guide.

Now, at forty-five, I walked the halls just as bewildered as before, but this time, it wasn't the building numbers throwing me off. It was my life.

Countless paths unfolded before me, speeding away from my present into myriad futures. I had no idea which path to follow. All I knew was I couldn't stay on my current trajectory. It ran right into a dead end.

Another ten minutes and I entered the Sloan School's main building. I darted down the corridor and up the stairs to the dean's office, eager to get this over with and move on. His office door was ajar, and I pushed it open so he could see me. He was on the phone and waved me in. I removed my coat, folded it over my arm, and sat in the chair on the opposite side of his cluttered desk.

"Yes. Yes, I understand. But the endowment simply does not cover those types of expenses. There's nothing I can do."

I glanced around his office and tried not to cringe even though my body was going through a visceral reaction to the mess. Stacks of books and papers littered the floor, and instead of neat rows on the shelf, books laid piled on their sides or askew, half-cocked out of their homes. Dirty coffee mugs adorned the windowsill, and old posters from a conference that had happened over a year ago leaned against the far wall.

Academia. There were reasons for the scatter-brained-professor stereotype, and the evidence occupied Tim Fletcher's office. I blinked hard to erase the chaos from my mind.

"All right, then. Yes. Thank you. Goodbye." He hung up the phone, took off his glasses, and rubbed his eyes. "There's a certain irony to my life." He replaced his glasses and gave me a tired smile.

His disheveled gray hair was in desperate need of a cut, and he looked ten years older than I knew him to be, face drawn like he hadn't slept in days.

Guilt seized me. The last thing I wanted to do was pile more stress on Tim's shoulders. He didn't deserve it. He already handled more than his fair share for the department. But I had no choice. I'd reached my breaking point.

"If someone would have told me how much time I'd spend dealing with the finances of the Finance Department, I'd have never become dean." I huffed out a chuckle. "What can I do for you, Anna?"

"I know the start of the semester is only a couple weeks away, but"—my stomach rolled—"I'd like to go on sabbatical."

The older man's head rocked back in surprise. "This is unexpected. And not exactly the best timing."

"I know. I'm sorry. I know it's a lot to ask, but I'm only scheduled to teach one, first-year class. Jack Owens said he'd be happy to teach it for me. He's taught it before, and he just finished that big research grant with the Fed. He was planning on taking it easy this semester. No research. I'm between grants myself."

He studied me as if he suspected I was a pod person and not really Anna Barone.

Before he could ask any questions, I cleared my throat and straightened my spine. I'd gone over my argument countless times the night before and was determined to get through my speech without interruption.

"I've been tenured for ten years, taught in this department for almost fifteen, and I've never taken a sabbatical. My publications are consistent in both quantity and quality, my research grants steady. I've taught every class the department has asked me to teach." I swallowed and blew out a heavy breath. "And if I don't get a break, I might—I might just quit."

His eyes widened, and his mouth fell soundlessly open. He studied me for a long moment before leaning forward and clasping his hands atop the desk. "This isn't like you, Anna. Is everything okay? What's going on?"

"I need a break, Tim. An extended break. From academia specifically. I—I'm not sure I want to do this anymore."

"I'm surprised. You have tenure."

He said tenure with such gravitas I almost second guessed myself. Almost.

"And not that it's any of my business, but what would you do instead?" The question was clipped like he took personal offense at the idea someone might not want to be entombed in the annals of academia.

But that was the question, wasn't it?

"That's part of the reason I want to take a sabbatical. I need some space, some time to think. I'm too burnt out to put a plan together. All I know is I want industry experience. I want to apply my research to real-world problems." He opened his mouth to interrupt, but I held up a staying hand, and he clamped it shut. "And before you say I already do that with data sets from industry, it's not the same. I want to work in an office without worrying about teaching or research or publishing."

"I see."

He sat back, steepled his fingers, and regarded me warily. "You do have an impeccable record of service to the department, and your research in financial modeling is unparalleled." The words came out more begrudging admission than sincere compliment, and I waited for the inevitable caveat. "You found someone to teach your class. Thank you for that."

"It was the least I could do on such short notice."

"But..."

And there it was. My stomach dropped, and my mind

raced through the different ways he might finish his sentence and destroy my plans. "But what?"

"I understand burn-out. It happens to the best of us. But I think this decision is ill-advised."

I scrunched my face. "How so?"

He removed his glasses and cleaned them with a handkerchief he lifted from his shirt pocket. "May I be frank, Professor?"

"Of course," I said, though I was sure I wasn't going to like whatever came next.

"You don't have the temperament to work in corporate finance."

His words punched me in the chest. I sat in stunned silence as decades-old self-doubt resurfaced to knock the wind out of my sails.

He spread his arms and shrugged. "Let's face it, Anna. You belong in academia. Can you really see yourself in a boardroom full of executives talking over each other and pushing agendas? I've never seen you get more than a word in edgewise at a professional conference. Not unless you were giving a talk, or someone asked you a direct question." He leaned forward. "You spent the last three department-industry mixers sitting at the bar with my admin!"

My cheeks heated, embarrassed by my personality for the first time in over a decade. He'd thrown my deepest insecurities in my face in less than a minute, transporting me back to graduate school and the chain of events that had led to this exact moment.

International finance is no place for a mouse. Better try accounting. Or maybe teaching.

The asshole executive who'd given me that "advice" at an industry meet-and-greet during my first year at Harvard Business School had lived rent free in my head for years. Funny how one stranger's off-the-cuff remark could destroy a person's confidence and change the course of their life.

And Tim Fletcher had just tried to do the same thing.

My temper simmered, poised and ready to boil over, but I tamped down the hot waters. Yes, he'd played on my insecurities to try and manipulate me into staying, but could I blame him? I'd just waltzed into his office two weeks before the start of the semester and thrown him a major curve ball. He was drowning in work and grasping for an easy way to keep his head above water, but I refused to take the bait.

I straightened my spine, folded my hands in my lap, and cleared my throat. "Be that as it may," I said, keeping my voice level and professional, "I'd still like to request a sabbatical. Will you approve it?"

He stared at me over a tight mouth, no doubt racking his brain for a valid excuse to deny my request. After a moment, he exhaled, and his shoulders descended. "Pending confirmation from Jack Owens he'll take your class... Yes, I'll approve it."

I sprang to my feet. "Thank you! Thank you so much! And again, sorry for the short notice. I'll send an email to you and Jack about the class and file the paperwork. Please let me know if there's anything else I can do."

He removed his glasses, waved them at me, and rubbed his eyes. "Good luck, Anna."

"Thanks, Tim."

I dashed out of his office and out of the finance building, making a beeline for Kendall Square. Long-buried memories fueled my hurried strides.

Smart, eager, and excellent with numbers, I'd always assumed my abilities would speak for themselves and never once considered my introverted, quiet nature would be seen as a liability. Not until that meet-and-greet. The event was intended to connect first-years with the big-name consulting and investment firms that ran up and down the East Coast. But instead of a potential employer, I'd received a slap in the face.

I'd cried myself to sleep that night, my dreams crushed beneath the heel of one man's dismissal. After that, I'd stood on the sidelines at every event, completely paralyzed, my confidence shattered. I'd bought into his rhetoric, convinced myself I didn't have what it took to enter his world.

Graduation sped toward me like a freight train and, with it, uncertainty about my future. My advisor suggested I transfer to MIT and pursue a doctorate instead of working in industry.

It's the best environment for your gentle temperament, Ms. Barone.

Gentle temperament. I snorted. She'd never seen me get into it with Jeff.

Which reminded me... I checked my watch. Twenty to one. Just enough time to make it to Harvard Square for a lunch meeting with my best friend.

Whether or not it was true, that conversation had been the final nail in the coffin of my plan to enter industry. I'd transferred to MIT after finishing my MBA at Harvard and never left.

The irony? I wasn't the nervous, mousey woman I'd been in my early twenties. Hadn't been for years. I'd grown. But like the elephant who'd been tied to a tree as a baby, I'd learned not to try and break free. The strong, independent woman I'd become remained tied to a stump.

Well, I just cut the rope.

A smile crept across my face. The suffocating dread that had weighed on my chest for weeks at the thought of another semester trapped inside those halls finally lifted.

I sped down the steps of the Kendall Square T stop. A burst of stale subway air and screeching rails heralded an oncoming train and my future. I was free. For the next six months, I was free.

Now, if only I could get a jump start on the rest of my life.

HARVARD SQUARE HUMMED WITH ACTIVITY. City workers stood on ladders to take down the holiday decorations still hanging from lampposts. Students reunited with friends. Fast-walking professionals skirted half-melted piles of dirty snow. I crossed the square to meet my best friend for lunch and attempt to rationally explain upending my career.

The glass doors of Scholar's Café opened with a whoosh. A wall of overly warm air blew my hair into disarray and had me blinking back tears. Coffee, sugar, and freshly baked bread filled my nostrils, and the familiar combination soothed my frayed nerves.

I ordered a cappuccino and biscotti and carried them to a table near the foggy glass walls. I wiped my hand through the condensation to watch the passersby while I waited for the inevitable reckoning with my best friend.

"Hey," Jeff said. "Sorry I'm late."

"You're not late. I just got here myself."

He slung his coat over the chairback, tossed his newsboy cap on the table, and ran his hand back and forth across the close-cropped, salt-and-pepper remnants of a once-full head of coarse curls. He must have walked, because his dark brown skin was ruddy from the cold at the tip of his nose and across his broad cheekbones. He patted himself down as if he'd forgotten something, and when he didn't find the missing item, sat in the chair across from me.

"Traffic was brutal across the bridge." He removed his

wire-rimmed glasses and cleaned them with the end of his scarf. "I forgot how busy it gets with all the kids back. It's like the cabbie was playing Frogger on Mass Ave. I couldn't take it. Got out at Central Square and walked." He inspected his handiwork and set the glasses back on his nose.

"That's why I take the T." I lifted my cappuccino in salute and took a sip of the milky goodness. "You look good. I haven't seen you since before break. You and Michael were in New York?"

"Yeah. He's still there. Alex is about to pop. Due any day now. I had to get back for work." Alex was Michael's sister, and with their tight-knit family, I wasn't surprised he'd hung back.

"Kinda stinks being the boss, doesn't it?"

He grunted. "How are your parents?"

"They're good. They send their love. Wanted to know when you and Michael are going to visit."

"When the scraps of hair I have left on my head aren't on fire."

I snorted. "Is CMG that busy?"

"Food first." Jeff had a singular focus at mealtimes, and it centered around his stomach. He scanned the café until he found a waiter, flagged him down, and ordered a cappuccino for himself and a caprese sandwich for us to split, a tradition as old as our friendship. "And yes, CMG is that busy. Hence this last-minute lunch."

He placed his palms flat on the table. "Okay," he announced in his I'm-The-President-Of-Cambridge-Management-Group voice.

I eyed him cautiously.

"A new job came in yesterday. I usually do the work for this client myself given his high-profile and non-disclosure requirements, but—and I can't believe I'm about to admit this

—I don't have the expertise to do this work on the timeline he needs. But you do."

I arched an eyebrow over the mug I held poised at my lips.

He raised his hands, conceding an unspoken point. "I know the semester starts in two weeks, but I'm really in a bind. The type of financial modeling this job requires is way outside my wheelhouse. I wouldn't even know where to start. At a minimum, I'd need you to come up with a plan, but even then, it would take me twice as long to do the work, if not longer, and my client wants results fast."

"What type of modeling? What's the objective?"

He shook his head. "I can't tell you that. Not until you meet with him and sign an NDA. But I can tell you that your research is directly applicable. It's an international, privately owned company, and the work is for their European branch. Frankly, I can't do this without you."

A rush of adrenaline shot through my body and surprised the hell out of me. It took me a moment to register where it came from, but I finally recognized it as genuine excitement at the prospect of doing something, literally anything, different than research and teaching.

"I know the timing is terrible, but this project has a short fuse. And there are still two weeks before classes start. You said you had a light teaching load this semester, right?"

"It's lighter than you think."

Jeff's eyebrows drew together. "What do you mean?"

"I'm taking a sabbatical."

And just as quickly, they launched to his non-existent hairline. "What? Since when?"

"Since about"—I checked my watch—"an hour ago. Give or take."

"Two weeks before the start of the semester?"

"Yes."

"Is it your parents? I thought you said they're okay."

"No, it's not my parents. They're fine."

Concern etched lines in my best friend's face. I sipped my cappuccino, searching for comfort, strength, and the right words.

"I don't want to be a professor anymore," I blurted before I chickened out.

Jeff's mug froze midair, and his eyelids moved through a slow blink. He set the mug down, and his mouth opened then closed. He pressed his lips into a line and studied me. It wasn't often Jeff's opinionated mouth was rendered speechless, but then again, I'd just dropped the Anna-equivalent of an H-bomb.

"My sentiments exactly," I said. "More so now after saying it out loud." I rested my elbow on the table and slumped my chin into my hand. "I don't want to do this anymore, Jeff. I'm so over it."

"You're over it?" His frozen shock shattered into a hysterical laugh, and he leaned forward. "Anna. You're a tenured professor at MIT, the best school in the world, and you're *over it*?"

"Yup." I nodded. "Over it."

He reclined in his chair, scrubbed a hand across his head, and glanced around searching for our waiter. "I think I'm going to need something stronger than coffee."

I gave him a wry smile. "You and me both."

"Seriously, Anna. What's going on?"

"Seriously, I just told you. I don't want to be a professor anymore."

"Since when? You've wanted to be a professor since grad school."

I nodded vigorously and swirled the last bit of biscotti in my coffee. "I know. It *is* what I wanted." I lifted the biscotti out of the mug and held it midair sodden with milk and espresso and my dreams. A chunk fell off and landed back in my mug. "Or, at least, it's what I thought I wanted." Defeated, I popped the soggy end into my mouth and pushed the remains of my biscotti-laden cappuccino away.

He leaned forward and narrowed his eyes. "Is this some sort of midlife crisis thing? Is that what's going on here? Because Michael went through that two years ago. I bought him a Porsche, and he started getting Botox, and now he's fine."

I snorted. "I hate that term—midlife crisis. This isn't a crisis. It's an awakening. And I don't think Botox is going to help."

He sat back and folded his arms across his chest.

"Your caprese sandwich," the waiter interjected and placed our food on the table.

I smiled at the waiter, grateful for the interruption and a chance to gather my thoughts. Jeff, on the other hand, dove right in. He licked his lips, lifted his half of the sandwich, and took a huge bite.

I popped a chip into my mouth and chewed thoughtfully. "I haven't been happy in months. There's been this... this antipathy brewing. Antipathy and... resentment."

I picked up my sandwich, sunk my teeth into the freshly baked bread, tomato, and mozzarella, and let the perfect combination of basil and balsamic dance across my tastebuds. I groaned dramatically and rolled my eyes back. "How is this consistently so good?"

Jeff grunted, shrugged his shoulders, and shoved a few chips in his mouth. Forty-six and he still ate like a teenager.

"My birthday brought some clarity. I think. I know it's irrational, but something about the number forty-five." I hesitated, but I couldn't keep the tornado of troubling thoughts bottled up any longer. "There's this sense of urgency. Like I— like I need to live. Right now."

He frowned. "You are living."

I sighed dramatically, exasperated trying to explain something I didn't fully understand myself.

"I spent the entire winter break in Amherst," I said.

"You don't usually do that."

"Exactly. But this year I needed to be with my parents. In my old house."

The admission made my chest ache. I never wanted to spend time in Amherst or with my parents. One week with them in Italy the previous summer and I was ready to jump off the train. But now? I'd been back in Cambridge a little over a week, and I already missed them. I craved my family.

"A few days after Christmas, my parents took me to a new restaurant in town. They thought I'd enjoy it. *It's where all the kids your age hang out.*"

"Kids," he chuckled and shook his head.

"They weren't kidding. The place was packed with people our age. I ran into one of my friends from high school. Melissa —remember her? We went to Amherst together for undergrad?"

"Oh yeah... Melissa. The one with the..." He wiggled his finger at his face. "The nose ring."

I huffed. "An accomplished nurse practitioner and that's what you remember? The nose ring?"

He shrugged, grabbed a fistful of chips, and crammed them into his mouth until his cheeks puffed out.

I made a face at him, and he managed a "What?" through the mouthful.

I chuckled. "Disgusting."

He gave me a self-satisfied grin.

I shook my head and soldiered on. "She has a kid graduating high school this year. The other one's going to be a freshman. Her and her family were at this big table with two other couples. They all had kids, and they were coloring, and—" I choked up. The back of my throat burned with emotion, but I held back the welling tears.

"Oh, Anna." He reached out and placed his hand over mine, his eyes filled with deep understanding. "Is this about kids? I thought you'd made peace with that."

"I did." I swiped at my eyes before the tears spilled over. "It's—it's not about kids. It's..." My breath shuddered as I tried to breathe through the heartache. I'd made peace with my infertility years ago, but that didn't mean it wasn't still painful. I shook my head, trying to clear my thoughts and get back on track. "It's not about kids. It's about what they represent."

I sipped my water, trying to ease the tension, and searched for words among the flurry of emotions, but I couldn't find anything louder than the growing ache in my chest. I had to get it all out.

"Did you know I bought readers?"

Jeff's head jerked back.

"The words don't stand out on the page like they used to. And after a day staring at a computer screen..."

He tossed his napkin atop his empty plate and narrowed his eyes, exercising heroic levels of patience while I took him on this wild ride.

"I slept with David."

"Lancaster?"

"Yeah."

"That's not a face I'd want someone to make while talking about having sex with me."

David Lancaster was a professor of chemical engineering at MIT who I'd met through my running club. We'd been on a few dates, the last of which had ended in a less than remarkable trip to the bedroom.

I pointed my sandwich at Jeff. "And yet, it pretty much sums up the experience." I widened my eyes and took a bite.

He winced. "Ouch."

He scrubbed a hand across his scalp. "All right. I don't have a doctorate like some people..." He winked, and I snorted. "So, I'm gonna need you to help me out here because I'm not following. Your parents, kids, glasses, bad sex... What does any of this have to do with taking a sabbatical?"

I swallowed. This was the hard part. The part I hadn't admitted to anyone. The part that made me feel old and lost and frantic. "They're reminders. Reminders that the clock is ticking. My eyes aren't as good as they used to be. What's going to go next? My love life continues to underwhelm. I'm starting to wonder if I'll ever get to experience true love, and that kills me. I don't have a family of my own, just you and my parents, and they're not getting any younger.

"Time isn't stopping, Jeff. It's speeding ahead like a bullet train, and I keep asking myself, is this it? Is this really all there is? Is my life just my career?"

He raised an eyebrow. "A pretty spectacular career."

"Yes." I nodded. "And don't get me wrong. I don't regret it. At all. I've loved teaching. It's been rewarding helping the kids, especially the ones who really need it. And I've been successful with my research."

"Understatement."

"But I feel—I feel trapped. Limited. And I can't pretend that my career wasn't shaped, in part, by what other people told me I could and couldn't handle."

"Now, wait a minute, Anna—"

"Dean Fletcher emailed me right before the break and let me know I'd been passed over for the Deloitte partnership. They gave it to Jeannie Craft. I have no delusions as to why they did it, and spoiler alert, it's not because she's more qualified."

Jeff scowled. "That really pisses me off."

"Yup. And over the break, I kept thinking about how

many days were left until the start of the semester and I had to teach again and hold office hours and file my grant application and this..." I shook my hands searching for the right words, my shoulders tensing. "This impending sense of doom, this overwhelming dread, it took over and it kept getting worse and worse. This sense of urgency I have to live my life, it won't let up. I don't want to feel trapped anymore."

My breath came in short gusts. I closed my eyes and rested a hand over my heart to calm the panic that rose every time I thought about my future. When I opened my eyes, Jeff's were filled with empathy and worry.

"We only get so much time on this planet, and that clock keeps on ticking. Every. Single. Day. And if the only thing I have is my career, if that's all I've got to show for it, why am I living according to someone else's definition? What the hell have I done with my life?"

"Jesus, Anna." He took off his glasses and rubbed his eyes. I reached for my water with shaking fingers, but he intercepted my hand and held it. Steadied it. Steadied me. "You weren't kidding. We're way past Botox."

"Tell me about it."

"I had no idea you were going through any of this. Why didn't you say something?"

"I don't know. I thought I was being self-indulgent. Figured this was a phase, that these feelings would go away. But they haven't gone away. If anything, they've gotten worse."

"I'm a terrible friend. I should have read the signs, but..." He blew out a slow breath. "I don't know. The quiet life of a professor always seemed to suit you. You aren't exactly a social butterfly."

I released his hand and grabbed my glass, hoping a sip of water might wash down the bitter taste of Jeff's words. "True.

But I'm not the painfully shy woman you met back at Harvard either. Remember how badly I used to clam up?"

"I haven't seen deer-in-the-headlights Anna in years." The corners of his eyes crinkled with the teasing.

"Exactly. I'm never going to be the outgoing life of the party. That's just not me. But I can hold my own, especially when it comes to work. And I don't want to get to my parents' age and regret not having pursued my dream to work in industry.

"I know it's not going to fix my eyesight. And Prince Charming isn't going to swoop in on a white stallion to give me mind-blowing orgasms." Jeff's shoulders shook with laughter. "But it's a start. It's something. And at least I can say I tried."

"I'm so proud I get to call you my best friend." He beamed a wide, sparkling smile, and the truth of his words reflected in his eyes. "You're a remarkable woman, Anna. You know that, right?"

My heart squeezed with the warmth of his sincerity. "Thanks. Right now, I feel remarkably lost, but thanks."

His smile took on a mischievous bend. "Lucky for you, your best friend owns Cambridge Management Group. This couldn't be better timing. Come work for me. You can take that job yourself now that you're on sabbatical."

A new challenge. A chance to break out of my rut. An opportunity in the real world. My stomach fluttered with anticipation. "When would I start?"

"I'll call DeVita Enterprises International after lunch. I have no doubt Marco would want you to start right away. Like I said, it's urgent."

The flutter expanded into a steady beat, and my body came alive with excitement and hope. "All right. I'm in."

He lifted his glass like it held champagne instead of water. "Here's to it, then. The next chapter."

I lifted my glass, clinked it against his, and a smile matching Jeff's spread across my face, so wide it made my cheeks hurt.

One of the countless paths in life's labyrinth unfolded before me. I had no idea where it would take me, but I'd be damned before I wasted one more minute spinning my wheels in this rut. I was ready to break free. I was ready to reshape my future.

Chapter Three

Anna

A gust of arctic air smacked me across the face and whipped my hair into a frenzy at the top of the Arlington Station stairs. The sky was a clear, pale blue, the crisp winter day blissfully free of clouds and snow. Just a fresh, clean scent that matched my optimism and a cold sting of the north wind that matched my doubt. It needled my confidence and reminded me I was sailing into uncharted waters.

The chaotic sounds of downtown traffic replaced the rumble and screech of the T. I dodged an oncoming businessman who checked his watch while *bahking* words thick with the Boston accent into his cellphone.

"Excuse me," I grumbled over my shoulder at his retreating form. "Sheesh." He hadn't even noticed me. Typical.

Not today, Satan, I thought, catching the pity party before it started. The Anna who'd liberated herself from academia didn't blend into the background. People noticed liberated-Anna. That guy was just a self-absorbed jerk.

I landed awkwardly on my pointy heel and stumbled. "Dammit!" I winced and crouched to rub my twisted ankle.

My professor-wear consisted of jeans, V-neck t-shirts, and running shoes. I could count on one hand the number of times I'd walked these streets in heels. Luckily, Terme di Boston was only a few blocks away, just past the bend in Boylston Street. I stood, held my head high, and resumed my tentative, wobbling steps.

Past the Public Gardens on my left and the unending wall of the Four Seasons on my right, a columned portico came into view followed by the stone edifice that was Terme di Boston. The luxury hotel and European spa extended the entire city block, looming over the southern border of the Boston Commons.

Intricate carvings adorned the cream and brown stone, and mosaic tiles decorated the corner pillars and window frames. Two wide, square towers rose on either side of the covered entrance crowned with sculpted balustrades. The east and west wings of the building were set back from the entrance, and French doors opened onto street-level patios. Behind the two floors of the northern façade, the building dominated the skyline with tiered balconies and extensive outdoor living spaces. Above the portico roof, TERME was carved into a solid piece of creamy marble, the capital lettering reminiscent of ancient Rome.

"Good afternoon, ma'am," the doorman said. "Benvenuta a Terme di Boston." He tugged on the wrought-iron handle and ushered me inside.

The interior of the hotel was no less impressive than the exterior. Marble floors and countertops glinted under bright lights. Plush, cream-colored cushions edged with gold thread topped stone benches. Tall orchids and lush ferns emerged from planters on columned bases. The vaulted ceiling was inlaid with the same mosaic tiles that blessed the exterior, and distressed frescoes decorated the walls.

Instead of students, affluent guests hurried across the cavernous lobby, and my heels clicked loudly on the marble floor, reminding me I wasn't in the finance building anymore. A splinter of doubt wedged itself firmly inside my excitement.

I approached the concierge desk, nervous like the first day of school. The man behind the desk met me with a bright, welcoming smile. "Can I help you?"

"Yes. I'm Dr. Barone with Cambridge Management Group. I have a three o'clock appointment with Mr. DeVita."

"Ah, yes. Just a moment." He picked up the phone, and suddenly, the meeting with my new boss was no longer a distant idea but an imminent reality.

The frescoed walls started to close in on me and sent me into a panic. Had I made a mistake? Forty-eight hours ago, the sum total of my experience had been confined to the Sloan School, classrooms, and the same twelve-by-twelve square foot office I'd occupied for the past fifteen years.

"Dr. Barone?" A woman's velvety voice interrupted the rising tide of my anxiety. I followed the sound of my name to a woman walking toward me with all the grace of a 1920s Vanna White. Her chin-length blonde hair was expertly styled in pin curls, not a strand out of place, and her pale skin was flawless, like porcelain. The retro style of her hair and makeup matched her clothing—a maroon dress with three-quarter-length sleeves, a collared bodice, and a flowing skirt that ended below the knee above what appeared to be vintage t-strap pumps.

What I wouldn't have given for a fraction of her style and confidence.

"Yes. I'm Dr. Barone."

"Right on time," she said and flashed a beauty-pageant smile. "I'm Ms. Connelly, the General Manager of Terme di Boston. Mr. DeVita's assistant left early for the weekend, so I'm to escort you to his office."

She held out her hand, and I shook it. Her voice had a hint of an accent I couldn't place—British, perhaps? My nerves mellowed at her unmistakably welcoming tone.

"Please. Call me Anna."

"Anna. I'm Siobhán. A pleasure to meet you. Let's check your coat—you must be boiling—and then we'll head upstairs. We run a tight schedule here at Terme."

She wasn't wrong. The layers were unbearable now that I was inside, and the tight schedule comment only served to turn up the heat. I stripped off my coat, scarf, and gloves, and deposited them with the bellhop before following Siobhán to the elevators behind the front desk.

She hit the penthouse button. "Mr. DeVita tells me you'll be with us for several weeks. There aren't too many women at the executive level. Let's do lunch or…" She arched a perfectly manicured eyebrow. "Happy hour? If you're into that?"

"Absolutely."

"Fabulous."

The elevator glided to a stop, and its doors opened into a wide, semi-circular foyer. Floor-to-ceiling windows provided an unobstructed view of the Commons below, the commotion of the streets silenced by some magical soundproofing. The only sound came from a sculpture of a nude woman trickling water from a jar into a shallow pool at her feet.

Behind her, the rounded wall was made of porous stone and reminded me of the ruins I'd visited on my last trip to Italy. It curved inward in a wide arc, connecting the windows to where we stood in front of the elevators.

Between the fountain and the windows was a set of double doors, cherry, inlaid with copper knobs, knockers, and a mail chute. A matching doorbell and intercom were set flush into the stone to their right. The entryway looked like something out of a tourism brochure for a luxury bed and breakfast.

On the opposite side of the statue, a matching cherry desk topped with a curved monitor, office phone, and ink blotter sat empty beneath silver letters mounted directly into the stone: *DeVita Enterprises International*. Beyond that, a single, nondescript office door with a stainless-steel handle appeared oddly mundane.

"Wait here," Siobhán said. "I'll let Mr. DeVita know you've arrived." She knocked on the office door.

"Yes!" a deep voice boomed across the distance.

She opened the door enough to squeeze into the room while still holding the handle.

Nervous energy heated my chest, neck, and face despite the coolness of the foyer. I smoothed my sweaty palms down my skirt, dreading the inevitable clammy handshake.

But my self-doubt was no match for the excitement inspired by an actual office and the chance at a real-world application of my skills. Twenty years ago, I'd set my heart on working in corporate finance, and this was my chance. Nothing was going to prevent me from realizing my dream.

Siobhán ducked back into the foyer. "Mr. DeVita will see you now. I'll be in the lobby when you're finished."

"Thank you," I said even as a fresh wave of adrenaline had my stomach doing flips.

She grabbed my hand on her way to the elevator. "Girl," she whispered and squeezed my fingers, "you look like you're about to pass out. Breathe." I let out a tremendous sigh, and she smiled with understanding. "Don't worry. He doesn't bite." She winked and got on the elevator.

"Right." I lifted my chin and strode into Mr. DeVita's office with as much confidence as I could muster.

The office echoed the décor of the foyer but held the faint scent of cigar smoke and leather. To my right, a ceramic urn sat next to a leather recliner and a side table. To my left, a bookcase spanned the entire wall, and the small bar set in its middle was topped with crystal decanters and glassware. Straight ahead, two gladiators grappled in a Renaissance fresco under the soft illumination of track lights. And beneath their epic battle, a man around fifty sat behind a cherry desk staring intently at his computer screen while banging away at a keyboard.

I'd always had a type; my kryptonite took the form of tall, dark, and Italian. I thought I'd developed an immunity after multiple failed attempts at relationships with that make and model, but apparently, my antibodies were no match for Marco DeVita.

Thick, glossy waves of dark brown hair were threaded through with silver as fine as the lines of his pinstripe suit. He kept the sides and back cropped close and neat, matching the clean shave of his smooth, olive-toned skin. Like ancient marble come to life, the hard, chiseled lines of his jaw and cheekbones complimented the prominence of his Roman nose. His bearing demanded obedience, as if Caesar himself had been plucked from history and deposited into that office to rule from a high-backed, leather executive chair.

My sweaty palms redoubled their efforts in the presence of such devastating masculinity. I wiped them on my skirt and reminded myself why I was there—an opportunity to reshape my career. I focused on my breathing to slow my heart rate and realigned my thoughts. Now was not the time for lusty gawping.

"Dr. Barone." Mr. DeVita's deep baritone filled the space between us. "Have a seat." The words were an order, not a request, and although he didn't spare me as much as a glance, I knew he expected me to obey.

I sat in one of the two chairs opposite his desk and surreptitiously wiped the sweat from my palms by smoothing my skirt, but his eyes never left his screen. His left hand enveloped the mouse, making it look unnaturally small. No wedding band. Just a fat gold ring on his right pinky finger. My stomach flipped.

Get a grip, Anna.

He clicked the mouse with finality and turned to face me. Dark eyes widened slightly beneath thick eyebrows. Someone else might have missed the subtle sign of surprise, but I'd seen that look before. He'd been expecting a man.

"Dr. Barone. I'm Marco DeVita," he said, not missing a beat. He made no move to rise, instead folding his hands on his desk and staring at me with unnerving intent. Eyes of the deepest brown met mine without hesitation and captivated me with the depth of their darkness.

"Anna," I breathed. "Please."

"Anna." My name in his deep voice sounded sinful, and a shiver pebbled my skin. "Before we get into the details, I require a signed non-disclosure agreement. CMG has already agreed to this contract, but Mr. Levitt explained this is your first consulting assignment. He's asked that I provide you with the right of refusal if the work doesn't align with your career objectives. After you sign, I'll explain the details, and you'll have an opportunity to decline."

"I have no problem with that. Jeff—excuse me—Mr. Levitt mentioned you'd require an NDA. I've signed them in the past, and I want to assure you I approach all working relationships with discretion. This will be no different."

"Even so," he said with dry skepticism, "I have rather particular requirements, and I expect thorough compliance." He punctuated those final words as if I needed the extra clarity.

"I understand."

He slid a manila folder across his desk. I took it and leafed through the papers inside.

"Read carefully. I require a signature agreeing to full cooperation before we proceed. If you are unwilling or unable to meet the terms, I will take my business elsewhere. If at any time during the contract you violate the terms, the contract with CMG will be terminated, and I will take my business elsewhere. Understood?"

Intimidated by a tone that brokered no debate but irritated by the implication I lacked the professionalism to adhere to an NDA, I nodded and started to read.

Boilerplate legalese filled the first two pages, content I'd seen before in my partnerships with industry while at the university—use of identifying names, titles, and data sets in publications or presentations strictly prohibited—standard and unsurprising. I flipped to the third page where *Additional Mandatory Clauses* was printed across the top, bold and uncompromising. Below the heading, titles were listed with spaces for my initials. I frowned and flipped through the remaining pages. Six in total, the final of which contained a declaration of compliance with a blank line for my signature and the date. I puffed out my cheeks, exhaled, and turned back to the first page.

My eyebrows lifted at the first title.

No Pictures

What an odd requirement for a finance NDA. And the paragraph that followed didn't make the clause any less strange.

The signatory agrees to refrain from any and all use of digital or analog photography, videography, and audio recordings, including those functions provided by cellular telephones, while on any property owned or operated by DEI. The signatory agrees to refrain from taking digital or analog photographs, videos, and audio recordings of the

DEI Chief Executive Officer, Marco Luciano DeVita, at any time while under contract or thereafter.

My eyes scanned the other bold titles. They had just as little to do with data breaches and intellectual property violations as *No Pictures*.

Do Not Name DEI as Your Current Employer

Do Not Discuss Your Contract with Other DEI Employees

All Personal Travel Must be Preapproved for the Duration of the Contract

What the hell?

"Excuse me, but I don't understand how my personal travel plans have any bearing on my ability to discreetly fulfill the responsibilities of the contract. Is this clause really necessary?"

"Every clause in the NDA is necessary. It's your choice whether or not to sign it."

My jaw tightened with the realization I'd asked the wrong question. Of course, he thought the clause was necessary; he wrote it. What I should have asked was why. But after his terse response and given the set of his impassive features, I knew asking the question would be pointless.

I had a choice. I could either agree to the terms or find another opportunity. But there was no way my pride was going to let me off the hook. I wanted to prove Tim Fletcher wrong, prove I could handle whatever bizarre situation the corporate finance world might throw at me, even if I was only proving it to myself. Not to mention, I really wanted to know the details of this job and the modeling it required. I hadn't been this excited about work in a long time, and if it wasn't as interesting as I hoped, I could always back out. Jeff had given me that luxury.

Tick, tock, Anna.

I initialed, signed, and dated the ridiculous NDA and placed the envelope back on his desk.

He eyed me suspiciously, picked it up, and pulled out the papers. He scanned them and must have decided they were in order, because he tapped the papers along their edge, placed them back in the envelope, and slid it into his desk drawer. He sat back in his chair, steepled his fingers, and regarded me with a dark, penetrating stare. I squirmed in my seat under the intensity of his undivided attention.

"I suspect one of my employees is stealing from me."

My head snapped back, and I blinked. I wasn't sure what I'd expected, but it certainly hadn't been corporate larceny. "Why—" No, that wasn't the right question. I gathered my thoughts. "What does that have to do with Cambridge Management Group? I'm not a private investigator."

He rocked his head from side to side. "Debatable."

I shook mine in genuine confusion. "I don't understand."

"My European properties are taking significant financial losses, and it's starting to impact the rest of my business. Based on the performance of my properties in the States and Canada, Europe should be doing at least as well. My COO assures me the difference is due to culture, expectations, and spending habits of the European consumer, but—" He paused, and a muscle in his jaw twitched. "I lived in Italy for years. I don't think that's it."

"You think someone is skimming your profits."

"And doing so in a way that isn't obvious to my accounting department." He canted his head. "Or someone in my accounting department is involved. Either way I need to find the leak. And fast. I recently signed the deed on a new property in Tuscany, and profits from my European office were earmarked to cover the acquisition and renovations. Now, I have to use Terme di Boston capital. Normally that wouldn't be a problem, but I'm in talks with city hall to purchase a significant amount of real estate in the financial district. I have it on good authority there's another interested party." His eyes darkened, and the twitchy muscle in his jaw ticked. "And I can't let them outbid me."

I nodded like everything he said sounded perfectly normal and not completely paranoid. Something about the heaviness of his mood and the weight in his words told me I shouldn't question his suspicions. A nervous seed formed in my belly.

"Was Mr. Levitt appraised of your situation?"

"Yes. Mr. Levitt and I have a standing, two-way NDA."

"Ah," was all I could manage. My first foray into the world of corporate finance, and Jeff had thrust me into the plot of a poorly written corporate thriller. "And you want CMG to..."

"Over the years, I've come to appreciate CMG's unique skillset. My understanding is you can create complex financial models to uncover potential optimizations, correct?"

"Yes. We use models to determine how companies can become lean, improve staffing and budget plans to increase gross and net profits, minimize unnecessary losses resulting from unoptimized cash flows—" I stopped mid-ramble, my brain connecting concepts in ways that had never occurred to me, in an application of my research I'd never considered.

Jeff was right. He couldn't have done this without my help. The nervous seed sprouted into eager fascination.

"You want me to create a financial model of your European office to identify discrepancies between what should be and what is." My eyes widened. "You want me to pinpoint the leak, and the thief, using a financial model."

The corner of his mouth turned up in the slightest hint of a devious smile. "Precisely."

I reclined in my chair and stared into the bookcase,

chewing the side of my fingernail. *Follow the money*. I'd never used my research for this type of application, but it made sense. Understanding how cash flowed was the first step in understanding why.

Gears turned and picked up speed.

I'd created hundreds of complex models over the course of my career; this would be no different. It had been a while since I'd constructed a model based in the European economy, but that was like riding a bike.

Model parameters took shape, and the growing seed of excitement took root.

"Anna?"

"Hm?" My eyes snapped to meet the source of my name.

Mr. DeVita stared at me with a raised eyebrow.

My cheeks heated. I'd forgotten where I was and who sat across from me, lost in my thoughts. Classic Anna. I dropped my hand and smoothed it over my skirt. "Sorry. I was thinking about how to formulate the model."

"Before you get started, we need to discuss the parameters of your work. I can't explain the sudden appearance of a financial analyst without raising suspicion, and I don't know if this is an inside job or an outside shakedown."

Shakedown? I scrunched my nose. "Yes, I suppose that would defeat the purpose," I said, humoring him. At least his paranoia explained why he didn't want me talking to other employees about my work.

"Starting Monday, you'll pose as my administrative assistant."

My eyebrows launched past my forehead. "Excuse me?"

"My assistant Diane is visiting her sick sister in California. You'll serve as her replacement, supplied by CMG, a firm I regularly use for temporary staffing and IT services. As my assistant, you'll conduct your work at the desk in the foyer"— he lifted his chin toward the office door—"as well as any administrative tasks she'd normally perform. You'll direct any questions or requests for information to me, and I'll provide access to my company's data."

My lips parted, but I was stunned silent by the idea of posing as this man's secretary while performing insider corporate espionage. The logistics alone were going to be a nightmare, not to mention the work itself.

"But my software... My computer... My—my notes... My models are huge, and—and the simulations computationally intensive. I can't just run them on a commercial desktop. I mean I can, but—"

"I have no doubt you'll figure out how to make this work. In fact, I'm paying CMG for you to figure out how to make it work. That's the job. Mr. Levitt asked me to provide you with an opportunity to decline. Are you in or are you out?" His black eyes bored into me, waiting for a response to his challenge.

My breath caught. This is what I wanted, wasn't it? A nine-to-five? Go to the office every day? Use my research outside academia? I just hadn't anticipated corporate larceny, posing as a secretary, and a gorgeous, overbearing boss. The situation was far from ideal, but I could make it work, and the unique application of my research was too tempting to ignore. I let go of my breath.

"I'll need to bring in some equipment."

"That's fine, as long as it's minimal. I don't want anything to appear out of the ordinary. You're my admin after all." His lips twitched.

I narrowed my eyes. Was he teasing me? Enjoying the idea of me serving as his secretary?

"In or out, Dr. Barone?"

"In," I said definitively.

"I start work at eight. I'll expect you at your desk no later than seven thirty. Do you have any questions?"

"I... No."

"Siobhán will help you with anything you need on your way out. See you Monday."

Flustered by the abrupt dismissal, I remained stuck in my chair searching for words amid the awkward silence.

The desk phone rang, my shrill savior.

"Yes," Mr. DeVita answered.

My shoulders relaxed as soon as he diverted his attention away from me and to his call. I stood, smoothed my skirt, and spotted my purse on the floor next to the chair. Right. Wouldn't want to forget that. I bent to retrieve it, teetering on my heels.

I rose and turned toward Mr. DeVita to signal my departure, and his eyes were fixed—obviously and with zero shame —on my ass.

A surge of heat rushed my body, making my neck and cheeks flush. He continued his conversation with whomever was on the line and dragged his eyes up my body to where my fingertips pinched my necklace right between my breasts.

He lingered for a moment, and an ache formed deep in the base of my belly. His dark eyes finished their languid journey to my face, and he held my gaze with guileless ease. After a breath that seemed to take an eternity, his focus shifted back to his computer screen.

I didn't waste another second. I marched out of his office and closed the door behind me, mortified by my reaction even more than his audacity. I should have been pissed off, or at the very least, grossed out. I'd just been eyed like a side of beef by a man who, for the next several weeks, was going to be my boss. Instead, my insides were on fire, every nerve ending lit up from being stroked by his attention.

The elevator doors closed, and as I descended to the ground floor of my new office building, I decided the interlude had been a fluke, an inappropriate lapse of judgment that a professional like Mr. DeVita would never repeat. And if that wasn't the case? If leering was his MO? To hell with him and his fancy job. I'd take my brains elsewhere and find an opportunity to reshape my career that didn't come with a side of tall, dark, and Italian.

Chapter Four

Marco

Darkness descended over Boston, a blanket of night through which windows, streetlamps, and headlights twinkled like stars. I flipped up my collar against its cold, sharp edge.

Vito leaned on the hood of my Range Rover, smoking a cigarette. With his scruffy beard, knit beanie, and fleece hoodie, he might as well have been down at the docks unloading the day's catch. He spied my quick steps, tossed the smoke, and ground it out beneath the toe of his boot. I slid into the passenger side and thanked God for heated seats.

Rush hour traffic around the Commons was a complete cluster, and tonight was especially fucked. Figured. My sister expected me at seven for dinner. We made a point of having dinner together at least once a week. Our immediate family was small, and our parents were living in Italy, having remained in Boston as long as they could without anyone noticing they'd frozen in time. It was a balancing act, managing two estates and swapping our lives every few decades, but we made it work. We had no choice.

I'm running late.

She thumbed-up my text, and I shoved the phone back in my pocket.

We inched along the packed city streets, lights and horns flashing in a cacophony of sights and sounds, none of which could distract me from my current fixation.

"The consultant from CMG starts Monday," I said.

"Good."

Vito'd never been one for idle chitchat, but his one word response captured my sentiments. I'd let this bullshit with my European office go on long enough.

What wasn't good? Distraction. Lips parted in surprise. Fingertips resting on the neckline of a red sweater that plunged between ample breasts. Anna Barone's image lengthened my fangs and hardened my cock.

She'd known I'd been leering. Her cheeks had colored, and the rush of her blood had resounded like a surging river. I licked my lips not knowing what plagued me worse—my hunger for her blood or my hunger for her cunt.

My semi-hard strained against my suit pants. I shifted uncomfortably, trying to relieve the pressure, and concentrated on retracting my fangs.

My hunger didn't fucking matter. What mattered was the success of my business and my ability to protect my crew. I unbuttoned my coat and cracked the window, hoping the cold blast of air would calm my fires.

The towering monoliths of Boston's financial district crept by, our progress slower than my reaction to the mess with my European office.

"We're out of time," I said.

"We have a few weeks."

True. Boston's zoning commissioner hadn't officially agreed to my plan or the special provisions I needed to make it happen. The financial district wasn't zoned for nightclubs, but tens of thousands of dollars' worth of gambling debt made it a done deal. Unless Shaughnessy got to him first.

"You don't know what kinda heat he's getting from the Irish."

"Neither do you."

Also true. And why Vito Balistreri was my consigliere.

I wanted that property. Bad. That end of the city was a cash cow waiting to be milked, and I'd be damned before I let the Irish get their hands on it. A few clerks we had on payroll down at city hall tipped us off that someone from Shaughnessy's crew had been poking around, asking questions. Word on the street was the Irish were looking to expand their gambling rackets. No gang had set foot in that part of the city. Not yet. I was determined to turn the financial district into an Italian stronghold. But I couldn't do it without the capital to make the multi-million-dollar deal.

"We need to find out if they're behind that leak. If they've got someone on the inside. If we've got a fucking snake."

"That's why you hired the expert, boss. Patience."

My phone vibrated. I glanced at the illuminated screen. A new encrypted email from my cybersecurity officer, a paranoid recluse Jeff found for me after the guy'd gotten himself kicked out of MIT for hacking their records database.

Anna Barone Dossier

I didn't like being caught off guard, and finding out Dr. Barone was a woman had caught me off guard.

Aside from the cybersecurity position, Jeff took care of my contracts himself. He understood the importance of discretion and anonymity in my line of business. Not to mention he owed me no small debt for past favors. I trusted Jeff, and Jeff trusted her. That went a long way, but not far enough. I'd ordered the workup as soon as he'd informed me he was bringing in an expert.

Better late than never.

Advanced degrees. Awards. I scrolled through pages of publications, guest lectures. A single headshot used for papers, conferences, and... her department website? A tenured professor at MIT's Sloan School?

Pictures from what looked like Jeff and Michael's wedding. A recent photo with an older couple in Rome. Her parents?

At first glance, accomplished and under the radar. No red flags. Perfect.

Strange, though. No marriages, no children, not so much as a single picture with a boyfriend.

She was an attractive woman. Straight, chestnut hair cascaded past her shoulders. Its rich, silky sheen reached her mid-back. Thick eyelashes accented the almond shape of her light brown eyes. The softness of her Mediterranean complexion was blessed with two beauty marks on her right cheekbone, and wisdom was etched in lines across her forehead and around the bow of her full, rosy lips.

Petite with delicious curves, the red sweater she'd worn had barely contained the swell of her breasts, and her tight skirt had stretched around a plump ass. My hand fisted.

I put the phone back in my pocket and glanced out the window. I'd waited too long. I needed to feed. Or fuck. Probably both. I stretched my neck from side to side.

We rumbled down a cobbled side street on the outskirts of the North End. The flicker of poorly maintained streetlights hid the sidewalks in shadow. A few pedestrians walked with their heads down, hands shoved into pockets against the cold.

At the intersection, the hurried movement of silhouettes caught my eye. I narrowed my focus to an alcove dimly lit by the stoplight's red glow, and through the steam rising from a nearby sewer grate, shadows solidified into men. They grappled between the two buildings, one noticeably larger than the other. The big guy slammed the little guy into the side of a building and landed a fist in his gut. The little guy slid down the brick until he sat slumped, dazed or unconscious—I couldn't be sure. A gust of wind cleared the steam long enough for me to see Big Guy rifling through Little Guy's coat.

"Goddammit," I muttered under my breath.

The stoplight turned green, and Vito pulled forward.

"Stop the car!"

I was halfway out the door when Vito hit the brakes. Anger propelled me forward, and my eyes flared to life. I lowered the brim of my hat to mask their demonic glow. Luckily, the two men hadn't noticed the devil approaching.

The attacker's arms bulged against his puffy coat, and a tight knit cap made his head look like a cue ball, tiny atop a thick neck. He dragged the victim to his feet, pushed him into the wall, and went for his back pocket.

Little Guy grunted, his swollen, bloodied face flat against the red brick. I lifted my head, and his hooded eyes widened when they met mine. He slammed them shut, and my fangs descended to their full length in an angry sneer.

I tore the mugger off his victim and tossed him across the alcove. He hit the brick wall with a grunt, and I positioned myself between him and Little Guy. Little Guy tried to stumble toward the street but failed. He slumped against the building and spewed his guts onto the sidewalk.

Big Guy cracked his neck, flexed his hands, and launched off the building, coming at me like a linebacker. His shoulder rammed into my middle and knocked the wind out of me. He was a big fucker, I'd give him that, but for every ounce of muscle he had, he was short a few brain cells. He wrapped his arms around my torso, leaving my arms free. Big mistake.

I drove my fist into the side of his meaty head. It was an odd angle, but I had more than twice the strength of an average human, and even with his thick skull, that had to hurt. He released me and staggered back, unsteady, and I took the opportunity to catch my breath.

He recovered quicker than I'd anticipated, and his ruddy face was twisted with hatred. Not too smart, he came at me again, this time with his fists up.

My eyes flared, eager for a fight.

"What the fuck?" he shouted.

I stood to my full height and flashed a toothy sneer. "Ready for more?"

"Freak," he growled and threw a punch.

Easily blocked. Decades of training in Vito's boxing ring on top of superhuman speed, reflexes, and strength? This idiot didn't stand a chance.

I let him throw a few punches, tire himself out, then hit him with a wicked left hook. He spun with the punch and stumbled back until he sagged against the wall.

A pained groan cut through the silence. I glanced over my shoulder. Little Guy held his stomach, his head lolling from side to side. I moved to help him, but thick fingers clamped around my wrist. I spun back to face their owner, and my jaw met the blunt impact of Big Guy's gloved fist.

The hot, metallic taste of blood filled my mouth, and my anger erupted into rage. He moved to throw an opposite hook, but I swatted his arm away like a gnat. I picked him up by his puffy coat and threw him into the far wall, harder than before, the power of my fury fueling my strength. He tried to regain balance, but I drove my right fist into his gut before hitting him with the full force of my left cross.

My fist connected with a crack. The man's head snapped to the right and blood spurted from his mouth and splattered across the brick. His knees buckled under the weight of his limp body, and he sunk to the ground.

Cazzo, that hurt. I shook my hand and watched him, making sure this time he was down for good. But that had been a brutal punch. He was out.

I strode back into the street, amped from the fight and angry as hell that shit still happened in my neighborhood. Vito was leaning against the passenger-side door of the Range Rover, ankles crossed, smoking a cigarette. Like he was picking me up from an appointment. Asshole.

I swiped the blood from the corner of my mouth. "The fucker split my lip."

He lifted a shoulder. "You dropped your guard."

I glared at him. "Call an ambulance."

"What about the police?"

"Let the medics handle it but get the little guy's information." I'd cover his medical expenses. He was in a bad way, probably out of work. Can't take care of yourself if you're out of work. "As soon as you hear the black-and-whites, get the hell out of here. We don't need complications. I'm going to walk this off."

"You got it, boss."

I buttoned my coat, shoved my hands into my pockets, and started toward my family home. I hadn't taken more than a few steps before I stopped short, my adrenaline fueling a train of thought I couldn't ignore.

"Vito."

He looked up from the cigarette butt he was putting to rest with his boot.

"Put a tail on Anna Barone. I want to know where she goes, who she talks to, and if anyone is watching her."

He answered with a nod, took out his cell, and made his way toward the alcove.

The cold night air and my brisk pace burned off my

remaining rage. My fangs retreated, my breath slowed, and my heart stopped pounding against the cage of my ribs. That asshole was lucky I hadn't killed him. But I didn't need police entanglements, and dead bodies always led to police entanglements.

Protection came in different forms. Most of the time, people paid for protection, and the Lord knew I'd worked over more scumbags for fucking with the wrong person than I could count. Other times, like tonight, it was just the right thing to do because we lived in a shit world with shit people, and someone needed to keep it in check.

I turned the corner onto the street where my family had lived for over half a century. Despite Gina's assurances the neighborhood had changed, these streets were still dangerous. I'd just seen the evidence firsthand, and I'd taken an oath to protect them.

Gina's silhouette moved behind the kitchen drapes and made me smile. It tugged on my split lip, and I winced as I walked up the steps. I keyed open the door, and the light, warmth, and mouth-watering aroma of chicken piccata started to cleanse me of my foul mood. I hung my coat and hat, and my sister stepped out of the kitchen wiping her hands on a dish towel.

"Ciao, Gina." I moved to kiss her cheek, but she held me at arm's length and examined my face.

"Marco! Your lip! What happened?"

"It's nothing." I swiped my thumb across my bottom lip. It came away with a bloody smear. I shrugged and took her shoulders again, trying to greet her with a kiss.

"No dire cazzate," she swore and swatted me with the dish towel. "It's not nothing. Sit." She pointed at Papà's recliner, her stern tone reminding me of Mamma, and stalked off into the kitchen.

I knew better than to disobey. I shrugged out of my suitcoat, tossed it over the back of the chair, and eased myself into the old leather recliner, suddenly very tired and very hungry.

Gina came back with a crystal single of whiskey and an ice pack.

"What about dinner?" I asked.

"Dinner can wait." She handed me the drink and the ice. "Drink that and ice your lip while you tell me what happened."

"I don't need ice."

She lifted an eyebrow. "Humor me."

"Bossy little sisters," I grumbled and swigged the whiskey. I lifted the ice to my lip. The wound was almost healed from the power in my blood, but I had to admit the warmth of the whiskey and the chill of the ice eased the remaining discomfort and a lot of my tension.

She leaned back in the rocking chair and folded her arms across her chest. "What happened?"

"I pulled a mugger off a guy on Salem Street. He landed a lucky punch." I moved the ice from my lip to my knuckles and threw back the rest of the whiskey. "I landed more."

"No doubt," she said, her tone sharp.

She narrowed her eyes, but before she could begin with a barrage of questions, I lifted my hand to hold her off, ice pack in tow.

"They're both alive. Vito's handling it."

The tension in her shoulders eased. "Did anyone notice you change?"

"Yes, but you know they won't say anything. Even if they do, no one will believe them."

She nodded and stared into the empty fireplace, worrying her lip.

For the most part, blood demons hid in plain sight. We didn't flaunt our extraordinary abilities, and human Sources were as motivated as we were to keep our secret. They didn't want to lose their income or, for some, their kink fulfillment. But more importantly, the average human didn't want to believe in the supernatural. They'd explain away most paranormal experiences, convince themselves there had to be a rational explanation. No one wanted to be labeled crazy.

Gina's focus drifted back to my face, and she examined me with the unnecessary intensity typical of overprotective sisters. "You look pale. You haven't fed in a while, have you? You shouldn't wait so long. And now this? You need to feed, Marco."

"How's work? Is everything lined up for the Foundation gala next month?"

"Dannazione," she snapped. "Don't change the subject. You've always had such a hang-up about feeding. I don't get it. It's not like we didn't grow up in the same house. You should be feeding at least once a week."

She wasn't wrong on either account. I did have a hang-up about feeding, but I wasn't about to admit that to her or explain why.

I dropped the ice pack into the tumbler I'd left on the end table and pushed myself out of the recliner. I knelt before my sister and took her hands. "I'm fine. I'm just hungry." She scoffed and looked away. "For *food*, Gina."

She turned back to face me, still chewing on her lip.

I squeezed her fingers. "I promise I'll feed tonight, okay? But after dinner. Per favore," I whined. "I'm starving."

She swatted my arm, this time with her hand, and a genuine smile transformed her worried face. "All right, all right."

I stood and pulled her to her feet.

"Vino?" she asked over her shoulder before disappearing into the kitchen.

"Yes," I called back.

I picked up the empty glass and ice pack from the end

table and paused, running my tongue over the fading cut in my lip. It already felt better. So did my hand. Still, I was drained.

Had it already been a week? I'd lost track of time dealing with my European office, extorting permits out of city hall, and planning the new front I was determined to build in the financial district. I needed blood more than the food I was about to eat, and I wouldn't regain my full strength until I fed. I pulled out my cell and texted Vito.

> I need to visit Sarah. I'll text you when I'm finished with dinner.

Sarah was hearty and athletic. I could drink my fill. And our transactions were detached and professional, just the way I liked them.

Anna Barone appeared in my mind's eye, writhing in ecstasy, my teeth buried in her neck, my cock plunging into her wet cunt.

What the fuck?

My mood darkened with each step toward the kitchen. My European office was hemorrhaging money, and the Irish were sticking their noses where they didn't belong. The last thing I needed was a distraction, someone upending my routine.

I paid for blood, and I paid for sex. Never at the same time and never with the same woman. No matter how enticing the temptation.

Chapter Five

Anna

Morning peeked over the downtown skyline and shined bright through the glass wall of the penthouse floor. The sunlight matched my outlook—eager and optimistic—and I fired up the computer to start my first Monday in the world of corporate finance.

The computer booted with a low whine, and I reached into my new Louis Vuitton tote to retrieve my water bottle and the external hard drive I needed to make this ruse work.

What a gorgeous bag, I thought for the millionth time since I'd bought it. I'd never purchased anything so indulgent. Frankly, I really couldn't afford it, especially given I was making only a fraction of my salary while on sabbatical. But if I was going to do this whole midlife awakening thing, I was going to do it right, and that bag was a hell of a lot cheaper than Michael's Porsche.

First thing first—how bad was the computer situation? I navigated to the system settings, relieved the desktop wasn't a cluttered mess. The window opened and so did the office door behind me, giving me a start. I swiveled my chair.

Mr. DeVita leaned against the door jamb, one ankle

crossed over the other, dominating the space between us with easy authority and smoldering good looks. He folded his thick arms across his black waistcoat, and his biceps strained against his white dress shirt.

He tilted his head and examined me from my hair, carefully arranged in a bun at the nape of my neck, to the Band-Aids covering the blisters on the backs of my heels.

I shifted, nervous under his scrutiny. *Is he judging my clothes? Did I get "executive admin" right?* My palms started to sweat.

"I like your hair better down."

The fresh curveball silenced my racing thoughts. Heat moved like a tidal wave up my chest, the telltale sign my cheeks were about to turn an obnoxious shade of tomato. I touched the neat bun I'd painstakingly pinned at the nape of my neck and tried to make sense of a statement that sounded more like a command than an observation.

Should I be offended or flattered he'd noticed my hair enough to have a preference? We were at work. He was my boss. My hairstyle was immaterial to my performance, and he shouldn't be commenting on my appearance anyway. Wasn't that in some HR manual somewhere?

"What do you need to get started?" he asked.

My brain short-circuited with Marco DeVita induced whiplash. I gaped at him, unable to form coherent thoughts, much less words. I couldn't remember the last time I'd clammed up so badly.

I swiveled my chair to face the computer, desperate for a reprieve from the severity of those dark eyes. My hand shook as I reached for my water bottle. At least the long, soothing drink bought me time to gather my thoughts.

"I—I'm not sure," I said, finally, my eyes safely fixed on the screen. "I brought an external hard drive with my software, tools, and notes, but I need to understand this computer's performance capabilities first. If it's powerful enough, I won't need additional equipment, just information to construct the model." I clicked through menus until the processor speed and memory appeared.

"And what goes into building the model?"

Surprised by the nearness of his voice, I glanced over my shoulder. His big body towered above me, right behind my chair, close enough to feel his body heat and smell a hint of cigar smoke and leather.

I shifted my focus back to the monitor and pretended to study the numbers. Instead, I closed my eyes and regulated my breathing.

Just answer his question, Anna. Talk about your work. You can do that in your sleep.

"The business strategies used by your European office as well as EU sector performance," I said. Robotic, but true.

His eyes never left me. They bored into the back of my head.

"I'll use that information to construct parameterized model elements. I'll piece those together to represent the entire financial system." My shoulders started to relax. "Then, I'll run the model through scenarios to determine if the expected behavior deviates from the actual, observed performance."

Recentered, I opened my eyes and glanced back over my shoulder.

He gave me a terse nod. "Let me know when you need something specific."

"Will do."

He moved for his office, and I exhaled, relieved to be left alone with my work.

"Before you get started..."

I swiveled my chair to meet the interruption.

"I'll need my breakfast."

The statement came out so matter-of-fact, I nodded in agreement. Of course, he needed his breakfast.

And then it hit me. I shook my head and blinked. "Excuse me?"

"My breakfast. Coffee and a pastry. Pick it up from Caffè del Vecchio Mondo."

This time it wasn't self-consciousness that threatened to turn my face bright red. He'd just pushed the only button that sent my temper straight to DEFCON 1.

"You want me... to get you coffee." The words came out slow and searing, vitriol equal to his demeaning request.

He released his grip on the door handle and shifted his weight to face me in full. "Yes. I take my caffè americano with a splash of cream. And today I want a cornetto."

My jaw clamped shut, teeth clenched so tightly they hurt. He had to have heard the tone in my voice and seen the redness that burned my cheeks, yet he mocked me with an air of indifference. My neck and face heated like a volcano ready to erupt.

"What type of filling?" I asked with enough deathly sarcasm to murder his ears.

Neither his body nor his face displayed any hint of remorse. "Vuoto," he said after a moment. As if he'd truly considered what he wanted. As if my insincere question deserved a sincere answer. His response ripped through my remaining decorum like an armor-piercing bullet.

"I'm trying to figure out if this desktop can meet the computing demands of running stochastic simulations of complex financial models, and you want me to walk three blocks in these heels to get you coffee?" My voice gained volume with each outraged word.

He folded his arms across his chest. "Yes."

Indignation forced me to my feet. Every instance of being mistaken for someone's admin, every assumption I'd be the one to take notes in a meeting, every casual request to bring in coffee and donuts roared into my head, and lava spewed out the mouth of the volcano. "There's a Dunkin' Donuts around the block!" I pointed at the elevator. "Get your own coffee!"

The muscle in his jaw twitched, the first and only sign my words had any impact. He dropped his arms and stepped forward until only inches separated us, the heat of his body stoking the heat of my anger.

"That coffee is American trash. And you are my administrative assistant." He over-enunciated the *t*s in his last two words and canted his head. "Remember?"

My chest heaved with furious breath.

"My admin gets my coffee and breakfast every morning, and it comes from Caffè del Vecchio Mondo." He leaned in, forcing me to look up to maintain eye contact. "And if we want everyone to believe you are her replacement, you'll do the same."

I ground my teeth on my nonexistent retort and the bitter taste of the truth and concentrated my disdain into a single venomous look. I grabbed my new handbag and marched to the coat rack, fuming.

"Make sure it's extra hot," he called after me. "I hate cold coffee."

My head snapped back to slay him with a fresh wave of daggers, but he'd already walked into his office, and I impaled the closed office door instead.

"I was going to wait until the next time we had lunch"—I brushed past Jeff into his Back Bay townhouse—"but after today…"

I wobbled a few more steps so I could set my new bag on the entry table instead of the floor even though hard leather rubbed mercilessly against my little toes and cut into the backs of my heels. I stumbled for what must have been the hundredth time that day and yelped in frustration. I kicked off the obnoxious shoes and sent them flying to bank off the wall.

"I fucking *hate* those things!"

Jeff's dog Lady trotted over to where they landed next to the door and sniffed the offensive torture devices.

"Tough day at the office, love?" Michael called from the kitchen.

I didn't respond. I was too busy glaring at Jeff. My best friend eyed me warily.

"You could have warned me, you know," I said.

He pretended to watch the pug-boxer nose my shoes, but she lost interest and wagged her tail into the kitchen.

"Given you've obviously met Marco and likely signed one of his NDAs, you know I couldn't."

"Bullshit." I narrowed my eyes, concentrating my irritation into a tight beam of hostility. "You're not getting off that easily. You could have said *something*. I had no idea what I was walking into. None. Can you guess how that went, Jeff? Hm?"

He winced.

"Exactly. It went about as well as you'd imagine. I clammed up worse than I have in over a decade. He probably thinks I have a speech problem."

"I'm sorry, Anna, I—"

"And then, to add insult to injury, you know what he had me do today?"

Jeff showed his teeth in an exaggerated grimace.

I craned my neck as I enunciated each humiliating word. "Get. His. Coffee."

"No!" Michael exclaimed from the kitchen.

I spun around and pointed at Michael. He hovered near the stove with a wooden spoon and looked over his shoulder, face twisted in horror.

"Yes!" I exclaimed and turned back to Jeff while still waving my finger at Michael. "*That* is the appropriate response, for the record."

"All right." He held up his hands in surrender. "I'm sorry. Let's... Why don't you take off your coat and snuggle Lady on the couch. Okay? I'll get you some wine."

"I guess," I snapped.

Lady jumped onto the couch as soon as I sat down and rested her head on my leg. Jeff handed me a glass, sat next to me, and squeezed my shoulder.

The luscious Sangiovese started to melt my tension and took the shrill edge out of my voice. "Seriously, Jeff, how do you even know this guy? He said you have a standing, two-way NDA." I shook my head. "It was like having a conversation with an Italian gangster out of a movie. What's his deal?"

Jeff stiffened and shifted his focus to Lady. "He gives CMG a lot of business. Values his privacy. I handle his contracts myself to protect that privacy. You're the first exception to the rule because I trust you, and Marco trusts me."

He hadn't answered the question, not in any meaningful way. But then again, he was under an NDA. NDAs didn't care about your best friend's feelings or personality quirks. They didn't include the clause, "Don't say anything, unless your best friend needs a heads-up, so she doesn't turn into a mute."

"Would've been nice to have some idea what I was getting into. I was completely caught off guard."

"Come on, Anna. You know I couldn't give you any details until you signed the NDA."

"I'm talking about Mr. DeVita."

"Oh." He snorted and gave me a wry smile. "Yeah, Marco can be a bit... extra." He ran his hand across the top of his buzzed head, sprang off the couch, and made his way into the kitchen. He peered at the stove over Michael's shoulder and wrapped his arms around Michael's waist.

"Stop it!" Michael wiggled out of Jeff's hold. "You're distracting me from stirring. Stirring is key, or it won't be creamy."

"Risotto?" I asked.

"Yes. With truffles." He glanced over his shoulder and winked.

"It smells amazing."

"I know."

I chuckled. Michael was one of the most self-assured people I knew, and I loved that about him. I'd give anything to channel a fraction of his unshakable confidence.

"I mean..." Jeff leaned against the counter and folded his arms, his face smug. "The work is right up your alley, isn't it?"

Excitement crept up my spine. My shoulders tingled with it. "It is," I admitted. "It really is." *Corporate larceny and paranoia aside...*

"See, there you go."

"I have to pose as his assistant, though."

He raised his eyebrows.

"Hence the coffee."

He moved his hand in front of his face to adjust his glasses, but I knew better; his shoulders were shaking, and he snorted.

"God, you are such an ass," I said.

He stopped trying to hide his face and doubled over laughing.

"Isn't he?" Michael called out.

"Sorry," Jeff managed while he stopped to breathe. "Sorry. It's just..." He stood up straight and wiped the tears from behind his glasses. "You? A secretary?" He shook his head and snickered. "I'm just imagining you bringing Marco DeVita coffee in those heels." He threw his head back and resumed cackling.

"Laugh it up, jerk. But when I ruin one of his expensive suits, I'll have him send the dry-cleaning bill to CMG."

Which, of course, made him laugh even harder.

"Whatever." I crawled out from beneath Lady's head and walked into the kitchen. "If this is the price I have to pay not to be holed up at MIT all semester, I'll make the damn coffee myself." I poured another glass of the smoky Sangiovese and drank in its fragrant earthiness. "Oh, this is good."

"Right?" Michael said. "It's going to pair perfectly with the wild mushrooms and truffle."

"You're an artist, Michael."

"I am. Remember that, Jeff. You're a lucky man."

Jeff regained his composure enough to lean across the distance and kiss Michael on the cheek. "The luckiest."

I left the two lovebirds and reclaimed my seat on the couch. Lady joined me.

Jeff and I had been best friends since grad school, and I'd happily inherited Michael along the way. They were so in love, had been for years. I sighed and ran my hand over Lady's wrinkled head. I'd be lucky to find even a sliver of the happiness they shared.

I had another date with David Lancaster that upcoming weekend, but I wasn't looking forward to it. Everything about the relationship, including my nonexistent feelings for him, was unremarkable. And, unfortunately, that single word summed up my love life for the past two decades. Unremarkable.

My eyes wandered back to the kitchen. Jeff resumed his quest to wrap his arms around Michael's waist, and Michael continued to swat at him like a fly. Michael finally relented and tilted his head to allow Jeff to nuzzle his neck. He looked up from his risotto to his husband, and my chest ached at the depth of love in Michael's eyes. He smiled, kissed Jeff on the lips, and returned to his stirring with Jeff's chin resting on his shoulder.

"I love how much you two love each other," I said wistfully, my eyes misty with tears.

I wanted to look at someone the way Michael looked at Jeff. I'd had my share of partners and relationships, but they'd always fallen flat. No one had ever stirred my emotions or touched my heart.

Jeff lifted his gaze to meet mine, and his mouth turned down in a sympathetic frown. I'd laid a lot on my best friend last week at Scholar's, but unlike my career, he didn't have a solution to my unremarkable love life.

"It's not all sunshine and roses, love," Michael said. "Remember that. Do you know how hard it is to stay wrinkle free when your beauty sleep is interrupted by a human chainsaw?"

"Hey!" Jeff slugged Michael in the arm.

"You love it," Michael quipped.

I huffed and shook my head. One step at a time. Career first. Love life... Well, some things you just couldn't work at fixing.

I sipped my wine, and the slight burn from the alcohol heated my chest and cheeks. The last time I'd felt flushed like that was Friday when I'd caught Mr. DeVita staring at my ass. He'd known I'd caught him, but that didn't stop him from finishing what he'd started. He'd practically undressed me with his eyes, and I swear the intensity of his gaze made it feel as though he'd used his hands.

And God, he'd looked so good in his white shirt and black waistcoat. I bit the rim of my wineglass. I could almost smell the cigar smoke and leather, and a rush of desire zipped up my spine and made me shiver.

The way he'd spoken to me, the way he'd commanded me to serve him, had put me into a rage of righteous feminism. But two glasses of Sangiovese later, I was horrified to admit that as much as it still pissed me off, it turned me on. I had zero desire to examine the reasons why; I wasn't sure I'd like the answer.

Marco DeVita was domineering and inappropriate and devastatingly handsome. But he was my boss, and I wasn't about to harbor any fantasies about a man who was my gateway to a fresh start at my career. No way. Everything between me and Mr. DeVita would remain strictly professional. Simple as that.

Chapter Six

Marco

A soft knock at the door interrupted my focus. It was Wednesday afternoon, and I was scrambling to finish my review of the construction contracts for my new property in Tuscany before I flew to Rome Friday to sign the paperwork.

"What is it?" I barked and noted my place on the page.

The door opened just enough for Anna to slip into my office. She stood in front of the door holding the handle behind her back. She'd removed the sweater she'd been wearing, and her chestnut hair spilled onto her white blouse, sheer enough and unbuttoned enough to draw my attention a beat too long. Annoyed by the interruption, the distraction of her breasts only added to my irritation, a reminder that her abilities came with unwelcome temptation.

Worry creased her forehead with deep lines, and her sun-kissed complexion was a shade paler than normal. Her eyes darted around the room, and the delicate skin of her neck bobbed beneath the pressure of a hard swallow.

Anna was a nervous woman, but that type of reaction didn't come from nerves. It came from fear.

"What is it, Anna?"

"There's—uh... There's a Mr.—a Mr. Vincenzo Valenzano here to see you."

What the fuck?

Almost a century of practice guarding my emotions was the only reason I didn't yell that out loud. No wonder Anna looked like she'd seen a viper. She had. He was slinking around my foyer.

Vinnie knew better than to show up at Terme. In the middle of the day. Unannounced. Suspicion drove my irritation to a peak.

"Send him in."

She frowned, but nodded, slipped out of the room, and left the door open behind her.

I had nothing to hide, not when it came to Vinnie, but Anna didn't know that. All she knew was a man whose face she'd probably seen on the local news wanted to meet with her boss.

Vinnie sauntered into my office with all the confidence you'd expect from the Don of Boston. And a three-piece suit to match. His hair was more salt than pepper—he'd started graying when we were in our thirties—but his thick eyebrows were as dark as his blood-demon eyes.

I picked up my letter opener, held both ends loosely between my fingers, and leaned back in my chair. He flashed his wolfish smile, and the door clicked shut.

"What? No handshake? Nessun bacetto?"

"What do you want, Vinnie? And why the fuck did you come here to get it?"

He unbuttoned his suit jacket and lowered his ample frame into one of the chairs opposite my desk. He wasn't as big as Big Frankie, but the apple hadn't fallen far from the tree. "You assume I want something." He opened his arms. "Maybe I'm just here to invite you for caffè."

"Spare me."

He chuckled. "Speaking of *caffè*, can you ask your secretary to get us some from that restaurant of yours downstairs? I could use an espresso."

The innocent request added another layer to my foul mood. Anna'd probably quit after this fiasco.

"Anna!"

She opened the door enough to peek in and eyed Vinnie like if she looked anywhere else, he might strike. "Yes, Mr. DeVita?"

"Mr. Valenzano would like an espresso from Vittoria."

"Vittoria?"

"The restaurant downstairs."

"Oh. Right. Sorry."

"A double espresso, *sweethaht*. Two *sugahs*," Vinnie said in his thick Boston accent.

She looked at me, eyes flashing with contempt. "Can I get you anything, Mr. DeVita?" The words cut with a sharp edge of disdain despite the shake in her voice.

"No."

She gave me a terse nod and closed the door.

I let the tip of the letter opener fall to the blotter and spun it on its pointed end. "You're supposed to text if you want something. Set up a meeting. Somewhere safe."

He eyed the spinning blade. "What place is safer than Terme?

"Safe from eyes, Vinnie."

He shrugged. "They watch me no matter where I go."

His cavalier attitude made me want to stab him with the damn letter opener, but I let it go. A swift end to the conversation was more important than proving my point. "What do you want?"

"I don't want anything. But I do have something for you."

I cocked an eyebrow. "Forgive my skepticism."

He frowned, dropped his Don-of-Boston persona, and narrowed his eyes. "What's with the venom, Marco? What the hell did I do?"

The valid question snapped me out of my attitude problem. I sighed, let the letter opener fall to my desk, and pressed my thumb and forefinger into my eyes before pinching the bridge of my nose.

I was on edge, annoyed by Vinnie's unexpected visit, but he wasn't the enemy. He wasn't exactly a friend, but I'd known the man since I'd started working for his father eighty years ago. We shared an understanding and mutual respect.

No, this had to do with the fear I'd seen in Anna's eyes, her reaction to the boss of the Boston Mafia showing up at her desk. It had triggered a response, some sort of instinct I didn't want to examine. And it was making me act like a dick.

"Nothing. Sorry." I dragged a hand down my face. "I'm flying to Italy Friday, and I have to finish reading this contract." I waved a hand over the papers strewn across my desk.

He arched an eyebrow. "Now it's my turn to be skeptical."

I stared him down, done with the banter. "What do you have for me, Vinnie?"

He smirked but took the hint. "A business proposition."

"I gathered. Which business?"

"Sources."

I folded my hands in my lap and reclined in my chair. "I'm listening."

"It's important to me, you, and our community to have consistent and affordable access to Sources."

"For a price."

"Of course, for a price. This is business."

Where there was a need, there was a way to make money, and enterprising blood demons like the Valenzanos had been cashing in on our need for hundreds of years, brokering

Sources for those without a spouse or the connections to find one themselves. Boston housed the largest population of blood demons outside of Italy, and with it the largest Source market.

"The one demone del sangue crew under my control handles the clients, connects them with Sources, and collects and distributes payments. Same as when you worked for my father. But..." He lifted his hands and shrugged. "Demand is up. More and more demoni del sangue are settling in Boston every year. And now we have high-end clients with loftier expectations. Times are changing, and we need to change with them."

Willing Sources weren't as hard to find as one might imagine. Unbonded blood demons in need of extra cash. Humans intrigued by the darker side of nature, or the pleasure induced by our venom. But the key word was *willing*. Feeding from another soul without consent was a sin akin to rape.

My brow furrowed. "You worried about an uptick in nonconsensual feedings? My lawyers haven't mentioned they're getting any more requests than usual from the community."

If demand was up, supply had to follow. Desperation led to attacks in the night, dark alleys, and shadowed corners. Most of the time, anyone claiming to have been attacked by a "vampire" was dismissed as crazy, but that didn't mean victims couldn't claim assault. And if too many vampire accusations started flying around, no matter how unhinged, we'd have a real problem—unwanted attention. Federal unwanted attention.

"Not yet. We've recruited new soldati demoni del sangue to handle the increase in volume, and so far, we've kept up. But I'm pushing the boundaries of how much I can grow that crew, Marco. You and I both know there's a reason my father agreed to let you out."

Vinnie leveled me with a heavy look equal to the weight of his words, but he didn't need to remind me of Big Frankie's motivations. Every favor granted in Cosa Nostra came with a price.

The mixed bag of humans and blood demons that was the Boston Mafia back when me and Tony joined had been a risky business. Not all humans were as accepting as Big Frankie. Enforcing omertà when a soldier's world was rocked by learning the supernatural existed was no easy task. Especially given the feds were breathing down our necks and hoping to put the screws to a rat.

Big Frankie had been well aware of his mortality, and that his blood demon son would soon become Don. The Mafia garnered enough attention without the added bonus of potential vampire accusations. He'd decided separating the ranks would deflect any unnecessary scrutiny while keeping Boston under Valenzano control. But he also wasn't about to give up one of his most lucrative rackets.

So, we struck a deal. He let me out, and I took the blood demon capi and soldati with me. The Valenzano demoni del sangue were limited to Vinnie and the capo and crew responsible for the Source racket. The rest of the Boston outfit was human and kept in the dark about the true nature of their boss.

"What's the problem, then?" I asked. "Sounds like you're meeting demand. And probably earning a shitload in the process."

"Like I said, times are changing. If we can't keep up with expectations, won't matter if we have enough Sources."

Suspicion hardened into a sinking rock in my gut.

"The fronts in Revere and Saugus do steady business, but not all our clients, or Sources for that matter, want to be seen at a strip club. Others feel uncomfortable bringing a Source into their home since many of them are doing it for the money, not the kink. Options in the city are limited outside the North End."

The sinking rock bottomed out, and I stiffened, realizing why Vinnie'd come to Terme.

He quirked a smarmy smile. "Some of the new Sources signed up thinking they could charge more for high-end experiences. Thing is, I don't wanna stop 'em. Clients are willing, and it's a bigger tax." He shrugged. "There's more money to be made in this racket than ever before. If I can find the right venue."

I ground my teeth and picked up the letter opener, needing something to squeeze beside Vinnie's neck.

"An upscale venue where refined clients and Sources can conduct business. A venue friendly to demoni del sangue where both parties feel comfortable and safe—"

Two knocks came at my door before I had a chance to unleash my own interruption.

"Yes," I barked.

Anna slipped into the room carrying a small, insulated cup. She tentatively stepped to where Vinnie sat, relaxed and waiting to be served. She held out the cup, and it trembled in her fingers.

"Grazie, sweetheart." He looked her up and down, and I loathed him in that moment. "You ever get sick of working for this wiseguy, you gimme a call, capisce? I could use more Italian women like you on my staff." He flashed his wolfish smile and winked.

Anna wrung her hands, and her face paled like she was going to be sick. Not that Vinnie noticed. He was too busy feeling her up with his eyes. I strangled the letter opener.

Anna nodded. "Excuse me," she said softly and turned to leave.

Vinnie tracked her backside as she hurried out of my office. "She'd make a great Source," he said as an afterthought.

The door closed and he turned back to me, brow raised as he sipped his espresso. "Healthy. Italian. She'd be a top earner with that ass and those tits—"

I stabbed the letter opener into the blotter. It cut through the leather and wedged itself deep in the hardwood. My breath came fast and heavy, and the heat in my blood threatened to turn my eyes.

"Cosa?" Vinnie exclaimed and opened his arms. "She your goomar or something?"

"She's my assistant," I snarled, "which means she's part of my crew and off limits." The thought of my connections corrupting Anna's safe, mundane world made me want to commit acts of violence. "Get to the point, Vinnie."

He eyed me suspiciously, mouth twisted in an unhappy sneer. "My point is, if I had a venue like Terme di Boston—"

"You could charge more," I interrupted, my temper overtaking my patience. "And you'd have a reputable business through which you could launder your profits."

The constancy of his stare and the twitch of his upper lip were his only answer.

"In other words," I continued, my words clipped with malice. "You want to turn Terme into a brothel and me into a pimp."

Vinnie scoffed and looked away. "Don't be crass."

"Well, that's what you're asking for, isn't it?"

He turned back to face me. "You've always had an interest in protecting our people." His lip twitched again, and he tried to cover it up with an ingratiating smile.

Vinnie'd had that tell as long as I'd known him. That lip twitch told me everything. He thought he could bait me by framing this entire scheme as some altruistic service to the community. He should have known better than to think I'd buy such thinly veiled bullshit.

"Let's call it what it is, Vinnie. You want to expand your

Source racket, but you need a high-end front with a large enough cash flow to do it."

"A small price to pay to protect the community." There was that twitch again. He wasn't even trying to hide his bull-shit anymore.

"Ah," I said through a cynical laugh. "Okay." I yanked the letter opener out of my desk and tossed it on the blotter.

"You'd get a sizable cut of the tax. And for what? Nothing illegal. Sources are willing."

"Nothing illegal? Really? Laundering prostitution money? No, nothing illegal about that."

"That's a rather pejorative way of looking at it. Not to mention, you've never had any issue paying for Sources."

No matter how he spun it, the Source racket was orga-nized prostitution, and I did not take that shit lightly. Yes, I participated, but out of necessity. I took no pleasure in the act and gave those transactions the respect they deserved.

I gripped the edge of my desk and leaned forward. "I'm not going to rot in jail from blood starvation to launder *your* money. Or house an illegal brothel, which, if the feds find out, is exactly what they'll call it."

He pressed his lips together and folded his arms.

"Come on, Vinnie. I have no moral quandary with the service you provide. You know that. But I already have Agent..." I waved my hand through the air.

"Agent Johnson."

"Agent Johnson following me around, trying to build a RICO case. The last thing I need is more traffic in and out of Terme. Especially Sources. I'm not willing to risk a federal indictment."

He scoffed. "You know we have provisions in place to handle jail time and the feds. Managed by your lawyers, in fact. You're being shortsighted. This is an opportunity for both of us to make a lotta money."

"I broke financial ties with the Valenzanos years ago. I'm not going to be pulled back in now."

"I never understood why."

"You know my reasons. I never hid them from you or your father."

He stood and stepped to the edge of my desk. Challenge flashed in his eyes. "You should take this deal, Marco. It'll be good for business."

"My business is doing just fine."

"Is it?" Vinnie smirked. "I hear it could be doing better. Not to mention the Irish movement lately. We can't afford to give up any more territory."

His eyes drilled into me, but I held my composure, determined not to give him any reason to believe his words landed like an uppercut. Did I have a rat in my crew on top of everything else?

"Think of your family."

"Is that a threat?"

"It's not a threat, and I resent the implication." He pointed a meaty finger in my face. "You're a made man, Marco. I would never threaten a made man. It's just a fact. I'm giving you an opportunity to grow your business and protect your community. That includes your family. You should take it."

Our eyes locked in silent battle, two blood demons, both nearing a century old and neither willing to compromise.

Vinnie knocked his knuckles twice on the edge of my desk and backed away, buttoning his suitcoat. He spun toward the door and walked out of my office.

I pushed out of my chair, loosened my tie on the way to the bar in my bookcase, and poured myself a finger of whiskey.

In typical Valenzano fashion, Vinnie knew right where to hit me and when. No way this was a coincidence. Coming to me with an offer like that when profits were down and I was on the verge of a major territory acquisition? And the fact it was a good offer just pissed me off even more.

He'd been on the right track, too, playing to my sensibilities. Safe, affordable access to Sources was critical to minimizing nonconsensual feedings and keeping law enforcement out of our business. It was an important part of protecting our community and our secret. As much as I knew it was a ploy, the reminder landed hard.

But he hadn't quite hit the mark. Not all Sources gave up their necks willingly. Some did it out of necessity, for survival. Those were the people I wanted to protect. The people who had no choice. Like my mother.

I shot back the whiskey, trying to ground myself in the present, but those images I hated so much barreled straight through my defenses and forced me to watch.

Pumping my short, eleven-year-old legs, I sped down the alley as fast as I could despite the slick, ice-covered cobbles. Italy had declared war on the United States, and the school sent us Italian kids home early, worried about unrest in the North End. I slid to a stop in front of the stairs that led to the basement room where I lived with Mamma, Papà, and my baby sister, Gina.

The cracked wooden door opened with a creak. It wasn't much warmer inside, but I slammed it shut to save the heat. "Mamma—"

I froze. Mamma sat at the table, head tilted to the side. Two fading welts and a single drop of blood dotted her neck. A finger swiped the blood away. It belonged to a man I'd never seen before. His eyes glowed a deep red, and he licked the remnants of his meal from his finger.

His eyes landed where I stood in front of the door. Then they fell to the floor, and his shoulders slumped. He stepped back, pulled two dollars out of his coat pocket, and handed it to Mamma. "Grazie," he said.

Mamma's eyes held mine, and she shoved the two dollars into the pocket of her tattered sweater. "Prego."

The man stepped past me and out the door.

Mamma and I stared at each other.

Gina let out a wail from her basket. Mamma got up, slowly, exhaustion weighing down her slight frame. She picked up my baby sister and bounced her on her hip until she stopped crying, then sunk back into her chair.

"Vieni qui, Marco."

I met her where she sat, trying to make sense of what I'd seen. Bonded blood demons didn't share their necks. Mamma and Papà only drank from each other.

She took my hand. Her fingers were cold and bony; Mamma had grown so thin. But her grip was firm and steady.

"That two dollars will feed this family for a week. Longer if we're lucky. My blood is a small price to pay. But we can't tell your papà. It would kill him. He works so hard." Her strained voice cracked with the truth, and her eyes filled with tears. But Mamma was too strong to cry. She swallowed and cleared her throat. "I do what I need to do to provide for this family. Do you understand?"

"Yes, Mamma."

"Good. Now, why are you home so early?"

I slammed the rest of my whiskey and poured another.

Mamma and I never spoke of that day. No one else knew she'd sold herself so we wouldn't go hungry. But the image was branded into my memory.

The love and devotion between my parents had been the only steady force in an otherwise unsteady life. When you're poor and your stomach aches from hunger, when you watch your father leave every day to find work only to come home empty-handed, when you're eleven years old and life is that uncertain, there's a constancy in your parents, at least there had been for me. And walking in on another man at Mamma's neck had rocked my foundation.

From that day on, blood demons fed out of necessity; there was no room for pleasure. Sources provided a service purely transactional. Decades later, I understood life wasn't so black-and-white. I understood desperation, sacrifice. But the die had been cast. Those beliefs had anchored my formative years, and I'd held on to them for so long, they'd become my truth.

A knock at the door snapped me back into the present.

"Yes."

Anna, quiet as a mouse, slipped in through the door and closed it behind her. She looked down at her hands, clasping and unclasping them, her face still etched with worry.

"What is it, Anna?"

She cleared her throat and lifted her eyes, the light brown nearly consumed by her dilated pupils. "Was that..." She balled her shaking fingers into fists, and her nervous energy did uncomfortable things to my chest. "Was that *the* Vincenzo Valenzano?"

"Yes." I sipped my whiskey, hoping to deaden the impulse to take her into my arms and tell her she shouldn't worry, that I'd protect her.

She nodded and tried to appear relaxed even though her hands flexed open and shut. I could have strangled Vinnie.

"Does he..." She swallowed. "Does he come here often?" She asked her question quietly, as if whispering the words might ensure she wouldn't receive an answer she didn't want to hear.

"No. Never, actually."

She nodded again, then looked askance and tucked an errant piece of hair behind her ear.

"He was here to offer a business deal," I said, answering her unspoken question.

Her face paled, imperceptible to the human eye, but I was attuned to the flow in her veins.

I wanted to ease her anxiety but didn't have the words. Vinnie was a known criminal. Son of the infamous Big Frankie Valenzano and Don of the Boston Mafia. And he'd just been in my office.

"I declined."

Her shoulders relaxed, and she nodded vigorously, more of a comfort to herself than a message to me. She reached for the door.

"You're Italian," I said, and the casual comment surprised me.

She dropped her hand from the knob and turned back. "Yes," she said tentatively.

"What part of the boot?"

The corner of her mouth twitched. "My mother's parents are from Palermo, and my father's are from Naples."

I quirked a knowing smile "I should have guessed you were half Sicilian." She let out a short laugh and looked down at her feet, and her hair tumbled on either side of her amused face. "You have that spark."

"If by spark, you mean temper." Her gaze settled back on mine, and a playfully guilty smile brought the color back into her cheeks and brightened her eyes. The tightness in my chest started to unwind.

"Second generation, but full-blooded Italian. Not that I doubted." I narrowed my eyes. "Signature dish?"

"Hmm." She bit her lip and rocked her head back and forth. "I'd have to go with... spaghetti alla puttanesca. My father's recipe."

"Ottima scelta. Especially since your father's from Naples."

"He prides himself in his heritage."

I nodded. "The best recipes are brought over from the old

country, passed down from one generation to the next. I'm a terrible cook, but at least I can make a decent Sunday gravy thanks to my mother's unending supply of patience." I lifted my glass in mock toast, and she laughed. "We're not so different, you and I."

She stuck out a hip, wrapped an arm around her waist, and picked up the gold chain around her neck. She ran it between her thumb and forefinger, regarding me with a raised eyebrow and a skeptical tilt to the bow of her lips.

Her hand at her chest drew my attention, and for a heartbeat, I admired her breasts beautifully framed by the clean white lines of her blouse. I sipped my whiskey and lifted my eyes.

"What I mean is, you understand the life of immigrants and the importance we place on community. You were raised, at least in part I assume, Italian."

"True. My parents were involved with the Italian-American community where I grew up outside Amherst. I've traveled with them to Italy a few times to visit their aunts and uncles. Certain aspects of the culture were very much a part of my upbringing."

"Those experiences shape a person. Like I said"—I lifted my glass—"we're not so different." I took another swig and set it down on the bar top. The warmth of the whiskey and the easy conversation softened the remaining tension in my chest and neck. "The Italian-American population here is small when you consider the size of the city. The DeVitas and Valenzanos go way back, and regardless of Vinnie's business pursuits, he does tremendous work for the community. He crossed a boundary coming here today, but he was here for the community."

Her lips pursed and jaw worked as if chewing on the idea. "I—I can see that." She shifted her weight and dropped her necklace, clasping her hands in front of her. "I just wasn't expecting someone I've seen associated with the Mafia walk off the elevator at my job and ask to see my boss."

The quaver in her voice belied her dry tone. She was still unsettled. It bothered me more than I expected and more than it should.

"Yes, I can imagine how that might have been a touch jarring."

She huffed. "Just a touch."

"I can assure you it won't happen again."

She nodded. "Did you need anything else, or…" She gestured to the door.

"No. That will be all."

She stepped toward the door.

"Although," I continued, and she paused. "To spare you any more surprises, tomorrow morning, I'm going to city hall to meet with the zoning commissioner. I'd like you to come with me."

"Is this about the property in the financial district?"

"Good memory."

"Okay." She smiled, warm and genuine, and it stirred those uncomfortable sensations in my chest. "Thanks for the heads-up."

She left my office and closed the door behind her. I walked behind my desk, slumped into my chair, and picked up the contract I'd been reading.

My focus was shit, the words a jumble on the page, and I tossed the papers back on my desk. They landed on the letter opener I'd abandoned atop my punctured blotter. I dragged a hand down my face and reclined in my chair, resting my head against the soft leather.

Vinnie knew I was having financial problems. He was also expanding his Source racket and wanted to give me a piece of the action. And after eighty years, I was tempted to sink my fangs into a woman's neck for a reason other than necessity. What an afternoon.

I closed my eyes and let out a long, slow breath. These contracts weren't going to review themselves, and I had a zoning commissioner to shake down in the morning and an international flight to catch on Friday. Vinnie and Anna and all my unresolved issues would have to wait. The clock was ticking.

Chapter Seven

Anna

Mr. DeVita's driver slowed to a stop along the curb in front of City Hall Plaza. The concrete behemoth loomed outside the Range Rover's backseat window and dominated the Government Center skyline. Everyone but the driver opened their doors, and the cold wind whipping and snapping the flags in front of Boston's most notorious eyesore wreaked the same havoc on my hair.

I brushed the frenzied strands out of my eyes and gathered them into a fist. I steadied myself with my free hand, wondering how to orchestrate a graceful exit from the ginormous SUV in heels.

Mr. DeVita appeared, a knight in shining armor, and offered me his hand.

I stared at him, paralyzed by his chivalry. And the thought of holding his hand. The drive from Terme to city hall had only lasted fifteen minutes, but he'd been so close in the back seat. Close enough to smell the hint of cigar smoke and musky aftershave. Close enough to see the details of the gold ring on his pinky finger resting on the center console. Close enough to feel the wool of his overcoat brush against the back of my hand. I shivered.

"Thank you," I said and reached for him. His thumb closed around my fingers with a squeeze, and I leaned into his support. His grip was steady and powerful, like him, and it struck some primal chord inside me, evoking trust, a sense of safety, and no small amount of attraction. I snatched it back, and his lips twitched at my reaction.

He shut the door and knocked twice on the window. The Range Rover sped away, and Mr. DeVita, Mr. Balistreri, and I started off across the sea of concrete between us and our meeting with the zoning commissioner.

Mr. Balistreri sped ahead, his long strides propelling him toward our destination faster than I could manage with my short legs and heels. Mr. DeVita fell back and walked alongside me.

"I assume I'm here to take notes?" I asked with an arch look that matched my tone.

"Something like that," Mr. DeVita muttered and pulled open one of the glass entry doors.

The foyer's warmth was a welcome reprieve despite the stale smell of government building. The hive buzzed with professionals, security personnel, and average citizens; they tread noisily across the glossed brick. Footfalls and conversations echoed off tiered floors of the same emotionless concrete I imagined they'd used to build the county jail.

We rode the slow, clunking elevator to the ninth floor, and Mr. DeVita led us down a hall to a low-partition cubicle farm. The plastic nameplate on the welcome desk read "Planning and Development Agency."

"Marco DeVita here to see Doug Heller."

"Around the corner to your right." The woman behind the desk didn't bother to look up and instead pointed a finger ending in a manicure as sharp as a dagger. "Second door."

We followed the walkway between the cubicles and offices to a half-open door. Mr. DeVita rapped a knuckle against the wood even as he pushed his way inside.

"Hello, Doug," he said in a familiar tone.

The wiry man behind the desk jumped, and his thick, tortoiseshell glasses did nothing to obscure the surprise in his eyes. "Mr. DeVita." He pushed his glasses up his nose and rocked a pen between twitchy fingers. "I—I wasn't expecting you."

Hadn't Mr. DeVita mentioned an appointment?

"We were in the neighborhood. Thought we'd stop by, see how things are coming along with the waiver I requested for that property in the financial district."

The commissioner turned an unnatural shade of white and launched to his feet. He scurried around his desk and past the three of us. His eyes darted up and down the cubicle walkway before he hastily shut the door.

He quirked a sheepish smile, gestured to two guest chairs, and rounded his desk to reclaim his seat. He leaned back, affecting a relaxed posture, but he held onto his pen like a cigarette, rocking it between his fingers.

"You remember my lawyer, Vito Balistreri?" Mr. DeVita asked conversationally and took one of the two chairs. He glanced at me, a silent message, and I sat in the other.

Mr. Balistreri remained behind us, hands clasped and feet parted in an intimidating, authoritative stance. Mr. DeVita's lawyer stood about the same height as his boss, but with his stockier build, previously broken nose, and curly black hair, he looked like an extra from *Rocky*.

"Yes. Yes, of course." The cigarette-pen bounced between the commissioner's fingers. "Good to see you again, Mr. Balistreri."

"And this is my financial advisor, Ann Marone."

Ann Marone? A microdose of adrenaline shot into my

bloodstream. The lies rolled off Mr. DeVita's tongue as easily as the truth.

"Ms. Marone," the commissioner said with a nod.

"Hello." The evenness of my voice surprised me.

"Before I forget..." Mr. DeVita reached into the right breast pocket of his suit jacket, pulled out a cigar case, and extracted one of its fragrant inhabitants. He placed the cigar on the desk, then reclined into the old, plastic office chair like a king on a throne. He tossed one ankle over his knee, tucked the case back into his jacket, and folded his hands in his lap.

The cigarette-pen froze between the commissioner's fingers, and he stared at the cigar as if Mr. DeVita had deposited a venomous spider on his desk.

"It's one of those Cubans I gave you at Vesuvio," Mr. DeVita explained with a charming smile. "Remember? With the port? Thought you'd appreciate another."

The commissioner looked up from the cigar. "I can't accept that," he said quietly and shook his head.

"Of course, you can." Mr. DeVita held the commissioner's eyes in silent challenge, and the feigned smile fell from his face. "I insist."

The commissioner swallowed, picked up the cigar, and lifted it in toast. "Thank you," he said and tucked the contraband into the pocket of his button-down.

"Now, tell me about the waiver."

The cigarette-pen resumed its rhythmic bounce. The commissioner's eyes darted to me, behind us to Mr. Balistreri, then back to Mr. DeVita. "I—I haven't made much progress. These regulations weren't meant to be altered on a per-property basis. To waive a land use restriction in the way you suggest..." He shook his head and frowned. "The system wasn't set up to do that."

"Come on, Doug. I've given you plenty of time. We

wouldn't want some other party buying that property before you figure this out now, would we?"

The commissioner shifted uncomfortably in his seat. I didn't blame him. My growing discomfort with this conversation was making my palms sweat and my heart race. That cigar seemed a lot like a bribe, and Mr. DeVita's question a lot like a threat.

"I'm not sure I can do this." The commissioner's voice wavered across his mumbled words.

A taut silence held the room in wait. The cigarette-pen tapped against the desk. I bounced my heel in and out of my shoe. Yet, the hard lines of Mr. DeVita's face remained impassive, the easy recline of his powerful body unperturbed.

"Vito. You watch the Pats game Sunday night?" Mr. DeVita's question cleaved the tension with startling force. "These division playoffs are really heating up."

"Sure are."

Mr. DeVita glanced in my direction. "I had a grand riding on the Pats," he said in a commiserating tone. "Losing hurts worse when you've got money riding on it." He turned his attention back to the commissioner and leveled him with a heavy stare. "Wouldn't you agree, Doug?"

Beads of sweat on the commissioner's forehead glinted beneath the fluorescent lights.

"Who'd you take in the game?" Mr. DeVita's question was rife with knowledge.

"The Pats," Doug croaked.

"Shame."

The word delivered an unspoken warning, and Mr. DeVita stared the commissioner down until it grew and consumed the office. Nausea gripped my stomach under its weight, and my hands, already clammy with nervous sweat, started to shake.

"But enough about football." Mr. DeVita's stoic features

broke into a wide, predatory grin. "We were talking about a waiver."

Doug nodded, jarring a bead of sweat loose. It trailed down his temple, and he blotted it with the cuff of his button-down. "As—uh—as I mentioned, I'm having difficulty finding a way to waive the land use restrictions on a per-property basis. I'm sure—" He swallowed. "I'm sure there's a way. A loophole or a statute I'm not aware of, but I haven't found it yet. I need more time." He made the desperate plea through clenched teeth.

"That's why I brought Vito."

The commissioner's eyes darted to where Mr. Balistreri stood behind us.

Mr. DeVita thrust his wrist out of his coat sleeve and glanced at his watch. "Huh. Just about time for my mid-morning caffè." He pushed out of his chair, and I scrambled to my feet. "Vito will stay and assist you in your search. I'm confident, after a day together, you'll find a way to waive the zoning regulations."

The commissioner's pale face went a touch green.

"Before we go, Ann will ensure all required fees are paid and paperwork filed in advance so I can make the purchase as soon as the waiver is in place." Doug frowned and opened his mouth to interject, but Mr. DeVita steamrolled right over him. "The last time we met, you mentioned the building's historic classification, that the city won't allow the seller to consider bids without sufficient capital and proof of solvency. Ann will provide any documentation you need."

I would? I scrambled to pull the notebook and pen from my purse. "Yes. Uh—what is required? And your—your contact information? Please?" Not exactly the notetaking I'd been referring to when I'd asked him why he'd brought me along, but I jotted down the barrage of form numbers and his email address regardless.

"Enjoy the cigar." Mr. DeVita grabbed the doorknob. "We'll talk soon," he said and walked out of the office.

"Thank you," the commissioner mumbled to Mr. DeVita's back.

I spared a final glance at the nervous official. The resignation in his voice matched the defeated downturn of his mouth. His wary eyes tracked Mr. Balistreri as the big man removed his coat, unbuttoned his suit jacket, and lowered his bulky frame into one of the chairs opposite the commissioner's desk.

I hurried after Mr. DeVita, walking as fast as I could despite my heels and the nervous energy turning my legs into noodles. I caught up to him at the elevators, and we made the rest of our exit in silence. Fine by me; I was at a loss for words.

The bracing cold and gusting wind shocked my system out of its caged feeling from being trapped inside the jail-like building. I took small, quick steps to keep up with Mr. DeVita's long strides, and the icy air brought a measure of calmness and clarity to my flustered mind.

"You know, I really could use a caffè," he said easily, as if he hadn't just bribed and threatened a city official. "There's a bakery across the street." He gestured to the south end of the plaza. "They make a decent cappuccino. We'll stop there before I call my driver."

"Are we going to talk about what just happened?"

"What just happened?"

"Not to put too fine a point on it, but..." The words to describe what I'd witnessed slowly solidified, and the clarity grew my anxiety into something just short of panic. "That entire conversation sounded very much like extortion."

"Interesting take. Which part exactly?" He glanced down at me, his brow furrowed in genuine curiosity.

I stared back at him, awed by the complete lack of culpability. "For starters, the cigar. The *illegal* cigar, I might add. Your intimidation tactics—showing up unannounced, Mr.

Balistreri, the talk about football and making bets. That poor man looked like he was going to be sick!"

"Doug's a nervous guy. He always looks like that."

I gave him my best I-call-bullshit look.

"There are ways of obtaining Cuban cigars these days that aren't illegal. As for the football? He's a fan. I was making small talk."

"You can't possibly think I'm that naïve."

"No. Far from it." He captured my eyes in that way he did, holding them to make sure his message landed. "I think you're intelligent enough to know when not to ask questions. You may not want to hear the answers."

"That's rather ominous."

"Just a fact."

"You're not helping your case, you know."

"I didn't realize I had a case."

I glared at him. "You told me you had nothing to do with Mr. Valenzano."

"I don't."

"Well, this entire visit and your cagey answers sound a lot to me like Mafia scare tactics."

"You've watched too many gangster movies."

I scoffed and looked away. Unbelievable.

We'd been walking south across the plaza and the abrupt rise of buildings to the east reminded me where we were— Government Center. My pace slowed, and I stared at the block of buildings I'd once thought held my future.

"What?" Mr. DeVita asked.

"Nothing." I hurried back into step alongside him. "It's nothing."

"Tell me."

"So demanding," I said exasperated.

He raised an eyebrow.

I chewed my lip before answering, selecting my words, not

wanting to give away too much. "I—I always thought I'd work down here when I was younger. That's all."

"You don't strike me as the government and politics type," he said dryly.

We darted across the busy street like good Bostonians, completely ignoring the crosswalk and traffic signals.

"I'm not," I said, when we reached the other side. "I'm a researcher at a university." I lifted my chin toward the cluster of buildings directly south of City Hall Plaza. "But a lot of the big financial consulting firms are headquartered there."

"Ah. Still a far cry from academia."

I huffed. Didn't I know it.

The wind whipped down the corridor created by the tall buildings. I lowered my face to shield it from the icy blast, but struggled to keep up, my short steps more tentative than usual under the onslaught of gusting wind.

"Here," Mr. DeVita said and held out his elbow.

I looked up at his handsome face, the clean lines of his shaved jaw, the dark lashes over darker eyes, and slid my hand inside the crook of his arm. His bicep bulged beneath the soft wool of his overcoat, and I squeezed it to steady myself, pulling his warmth closer. "Thank you."

He nodded, and we continued down the block until the clean white façade of a French bakery materialized.

"I had no idea this was here," I said.

He opened the glass door and ushered me inside. "I'm always on the lookout for decent caffè. And I like their croissants."

The warmth of the bakery replaced the warmth of Mr. DeVita's arm, but his absence was no less palpable. I ignored my unhinged desire to reclaim his arm and stepped up to the display case instead, placing my gloved hands on the glass. The pastries were perfectly shaped, and their buttery sheen glistened under the lights. My stomach growled. Loudly.

I laid my hand over the beast and looked up.

Amusement danced in Mr. DeVita's obsidian eyes. "Hungry?"

"Apparently."

"Order whatever you'd like."

We ordered, he paid, and we carried our decadent mid-morning snack to a small table by the window.

I peeled off a swath of the flaky croissant and popped it in my mouth. It melted like butter on my tongue. I washed it down with a piping hot sip of cappuccino. The rich, soothing flavors and the quiet of the empty bakery did their best to calm my riotous nerves.

Coffee with Mr. DeVita. My stomach flipped, but I swatted at the butterflies, reminding myself I'd just witnessed an act of extortion.

"What about Mr. Balistreri?" I asked.

"What about him?"

"You left him there to intimidate that man."

"Are we back on this again?"

"I don't want to be involved in anything illegal," I hissed under my breath, and a touch of the nausea that had gripped my stomach in the close confines of the commissioner's office returned.

Mr. DeVita sat back in his chair and crossed his arms. "I left him there to help find a solution. I am extremely moti-vated to secure that property, and Vito has decades of experi-ence navigating regulations and bureaucracy. That's not illegal."

"Extortion is illegal." My whispered words remained firm.

He reached for his croissant with relaxed indifference. "Did you hear me threaten anyone?" He raised an eyebrow. "Cause I didn't." And took a bite of croissant.

He was right, of course. He'd been pushy, arrogant, and domineering, but he hadn't threatened anyone.

I narrowed my eyes. "Why did you ask me to come along?"

"Because I want you to read through the permits, help me understand what type of financial information they need, and make sure, leak or no leak, I have enough capital for escrow."

"Don't you have a CFO or an accountant for that?"

"I'm the CFO. And I already told you, I don't trust my accounting department right now." He sipped his coffee, and the bend of his mouth turned smug. "Don't forget, the contract you signed did specify you'd be asked to perform tasks usually done by my assistant."

I twisted my lips into a skeptical smirk. "Your assistant is a financial advisor?"

"No, but if she were, I might ask her to help."

I huffed out a laugh despite myself and shook my head. Infuriating man.

He pulled out his cellphone, hit a button, and held it to his ear. "Ten minutes. The coffee shop on Washington," he said and, after a beat, tucked the phone back into his pocket.

He sat back and stretched one leg out in front of him. "What is a tenured finance professor from MIT doing working for Jeff Levitt?"

I inhaled a flake of croissant and unleashed an epic coughing fit.

An eternity passed while I tried to regain composure, my mortification growing with each gasp for air. Mr. DeVita just sat there, patiently awaiting the end of my episode. What I wouldn't have given for a black hole to appear beneath my chair and swallow me into oblivion.

"Sorry," I croaked, and soothed my throat and my ego with coffee. I dabbed the tears from my eyes and soldiered on. "First of all, how do you know that?"

"It's my job to know things."

"That's cryptic."

He shrugged.

"Well, for starters, Jeff is my best friend."

"I figured based on the pictures."

"What pictures?"

"The pictures from the profile I had made up for you."

I opened my mouth to protest, but quickly snapped it shut. I scowled, and the corner of his mouth turned up in a sly hint of a smile.

Of course he'd had a profile made up. Probably knew my childhood dog's name and bra size. There was no point arguing; it was a done deal, and my emotional well was already drained from the extortion.

I sighed and waved my hand through the air like what I was about to say was no big deal. "I'm considering leaving MIT."

He blinked the same surprised hesitation I'd seen on his face that first day when he realized I was a woman.

"I'm on sabbatical. Jeff offered me this job because the work aligns with my research. This is my chance to try on the real world, see if it fits."

He looked at me as if I'd grown another head. "The real world? You're a tenured professor. Sounds real to me."

I studied the last dregs of my cappuccino and grabbed my necklace, running the chain between my thumb and forefinger. I'd had enough trouble opening up about my dissatisfaction with Jeff, yet here I was about to launch into my midlife awakening with an overbearing stranger. Maybe I was too drained to clam up. Or maybe it was the genuine interest I'd seen in his face and heard in his voice.

"When I was in grad school, people told me I'd never make it in industry. International investments and corporate finance aren't places for a wallflower."

He arched an eyebrow.

"Those were my advisor's words, not mine."

His lips flattened in a tight line of displeasure.

"What I said earlier? About working down here? That's why I never did. I believed them."

My stomach rolled admitting my deepest regret to someone I barely knew. But then again, there was freedom in putting it out there so plainly. Like I was finally owning my destiny. I huffed out a breath, surprised by the revelation, and finished my coffee.

"The car's here," he said, glancing over my shoulder.

We put on our coats, and for the third time that morning, Mr. DeVita donned his chivalrous persona and offered his hand to help me into the back seat. The doors slammed shut, and the Range Rover lurched forward into Boston traffic.

"Instead, you became an esteemed professor at the most prestigious university in the world. I've seen the awards. Impressive doesn't begin to describe your accomplishments."

Over the years, I'd learned to take compliments about my career, but coming from Mr. DeVita, the praise landed with a weight I hadn't expected. I gave him an embarrassed smile. "Thank you."

"You've made quite a career for yourself. I don't understand why you'd want to leave that now."

I looked out the window. It was nearing lunchtime, and the busy sidewalks and streets seemed so far away from our quiet conversation. We drifted through the melee in a bubble, just the two of us, separated in time and space from the chaos of the outside world. It felt safe and secure, and the explanation I'd been holding inside clawed its way out, desperate to be heard.

"It's easy to look at someone," I said to the window, "and based on their job and their accomplishments assume they have it together, that they're in control and have everything they want." I shook my head. "But you don't know. All you see is their highlight reel. You don't see what they're missing."

He shifted in the seat behind me, and I sensed I'd struck a chord, but I needed to get the rest of my truths off my chest.

"Prestige doesn't equate to happiness, or even satisfaction. Neither do awards or tenure. Just because someone's job seems impressive or noble, that doesn't mean they're happy." I swallowed down a surge of emotion and turned to face him. "If it did, I wouldn't be sitting here."

The lines around his mouth and across his forehead softened, and his lips parted as if my words had torn open their tight restraint. "You were cast in a role, and you're done playing the part. You want something more."

"I do."

"You want what's missing."

"Yes."

"There are things you told yourself you couldn't have. Because what you've been doing? That's all you're supposed to do. And you've been doing it for so long."

I swallowed.

"Then one day, you wake up, and you realize... you want more." His voice was low and gravelly, barely above a whisper.

My eyes burned with unwanted tears. "How..."

He cleared his throat and turned to the window, severing our connection. "It's a common experience among people our age." He lifted his shoulder in a casual gesture that belied how his voice cracked halfway through his excuse.

The car lurched to a stop, popping our cozy bubble and thrusting us back into reality. The haze from our conversation lifted, and I patiently waited for Mr. DeVita to come around to my side of the car. He held out a hand and helped me out but avoided eye contact, and we walked through the lobby of Terme di Boston without another word.

An awkward silence rode with us in the elevator. It only released after the doors opened and Mr. DeVita put distance between us with quick strides. I took off my gloves and coat and hung them on the rack. I smoothed my hair, staticky from the cold, picked up my bag, and headed for my desk.

Mr. DeVita stood in the doorway to his office and watched me, his face a mask of cool control except for the slight tic of the muscle in his jaw. "I'm flying to Italy tomorrow on business. I'll be back in the office Tuesday after lunch."

"Okay." I unpacked my water bottle and notebook before tucking my purse under the desk. The awkward silence from the elevator returned and took over the foyer. "I'm..." *Wracking my brain for something to say.* "Hopefully I'll have a draft ready by the time you get back. Oh! And I'll look over the financial requirements for those permits, too."

He shoved his hands in his pockets and nodded. "Siobhán will help you with anything you need while I'm out. Unless it has to do with your contract. In which case, contact me on my personal cell. I'll email you the number."

"Sounds good," I said, thinking we'd finally reached the end of uncomfortable. But he didn't move, clearing his throat instead.

"For what it's worth, I think you're doing a fine job in the real world. You came up to speed faster than I expected and have been making steady progress despite everything I've thrown at you. Any company would be lucky to have you on their staff."

Heat bloomed in my chest and threatened to color my cheeks. It's as if he'd known exactly what I needed to hear, except there was no hint of flattery, just sincerity. "Thank you, Mr. DeVita. That—that means a lot."

He nodded but hesitated. Part of me hoped he'd stay, hoped he'd lean into our connection. But then he dropped his head and walked into his office, and the door closed behind him with a soft *click*.

I stared at it for a moment, confused and unsettled. Of all

the morning's problematic developments, the warm sensation in my chest was by far the most troubling. Mr. DeVita's small acts of chivalry, his genuine interest in my background, and his sincere praise had me reeling.

I woke up the computer, initialized my software, and tried to concentrate on the tasks at hand—the remaining elements I needed to add to the first draft of my model and the list of permits I needed to research for the property in the financial district—but my mind had other ideas. It kept drifting back to the warmth that had settled in my chest and the mesmerizing hold of Mr. DeVita's obsidian eyes.

Chapter Eight

Marco

"Matteo! Guard!" Vito's warning boomed across the gym.

I walked out of the locker room, and Matteo's opponent connected a mean right hook with Matteo's left forearm. Lucky son of a bitch got his guard up just in time.

Shuffling and grunts came from the ring. The discordant clank of free weights rang out above the rhythmic thud of the punching bag. Stale sweat and disinfectant clung to my nostrils in a familiar mélange. Vito's gym was like a second home, a sanctuary where I reset my brain by punishing my body. And after today, I needed a hard reset.

I wrapped my knuckles and made my way to where Vito hovered over two stacks of receipts and an old-school printing calculator. The tape advanced, and he moved a small piece of paper from one stack to the other.

"That kid's gonna get his teeth knocked out if he doesn't learn to keep his guard up," Vito mumbled from behind the desk.

I grunted. "At least he'll learn his lesson. How'd we do last week?"

"Better than average. Everyone bet on the Pats."

"Excellent."

Football season was our busiest time. Gambling was a profitable racket all year round, but nothing came close to what we pulled in on football. Which reminded me…

"How'd it go with our friend?"

Vito finished adding the receipt he was holding, stopped, and looked up. "He either wasn't trying very hard or he's wildly incompetent." I snorted. "Either way, I think we identified a loophole that'll work. The waiver should be ready by late next week. Two weeks max. He'll email your assistant when it's ready."

"Good." Good for us, and good for Doug. He didn't have the cash to pay his debts, but lucky for him, his position guaranteed he could pay me back in other ways. "I want that shit locked down. Any word from the clerks on the Shaughnessys?"

The zoning commissioner wasn't the only member of city hall I kept on payroll. I had clerks in most departments feeding me information.

"Nothing. Just the initial tip. Confirmed by two clerks."

"Let's hope it stays that way. Last thing we need is those Irish fucks buying up that property before the waiver's in place."

"You worry too much."

"What about the European accountants? Find any dirt?"

"No smoking gun. One guy cheating on his wife." He shrugged. "Nothing that'd push someone onto a take. But not all snakes are born out of dirt."

Wasn't that the truth. Greed was just as powerful a motivator. What I couldn't get with dirt, I got with bribes.

"Keep digging. The timing's too convenient for coincidence."

His forehead creased. "Aren't you flying out tomorrow?"

"What?" I smirked. "Want me out of your hair or something?" He snorted. "I am. Needed to blow off some steam."

"Hit the bag," he said and returned his attention to the receipts. "I'm not going to be done for a while, and you'll KO those kids in about five minutes."

The bag would help, but not as much as getting in the ring. I wanted to fight. "It'll be good for them. No better teacher than getting your ass kicked."

"Marco."

I scowled at Vito's gruff admonition. "Fine."

He picked up a receipt and punched a few numbers into his calculator, and I headed around the ring to where the custom-made speed bags and heavy bags hung from steel chains mounted into a reinforced ceiling. Standard gear didn't hold up to blood demons.

I warmed up on the speed bag. The sweat forming on my brow and the burn in my shoulders released some of the tension that had been building in my body since earlier in the day. The furious speed of my fists drove the bag in a blur of maroon leather, but I wanted to hit something. Hard.

Doug wasn't moving fast enough with my waiver. I'd played nice so far, only using bribes and my reputation to scare him into action. But if he didn't hurry his ass up, I wouldn't hesitate to turn the screws. And if Shaughnessy got to that property before I did, I'd use his slimy face as a warmup instead of a speed bag.

With a final punch, I sent the speed bag flying. I rolled my shoulders and moved for the heavy bag. One of my men working it backed off, eyeing me warily. I threw up my guard, bounced on the balls of my feet, and unleashed a flurry of hooks and crosses that slapped and thudded against the thick leather. My chest heaved and arms burned with exertion.

Doug wasn't the only person who'd pissed me off. Anna's confession about her job, why she'd forgone her plans to work in industry... The regret in her voice and the tentative way she'd opened up about what had brought her to DEI... I wanted to strangle the person who'd squashed the dreams of such a brilliant woman.

I slammed my left fist into the bag, and the force of the impact jerked the chains securing it to the ceiling causing an ear-piercing screech.

"Jesus fucking Christ, Marco!" Vito yelled from across the gym. "If you rip through another bag, I swear to God..."

I backed off and faced him, opening my arms. "Then get your ass in the ring so I can fight!"

He shook his head, ripped the tape from the calculator, and set it across the two stacks of receipts. He stood, threw off his hooded sweatshirt, and climbed between the ropes into the ring. "Out," he barked at the two men still sparring. They dropped their hands, scrambled out, and hung on the ropes to watch.

I climbed in, and we squared off. We'd done this so many times, neither of us hesitated. We threw up our guards, hands wrapped, but no gloves, and Vito came at me with a mean right hook, no doubt irritated I'd interrupted his bookkeeping. I blocked the punch and smiled. Finally.

Anna's eyes had glistened with tears in the car, and my overwhelming need to comfort and protect her had resurfaced with a vengeance. The same feelings I'd had during Vinnie's unexpected visit.

Two quick jabs and an uppercut. Vito blocked them with ease and countered with a quick succession of jabs. I welcomed the onslaught of his fists, needing to get her out of my head. I swung a left cross, and he got his elbow up just in time. He danced away with a knowing tilt to his head. Now, we were moving.

What pissed me off even more was the sucker punch she'd landed on the ride back to Terme. Made me say things I hadn't meant to say, admit things I didn't want to admit. *Then one day, you wake up, and you realize... you want more.* The words had spilled out of me as if wrenched from my lungs by the force of their truth.

Round after round, we threw and blocked punches with the strength and speed only used when fighting another blood demon. We flirted with the edge of exhaustion, daring each other to give in first. Sweat-soaked and straining for breath, my anger, tension, and defenses melted away.

I had responsibilities. To my family, to my crew, and to my community. I protected. I provided. That's all that mattered. Was I happy? Was I satisfied? Who knew; it'd never mattered before. I'd been so busy carrying the weight of all my shoulds, I'd never considered there might be another way, that I might want something more.

Anna's fingertips trailed the length of her necklace to where it landed between her breasts. Her hair fell to the side exposing her neck. My fangs ached to pierce her delicate skin, and longing ripped through my chest.

Vito's left fist connected with my jaw.

"Argh!" A shock of pain lanced through my face to the back of my skull. I spun away and doubled over, holding my chin. It was shifted out of socket, throbbing to the beat of my rapid pulse. I took two deep breaths and on the third squeezed my eyes shut and snapped it into place.

"Cazzo! What the fuck!"

"Come here," Vito growled. He took my chin in his hand and examined my eyes. They stung from sweat and from having my fucking jaw dislocated. He turned my head from side to side, studying my face, and patted me twice on the cheek. "You're fine."

I breathed rapidly through my nose, jaw clenched despite the sharp pain, pissed off more at myself than Vito.

"But you shoulda blocked that," he said and gave me a disapproving look.

"No shit," I snapped and ran a hand through my sweaty hair.

Vito whistled and held out his hand. Matteo grabbed a couple of towels and a water bottle and climbed into the ring. He tossed me a towel, and I wiped the sweat from my face.

"All fired up and distracted. Dangerous combination, boss. If I didn't know better, I'd think you were hung up on some woman." Vito raised his eyebrows and squirted water into his mouth.

"Good thing you know better," I barked.

He handed me the water bottle and stared at me sideways. "She's not one of us," he said, only loud enough for my ears. "Don't forget that."

I squirted water on my face and in my mouth. I handed it back to him with a scowl and headed for the locker room. I slumped onto one of the benches and gripped the old wood on either side of my thighs, hanging my head while I caught my breath.

Distracted. From the fight right in front of me and the fight to maintain control of my empire. And by a human, no less. A fragile human who'd likely never been exposed to crime and had no idea blood demons existed.

The instinct to possess and protect this woman I barely knew was running roughshod over the tight control I kept on my appetite for blood and sex. I wanted her. To feed from and to fuck, an inclination I'd never experienced beyond a fleeting moment. It bothered me.

I rolled my shoulders, pushed off the bench, and stripped out of my sweaty clothes. I didn't wait for the water to warm up but stepped beneath the cold blast hoping to ice my unwelcome desires. I placed my palms flat against the tile, dropped my head, and closed my eyes. The water pounded the top of my head and shoulders.

Anna's beautiful face appeared—its two little beauty marks, the wrinkles at the corners of her eyes, the trusting expression she'd worn when she'd opened up.

Maybe she was right. Maybe there was more to life than responsibility. Maybe true happiness and satisfaction were possible.

Or maybe I couldn't afford those things. Maybe belonging and companionship weren't possible for an immortal criminal.

Chapter Nine

Anna

The blinking cursor waited for my command. I typed *start* at the terminal prompt, hit enter, and the compilation log flew up the screen. My first cut at a financial model of DEI's European office. I leaned back in my chair and sipped my coffee through a self-satisfied smile. The draft was rudimentary. It had holes, and I'd fill those holes over the next week or two. But a structure in place after only five days? Not too shabby.

The silence of the penthouse was both a welcome reprieve and a disappointing vacuum. Mr. DeVita's absence left an undeniable void.

The past two days had been illuminating, to say the least. Don Valenzano had visited my boss. He was, in fact, a close, personal associate of my boss. Then, the very next day, the same boss had attempted to bribe and threaten a city official. No matter how hard he'd tried to explain it away, that was extortion.

I shook my head and drained the last of my coffee. The model would take at least an hour to compile, and idle time was the devil's playground. Or something like that. Time for a little internet sleuthing.

Google returned surprisingly few hits on *Marco DeVita*. The same three pictures showed up over and over again, and suddenly the *No Pictures* clause of my NDA didn't seem so strange. A younger portrait used for official DEI publicity. A casual but blurred picture of him holding a glass of wine at a charity event that could have taken place two weeks ago or two years ago. And a candid shot of him leaving Terme di Boston.

Waves of dark hair with silver pinstripes immaculately styled above stern features. A dominating stature accentuated by the clean lines of a fine, tailored suit. And obsidian eyes, staring into the camera, commanding attention and respect. A pleasant tingle rippled down my spine.

Brief glimpses of empathy and vulnerability had broken through Mr. DeVita's domineering and arrogant exterior, and they tugged at the physical attraction I'd been trying to deny. Despite my best efforts to squash my growing interest, he'd become even more intriguing after the quiet moments we'd shared.

I shook off the warm sentiments, opened another browser tab, and continued my search. No mugshots or pictures of him with Valenzano. A sliver of relief cut through my suspicion and alleviated some of the guilt I had over my body's reaction to his picture.

The results revealed more about DEI and the six terme than Mr. DeVita himself. I tried his name in a few people-finder websites as well, but records of Marco DeVita in Boston were thin at best, especially without a birthplace or a date. There was no telling if any of the hits were an exact match.

Hard to believe someone with such far-reaching financial interests could fly so far under the radar. Then again, given the NDA I signed, maybe I shouldn't have been surprised. Mr.

DeVita probably spent a small fortune keeping his name under wraps.

I pulled up the picture of him walking out of Terme, and the pleasant tingle morphed into a simmering heat. I closed my eyes and remembered the feel of his thick bicep beneath my fingers as we walked to the bakery. The heat spread, quickening my heart rate and making me squirm in my seat.

My eyes shot open. I'd never responded so primally to a man before. I reached for my water bottle, unnerved.

The elevator dinged, and I jumped, quickly closing the browser and restoring the terminal window.

Siobhán sashayed off the elevator with all the style and grace of an early Hollywood starlet. Her tea-length skirt swished above a pair of heels I'd give anything to master. Her white blouse was tucked into her skirt, the ensemble cinched with a tight belt around her tiny waist, and once again her hair and makeup were perfectly set, white teeth gleaming behind ruby red lips.

I sighed and rested my chin on my hands, stars in my eyes as I watched her glide across the foyer to my desk. I'd always dreamed of being tall, confident, and graceful instead of short, awkward, and clumsy.

"Hi, Anna," she said, her voice light and friendly. She half-sat on the edge of my desk facing the window and folded her hands against her thigh.

We were around the same age, both career women, and she had an easygoing, nonjudgmental manner that reminded me a lot of Jeff. It made talking to her comfortable and effortless.

"Hi, Siobhán. What brings you up here?"

"You, girl. I'm here to take you to lunch. And to check on you." She winked. "Marco mentioned he was flying out this morning and asked me to pop in to see if you needed anything."

"Oh. That was... nice of him."

"He's a sweetheart." Her expression and voice reflected the warmth she obviously felt for the man.

I scrunched my face. "I'm not sure sweetheart is the word I'd use to describe Mr. DeVita."

The amusement in her smile reached her eyes, and they crinkled at the corners. "No, I suppose you might not. He can be a little intense when you first meet him."

"A little?" I raised my eyebrows and relaxed against my chairback. "He makes Godzilla look like a teddy bear."

She tipped her head back and laughed. "I can see how you'd think that, especially if you're not used to men like him. I, however, am used to it. Painfully so. My brother and all my cousins are just like Marco." She shrugged. "Most of the time those guys are teddy bears under their gruff exteriors." She leaned toward me. "Most of the time."

I tilted my head in question.

"You think Marco's intense? Wait until you meet Luca."

I grimaced. "With that endorsement..."

She chuckled.

"Who's Luca?"

"The Chief Operating Officer of DEI Europe and Marco's nephew. They're a pair, the two of them." She raised her eyebrows and dropped her chin. "The type of men you want on your side, but never want to date," she said with finality and a firm nod.

"I'll take your word on that. And honestly, after the past two days, I'm not sure I can handle much more intensity."

She narrowed her eyes, and worry-lines formed across her forehead. "What happened?"

I waved a hand. "Nothing. A trip to city hall yesterday and an unexpected visitor the day before. It was a lot."

Her eyes grew wide with understanding. "Right. Mr. Valenzano came by Wednesday. I saw him walk through my lobby."

"I—I wasn't expecting that." I swallowed back the anxiety that surfaced every time I thought about meeting a known criminal. "And his bodyguard, or whatever, he stood there all huge and menacing with sunglasses on like he was a Secret Service agent or something. I thought my heart was going to explode out of my chest."

"If it makes you feel any better, I've never seen Mr. Valenzano at Terme before. I was just as surprised." She leaned forward. "Knowing Marco, I'm sure he took care of it. I doubt either of us will see him again." She reached across the desk and squeezed my arm.

"And what's with the sunglasses?" I blurted out now that I had an audience for all my questions. "It wasn't just Mr. Valenzano's guy. Every day in the lobby there are at least two men like him stalking around. Same type of beefcake, and they're always wearing sunglasses."

She snickered. "Beefcake?"

I rolled my eyes. "You know what I mean."

"Marco staffs his properties with his own private security detail. He's a bit of a control freak."

"I hadn't noticed," I said dryly.

"Listen. Marco's a well-connected man, and in this city, being connected comes at a cost. He's protecting his interests, making sure his employees are safe. As for the sunglasses?" She straightened her spine and slapped her hands against her thighs. "I always assumed it was to make them look more intimidating. Like *Men in Black* or something."

I snorted. "You're probably right. I've spent most of my life in academia. I'm not used to all this intensity and connections and beefcakes in sunglasses. I think I got spooked by all the..." I waved my hands in a big circle. "All the real." I shook my head. "Anyway, lunch?"

"Lunch." She hopped off the desk. "And it's Friday, which in my book means it can be extra-long and include martinis. A couple of those should take your focus off the beefcakes." She winked and stuck the tip of her tongue between her teeth.

I laughed. "Sounds perfect."

I PUSHED the mushroom around my plate, unable to eat one more bite of marsala, but wishing I could so I'd have something to do while David prattled on about himself. It would have been rude to check my watch, but part of me was genuinely interested in how long the man could have a conversation with himself before realizing there was someone else at the table.

It was Saturday night, and I was on my fourth date with David Lancaster. He'd suggested Lombardi, an intimate Italian restaurant near Kendall Square overlooking the Charles. I didn't have the heart to tell him you didn't go out for Italian in Cambridge.

Mr. DeVita, on the other hand, wouldn't have hesitated. He probably would have fired off a string of Italian curses at the mere suggestion of dinner at Lombardi.

I speared the mushroom, brought it in front of my eyes, and stared at it for what felt like an eternity. Maybe I was caught in a singularity in the space-time continuum and time had stopped. Or maybe David was just that boring.

My love life. Boring and predictable. Just like my career.

"And that's how I ended up with my *second* National Academy of Engineering award." David's eyes settled on my face with his declaration, and I tore mine away from the marsala-drenched mushroom to smile and nod.

At least Mr. DeVita had been genuinely interested in me. We'd only known each other for a week, and he'd already asked about my family, my heritage, and my career. Meanwhile, I'd been seeing David for over a month, had known him from running club even longer, yet I was pretty sure he had no clue where I was from, much less that I was Italian. Thankfully, the server appeared to clear our dishes and gave me a moment to figure out my next move.

On paper, David was everything I should have wanted in a partner. He was successful, intelligent, and kind. We shared a similar education and career path. We both liked to run. He was handsome in an unassuming, traditional way. Healthy and fit. He had nice teeth.

Really, Anna? Nice teeth?

In reality, we had little in common and even less to talk about. And I'd just put his teeth in the "pro" column. Not to mention the orgasm-less trip to the bedroom after our last date. He may have had a PhD in chemical engineering, but there was absolutely zero chemistry happening in that bedroom, not with his vacant stare, stilted grunts, and robotic thrusts.

When he first asked me out, I'd been so hopeful. I was desperate to find connection, romance, and passion. But all I'd found with David were one-sided conversations, outings I'd rather have spent with Jeff, and unremarkable sex. A relationship with him was headed straight to nowheresville.

"Would you care for some dessert? Coffee?" David reached across the table for my hand.

Mr. DeVita held out his hand to help me out of the Range Rover. The image was quickly replaced by a closeup of his angular jaw. A muscle there twitched when his dark eyes settled on my breasts. A shiver went down my spine, and I blinked myself back into the moment.

God, I'm a horrible person.

David was being so sweet, trying to respect my boundaries. Ironically, that was part of the problem.

"No, thank you," I said and carefully pulled my hand away.

He turned to the waiter. "Just the check, please."

"Of course, sir," the man replied and walked away.

The bend of David's smile was sad but resigned. "This isn't working, is it?"

"No," I said with as much regret as I could muster despite my relief. "I don't think so."

He nodded and trailed his finger along the base of his water glass. "I thought you might say that." He lifted one shoulder and gave me a half smile. "It was worth a shot though, right?"

"Yeah." I smiled. "I think so." I scrunched my face. "I hope it won't be weird at running club."

He laughed. "No. It won't be weird. I promise."

I believed him. He was too kind and too boring to create any sort of drama.

Horrible. Person.

The waiter returned with our check, and David paid, waving me off even as I reached for my purse. We walked out of the restaurant, and he kissed my cheek, thanking me for a pleasant evening. Then, he stepped to the curb and hailed a cab.

Apparently, my midlife awakening wasn't taking any prisoners. Tonight's lackluster dinner had put an exclamation point on the fact my career wasn't the only thing in need of a makeover. In terms of dissatisfaction, my love life came in a close second.

I shoved my hands into my coat pockets and took off in the other direction, cursing myself for not wearing gloves. The crisp night air felt clean and refreshing against my face, like I'd broken free from another shackle holding me back. I wanted to soak in the freedom. My condo in Harvard Square was only two miles away. At least I wasn't wearing heels.

I loved walking through Cambridge at night. It was so much quieter than during the day when students carpeted the sidewalks like ants and cars raced and honked their way from one university to the next. It was peaceful at night and gave me a chance to reflect and enjoy the city's old-world charm.

Old-world charm. Mr. DeVita wore old world charm like cologne.

This was starting to become a bad habit, but I couldn't get the images of him offering me his arm out of my mind. Or how we'd connected in the backseat of the Range Rover. He'd understood me on a level I knew went deeper than the shared experience of people our age. I wanted to know more, but he'd thrown up his walls almost as soon as they'd come down.

And the undercurrent of danger that followed in his wake? It zipped through me like electricity. His unfiltered intensity was as sexy as it was intimidating.

Something tickled the hairs on the back of my neck. I snapped my head around to look over my shoulder. The street was empty aside from a handful of pedestrians and cars. But half a block later, I still couldn't shake the feeling I was being watched. My paranoia snowballed, and I darted across the street, speed-walking for Mass Ave, constantly checking my back.

The lights, traffic, and Saturday night bar crowd on the busy street eased my paranoia but didn't take it away. My over-active imagination had me on high alert ever since Don Valenzano had walked off the elevator with his meathead bodyguard. The visit to city hall and Siobhán's talk about "connections" hadn't helped. Despite assurances to the contrary, Mr. DeVita exuded mafioso, or at least, what I imagined was mafioso based on the movies.

I didn't want to be involved in anything illegal. I didn't want to put myself in danger. But a part of me I found appalling was excited, intrigued, and wanted answers. What was real and what was fantasy? What was the truth and what was my imagination? What would it feel like to be touched by a man whose very presence made my body come alive?

Anger and comfort. Outrage and lust. Fear and excitement. Marco DeVita caused such a conflict of emotions, I almost forgot he was my boss. He'd done what I'd grown to believe impossible. He made me feel, and I couldn't go back to unremarkable.

Chapter Ten

Anna

Mr. DeVita walked off the elevator Tuesday morning dragging a leather carryon behind him, a coat draped over his arm. He wore a pair of dress slacks and a long-sleeved button-down, which, despite him having clearly come from the airport, looked perfectly pressed. The only hint he'd traveled across the Atlantic was the thick stubble covering his jaw, and the sexy salt-and-pepper growth gave him an even rougher, don't-mess-with-me look than he normally wore.

He didn't spare me a glance, though I watched him like prey might track a would-be predator. He stopped in front of the double, wooden doors on the opposite side of the foyer and rifled through the top compartment of his carryon.

"Anna." My name on his lips was a command, and my body obeyed, coming to life in answer, desire zinging through my belly.

"Good morning, Mr. DeVita. Welcome back. I wasn't expecting you until after lunch."

"The pilot made up time in the air," he mumbled, distracted by his search. "Customs were fast. No traffic."

He triumphantly extracted a set of keys from the carryon,

wiggled one into the lock, and pushed open the door. He glanced over his shoulder, finally making eye contact. "I'll take my Americano and a cornetto," he said with unadorned demand. "Pistachio if they have them this morning."

His eyes slid down to the neckline of my red sweater, and for the beat they lingered on my breasts, I could have sworn they grew darker, almost glowing in their intensity. He blinked and walked through the door, closing it behind him.

Ordered around and ogled like a personal serving wench. But the really messed up part? My body was tingling with the anticipation of being submissive to his demands and the subject of his desire. I grabbed my coat but left my scarf and gloves, needing the winter air to ice my fiery insides.

The walk to the café and back burned off most of the heat, and I returned to Terme and my second week of work with Mr. DeVita determined to keep things professional.

I set his breakfast on my desk to fluff my hair, straighten my skirt, and smooth the fitted lines of my red sweater. The sweater I'd worn the first day we met. The sweater I knew would draw his attention. The sweater I'd washed the night before so I could wear it.

Oh, yeah. Totally professional.

I knocked on Mr. DeVita's office door.

"Yes," he called.

I balanced the coffee and cornetto in one hand to open the door and closed it behind me, impressed by my new-found stability in heels. I transferred the pastry back to my other hand and—

My breath caught and I froze.

His face was cleanly shaven, and the musky scent of expensive aftershave and cigar smoke filled the office, a custom aphrodisiac meant just for me. He leaned back in his chair, feet resting on the edge of his desk, one ankle crossed over the other. His dress shirt was unbuttoned at the collar, and dark hair peeked out from beneath the dip of his undershirt. His elbow rested on the chair arm, and he held a cigar aloft between the first two fingers of his left hand and his thumb. His sleeves were rolled up and an intricate pattern emerged from beneath the cuff of his white shirt, a winding track that traveled down his muscled forearm and stopped at his wrist.

All plans for focusing on work died with black ink etched into tan skin.

Smoke trailed from his parted lips making him inexplicably more sexy. He surveyed the length of my body through the cloud, and my nerve endings sparked from the unapologetic appreciation behind his hooded eyes.

I forced my legs to move and set his breakfast on the desk. I wiped my sweaty palms down my skirt, and his eyes followed my hands to my hips, reigniting the heat in my belly.

He tapped the glowing end of his cigar on the ashtray.

"You're welcome," I said.

He raised an eyebrow and brought the cigar back to his mouth. He bit its end and held it between his teeth while he took another puff.

"You shouldn't smoke." The challenge flew past my lips before I could cage it. I'd never say something like that to anyone but Jeff or Michael or my parents. But Mr. DeVita baited my boldness and made me reckless.

"Why not?"

I frowned. "It's not good for you."

He smiled around the cigar. "I'll take my chances."

I huffed. "What about secondhand smoke? It's not all about you, you know."

He wrapped his forefinger around the cigar and removed it from between his teeth. "This room has a top-of-the-line ventilation system." He placed the cigar between his lips and took a long, slow drag, never breaking eye contract. He made an *O* with his mouth and blew a lazy train of smoke rings into the room. Biting the cigar between his teeth again, he leveled me with the most arrogant, shit-eating grin imaginable. And damn, if I didn't find it sexy as hell.

"Doesn't matter if you're blowing it in my face." I glared at him and folded my arms. His eyes traveled to my breasts; I'd inadvertently pushed them together with my defiant gesture. I dropped my arms and balled my fists, heat surging up my neck.

He chuckled, plucked the cigar from between his teeth, and ground its glowing end into the ashtray. He gave me a look that said, "Satisfied?" and leaned back in his chair, folding his hands across his stomach.

I narrowed my eyes, and we stared at each other for several heartbeats before he broke the standoff.

"How's your model coming?"

Thank God he wanted to talk about work. I needed to cool down. In more ways than one.

"I finished the preliminary draft on Friday," I said and relaxed into one of the chairs opposite his desk. "You have a sound organizational structure, each office with its financial autonomy. It made the base elements easy to construct. I'm impressed."

He nodded, acknowledging the compliment. Which he deserved. Privately owned companies were often a spaghetti mess of financial and organizational interdependencies. DEI's structure was clean and calculated, just like Mr. DeVita. He had a sharp tongue, but he also had a sharp mind for business and finance.

My curiosity got the better of me. "Where did you go to business school?"

He looked at me like I was from another planet. "The school of hard knocks."

My cheeks heated, and I groaned inwardly at my awkwardness. Classic Anna.

"I—I'd never have guessed." Not the most graceful recovery, but I cleared my throat and shook my head, determined to stay on track. "Anyway, it's a matter of refinement. The more details we add, the higher the fidelity. I want to capture as accurate a representation as I can before I run the Monte Carlo analysis. That's the best chance we have at pinpointing any deviations and their sources."

"How long?"

I scrunched my face and stared at the ceiling, running down the list of elements I needed to add. "Another week? Then I'll work out any kinks using test data before I start the simulations, so..." I rocked my head. "Two weeks before we start seeing results?"

"That's faster than I thought."

"To be fair, the preliminary results will only provide a list of discrepancies, deviations between predicts and actuals. We'll need to investigate to see if they're false positives. And, of course, that doesn't include how it's being done. Or by whom, for that matter."

His energy had shifted while I rambled. He regarded me curiously, as if impressed by my progress but preoccupied by something more important than the finances of his multi-million-dollar company. He seemed distracted, but he was so difficult to read with his impenetrable poker face.

"How was your date Saturday night?" His question came out like an accusation, and my mouth fell open trying to process how wrong it was on so many levels.

The old Anna resurfaced, flustered by a sea of racing thoughts and unable to form a coherent sentence, much less sharp reply. "Wha—What are you talking about?"

"You went on a date this weekend. To Lombardi. Not the best Italian in the city. Not even the best in Cambridge. But they do have a decent view of the Charles. How was it?" There was an edge to his voice, like I'd done something wrong by going on a date.

A flurry of reactions played tug-o-war with my emotions. Flattered by his possessiveness, outrage at his presumption, alarm at his knowledge of my whereabouts—

"Oh my God," I whispered. "You had me followed."

Lava traveled up from my belly and headed for my face. I ground my teeth to suppress the impending eruption. "You had me followed." This time the words came out throaty and molten, and I surged to my feet.

The corner of his mouth kicked up as if he found my outrage amusing. "There's that spark."

"I knew it!" I squeezed my hands so tightly my nails cut into my palms. "I knew someone was following me! How dare you? How dare you invade my privacy? You had no right!"

"No right?" His eyebrows lifted, and he removed his feet from the desk. He stood and prowled like a cat until his powerful body loomed over me.

Adrenaline electrified my insides, and I stiffened, nerves slicing through my anger to paralyze me.

"I had every right," he growled.

My breath came fast and heavy, anger burning my cheeks as I stood my ground against the righteous authority flashing in his eyes.

"You signed an agreement granting me permission to utilize surveillance to protect my company's assets, and I am exercising that right. I need to know if you are at risk, if someone thinks they can use you to get to me." His breath came faster now, his voice low and gravelly. "That's my end of the bargain, and I take that responsibility seriously. I will protect you."

"Protect me from whom?" I shouted. "Seems to me, you're the one I need protection from!"

He looked at me like I'd slapped him across the face, and his eyes went dark with menace. "There's more danger around you than you know, Anna, and I will do whatever I deem necessary to ensure your safety."

The promise in his voice created fresh turmoil, the invasion of privacy taking a backseat to his declaration he'd protect me. My pulse pounded in my ears, an incessant drum of confusion. I was so emotionally flustered I couldn't move or speak or think. It was like my brain had disconnected from my body.

He must have sensed my deep freeze because he backed off and moved to retrieve the coffee from his desk. The second he broke eye contact, I released the hold on my shoulders and sagged against the side of my chair, unsteady on shaking legs.

"So." He reclined against the edge of his desk. "How was it?" He sipped his coffee, giving me whiplash with his charming smile and mild tone.

I scoffed and turned my attention to the bookcase.

"That good, huh?"

My head snapped back to meet his taunt, and I scowled at the amusement in his black eyes.

He shrugged, a surprisingly easy gesture on his powerful frame. "You wouldn't be so put out if you'd had a good time."

He was right, of course, and it rankled. Especially since I'd spent the majority of the night thinking about him.

I lifted my chin in defiance, refusing to give him the satisfaction of knowing he'd hit the nail on the head. "It was lovely," I lied, cold and haughty, and ran my fingers back and forth along the length of my necklace.

"You're a terrible liar, Anna." A playful menace danced in his eyes, and they travelled to where I fidgeted my necklace. "More tells than a sinner in church."

I dropped the necklace, but his eyes lingered, focused on where my chest rose and fell to meet the demands of my rapidly beating heart. Maybe the red sweater hadn't been the best idea.

"Stop that," I whispered.

"Stop what?"

"Stop looking at me like that. I—I can't think when you look at me like that."

"Like what?"

My mouth went dry. I licked my lips, searching for an answer, but my brain had lost the ability to form words.

"Like what, Anna?"

"I..."

He pushed off the desk and stepped forward until his face hovered inches above mine. Cigar smoke and aftershave and masculinity dominated my world, his energy humming with an unapologetic and desirous intent. "Like I want to worship your breasts with my eyes?"

My lips parted in shock.

"Maybe you'd rather have me use my hands. Or my tongue?"

I sucked in a ragged breath, his brazen words conjuring images of him running his tongue over my nipples. Aching need pulsed between my legs, and I swayed under its merciless attack. A groan formed deep in my chest, but I caught it before it escaped.

"That's—That's sexual harassment." The whispered words sounded ludicrous, but I needed to douse the flames threatening to engulf me.

His chest rumbled with deep, cynical laughter. "No, it isn't."

"Then what is it?" I asked, my voice breathy with desire.

He leaned forward, and for a moment, I thought he was going to kiss me and end my silent torture.

"It's called flirting." His gaze travelled to my breasts again, and his warm breath tickled the naked skin of my chest. "And if you don't like it, maybe you shouldn't have worn that sweater."

My cheeks flared with heat, embarrassment and lust battling for control. I scrambled for a pithy recovery, but all that came out was, "I don't know what you're talking about."

"You know exactly what I'm talking about." He backed away with a devious grin. "You started this game when you put that sweater on this morning."

A hysterical bark of laughter escaped me. Was I that obvious?

He resumed the easy lean against his desk. "And if you can't recognize a little flirting, you're just not dating the right men." He picked up the cornetto and took a monstrous bite. "Am I wrong?" he asked through a mouthful of pastry.

I held up both hands and backed away, eyes wide and head shaking, astonished by his audacity. I spun on my heel, walked out of his office, and shut the door, hating myself for being disappointed he hadn't kissed me.

By three o'clock, another revision of my model was complete. It would take the rest of the workday to compile, but in the meantime, I could construct a plan for how to refine it in the next iteration. Anything to keep my mind off cigar smoke and aftershave and the warm caress of breath against my cheek.

The elevator dinged, and a tall man with broad shoulders stepped off the elevator. He ran his hand through a mop of chin-length, dark-chocolate brown hair. He dropped his arm and lifted his head to shake the thick mane off his forehead.

He was drop-dead gorgeous. Magazine-ad beautiful with perfectly proportionate features. A straight nose, high cheekbones, and an angular jaw, all blessed with a blemish- and wrinkle-free tan. His pouty lips invited sin, and his large, almond eyes under long lashes reminded me of Marco's in their intense darkness.

He stopped when he saw me and flashed his straight, white teeth, and the affected smile undermined his beauty with pretense. "Hello," he said, his voice rich and silken. He removed his leather gloves one finger at a time. "I didn't know Marco had a new assistant. I'm Luca. Luca Moretti. And you are?"

The infamous Luca. Jesus, Siobhán hadn't been kidding. Talk about intense. I'd never met anyone so staggeringly handsome.

And that name. My brain snagged on his last name. Moretti.

"Anna." I cleared my throat. "I'm Anna."

"A pleasure to meet you, Anna." The words dripped off his tongue like honey, but I suspected they were tantalizing bait offered by a camouflaged viper.

"You as well." I glanced at the office calendar. "Mr. DeVita doesn't have any appointments today. Is he expecting you?"

His smile turned patronizing. "No. It's a surprise." And then the viper winked.

I clammed up, classic Anna, no idea what to say, and I gaped at him in awkward silence.

"Luca!" Mr. DeVita's voice boomed into the foyer, coming to my rescue.

"Marco! Ciao, zio!"

The two men embraced with back slaps and kisses. Mr. DeVita pulled back, but held on to Luca's shoulders, squeezing and patting them. "Nipote, I wasn't expecting you till the weekend."

Luca shrugged. "I flew in early to take care of some business in Saugus."

"I'm glad you're home. Gina will be happy to see you."

Mr. DeVita patted Luca's shoulders again before dropping them.

"I'll call her as soon as I'm finished here. I thought we could have a cigar, get a drink, catch up."

"As much as I'd like that, I flew in from Roma this morning. I won't be good company. Tomorrow, nipote, after lunch. Vesuvio at two."

"Perfetto, ci sarò."

Mr. DeVita glanced down at me as if he suddenly remembered I was there. "You've met Anna?"

"Yes." Luca looked at me and smiled like we shared a secret. "We just met."

"Anna's temping for Diane while she's in California. She's only been on staff a week, so best ask Siobhán if you need anything while you're in town."

Luca's eyes darkened. "No problem," he said through a devilish grin before returning his features to their mask of charm. "I'm off then." He tugged his gloves back on and turned for the elevator. "I'll visit Gina, now."

"Bravo ragazzo." Mr. DeVita slapped him on the back. "That will make her happy. She misses you."

Luca smiled an unaffected smile. It softened his veneer and for a moment gave me a genuine glimpse at the man behind it. A far more charming and sincere man.

"Ciao, zio."

"Ciao, Luca."

The elevator doors closed, and I raised my eyebrows at Mr. DeVita.

"That was Luca Moretti, the Chief Operating Officer of DEI's European branch. His father and I were best friends." He sounded proud when he announced Luca's title, but melancholy entered his voice when he mentioned Luca's father. "He's in town for our quarterly review, which is next week, by the way, but I'll brief you on that another time. I'm done for the day."

He pulled out his keys and walked around my desk to the double doors of his penthouse. "Oh. Email me a summary of what you found out about those permits. We never did get around to that."

"Please," I said with emphasis.

He grabbed my eyes, smirked, and closed the penthouse door behind him.

I huffed and turned back to my computer.

Luca's intense good looks combined with his affected demeanor rubbed me the wrong way. Siobhán had warned me, but meeting DEI's European COO in the flesh was next level.

Moretti.

It was a common enough Italian surname. Why did it keep nagging at my brain? My model was still compiling, and Mr. DeVita was gone for the day... Time for more internet sleuthing.

Luca Moretti returned almost as few hits as *Marco DeVita*. A handful of paparazzi shots in Italy with runway-model women hanging off his arm. No surprise there given his good looks and money. But, like Mr. DeVita, I could count on one hand the number of links to any real information.

An article from an Italian magazine featured him in a set of staged photos amid a wall of Italian text. Thank God for my browser's translation plugin; despite my heritage, I didn't know more than a handful of Italian words.

The article introduced Luca as the man behind Terme di Roma and Terme di Sicilia, the face of high-end, European resorts from Italian-American entrepreneur Marco DeVita. It lauded the innovative blend of Italian and American cultures, their financial success, and the benefits to the community. I skimmed the rest of the article until I reached a short paragraph at the end.

Luca Davide Moretti is from Boston, Massachusetts. He is the grandson of former Italian citizen, Antonio Moretti, who emigrated to the United States in 1935. Since then, the Moretti family has been involved with the lucrative Valenzano Trading Company and an integral part of the Italian-American community.

A sinking feeling attacked my stomach. I read the paragraph again, and my stomach collapsed into my feet.

Antonio Moretti. *Tony* Moretti. Notorious member of the Boston Mafia. Capo under Big Frankie Valenzano. Every Italian-American in Massachusetts knew of the two mobsters and their bloody history.

The unease that had taken root after Don Valenzano's visit and our trip to city hall finally transformed into panic. My mind raced down paths I didn't want to explore. Mr. DeVita had sworn he wasn't involved with the Mafia, had explained away his connection to the Valenzanos as an artifact of the small Italian-American community. But he'd conveniently left out the part where his best friend and his European COO were Tony Moretti's progeny. It was a small world, but it wasn't that small.

I checked the terminal window. The compilation finished with no errors. Thank God. I needed air.

I collected my things, rode the elevator down to the lobby, and walk-ran out the front door. The winter air hit me in the face, and I welcomed its cleansing slap. I bolted across the street to the Commons and pulled out my cellphone.

"Hey, Anna." Jeff's voice sounded distant through the blood thumping in my ears. "What's up?"

My voice trembled as much as my hand holding the phone to my ear. "What the hell did you get me into?"

Chapter Eleven

Anna

I opened the door to my condo, and Jeff pushed past me, determination etched in the lines of his flushed face. "Stay away from this, Anna. I'm telling you." He paced my living room with clenched fists.

I closed the door behind me. "First of all, calm down," I said, more chiding than I'd intended, but I was the one who was supposed to be freaked out. It was his fault I'd even met Marco DeVita. "I've never seen you like this before. Okay. Maybe once, the night before your wedding, but seriously, Jeff, you need to slow down and breathe."

He stopped, took off his glasses, and rubbed his eyes. "Sorry. I'm sorry." He took a deep breath and exhaled long and slow.

"Second," I snapped, "you can't come in here and tell me to stay away from a thing when I don't even know what the thing is. And the cryptic phone conversation this afternoon didn't help."

Walking through the Commons after fleeing the office, I'd asked him straight out if Mr. DeVita was involved in the Mafia. He'd responded with silence. When I'd pushed, he'd said, "We'll talk about this tonight. I'm coming over. Don't say anything like that over the phone. Or to Marco." His voice had been low, words clipped.

He put his glasses back on and straightened them atop his nose. "Okay, okay," he said. "You're right. I'm sorry. But Anna, these are not things you want to know about. Your assignment has nothing to do with any of that." He waved his hand as if he could brush away my newfound knowledge. "And you want to keep it that way."

"Don't." I crossed my arms and scowled. "Don't you dare do that to me. You know better than to tell me what I don't want to know, what you think I'm not capable of handling. You aren't getting out of this without an explanation."

Jeff scrubbed a hand over the remnants of his hair and sunk into the couch. He let his head fall back and stared at the ceiling. Sophie, my long-haired, gray and white fur baby, climbed into his lap, and kneaded his thighs, purring so loudly I could hear her over Jeff's exaggerated sighs. He lifted his head to pet her, and she finally lay down on her second favorite lap, hiding her eyes beneath her paw. He calmed as he stroked her fur.

I went into the kitchen, poured two glasses of Chianti from an open bottle on the counter, and returned to sit cross-legged next to him. "Why don't you start from the beginning," I said and handed him the wine.

He downed a mouthful, winced, and his expression turned serious. "We both signed NDAs."

"We did."

"So, this stays in this room." He held my eyes with a weighty stare. "No matter what."

He was so tense, I reached for his hand and squeezed. "I promise. Nothing you say will leave this room."

He nodded and resumed stroking Sophie's fur. "I think you've figured out by now, Marco DeVita is connected, but I want to be clear—don't mistake being connected for being involved. He's a good man, Anna. One of the best I've ever known. He does a lot for his community. You don't need to know the details. Can't you trust me and accept that?" His voice was confident in its sincerity, tone heavy with respect, no trace of hesitation.

"In the past two weeks, I've met the head of the Boston Mafia and participated in what I'm pretty sure was extortion of a city official. A week later, the grandson of Tony Moretti turns out to be the Chief Operating Officer of DEI's European branch. There's no way that's coincidence." I shook my head. "I trust you. You know I do, but I can't keep doing this job knowing I might be involved in something illegal. I won't do it. So, unless you want me to delete my model and never go back to Terme di Boston, you better start talking."

"I know for a fact Marco isn't involved with the Valenzanos. Not in the way you're thinking. If anything, he actively distances himself from them."

"How could you possibly know that? In fact, how do you know anything about this? The Mafia, Jeff? Really?"

His shoulders slumped and his head dropped, and he stared into his wine, moving the glass through slow circles.

"Do you remember when I expanded CMG?" He pushed his hand deep into Sophie's fur as if anchoring himself to the present while he traveled back in time. "It was right after Michael and I got married. Neither of us had any money. I'd put every penny I'd earned at McKinsey into starting the company, and we were finally turning a profit."

"I remember eating a lot of grilled cheese and tomato soup at your apartment."

His mouth quirked, attempting a smile, but unease held his features hostage. "I got impatient, wanted to expand. I knew how much money I could be making."

Sophie lifted her head and glared at Jeff. He'd started

bouncing his knee, and she did not appreciate being jostled. We'd never kept secrets from one another, not once in our twenty-four-year friendship. And now he slugged down his wine while trying to still his leg so Sophie would lie back down.

"There was no way I could get a loan. Michael was mired in student debt. I'd barely dug myself out of mine. The only collateral I had was CMG itself. No bank was going to give me the money I needed to expand." He looked at me with haunted eyes. "So, I went somewhere else for a loan."

Sickening suspicion seeped into my gut.

"I wasn't always as fortunate as I am now. You know I grew up in Southie. A Black kid in a poor Irish neighborhood?" He shook his head. "I hung out with the kids I needed to hang out with to stay safe." He downed the rest of his wine and stared into the empty glass. "But I was lucky. I had brains. I had a way out. Most of the neighborhood kids? They never left." He placed the glass on the end table and folded his hands in his lap, picking at his thumbnail. "So, I made a few calls to old high school friends who knew where to go when you needed a loan. They knew cause, back in the day, they were runners for the Shaughnessys." He lifted his eyes to meet mine. "Runners for the Irish mob."

My jaw dropped. I'd never known how Jeff had expanded his company. He'd never told me. Apparently, he'd gotten a loan from the most ruthless gangsters in Boston. I stared at my best friend like I'd never seen him before, wondering what else he was keeping from me.

He eased Sophie off his lap so he could rest his elbows on his knees. "The thing is, the thing they don't tell you, you have to pay it back on their terms and on their schedule. With interest. One of the Shaughnessy goons came to collect earlier than I anticipated, and..." He exhaled slowly, hanging his head. "The money was gone. I'd spent it all. Hiring consultants, marketing, renting office space, computers. It was going to be a year before I broke even, longer before I turned a profit. I put them off as long as I could, but after six months, they decided they were tired of waiting."

He took a shaky breath, and I squeezed his leg, comforting myself as much as him, certain his story was about to get much worse.

"Marco was a client, although I didn't know anything about him or who he was at the time. He'd hired us for cyber-security. Even back then he would only deal with me, wanting to minimize the number of people who knew about our arrangement. We had a meeting. It was on a Monday." Jeff's voice cracked, and his eyes grew distant. "The Monday after the first time Shaughnessy's goons shook me down."

My hand flew to my mouth and tears burned my eyes. He met my horrified expression, his own eyes glassy with unshed tears.

"Marco didn't say anything that first time, but he'd noticed. By our third meeting, things had escalated. I showed up with a broken arm, a cracked rib, and a black eye. He never asked what happened, just took it upon himself to investigate."

"You told me you were in a car accident," I whispered.

Memories of Jeff's bruised and broken face resurfaced. In the weeks before the accident, he'd become distant, elusive. He'd pushed me and Michael away. We'd assumed he was overworked.

Silent tears fell down Jeff's face and landed on his sad smile. He removed his glasses to wipe them away. "I'm sorry I lied, but... God." He looked at the ceiling, and his throat bobbed through a swallow. "I felt so guilty, so ashamed. I was scared. For myself, for you, for Michael. I lied to protect you." He reached for my hand, and I gave it to him, squeezing his shaking fingers. "It didn't take Marco long to figure out what was happening. He came to my office a week later.

"Anna, what I'm about to tell you…"

Jeff's brown skin paled. The flush from the winter cold and its usual glow were gone, and the whites of his eyes were glassy and bloodshot.

"You know you can trust me."

He let out a shaky breath. "Marco went to Pádraig Shaughnessy. Paid off my loan and the interest. Told him I was under DeVita family protection, that I was one of his people, and if anyone tried to shake me down again, it would be seen as an Irish move against the Italians."

My stomach bottomed out. "Jesus, Jeff."

He nodded somberly and squeezed my hand. "I know. I've never been so scared in my life." His gaze grew distant as if he was reliving that day.

He grunted after a moment, and the corner of his mouth ticked up. "And then I got the lecture of a lifetime."

I let out a nervous chuckle. "Knowing Mr. DeVita, I can imagine."

"He told me how hard he worked to stay out of Mafia entanglements, how he refused to be dragged back into the *game* as he called it. And that even though the Valenzanos knew he wanted no part in it, the Shaughnessys didn't, and that's what saved me. He broke a promise to himself to save my ass, Anna, and he made sure I knew it.

"Everything comes at a price in their world, and this was no different. He didn't want his money back; he wanted my allegiance. That's why I signed the NDA. I've been providing Marco with whatever he needs since."

My mouth gaped in horror, speechless at the thought of Mr. DeVita exploiting Jeff. It shouldn't have surprised me, given what I knew. That was the Mafia's MO, wasn't it? Find a weakness, leverage it to get a person in debt, then hold that debt over their head, squeezing them for every last cent. Just like the zoning commissioner.

Extortion landed differently when it was happening to your best friend. The idea of Mr. DeVita using Jeff upended everything I wanted to believe about my boss, making it hard to breathe.

Jeff's eyes widened. "Oh, God. No. Anna, it's not like that. That came out all wrong." He grabbed my wine glass, set it on the coffee table, and took both of my hands. "The Shaughnessys would have killed me. Do you understand that? If it wasn't for Marco, I would be dead right now."

"I can't believe you pulled me into this," I whispered through my shock.

"I had no choice. Marco needed help. I owe him. You're the only person who could have done this job on such a short timeline. I didn't have the option not to pull you in."

"You're making excuses for him? Seriously, Jeff? It's called extortion. He's using you!"

"No." He vehemently shook his head. "That's not how it is. I have no problem doing the things I do for Marco. In fact, I'm happy to do them. I owe that man my life. He's never asked me to do anything shady. We staff his cybersecurity needs, provide the occasional financial audit. What you're doing for him isn't criminal, is it?" He held my gaze without shame because he already knew the answer.

Everything about this conversation had me on the edge of panic, but Jeff was right. Nothing about my financial modeling or even the permit research was illegal. And after the nightmare situation Jeff had gotten himself into with the Shaughnessys, I felt like I owed Mr. DeVita for saving my best friend's life.

"The work I do for Marco has nothing to do with the Mafia. It never has. That's how I know his COO couldn't be tied up with the Valenzanos. Marco wouldn't allow someone connected like that on his staff. As for Mr. Valenzano? I don't know why he was there, but I promise you, Marco wouldn't be in business with him. No way."

My shoulders relaxed as I willingly bought into Jeff's words. Until that moment, I hadn't realized how badly I'd wanted him to explain away my misgivings about Mr. DeVita. I needed to believe he wasn't involved in the Mafia. I needed to believe however dark and dangerous, his intentions and integrity were good and true. I needed to believe I wasn't falling for a monster.

Chapter Twelve

Anna

A snowstorm had attacked the city in the early morning hours, and the blanket of fresh white reflected the bright sun shining in a cloudless sky outside the penthouse foyer's windows. So clean. So pristine. So unlike the jumbled mess of my emotions.

I sipped the double latte I'd bought for myself along with Mr. DeVita's breakfast and set it on my desk. I hadn't slept well, not after my conversation with Jeff. There were still too many unanswered questions, too many ways we might be in danger. My racing thoughts had kept me awake following leads and exploring rabbit holes until physical exhaustion forced me into a fitful sleep.

I delivered Mr. DeVita's breakfast without words. He was engrossed in something on his computer screen and didn't spare me a glance, but I hesitated before heading back to my desk. Neither his handsome face nor his commanding presence had changed overnight. He was the same man he'd been before I'd learned of his influence in the world of organized crime or how he'd used that influence to save my best friend's life. If anything, the power I now knew he wielded grounded his self-possession, legitimizing it and making it even more alluring.

I settled behind my desk with my caffeine to start the tedious process of assembling input files while waiting for my model to compile.

Hours passed sifting through megabytes of data, separating input streams, formatting files for ingestion. I found the first data hole just before lunch.

Mr. DeVita,
I have complete housekeeping expense reports from January of 2022 through December of 2023, but June through August of 2023 are missing. Maybe an ill-formed query?
Anna

His reply appeared in my inbox only a few minutes later.

Missing months attached.
You're wearing a turtleneck today.
M

My lips twitched, fighting a smile. He hadn't even looked up when I'd brought him his breakfast. How had he noticed what I was wearing? One thing was certain, regardless of my newfound knowledge or my near-sleepless night, my attraction to the man hadn't changed.

Thank you.
Local and state taxes are not included in your expense reports. Do you bookkeep those separately? I'll need that information as well.
??? It's cold, and someone makes me walk three blocks every morning to get his breakfast.
Anna

I sat back in my chair, smug, and played with my necklace, watching my inbox for his reply. I didn't have to wait long.

All foreign taxes are journaled separately. Attached.
How am I supposed to stare at your tits if you're wearing a turtleneck?
M

"Oh my God!" I mouthed through a shocked smile and pressed the backs of my cold fingers against my unbearably hot cheeks. That man was turning me into a pre-teen at a boy band concert. Ridiculous.

I shook out my hands, shifted in my chair, and brushed the hair out of my face. "Okay," I mumbled to myself. Resettled, I chewed my lip and considered my reply.

Tsk, tsk. There's that sexual harassment again. Careful or I'll file a complaint with the management.
Anna

The little angel on my shoulder told me I shouldn't be encouraging him, that I should put an end to this dangerous game of cat and mouse. But his sinful attention was too powerful a temptation. It excited me, good sense be damned.

Fifteen minutes with no new emails and I regained enough focus to work on the input files instead of mindlessly clicking through the internet. Ten minutes later, the office door opened, and Mr. DeVita strode into the foyer with his coat and gloves.

"I got your message about the permits and the paperwork required for the financial district purchase," he said and leaned against the side of my desk. "I emailed you the information about my prime contractor in Italy. They'll be managing the renovations of the new Tuscany property I finalized last week. The signed contract as well as receipts from the initial deposit are attached."

"I see them."

"That should be the last piece of information you need to determine if we can meet the city and seller's escrow and solvency requirements."

"Let me look." I opened the email and pulled up the attachments. "The permit fees themselves won't be a problem," I mumbled as I scrolled, looking for the bottom line. When I reached it, I blinked, dizzy from all the zeroes. "How—" I swallowed. "How big is this property in Tuscany?"

"Twenty acres."

I swiveled my chair to face him. "Twenty *acres*?"

"Yes. The property has tremendous potential. The villa will need to be expanded, and a spa added to match the other properties, but the acreage provides an opportunity I don't have with my other locations—land." The nonchalance with which he described his new, quarter-billion-dollar piece of real estate was enough to make my head spin. "It was too good a deal to pass, even with the poor performance of Rome and Sicily."

I stared at him, awestruck. No wonder his reserves were low. The down payment on a quarter-billion-dollar property was an outrageous amount of money.

"I'm going to have to look at these numbers. Obviously,

this changes your liquidity," I said dryly, "and your debt-to-income ratio."

He nodded. "I need an answer by this evening. I'd like the escrow in place as soon as possible; the waiver could come through as early as tomorrow. The zoning commissioner will email you when it's ready."

"I can have an answer for you by the end of the day, and setting up the escrow will take no time at all, but..." I pursed my lips and furrowed my brow, not wanting to stick my nose where it didn't belong, but he *had* referred to me as his financial advisor at city hall. "This is a huge amount of outgoing liquid assets in a short amount of time. I'm not sure I understand the urgency, especially given the performance of your European branch."

He studied me, perhaps deciding how much information to share. It was hard to tell. The stone wall of his expression gave nothing away.

"I've mentioned another party is interested in the property?"

"Yes."

"I don't think the drop in my liquidity right before I'm about to make this purchase is a coincidence."

"You think this other party is somehow behind the leak," I said with no small amount of skepticism. "That they're trying to sabotage your purchase."

"I think it's a strong possibility."

"But it would take months, a year even, to create a drain like this. And that's if there really is a drain."

"The property went up for sale nine months ago. I've been in talks with city hall for almost that long."

"But why? Why would someone go to those lengths to prevent you from buying a piece of property?"

"To get a foothold in the financial district. To prevent *me* from getting a foothold in the financial district."

I frowned. Was that what this was about? Gang territories?

At every turn, new evidence pointed to Mr. DeVita being entangled in Mafia affairs, and at every turn, I found rationalizations to explain them away. Mr. DeVita was hinting at territory expansion, and there I was trying to convince myself he must be referring to wine bars and fine dining.

"I'm not going to lie. This is going to be tight. And you're right—it wouldn't be if your European office was performing. But I'll dig in this afternoon and email you as soon as I know for sure."

His jaw muscle ticked as if he chewed on my words, and the downturn of his tight mouth told me he didn't like their taste. "Rome and Sicily should be doing better than Montreal and Vancouver." His voice rumbled with frustration. "We need to find the leak."

"Numbers don't lie. If there's a leak, we'll find it."

His eyes darkened, and he ground his fist into the edge of my desk, knuckles white from the pressure. "I want to know who."

Passion simmered just below the surface of Mr. DeVita's steely veneer, and for the first time, he allowed it to break free in my presence. He was angry, that much was certain. But it wasn't just anger coming across in his flared nostrils and flashing eyes. It was hurt. He felt betrayed.

This time, I held his eyes, determined to give him the support he needed. "I'll find the leak," I said. "I promise."

His fist unclenched, and his jaw relaxed, my promise easing the tension holding his body taut. And just as quickly as it had vanished, his mask of control snapped back into place. "I'll be out the rest of the day. Off-site meetings. You have my number if you need me."

"Okay."

"I know you have a lot on your plate with the permits and

the model, but I could use your help with one other thing. If you're up for it?"

"Mr. DeVita! Are you *asking* me for help?" I feigned shock and hoped the gentle teasing would lighten his mood.

His lips twitched, and he raised an eyebrow. "I'm hosting a charity gala here at Terme. Not this weekend, but the next. Before this arrangement, Diane was helping Siobhán with preparations. It slipped my mind, but Siobhán asked if you're available."

"What do you need me to do?"

"Call Siobhán." He pulled on his coat and stepped toward the elevator. "She'll let you know what she needs."

"Will do.

"Oh. I almost forgot." He walked over and placed one hand on the back of my chair and one on the edge of my desk. His big body hovered over mine, and his dark eyes simmered with intent. "I am the management, and you don't have a case."

I licked my lips, my body held captive by his hungry gaze. "I don't?"

"No." He lowered his eyes to my chest, and when he looked back up, they burned with desire. "Not when your nipples harden every time I look at your chest." He brought his lips to my ear, so close they tickled its ridge and made me shiver with lust. "Like they're straining for my mouth."

I gasped on an intake and held on to the air like it was my last breath.

He lingered a moment, letting his warm breath caress my ear in a sultry promise I desperately wanted him to keep. Then, he pushed off the chairback and desk, his long legs carrying him across the foyer and onto the elevator. The doors swooshed shut.

"Jesus." I collapsed onto my desk, resting my forehead on the backs of my hands.

That man made every nerve ending in my body come alive. I was so turned on, my skin felt like it was on fire. I wanted to strip naked, run outside, and throw myself onto a snowbank.

All the warning signs were blazing red neon lights—his complete lack of boundaries, the way he ordered me around, his involvement, however unofficial, with the Mafia. Any sensible person capable of rational decision-making would run far, far away. Yet there I sat, unabashedly aroused, excitement coursing through my veins, not wanting the rollercoaster ride to end.

I was done with quiet classrooms filled with bored students. Done with stuffy department mixers and windowless offices with only my books to keep me company. Done with bad dates and even worse sex.

I'd escaped my rut. I was on a new path, a path fraught with danger and pointing me in the wrong direction, but I was willfully marching down that path with reckless abandon. I was taking risks, living life with the urgency it deserved. A phoenix reborn out of the fires of Marco DeVita's indomitable presence.

Who was this woman emerging from my midlife awakening? Liberated-Anna shocked the hell out of me. Even more surprising? I liked her.

Chapter Thirteen

Marco

Faneuil Hall was a twenty-minute walk from Terme. My meeting with Luca in the North End wasn't till two, but I needed to clear my head. Of Anna, the Irish, my European office. Of everything.

The wind whipped across the Commons, and the overcast sky blocked even the slightest breakthrough sun. Homeless people gathered their belongings close. Runners tugged on their winter gear to cover their faces. A few businessmen charged through the streets, heads lowered to the wind. It was going to storm again tonight, maybe even this afternoon. The air was thick with humidity, and the dense clouds loomed heavy in the sky, readying themselves for release and doing nothing to lift my dark mood.

The empathy and determination in Anna's eyes when she'd promised to find the leak had eased something in my chest. She was giving me the partnership I'd been missing, and it made my heart ache with a tenderness a man in my position couldn't afford.

I hadn't been able to get her out of my head the entire time I was in Italy. I'd jerked off more times in the past week than I had since I was a teenager. And when I'd found out she'd been on a date? Thank God I'd been in my hotel room when Vito's email came in. One thought of another man's hands on Anna's body made my eyes flare and fangs descend.

The way she fidgeted that damn necklace when she was nervous or too flustered to find words. The way she lost her temper each time I pushed her buttons. The way she shifted and stumbled, unsteady in heels. I smiled and shook my head remembering how she'd wobbled that first day.

She struck the perfect balance, a harmonious chord. Timid yet fierce; reserved in manner yet bold in brilliance; self-conscious yet undeniably sexy.

But to expect a sheltered, educated woman to accept a made man was delusional. Our worlds were too different. Right now, she skirted the periphery. Getting involved would put her in real danger, and that wasn't an option.

And when she found out I was a blood demon? I chuffed out a snort and yanked open one of the doors to Faneuil Hall.

I'd been worried about distraction, but this was bordering on obsession. If I didn't keep my eye on the game, things would get a lot worse than a dislocated jaw.

My favorite chowder stand was on the far end of the buzzing hive of vendors, tourists, and school groups. I found a seat at the counter and removed my gloves.

"Cup or bowl?" the grizzled old man in a Sox cap and dirty apron shot across the counter.

"Bowl."

Armed with his ladle, he spun around to a stainless-steel pot in a single choreographed motion, and within moments, the rich, comforting flavors of Boston soothed my hunger and my temper.

A vaguely familiar man on the opposite end of the counter stared at me with a wide, grateful smile. It took a second, but eventually the connection snapped into place—a newly immigrated blood demon. Gina was using DeVita Foundation funds to help him get settled in his new country. The chowder stand was a known friendly spot for our kind. Leave it to Gina to help a person feel right at home. I acknowledged him with a nod.

There were a lot of humans who found out about blood demons and accepted them as a fact of nature, just another part of our crazy world. Most were Sources who, for their own reasons, benefited from the knowledge. But the majority of the population refused to believe, their logical brains discounting the supernatural. They'd make any excuse to keep their understanding of the world intact.

Then there were the humans who found out about blood demons and the knowledge broke them. Discovering the world wasn't what they were taught to believe? That their understanding was an illusion? The abyss of their fear devoured them whole, and they couldn't escape.

Like Lucia. Fear had killed Luca's mother, God rest her soul. I couldn't risk Anna suffering that fate.

I tossed a twenty on the counter and checked my watch. Another fifteen minutes to the North End. I pulled on my gloves and, armed with a stomach full of chowder, braced myself for the cold.

The clouds had lost the battle to withhold their winter burden. Snowflakes kissed my cheeks, and a thin sheen of white blanketed the frozen landscape.

My capi from the West Coast and Canada would arrive tomorrow. We gathered in Boston for two weeks every three months to discuss business. We talked about the crew—who were the top earners, who was ready to be made, who was dead weight—how to expand our rackets, increase tributes. We played cards and shot pool, smoked cigars and drank whiskey, shared meals with our families.

I'd spent the morning trying to figure out how to break

the news, but there was no gentle way to say it. We were losing money, and there was more at play than poorly performing hotels and spas. I felt the truth in my bones as sure as I felt the oncoming blizzard. Vinnie's visit and the Shaughnessy interest in the financial district were too coincidental. But I needed proof. I needed Anna.

I walked past the entrance to Stanza dei Sigari, an iconic feature of Hanover Street and one of the last bastions of another time. A lot of the Italian immigrants had moved out of the North End over the past few decades, out to the suburbs where it was more affordable to buy a house. But there were holdouts, including my family and a handful of restaurants, delis, and bakeries who refused to relinquish the "Little Italy" of Boston.

Vesuvio dominated the second half of the block, windows dark, red marquee dim and waiting for twilight. The high-end nightclub was a front for where I really made money with the property—illegal card games and professional sports betting. The same setup I'd create in the financial district.

I turned down the alley, climbed the back stairs to the second floor, and punched in the door code. Enzo stood behind the bar cleaning glasses, and the only other person on the floor was Luca. He sat at the bar with a glass of scotch.

I tugged off my gloves and tossed them on the bar.

"Hey, boss," Enzo said and placed the pint glass he'd been drying on the shelf behind him.

"Enzo. Will you give us a minute?"

"Sure thing." He walked out from behind the bar and down the hallway to the girls' dressing room and lounge.

"Ciao, Luca." I slapped him on the shoulder and rounded the end of the bar to pour myself a finger of whiskey. "È bello averti a casa, nipote."

"Grazie, Marco."

The high-backed stool next to Luca creaked under my

weight. I pulled out two Nicaraguan cigars, and we went through the slow, methodical dance of retrieving our cutters and readying our smokes in the comfortable silence only possible with family.

The peaceful moment eased my worries. I needed him in Italy, but I wanted him in Boston. I might have called him nephew, but for all intents and purposes, Luca was my son, and when he was home, it was like a piece of my best friend was still with me.

Smoky cedar notes settled on my tongue, and I washed them down with a sip of whiskey. "How's Gina?" I asked.

"Mamma Gina's fine," Luca said, and a heartfelt smile softened his mask.

Mamma Gina. He still called her that after all these years. Tony had called her Mamma Gina when Luca was little, as if the nickname could replace the mother he'd lost.

"She made lasagna and bought cannoli from Mike's."

"She still spoils you."

He chuckled. "She does. I'm not complaining."

The comfortable silence returned while we enjoyed our cigars and drinks, but it didn't last long.

"That FBI agent was skulking around outside Terme when I stopped by yesterday," Luca said.

"Agent Johnson." I let out a tired sigh and closed my eyes. "Please tell me you didn't engage."

He snorted. "Non preoccuparti, zio. Didn't have to. Siobhán came out and read him the riot act. Told him he was impeding business and if he didn't leave, she'd call his supervisor." He chuckled and shook his head.

"She's got moxie, that one. Couldn't find a better GM if I tried."

Luca puffed on his cigar and gave me side-eye. I knew they didn't get along, but when it came to business, they both had enough sense to keep things professional.

"He been coming around a lot, lately?" Luca asked into his drink.

"No more than usual, but I'm not surprised you saw him yesterday." I blew out a mouthful of smoke. "Vinnie came to see me last week."

Luca's head snapped up.

"I know. I had the same reaction. I don't remember the last time he came to Terme."

Luca took a long drag off his cigar and swiveled his barstool to face me. "What did he want?"

"He wants to use Terme to expand his Source racket. Provide lodgings and meeting places for higher-end clients. Legitimize a portion of his income by laundering it through DEI. For a cut, of course."

Luca shifted and cleared his throat, his eagerness unmistakable. He'd always wanted to involve himself with the Valenzanos, follow in his father's footsteps out of some misguided sense of tribute or legacy. I thought he'd moved on. Apparently not.

"What did you say?" he asked.

I lifted my whiskey. "I told him I wasn't interested," I said and took a sip.

He swiveled back to the bar and stared into his drink, disappointment evident in the set of his jaw.

"Might be worth considering." Luca's words were muted with hesitation. I tilted my head and raised an eyebrow. "You know as well as I do Roma and Sicilia aren't doing well. Fucking economy. But the Source racket is steady, and he's offering you a cut."

"We've been down this road before, Luca," I said, my tone thick with warning. "I won't tie myself financially to the Valenzanos. I've been running my crew my way for longer than you've been alive, and I'm not going to jeopardize our independence now."

The muscles of his hard, angular jaw twitched. My involvement, or lack thereof, with the Valenzanos had been a recurring issue between us since he'd turned eighteen and decided he wanted to be made.

"It's not just the money. It's the alliance. The Irish are getting bolder. Expanding. Taking more business. It's only a matter of time before they encroach on Italian territory. You want them running books in the North End? Taking business away from Vesuvio?"

Fuck, no. Especially given my suspicion that the Shaughnessys had a hand in the poor performance of my European properties. But I didn't need Vinnie's help to put a stop to that.

"How about real estate development? Between you and Vinnie, the Italians have city hall and the unions, but how long will that last with those Irish cops Shaughnessy has on the take?"

"Law enforcement is the exact reason we shouldn't take this deal. You just finished telling me you saw Agent Johnson outside Terme. You think bringing Source traffic through there is going to make him less interested in what we're doing? You want to jeopardize the safety of blood demons on top of our rackets?" I shook my head. "Our lives are dangerous enough, Luca. Your father—"

"My father's been dead for almost forty years, Marco. Paddy Shaughnessy put a bullet through his head. Or have you forgotten?" Hesitation fled Luca's voice, leaving only bitterness. I chewed the end of my cigar and let him finish. "I'm tired of living in his shadow, and I don't need you to protect me anymore. All I'm saying is this might be a good move. For the money and the alliance. We should at least consider it."

When Luca was three or four, Tony made me promise if anything happened to him, I'd make sure Luca had options, that he wouldn't be forced into the life me and Tony had no choice but to lead. One of the strongest men I'd ever known, the worry and pleading in Tony's eyes when he'd made me promise had stayed with me every day since Pádraig Shaughnessy ended his immortal life.

Only two things could kill a blood demon—blood starvation and a head shot. Tony had fallen victim to the latter. I didn't want my adopted son to meet the same fate.

"I'm going to explain this one last time, Luca. One. Last. Time. Tying ourselves financially to the Valenzanos is off the table. Laundering money for something the feds will consider prostitution, regardless of whether or not that's what it is, is not a good look. Do you want to starve in a federal penitentiary? Do you want to put Gina through that pain? Watch her lose everything?"

"No. Of course not." The Luca I knew and loved broke through the anger, sincerity clear in his eyes and in the softening of his face. "I want to protect her as much as you, but we can't let this go. We can't let them win."

"You think the solution is making a stand against the Irish? Starting a war?" I shook my head. "I know you hate the Shaughnessys. The Lord knows I've tried to help you out of your anger since you were a kid, but you need to let it go. Before it consumes you. Before you end up with a bullet through *your* head."

His fury spread, glowing red streaks through the darkness of his eyes.

"Hey." I clasped his shoulder and squeezed. "Nipote. Come on. Finish your drink. Let's smoke these cigars and play some pool. Va bene? Take the edge off?" I patted him twice on the cheek.

He closed his eyes, ran a hand down his face, and pulled at his jaw. His lips parted, revealing the tips of his fangs.

"You're right," he said and opened his eyes. They'd

returned to their normal near-black. "You're right. I forgot myself for a moment. Just stressed about Roma and Sicilia."

He gave me one of his fake smiles, the ones he used when dealing with the public or his endless stream of women. He was still pissed. At me, at his father, at the world. But he'd school his emotions and erect his walls and I'd let him, hoping he'd never unleash the inferno of his deep-seated rage.

Chapter Fourteen

Anna

"Siobhán Connelly."

"Hi, Siobhán. It's Anna."

"Hey, girl. What's up?"

"Mr. DeVita told me you needed help with a charity gala? He asked me to call you."

It was Thursday, just before lunch, and this was the last loose end I needed to tie up before taking my break.

"Yes! Oh my God, thank you! There's only a week left until the event, and I have so much to do."

"What do you need?"

"The planning is done. It's just last-minute details. I'll send you a list to review. I'd like to meet and divvy up the work."

"I can do that, no problem. When do you want to meet?"

"Ugh," she groaned. "Today is a mess. My afternoon is shot. Department meetings. I have a few errands to run after work, but..." She drew out the *but*, and I sensed mischief. "We could go out tonight. A little late-night planning sesh? What do you think?"

"That sounds amazing. I could use a drink after the past couple days."

"That good, huh?"

"You have no idea."

She snorted. "It's a date. Meet me outside Vesuvio at eight."

"Vesuvio? As in the nightclub?"

"That's the only Vesuvio I know." I could almost see her sticking the tip of her tongue between her teeth.

"People like me don't go to Vesuvio, Siobhán. I'm not exactly a jet-setting partier. Are you sure that's where you want to go?"

"What? You don't like free drinks?"

"What do you mean?"

She laughed. "Vesuvio is Marco's club."

I sighed. Of course it was. "I don't know."

"Come *ooon*. It's different during the week. No DJ. No dancing. Just professionals having drinks after work. You'll be fine."

I did need a drink and some girl time after the previous day's Marco-DeVita-induced hot flash. What the hell. "Okay," I said, resigned yet doubtful.

"Yes! You'll love it. Promise."

I chuckled. "We'll see."

"See you at eight," she said and hung up.

I placed the receiver back on the dock and got up to retrieve my coat just as Mr. DeVita walked out of his office.

"Anna."

"Mr. DeVita. I was about to go to lunch. Did you need anything before I head out?"

"The escrow's in place?"

"Yes. I sent you an email with the account number and proof of deposit."

Turns out, Mr. DeVita did have enough capital in reserves,

and his debt-to-income ratio, while high, was well within the stipulations required by the purchase agreement. Although, had I actually been his financial advisor, I still would have recommended against the purchase.

"Excellent. I'm taking the rest of the day off, but I want to know as soon as that waiver comes through. If I don't answer my cell, I'll be downstairs in the spa." He walked across the foyer to his apartment.

"Enjoy your break," I said and meant it. That man was constantly working. He shot me a quick glance over his shoulder, and I stepped onto the elevator and headed to lunch.

The afternoon flew by with two iterations on the model and assembling input files, and suddenly it was four-thirty. I usually left the office around six, but since Mr. DeVita was gone for the day... I closed all the windows on my desktop, put my water bottle in my bag, and checked my email one last time.

There it was. A message from Doug Heller with the subject "Financial District Waiver Approved." I picked up my cell and called Mr. DeVita. Straight to voicemail. I texted him, waited five minutes, and called again. Nothing. I was going to have to go down to the spa. I sighed. So much for leaving early.

At the back of the main lobby, behind the front desk and past the elevators, a set of copper-clad doors led to the baths that gave Terme di Boston its name. I climbed down two flights of stairs that opened into a foyer with ivy-covered stone walls and trickling fountains. The air smelled clean but not artificial, a combination of eucalyptus and toasted almonds.

"Good afternoon," I said to the attendant at the front desk. "I'm Mr. DeVita's assistant. I have an urgent message for him."

"Yes. Ms. Barone. Mr. DeVita asked us to reserve the low-steam room for him this afternoon. If he's not in the main baths, he's likely there. Go past the full-length pool, but before you enter the hallway to the private men's and women's areas, you'll find the low-steam room on the left."

"Thank you."

"Of course."

I pushed through the second set of copper doors behind the front desk and stepped into the main baths.

An Olympic-sized pool occupied the center of a cavernous chamber surrounded by smaller pools, misters, tiled walkways, and a bar. A man in a speedo stroked lazily through its crystal waters under ivy that had ventured beyond its trellises to conquer the vaulted ceiling. Between the legs of foliage dripping from stone beams, chandeliers cast light across the rippling water, making it dance with reflection.

The attendant standing behind the bar handed a woman in a thong bikini and heeled sandals a glass of sparkling water. She carried her drink to a square plunge pool along the wall. "MINERAL" was carved into the stone in the same Romanesque lettering used on the front entrance. She kicked off her sandals, held her drink aloft, and descended into the bath, slowly sinking until she sat and rested her head against the lip of the pool. Her glass, beaded with condensation, dangled in her fingers above the water.

On the opposite side of the pool, stone benches protruded from the wall like organic growths, one of them occupied by two older men with noticeable paunches and receding hairlines. One of the men reached behind him and turned a copper knob. A gentle mist sprayed the area where they sat and rustled the foliage.

Mr. DeVita was nowhere in sight.

At the far end of the main room, another set of copper doors mirrored the set behind me. Right before the doors and past the smaller baths, "SAUNA" was carved into the stone over a glass door opaque with condensation.

I walked the length of the pool, kicking myself for having

never ventured down there before. The peaceful ambiance was soothing, and I wanted to stay and soak in the tranquility. But I was on a mission.

Sure enough, a Reserved placard hung from a suction cup stuck to the glass.

The door opened with a whoosh, and I stepped into the warm, hazy space. The low-steam sauna wasn't overly cloying with heat and humidity like a regular sauna. The air was thick, and condensation trailed down the tiled walls, but the room was set to a temperature you could tolerate for more than ten minutes, and visibility wasn't completely obscured by a wall of steam. Dim, orange lights reflected off a plunge pool set in the center of the space, its refreshing waters empty and waiting.

Against the opposite wall, Marco DeVita gripped the edge of a stone bench on either side of his knees. His head rested back on the tile, unmoving, but his dark, hooded eyes followed me like a predator tracking its prey.

The click of my heels ricocheted off the walls, a steady beat over the rapid pounding of my pulse. It quickened the closer I came to the full extent of his dominating presence, so primitive and exposed.

The wave of his hair, damp with humidity, was more pronounced, curls glistening and falling out of their ordered places. He was naked aside from the white towel wrapped around his waist, and sweat followed the curve of his muscled arms to where his hands gripped the edge of the bench. Neatly trimmed salt and pepper hair covered his broad chest. It trailed down an abdomen thick with muscle before disappearing beneath the towel. The tattoo I'd seen on his forearm was on full display, the "track" revealing itself to be scales on the tail end of a snake. The serpent coiled itself around his forearm and bicep, slinking up his arm until it rested its diamond-shaped head on the bulge of his shoulder.

My mouth went dry despite the humidity, and I licked

my lips. Sexual energy poured from his hungry eyes like the droplets of moisture sliding down the hard planes of his body. The heat of the sauna and the heat in his eyes combined to form a tidal wave of lust that crashed into me. But I was there for a reason that had nothing to do with the urgency developing between my legs, and I stopped a few feet short of the bench, not daring to venture any closer to temptation.

"You—you wanted me to notify you as soon as the waiver came through."

He lifted his head off the tile and stood. The towel wrapped around his hips only covered half of his thick thighs and exposed an indecent amount of his lower abs. He prowled toward me, and his muscles rippled under a thin sheen of sweat.

Jesus. I swallowed, trying in vain to slow my breathing as the alpha sex god eyed me like he was ready to feast.

"You didn't answer your phone," I mumbled.

He stopped close enough for me to see the muscles of his shoulders flex beneath his smooth, glistening skin. He held me transfixed, taking control of my body by the sheer force of his regard. I clasped my hands in front of me as if they clutched a life preserver in the sea of his dark intentions, but damn if I didn't want to drown.

"And?" he prompted with gravelly demand.

"The waiver's been approved. The commissioner attached a digital copy to the email, but you'll need the original to submit the paperwork. City hall is closed, so I can't file the permits, but you can alert the seller you're ready to purchase and provide them with the escrow."

A smile crept across his face, victorious and predatory, a wicked celebration of his illicit checkmate.

The devious bend to his mouth. The rough stubble across his jaw. The angle of his Roman nose, as sharp and defined as the muscled length of his body. Desire seized me, and rational thought fled.

His dangerous smile transformed into a sly, knowing grin, and his eyes gleamed with arrogance.

He closed the distance between us. His skin radiated warmth, and the heat it caused in my body made me dizzy. My lips parted, desperate for air.

He dragged his fingertips across my sweaty forehead and into my hair, moving the loose strands away from my face before wrapping his fingers around the back of my neck. He tilted his head and watched a bead of sweat slide down my cheek. It tickled my skin as it trailed downward. He swiped it away with a brush of his thumb and lowered his mouth to my ear.

"You should go now, Anna. You're getting wet."

Urgency surged between my legs and blood rushed my face. He knew how ready I was, how much he turned me on, and it only amplified the aching need of my desire.

He pulled back, just enough to watch a droplet of sweat travel down my chest and beyond the top of my silk blouse. He followed its path until it was lost between my breasts.

He lifted his sultry gaze, captured my eyes, and a roguish smirk formed on his lips. He backed away with slow, deliberate steps and stopped just shy of the plunge pool. His hands went to the towel around his waist.

With a flick of his fingers and no shame, he untucked the end. The towel fell to the tiled floor revealing the rest of his magnificent body and the overwhelming extent of his desire.

I sucked in a breath, lightheaded from the heat and the humidity and Marco DeVita's brazen beauty. Arms at his sides, weight shifted onto one leg, he stood unabashed, dominating the room like a Roman god sculpted to perfection, expertly carved out of marble and sin. I wanted to touch him, wanted to run my hands over his hard muscles and up and down his erection. I wanted to witness the statute come to life. I wanted to make him lose his impenetrable control.

He lifted his chin and stepped toward the pool, the profile of his naked body no less erotic than the front. I shamelessly enjoyed the view—the round curve of his firm buttocks, the thick muscles of his powerful thighs, the proud extent of his hard length.

He descended into the water, each movement a dark temptation. He sat, stretched his arms along the edge of the pool, and let his head drop back, closing his eyes.

Shock held me in place, but eventually the blood stopped rushing between my legs and returned to my brain. I stepped toward the door bemused, bewildered, and horny as hell.

"Anna?" I stopped short and glanced over my shoulder. His head still rested on the lip of the pool. "You better wear one of those turtlenecks of yours tomorrow, or I won't be held responsible for my actions."

My jaw dropped, but I slammed it shut before the groan percolating in my lungs escaped. I ripped my eyes away from where cool waters lapped his naked body. Where he made dirty promises I prayed he'd keep.

I walked out of the spa and up the stairs to the main lobby, plotting what I'd wear the next day. There was no way in hell it was going to be a turtleneck. I was ready for Marco DeVita to lose control.

Chapter Fifteen

Anna

Thick maroon drapes fell from the ceiling to the floor behind Vesuvio's tinted windows. Through the narrow gap between panels, the soft glow of chandeliers cast silhouettes onto the club's glass façade. Slick, black veneer outlined the windows and door, and lava-red Roman lettering announced the club's name, the second *V* an eruption that spewed forth from an outline of the notorious mountain.

If the name and aesthetic didn't make it obvious Vesuvio was Mr. DeVita's club, the bouncer standing outside the entrance was a dead giveaway—big muscles, a stern mouth, and sunglasses.

Siobhán waited for me looking like she'd stepped off the set of a *Great Gatsby* movie, beret tilted over pin-curled hair and a trench coat cinched tight around her waist. She held out both hands, and I took them, greeting her with air kisses.

"I love your style," I said. "I wish I could pull off something more daring."

"Pfft." She waved a hand and turned for the door. The bouncer opened it without a word. "Girl, with those curves, you could pull off anything."

We walked out of the cold and into a refuge of heat, moths to the flames crackling in the glass firepit opposite the bar. Soft jazz filled the mostly empty space, the atmosphere more subdued and sophisticated than I'd expected. Men in suits and women in business attire stood around high tops sipping at martinis and globes of wine. The soft light from the chandeliers and fire glinted off the delicate crystalware. Most of the lush leather booths on either side of the fireplace were empty, only one of the spaces occupied by a couple engaged in intimate conversation.

"Come on," Siobhán said, interrupting my survey. "There's a Super Tuscan I want you to meet." She stuck the tip of her tongue between her teeth and led me to the few empty barstools still waiting for customers. We hung our coats on the backs of the stools and settled in.

The bartender placed his hands flat on the bar top and gave Siobhán a knowing smile. "Hey, gorgeous."

"Hey, yourself," she purred. "Can I get two glasses of that fabulous Tuscano I tried last week?" She turned to me. "Is red okay?"

"Absolutely."

"For you and your beautiful friend?" He spared me a glance. "Anything." He winked and sauntered off to get our drinks.

Siobhán laughed, the sound as infectious as her presence. "What a flirt."

"You come here often, I take it?"

"I wouldn't say often, but regularly enough they know I manage Terme di Boston for Marco. I look at it as a perk of working for DEI." The lines bracketing the corners of her red lips deepened with her mischievous smile.

"Nice perk."

The bartender returned with wine poured into two crystal

goblets. I swirled mine under my nose, and my eyes widened with its powerful bouquet.

"Right?" She held up her glass. "Cheers."

We drank, and the robust red hit my tongue with a burst of flavor even bolder than its intoxicating aroma.

I could get used to this.

"Let's get to business," Siobhán said, switching into general-manager mode. "Do you have any questions about what needs to be done?"

We spent the next hour talking charity gala logistics. She assigned me a list of odds and ends—confirm the florist, coordinate day-of installation, pick up the engraved guest nameplates. Siobhán was no-nonsense when it came to her job.

"I can't believe I haven't asked this yet, but what does the DeVita Foundation do?"

"Marco and his sister started it about ten years ago. They fund employment and language services for immigrants living in Boston. English as a Second Language, skills development, job placement. I think they wanted to provide the types of services their family didn't have when they moved to this country."

Warmth spread across my chest. I wanted so badly to believe in Mr. DeVita's virtue, and this act of charity was a huge point in his favor. "That's incredible. And he holds this event every year?"

She nodded. "Last year, they raised over a million dollars. The DeVitas are dedicated to helping immigrants. Marco told me once they think of all immigrants as part of their community."

I sipped my wine, hoping the alcohol would steady me since I was practically swooning. Benevolence on top of what I'd seen in the spa? It was too much!

Siobhán's eyes widened, and her lips turned up in a playful smile. "Oh my God. You have a thing for Marco."

"I do not!" I yelped. Mr. DeVita's naked body appeared in my mind, and my cheeks flared to match my drink. "Absolutely not!"

I hid my face behind my wine glass and bit the inside of my cheek to prevent the guilty smile attempting to break free. Once composed, I set the wine back on the bar and turned to face my accuser.

"You totally have a thing for Marco," she said with a knowing smirk. "I don't blame you. He's a good-looking man. He's generous and protective. Rich. Powerful. But..." She sighed, and her mouth bent into something just short of a frown.

"But..."

"Look, I love Marco like an uncle, but I've said it before, and I'll say it again—he's the type of man you want on your side, but not the type of man you want to date. The machismo in and of itself is..." She fake-shuddered.

I chuckled even though Mr. DeVita's unbridled masculinity was one of the things that turned me on about him. Much to my own mortification.

"Not to mention, those men don't understand the concept of fidelity." Her tone took a bitter turn. "They have their *goomars*"—she rolled her eyes through the Italian-American slang—"and don't give cheating a second thought."

She paused to drink her wine, and a new source of misgiving wedged itself between all the warm feelings I was developing for Mr. DeVita.

"Sorry," she said with a wave of her hand. She placed it atop mine, and her face softened, concern touching her pale blue eyes. "Just be careful, okay? In the years I've worked at Terme, I've never known Marco to date. I wouldn't want you to get hurt."

I sipped my wine and considered that surprising tidbit. "Well," I said with finality, "you absolutely do not need to worry about that. Absolutely nothing is going to happen between me and *my boss*. Absolutely not."

"Absolutely," she teased, eyes sparkling with delight. "Got it."

I scowled, and she laughed.

"Speaking of good-looking, you weren't kidding about Luca Moretti. Jesus." I fanned myself. "Talk about intense."

Siobhán's eyebrows shot to her hairline, but she quickly reined in her reaction and shifted her focus to where her fingertip traced the rim of her wine glass. "Luca's in town?" There was more than passing interest in her question; it leaked through the nonchalance I wasn't buying.

"For the financial quarterly. He stopped by to see Mr. DeVita on Tuesday."

She lifted her eyes as if waiting for me to say more, but I was distracted by the front door. It swung open behind her and let in a gust of cold air that whipped through the warm space like an icy fanfare heralding the man who followed behind it—Luca Moretti.

He glanced around the room, hands shoved into the pockets of his long wool coat, cashmere scarf hanging loosely in front of his unbuttoned suit jacket. His searching eyes landed on me, and after a beat, recognition snapped into place, and he donned his flashy smile.

"Speak of the devil," I mumbled.

Siobhán frowned and followed my gaze over her shoulder. Luca strode toward us with the effortless superiority of a model. His eyes shifted to Siobhán, who was fixated on his approach, and his dark stare turned predatory, his wide, inviting smile hungry and menacing.

She spun back to face me, swallowed a huge gulp of wine, and carefully curated her posture and face into a mask of casual indifference despite giving off an energy like she was preparing for battle.

Luca stopped behind Siobhán and rested a hand on the back of her chair. "Anna, right?" he asked over her shoulder. "Marco's new assistant?"

"Yes, Mr. Moretti, that's right. Nice to see you again."

"It's Luca. And same. Although, I do wonder about the company you're keeping."

Siobhán's head snapped up with a scowl.

He met the fierceness in her eyes with an intensity all his own, his pouty lips bending into a smile meant for pure seduction. Siobhán's steely glare and cool comportment melted in its aftermath. He leaned closer and with his free hand trailed a gloved finger from the top of her shoulder down the length of her arm. "Did you miss me?" he asked just above a whisper.

Siobhán shivered, and her eyes fluttered closed. I grabbed my necklace, uncomfortable and wanting to excuse myself, but they didn't seem to even notice I was still sitting there.

"Hm?" he prompted and leaned closer. "I missed you." He brushed an errant curl of her hair away with the tip of his nose. "Lucky for me you're still taking advantage of Marco's generosity, huh, Shamrock?" The words slowly took on a mocking edge, and when he said *Shamrock*, it had a derisive bite.

Siobhán's eyes snapped open. She pushed him away with her shoulder and flayed him with an angry glare. "I told you not to call me that," she said through gritted teeth.

"But that's what you are, right? Irish and Lucky?" He leaned in until their faces were an inch apart. "No matter how hard you try and change that accent."

"Asshole," she muttered under her breath and turned away, picking up her wine.

I shifted uncomfortably on my stool.

He chuckled and stepped back. "Have a nice night, ladies," he said and continued past us.

I followed his retreating form over my shoulder. "What just happened?"

Luca whispered something to one of Marco's sunglassed security guards. The man unclasped the red velvet rope hanging in front of the entrance to the narrow, spiral staircase at the far end of the club.

"And where is he going?" I turned back to Siobhán, and she was seething.

"And *that*"—she pointed to where Luca climbed the spiral staircase—"is why you don't get involved with those types of men! That man lives to vex me. Vex!" She downed the rest of her wine with a wince, and I decided it was not the time for any more questions about her and Luca. "And he's heading up to..." Her forehead wrinkled. "The other half of Vesuvio."

I craned my neck. "The other half of Vesuvio?"

"You signed one of Marco's NDAs, right?"

"Yes."

"The *members only* portion of the club."

I shook my head. "I didn't know Vesuvio had a private club."

"No one does. Well, except the members. And Marco's crew. It's not exactly advertised. Most people assume it's offices, which I suppose it kinda is during the day."

"Oh," I replied, completely lost. I sipped my wine hoping to cover up my naïveté.

Siobhán sighed and touched my hand. She filled her voice with a message I was supposed to understand by the slow articulation of her words. "The members like to play cards. Watch sports and horse racing. Enjoy half-naked waitresses who sometimes dance."

"Ohhh." My pulse quickened, the conflict of worry and excitement resurfacing in a rush. "I see."

An illegal gambling club right over my head. Another piece of evidence Marco DeVita was a closet mafioso. How was Siobhán so blasé about the whole thing? None of this seemed to faze her.

"Last call, ladies." The bartender's smooth voice interrupted my racing thoughts.

"We're good. Thanks, Eric," Siobhán said.

He nodded and walked out from behind the bar to the main floor.

"You okay?"

I forced a smile, not wanting her to think I was going to freak out and run to the cops or something. "I'm fine. Just surprised, that's all."

"I get it. I imagine it's jarring if you've never been exposed to this world."

And she had?

"Like I said, be careful with Marco. I know this is all new to you, and I don't want to see you get in over your head."

The front door opened, and Mr. Balistreri strode into the club followed by two men wearing telltale shades, one of whom I recognized as Mr. DeVita's driver. Mr. DeVita himself appeared next, his familiar, dominating swagger causing a rush of adrenaline that threatened to knock me off my stool. Two expensive suits filed in next. The first, shorter than Mr. DeVita and stout, his face shadowed by a fedora. The second, taller with features like a hawk. A final sunglassed security guard brought up the rear, and the seven men stood in the doorway like a scene out of the *Godfather*.

"I think that's our cue," I whispered.

She laughed, and the musical lilt drew Mr. DeVita's attention, but his eyes landed squarely on me.

He said something I couldn't make out, and the group strode through the club to the spiral staircase at the back while he and his driver made their way to where Siobhán and I sat at the bar.

"Ladies," Mr. DeVita crooned, peeling off his gloves one

finger at a time. "Did you enjoy your night?" His eyes never left mine, and I sat frozen, unable to speak, held captive by the conflict of danger and desire.

"The new Super Tuscan is fabulous, Marco. Excellent buy," Siobhán said and stood from her barstool. "I could have done without seeing Luca, but an otherwise lovely night. Thank you."

His eyes darted to Siobhán. "You two need to act your age around each other," he grumbled.

She snorted. "Tell him that." She took her coat off the chairback. "Anyway, we were just leaving."

His dark, sensuous eyes returned to me, and the air between us hung heavy with anticipation.

"Anna." Mr. DeVita held out his hand, never breaking eye contact. A spark zinged through me when our fingers touched and made my body rabid for more.

"Thank you," I said in an awe-filled whisper.

"Paulie. Take the girls home."

"You got it, boss."

"Oh, that's really not necessary."

"I insist," he commanded in his executive voice.

Siobhán's focus drifted to where my hand still rested in his. "Come on, Paulie." She shoved her arm into the crook of his elbow and pulled him toward the door.

Mr. DeVita released my hand and fetched my coat. He held it open, and I threaded my arms into the sleeves. He settled it across my shoulders, stepping closer as he wrapped it around my body. His powerful frame was a furnace pressed against my back, and his breath tickled my ear, sending a frisson of heat straight to the apex of my legs. I tilted my head to bring my face closer to his lips.

He hummed, a satisfied sound. "I changed my mind." He ran his hands up and down my arms. "Wear something low-cut to the office. Something tight that shows off your ass and those gorgeous tits. You're having dinner with me tomorrow night, and I want to engage in some sexual harassment."

A strange sound escaped me, something between a groan and a yelp, and my cheeks flared at the ridiculous noise. His chest rumbled with laughter, deep and sinful, and he squeezed my arms before releasing me and took quick strides to the winding staircase.

I walked out of Vesuvio in a daze, unable to process what had happened or the torrent of sensation attacking my body. Mr. DeVita's driver opened the backdoor of the Range Rover, and I slid into the seat. The door slammed shut.

"Girl." Siobhán gawped at me, her eyebrows approaching her hairline. "You are in so much trouble."

I THREW off the covers and picked my phone up off the side table. 3:00 a.m. "Ugh."

I swung my feet over the edge of the bed and slid them into my slippers. Sophie lifted her head and glared at me with the profuse judgment only achievable by cats. I didn't blame her. I'd go back to sleep if I could, but images of Jeff's bruised and swollen face and topless women serving drinks at poker tables plagued my dreams. I needed answers.

I pulled on a pair of jeans and an oversized sweater, threw my hair into a ponytail, and threaded it through the back of my Red Sox cap. Boots, coat, gloves? Check. I locked my front door and started the long walk to MIT.

Even if Marco DeVita wasn't currently a member of the Mafia—doubtful given the illegal club and the shakedown at city hall—I'd be hard-pressed to believe he hadn't been at some point. He wouldn't have been able to negotiate with Pádraig Shaughnessy otherwise.

My breath came in short puffs of steam against the cold

black night. Heightened awareness kept my mind busy and my eyes searching, nervous I was being followed. Whether by one of Mr. DeVita's men or someone keeping tabs on Mr. DeVita, I didn't know, and it didn't matter. It freaked me out all the same. I picked up my pace until I was safe within the walls of MIT's main library.

One of the benefits of working at a university? Twenty-four seven access to archives and primary source material not available to the outside world. A few students sat at wide wooden tables, hovering over open notebooks. Some were goofing off, playing board games. Others used their textbooks as pillows, having lost the battle against nature's inconvenient requirement that humans sleep.

Being in my forties, I remembered how information searches worked before the internet. Back then, looking up newspaper articles meant searching through a stack of index cards organized by keywords to find the correct roll of microfiche, then loading it into the viewer to access the article.

I removed my gloves and coat and placed them on the desk next to the index computer. I searched for Valenzano, DeVita, Moretti, and Shaughnessy. Most of the hits came from the *Boston Globe*, a few dating back as early as the 1940s. I printed the indexes from each decade predating the internet, retrieved the rolls, and settled myself in front of a viewer.

The articles themselves, especially the early ones, didn't tell me much more than I already knew about the history of the Boston Mafia or the key players like Big Frankie Valenzano and Antonio Moretti. Those two were local legends, especially among Italian-Americans in Massachusetts. But the pictures were fascinating.

The Valenzanos shared a strong family resemblance. Anyone with eyes could see Vinnie was related to Big Frankie. And the pictures of Vincenzo—Vinnie senior—looked nearly identical to the man who'd walked into Marco's office two weeks ago. Aside from the mustache, I couldn't tell them apart.

An article from 1962...

Italian Mafia Suspected in Cuban Cigar Heist

Famed mafiosos Antonio "Tony" Moretti and Marco L. DeVita are primary suspects in a missing truck shipment that contained over a hundred thousand dollars' worth of Cuban cigars.

That was a lot of money in 1962. And what was with these men naming their children and grandchildren after themselves? I shook my head and scrolled to the bottom of the page where two black-and-white pictures, one of Big Frankie and one of Tony, stared back at me.

Law enforcement believes Tony Moretti and Marco DeVita are capi under the current Don of Boston, Francesco "Big Frankie" Valenzano. At the time of printing, neither law enforcement nor the Boston Globe had a picture of Marco DeVita.

My stomach dropped reading Mr. DeVita's name in the newspaper even if it was referring to his... father? Grandfather? The DeVitas had been involved, that much was clear, and his legacy and fortune were tainted with blood. I shifted in my seat, but pushed my unease aside and continued my research.

By five in the morning, the only thing keeping me awake was anxious curiosity and my insatiable hunger for answers. Luckily, I'd reached the final index—an article from 1988.

Funeral of Antonio Moretti Draws Who's Who of New England Organized Crime

Italian businessman Antonio Moretti, Jr., son of Antonio "Tony" Moretti, Sr., famed mafioso and known associate of the Valenzano crime family, was shot in the head and killed last Saturday, sending shockwaves through the Italian-American community. Police found Antonio Jr. in the driver's seat of his Cadillac outside the Charlestown ship-yard. Authorities suspect the assassination was executed by the Shaughnessy crime family in retaliation for recent infractions involving gambling territories.

The article went on and on, detailing the Moretti family's involvement in organized crime since the 1950s as well as a laundry list of gangsters who'd attended the funeral. I skimmed to the bottom.

Antonio Jr. leaves behind son, Luca Davide Moretti. Luca's mother, Lucia, passed away in 1982 from complications during childbirth.

Below the article was a grainy, black-and-white photo from the funeral, taken at a distance, no doubt by law enforcement or the paparazzi. I couldn't imagine the family or the Valen-zanos allowing journalists at such a private event. The casket was closed, which I knew was an added insult. A young boy stared down at its black veneer.

Luca. My heart broke for the little boy in the picture.

He held hands with a man and a woman who stood on either side of him. A fat ring on the man's pinky finger caught my eye and turned my stomach.

I knew that ring. I'd seen that ring almost every day for the past two weeks. I swallowed and looked to the face of its owner. Marco DeVita's dark, passionate eyes were fixed on the casket.

I blinked rapidly. Exhaustion had my mind playing tricks,

and in my rush to leave the house, I'd forgotten my reading glasses. I squinted and tried to refocus, but I knew those eyes. They'd held me captive for weeks. The man in the picture was identical to the man I'd left only hours before, but that was impossible.

I sat back in my chair and chewed the side of my finger. What the hell was a fifty-year-old Marco DeVita doing in a picture from 1988?

Chapter Sixteen

Marco

I walked off the elevator and into the foyer. Anna looked up from where she sat behind the desk studying her screen. Her eyes weren't as vibrant as usual, her body not as tense. I knew the feeling; it had been a late night at Vesuvio. We were drinking and playing cards till well past 1:00 a.m. when Carmine's wife called and gave him an earful, forcing us to go home.

"Good afternoon, Mr. DeVita."

"Anna," I replied, trying to soften my usually gruff voice. "Any calls while I was out?"

"No."

Good. I didn't particularly want to talk to anyone. The low-grade headache from all the whiskey made me irritable.

I took quick strides to my office, but when I reached for the door, I stopped short, caught in the net of Anna's legs. Sheer black tights hugged her shapely calves, and a seam trailed up their backs from the spikes of her heels to where her little black dress met the middle of her thigh. Its long sleeves hugged her arms, and the square neckline was cut low, revealing the tops of her breasts. I tongued a fang, willing it to retreat, but the sight of all that creamy skin and tight, black silk made me ache with hunger and need.

She'd smelled so fucking good yesterday, the hint of rose she always wore amplified by the steam room. I'd been bold in my advances, but she'd played along, and the untapped passion in her eyes beckoned. She wanted me as badly as I wanted her.

I hadn't been drawn to a woman like I was drawn to Anna in decades. Not since Lucia died. Watching her waste away as fear ate at her like a cancer... Watching Tony lose the love of his life because of what he was... I never wanted to know that kind of pain.

This flirting was a risky business. The way things were going, there was no way we weren't going to fuck. Problem was, it couldn't be more than that. As much as I craved her companionship, I refused to bring her into my world and put her in danger, not even accounting for the possibility she might crumble under the weight of learning I was a blood demon. And if she didn't? Would she be willing to give up her life and everyone she loved to be with me? Was I selfish enough to expect that?

With all my issues, I couldn't feed from her unless we bonded. And that was a step I wasn't sure I'd ever be ready to take.

She looked up to where I hovered outside my office door staring at her while I spiraled.

"You dressed for dinner," I said.

"I did, but..." She leaned on the arm of her chair and ran her necklace between her thumb and forefinger.

"But what?"

"You could have asked."

"Asked what?"

"Asked if I wanted to have dinner with you." She raised an eyebrow. "Instead of telling me."

"It wasn't a request."

Her lips trembled, fighting a smile, but amusement danced in her eyes. "Yes, Mr. DeVita," she said in a coy, subservient tone undercut with sarcasm.

"You can call me Marco, Anna. I think we've moved past the business-only portion of our relationship." I raised an eyebrow. "Don't you?"

She had a mischievous glint in her eyes and bend to her mouth. "That wouldn't be professional, Mr. DeVita. I work for you."

"It's not any less professional than me staring at your tits. Or you staring at my naked body." She looked away, hiding her smile and the flush creeping up her neck. "Please. Call me Marco."

She turned back, eyebrows raised. "He does know the word!" I scowled, and she laughed. "Okay. Marco," she said breathily.

I wanted to skip work and dinner and drag her into my apartment. Instead, piles of paperwork forced me into my office.

Between organizing my notes for the quarterly and finalizing the permits for my new property, I was staring down the barrel of a busy Friday. And then there was Luca.

I leaned back in my chair and swiped a hand down my face. That kid was a ticking time bomb of rage. My fault, probably. I wasn't cut out to be a father. The Lord knew I hadn't asked Tony to get himself killed. I didn't know how to deal with a kid who'd lost both his parents, but I sure as shit never tolerated him hanging around Vinnie's nephews. That much I'd been able to control.

Kid. I snorted. He was a forty-two-year-old man. If he wanted to fuck around with the Valenzanos, there was nothing I could do to stop him. But he wouldn't be part of my crew.

Something bugged me about our conversation at Vesuvio.

He'd pushed the issue with the Shaughnessys, said they were aggressively expanding their territory, getting more cops on the take. But how much was true and how much was Luca's pent-up hostility?

Boston's blood demon population couldn't survive without Valenzano Sources. I didn't want to think about the consequences of an all-out war between the Irish and the Italians, especially if the Irish won. My people needed to feed, and I knew better than most what happened to your moral code when you were hungry.

I took out my phone.

> We need to talk.

The afternoon flew by, my attention occupied with financial reports, city hall, and the escrow company.

My phone buzzed. I glanced at the screen; 6:30 p.m. and a text message from Vinnie.

> 11 tonight. The usual.

He meant Vesuvio. Texting was dangerous. I had no doubt the feds monitored Vinnie's communications, and the last thing I needed was Agent Johnson hanging around Vesuvio like he hung around Terme.

> Ci sarò.

I undid my tie and tossed it on my desk, unbuttoned the top of my shirt, and tried to relax. Dinner with Anna and a meeting with Vinnie. I puffed out my cheeks and slowly released my breath. What a night.

I poured a finger of whiskey and tried to convince myself this was okay, that pursuing Anna when I had no fucking clue if I could manage a future with her wasn't a dick move. But my need to spend time with her, my growing need for partnership, was more powerful than common sense. I shot back the whiskey. As irresponsible as this was, I couldn't help myself. To hell with consequences; I'd deal with those later.

I walked out of my office. Anna was standing by the windows looking out at the city. Her head turned slightly when the door clicked shut, revealing a sliver of her profile behind the fall of her chestnut hair. The picture she painted, understated class and unparalleled Italian beauty, made my chest tighten with an overwhelming need to possess.

Fresh snow glistened under the bright lights surrounding the Commons and the buildings beyond. I crossed the foyer slowly, allowing myself time to drink in the curves of her delicious body against the picturesque backdrop beyond the glass.

I stood to her left, and we took in the winterscape in comfortable silence.

"What a beautiful view," she said wistfully.

"When I—" I caught myself and cleared my throat. "When my father built Terme, he had the foresight to line the entire north side of the penthouse with windows. I converted the floor from accommodations to my office and my home because of this view. I wanted to enjoy moments like this every day."

She turned her face up, and I glanced down to where she looked at me. Surprise colored her appreciation. "I don't blame you," she said. "This place is a retreat. The city can be too much at times. Loud and frantic. But up here, everything is much more serene, peaceful even, especially with the snow."

I placed my hand on the small of her back. "Shall we?" Without thinking, I ran my thumb up and down the curve of her spine, and her skin pebbled with goosebumps.

"Yes," she said with a shy smile. "Of course."

We entered the elevator, and the impulse to pull her into

me, tilt her head back and take her mouth, was overwhelming. Instead, I dropped my hand and shoved it in my pocket, afraid that if I touched her too long, I wouldn't be able to stop.

Vittoria was a three-star Michelin restaurant on the ground floor. I'd lucked out. During one of my extended stays in Rome, I'd found an up-and-coming chef eager to move to the US but waiting for the right opportunity. He'd jumped at my offer. I'd snagged my sommelier from one of the best restaurants in New York City. He'd wanted to move back to Boston to be closer to family. Done. Between the two, Terme was home to one of the best Italian restaurants in the country, and I couldn't wait to share a meal there with Anna.

We walked beneath the stone archway and the thin swirl of a wrought iron "Vittoria" nestled among climbing ivy. I nodded to the maître d' as we passed into the dining room and ushered her up the narrow set of stairs to the mezzanine. The single row of tables lining the exclusive level were all marked Reserved. I pulled out a chair for her at the center table, hoping she'd appreciate the view. It overlooked the dining area, and the French doors provided a grand view of the Commons and the blanket of fresh snow.

"Thank you." Her voice was shaky with nerves, and my unrelenting need to protect redoubled its efforts.

The warm candlelight highlighted the flush of her cheeks and the auburn highlights in her hair. I'd done nothing in this life to deserve sitting across from this angel.

"Good evening, Mr. DeVita. Ma'am." A waiter removed the Reserved placard from the table. "I'll let Chef know you've arrived. He has an excellent menu planned for you this evening."

"I have no doubt. I'd like a bottle of wine tonight."

The waiter eyed Anna. Kid needed to learn poker.

"Of course, sir. I'll get Mr. Klein."

"No need. My private collection is on reserve in the back.

Klein knows where to find it. Tell him I'd like a bottle of the 2012 Brunello. We're celebrating."

The waiter's eyes widened. "Yes, sir. Right away."

The corners of Anna's big brown eyes crinkled when she smiled. "What are we celebrating?"

"Pompeii."

She tilted her head in question.

"Well, I couldn't call it Vesuvio II now, could I? Too perfunctory."

She scrunched her nose, but after a moment, her eyes brightened with realization. "The purchase went through."

"It did. Escrow is thirty days, of course, but barring the seller pulling out, which I can guarantee won't happen, you're looking at the owner of one very large and very expensive piece of historic property in the financial district."

"Congratulations. I'll admit, I was skeptical you'd make it happen." Her expression turned knowing. "But I have a feeling there are very few things you want that you don't make happen."

"You're having dinner with me tonight, aren't you?"

She smiled coyly and reached for her necklace.

"I couldn't think of a more perfect way to celebrate."

She ran the necklace between her fingers and looked down at her place setting, her face glowing with contentment and her shy smile. "Such flattery." She traced the shining silver on black linen with her French-manicured fingertip, and her eyes sparkled playfully in the candlelight. "No menus tonight."

"Chef prepares a special menu when I dine. He knows what I like."

"And what if your date doesn't care for the selection?" She looked up, and her lips fought a smile.

I scoffed and leaned back in my chair. "Doubtful."

"What if I have allergies?"

"There's an EpiPen in the first aid kit behind the front desk."

She laughed, a throaty sound that went straight to my heart and made me smile in spite of myself. This woman.

"Your 2012 Brunello di Montalcino Riserva, Mr. DeVita." The waiter appeared, holding the bottle by its neck, and gently rested it against his forearm so I could inspect the label. A bus boy stood behind him with a crystal decanter and two red wine glasses.

I nodded, and with swift efficiency, he uncorked and decanted the wine, setting it on the table before pouring a small amount for me to taste. Perfection. I nodded again, and he poured both glasses.

He leveled Anna with a serious look. "You're in for a treat. Enjoy. I'll return with the first course shortly."

"No rush," I told him.

The waiter nodded and left.

"Perfect timing." I picked up my glass. "Alla salute."

"Alla salute."

She took a small sip, and her eyes widened into saucers. She gaped at the contents of her glass as if she might find an explanation for what she'd just tasted inside and took another sip.

"I think—I think that's the best wine I've had in my entire life." She reverently placed the glass on the table, laying her fingers across its crystal base.

I chuckled. Good taste, too. Could this woman be any more perfect? "Does this mean you'll trust me to order for you in the future?"

She laughed and shook her head. "No shame."

"Never."

She dropped her necklace, and her shoulders relaxed. "Is it expensive? The waiter looked like he was carrying a priceless artifact. I'm surprised he wasn't wearing white gloves."

"It's relative," I said with a shrug and swirled the glass under my nose. "2012 and 2013 were excellent vintages in the Montalcino region of Tuscany. 2012 is considered outstanding, hence the Riserva label. People buy them up, age them properly, and sell them for ridiculous amounts of money. But I like to drink the wine I buy. I purchased this case directly from the vineyard. They age best at twenty to twenty-five years, but you can drink them as early as ten."

"So, yes?" She brought the glass to her lips, and I became irrationally jealous of the glass.

"I suppose so, yes."

"Well, thank you for sharing it with me. It's divine."

"I'm glad you like it."

The waiter returned and placed two plates of antipasto on the table. Burrata and basil stuffed tomatoes drizzled in a balsamic reduction. One of my favorites. I took up my knife and fork.

"So, how's the grand experiment?" I asked.

She blinked. "The what?"

"The grand experiment." I circled my knife in the air. "Trying out the real world."

She swallowed her bite and gave me an arch look. "Well, I've had a few problems with the management."

I laughed, hard, picked up my wine glass, and tipped it in her direction.

"Honestly? I'm convinced, now more than ever, that I'm ready to move on."

"I'm that good of a boss, huh?"

She chuckled and took another bite of burrata, chewing slowly, a pensive expression on her face.

"For the past twenty-some years, I shaped my career, in part, based on what other people told me I could and couldn't handle. Believe it or not"—she pointed at me with her fork—

"I wasn't always the outgoing life of the party you see sitting across from you."

"I'm shocked."

"I know. Hard to believe," she said wryly and let out a sigh. "As much as I hate to admit it, after the past couple of weeks, I'm not sure I could have handled the intensity back then. I needed time to gain confidence. Time to develop the coping skills I use when I clam up."

"I've seen the clam ups. They're not as bad as you make them sound."

"Trust me—they used to be. Jeff called it deer-in-the-headlights Anna." She rolled her eyes, and I snorted. "Now, it just feels worse than it looks. Being a researcher and professor gave me an opportunity to develop those coping skills, and I'm thankful for that time."

"I sense a *but* coming."

She nodded while she chewed and washed her bite down with more wine.

"But it's time to move on. Don't get me wrong; being a professor has been satisfying in ways I hadn't imagined, and I'm proud of my research and my publications and the impact I've made on my students. But this? This is what I always wanted to do."

"This being..."

"Working in a corporate office, meeting new people, facing new challenges. Problem solving. It's exciting. I may be shy and an irreparable introvert, but that doesn't mean I don't get bored. I'm excited about coming to work every day, and that hasn't been true in a long time. And, turns out, I *can* handle the real world. I may be plagued with sweaty palms and the occasional stutter, but I've held my own. Even with the management."

I chuffed and gave my head a shake. "You certainly have."

The waiter swooped in to pour more wine and remove our empty plates.

Anna swirled her wine, took a sip, and let the glass dangle in her fingertips. "It's been refreshing working for such a capable businessman. You'd be surprised how many CEOs don't follow the financial performance of their own companies. I've worked with a lot of data sets over the years, and you, Marco DeVita, are an anomaly." She tipped her head and her glass toward me.

When you come up in the Mafia, one of the first things you learn is to count your money. Too bad that line of defense didn't protect you from snakes and cheats.

"If I were such a capable businessman, the performance of my European branch wouldn't be tanking." The bitter words left an unpleasant taste on my tongue.

She frowned, no doubt wondering how her compliment had gone sideways. "If there's a leak, if it isn't just the economy, you can't blame yourself."

"Can't I? If there's a leak, it means I brought someone into my family I shouldn't have. That or someone I trust betrayed me. Either way, the blame lies with me." The sting of failure burned my chest, and the look on Anna's face made it worse. I didn't deserve her sympathy.

"Sweet ricotta ravioli with an oxtail ragu," the waiter announced.

Anna's eyes widened, and she shifted her focus away from me and onto the steaming plates the waiter placed on the table. *Grazie a Dio.*

"Buon appetito," he announced and left us to our meal.

"This looks amazing." Anna closed her eyes, and a contented smile brightened her lovely features. "The smell..."

Warmth replaced the needling in my chest. The satisfaction of providing for her, of making her smile... It filled me with a sense of purpose and completeness.

"Knowing Chef, it'll taste even better."

We enjoyed our meal, and after several bites, Anna paused and lifted her fork. "Family is important to you."

I nodded mid-bite.

"Luca isn't really your nephew, is he? He's your best friend's son?"

I swallowed, relieved she wasn't heading back to the previous topic, and washed ricotta and ragu down with more wine. "That's right. But Tony and I considered each other brothers. Tony had Luca calling me zio as soon as he could talk."

"He doesn't look that much younger than you."

"Tony was older than me," *by a year*, "and he had Luca when he was very young," *by blood demon standards*. "And I'm older than I look," *by almost forty-five years*.

"How old?"

"Older than you," I said and winked.

Her sexy laugh floated across the table. "And a sister?"

"Yes."

"Younger or older?"

"Younger, although you'd never know by the way she talks to me."

"I'd pay to see that," she said through a devious smile. "Siobhán mentioned your sister is involved in your family charity? The one benefitting from the gala next weekend?"

"She is. Especially the ESL programs. Papà struggled with English."

Her smile warmed. "It's such a good cause."

"Speaking of which..."

I set down my knife and fork and held out my hand. She glanced at it, confused, then tentatively placed her hand in mine.

"Come with me to the charity gala next weekend."

Her eyebrows shot to her forehead. "I—uh—" She swallowed. "Are you sure?"

I ran my thumb over the backs of her fingers. "Of course, I'm sure. Why wouldn't I be sure?"

"Won't there be, you know, a lot of important people there? Won't they—won't they wonder why you brought your assistant?"

"You're an important person. To your students, to your field. To me."

She lowered her eyes, and a flush crept across her cheeks. Her hand twitched as if she meant to pull it away. I tightened my grip, and she seized her necklace with her other hand instead. "Thank you," she said shyly. "But you know what I mean."

"I do know what you mean. I never bring a date to these things, much to my sister's chagrin, but no one will be wondering why I brought you. They'll be wondering how I got so lucky."

She looked up, beaming. Her eyes sparkled beneath the candlelight and made my heart ache with affection.

"With an invitation like that, how can a girl say no?"

I squeezed her hand, fighting the urge to smile like I'd just been crowned Emperor of Rome.

We finished our meals with comfortable, easy conversation about the chef's talent, the sublime wine pairing, and the peaceful ambiance. Anna picked up her napkin, dabbed the corners of her mouth, and placed it on the table next to her empty plate.

"That was so good. I feel like one of those raviolis—totally stuffed."

"No room for dessert?"

Her hands went to her waist. "Even if I could, I'm not sure anything else would fit in this dress."

"You look stunning."

The color rose in her cheeks again, but this time, she didn't turn away or fidget. "Thank you. I rarely get a chance to dress up."

"You're welcome to wear that dress to the office any time you'd like. I won't complain."

She chuckled. "As much as I adore this ensemble—and I never thought I'd say this—I'm looking forward to my business attire on Monday. Much more comfortable. Oh! Which reminds me. I'm going to be late coming in on Monday, if that's okay?"

"Shouldn't be a problem."

"Sorry for the short notice. It slipped my mind. I'm not used to keeping regular hours."

"Another date?" I couldn't help the sardonic edge to my playful taunt.

"No. Not another date," she chastened with a dramatic eye roll. "It's my father's birthday. We're going to dinner Sunday night, and the Monday morning bus from Amherst doesn't arrive until nine thirty."

I laid my hands on the edge of the table and leaned forward, sure I'd misheard. "You're going to Amherst this weekend."

"Yes."

"By yourself."

"Yes."

"On a *bus*." I tried not to shout, but for all the God-forsaken ideas...

"Yes," she said quietly, and her eyebrows drew together in confusion. "I always take the bus when I visit my parents."

"Absolutely not."

She blinked rapidly. "Excuse me?"

"You are not taking a bus."

"Uh—yes, I am." Her voice rose with outrage to match my own.

We'd been here before; we both had hot tempers. But there was no fucking way I was letting her take a bus. "No. You're. Not." My knuckles went white from gripping the edge of the table, but I caught myself before I damaged it. "And why aren't you driving?"

"Not that it's any of your business, but I don't drive."

I sat back, my rage momentarily disarmed by surprise. "You don't drive."

"I don't drive."

"How do you get around?"

"The T. Walking. Cabs. *Buses*."

My fingers dug back into the wood, and I ground my teeth, trying to rid myself of the fear-induced rage she stoked being so cavalier with her safety. "How long has this been going on?"

"Uh—my entire adult life," she snapped. "And—shocking, I know—I've managed to keep myself in one piece since I was eighteen!"

"Well, that's changing. Starting tonight."

"What's that—" Her voice had risen to a pitch and volume so high she glanced down at the main floor with worry, then turned back and finished with hushed ire. "What's that supposed to mean?"

"It means that just because something hasn't happened yet doesn't mean it never will. It means that you are absolutely not taking a cab home tonight. It means that as long as you're in my life, I'm responsible for your safety, and you will let me make sure you get home safely." My voice hardened with each declaration, my breath quickening as I tried to contain my frustration.

"Did we not just talk about how I don't need people in my life telling me what I can and can't handle? Did we not just have that exact conversation?"

"This isn't about your abilities, Anna." My voice boomed

across the table and the restaurant, drawing more than a few glances.

Her jaw dropped as if she'd been struck by my voice, and her hand flew to her necklace. She sat back in her chair, looked out the window, and chewed the inside of her cheek.

Cazzo. I'd forgotten a shy, sensitive woman lived beneath the fiery armor of Anna's temper. And what a loud, demanding asshole I could be.

I swiped a hand down my face. "This isn't about your abilities," I said softly.

She wouldn't meet my eyes, and hers glistened in the candlelight.

"Hey. Anna. Mia bellissima Anna. Look at me."

She ran her fingers up and down the length of her necklace and turned to face me, but she continued to chew the inside of her cheek like she was fighting tears. That I caused. Fuck. Me.

"This isn't about your abilities, it's about your safety. This city is dangerous. You've been lucky nothing's happened to you all these years. A professional, single woman, travelling alone? You might as well have a fucking bullseye painted on your back."

She let out a shuddering huff and rolled her eyes. "You sound like Jeff."

"Jeff's a smart man." Jeff also knew how dangerous this city could be. Firsthand.

"Hey." I laid my hand palm up on the table. She stared at it with suspicion but placed her clammy fingers in mine. "Humor me, okay? Let me take you home tonight. I'll have my driver take you to Amherst tomorrow. I care about you. I don't want to see you hurt."

"You don't have to be such a—a tyrant about it," she mumbled.

"Yes, I do. It's part of my charm," I said and offered an apologetic smile.

She let out a nervous chuckle, and her shoulders relaxed. The waiter came to take our plates, and she pulled her hand away. I fought the urge to snatch it back.

"Dessert?" the waiter asked.

"No," I said. "Give my regards to Chef. Excellent meal."

"Of course, sir."

I pulled out my phone.

Bring the car around.

"Shall we?" I asked.

Anna nodded, a tired smile on her face, no doubt because I was a dick.

Regret pinched my chest. She didn't deserve to be barked at like a member of my crew. But I'd lost control, the overwhelming need to protect her making me crazy with an animalistic possessiveness. She may have needed more from her career, but I needed more from her. My feelings for this woman were evolving way past lust, and for the first time in my life, I didn't want them to stop.

Chapter Seventeen

Anna

A sea of headlights and streetlamps crept past the tinted backseat window of the Range Rover. I chewed the side of my nail, a nervous habit I thought I'd rid myself of years ago but reared its ugly head anytime I lost myself in thought.

He hadn't meant to upset me. I knew that. Fear for my safety had manifested as anger, and his anger was just another form of his passion. Loud voices rattled me, but more than that, his reaction to my taking the bus made me realize his flirting and advances weren't just a lark. Things had turned serious, and the gravity of my situation with Marco had caught me off guard.

He wrapped his big, warm hand around mine, and interlaced our fingers. My lips parted in surprise, and I looked up. Guilt softened the hard lines of his handsome face, and the corner of his mouth tipped up as he brought our combined hands to his lips and gently kissed the backs of my fingers.

The safety and comfort I'd known in his presence returned, and my body relaxed. I smiled, accepting his silent apology, and he rested our joined hands on the center console, running his thumb along the back of mine while we made our way across the river to Cambridge.

He helped me out of the Range Rover, and we walked through the courtyard of my condo complex to my front door.

Standing on the porch, I was as nervous as when I'd gone on my first date in high school, and my palms unleashed their sweaty fury, refusing to be outdone by the butterflies attacking my stomach.

He leaned against the front door, still holding my hand. "Thank you," he said. "For agreeing to be my date next weekend."

I let out a huff and couldn't help but smirk. "You've never said that to me before."

"What?"

"Thank you."

He raised an eyebrow. "I haven't?"

I bit the inside of my cheek, trying not to laugh, and shook my head.

His expression turned serious. He released my hand, pushed off the door, and threaded his fingers into my hair. His grip was gentle but urgent, and my head tilted up in response. Resting his forehead against mine, his eyes fluttered closed, and his warm, sweet breath caressed my face. My own eyes shuttered in response.

"Thank you," he breathed. "Thank you for being brilliant. Thank you for being brave. Thank you for not giving up. Not on this job and not on me." He tightened his grip in my hair, holding on like he thought I might disappear. "Thank you for making me feel."

My chest ached under the pressure of my expanding heart, his words destroying any remaining doubt I had feelings for the man who held me so desperately. I placed my hands on his forearms and squeezed.

We clung to each other, unmoving, breathing the same air,

sharing the same space. Bonded by our need to feel and not wanting our connection to end. Two souls, adrift, drawn together by fate at the right place and the right time to show the other what was missing, to be what the other was missing. And in that moment, we existed as partners, even if only for the night.

He lifted his head and pressed his lips to my forehead. He let go of my hair and ran his hands down my arms until they enveloped my clammy, shaking fingers.

"You're gone this weekend, and next week I won't be in the office. I have the quarterly with my COOs. We likely won't see each other till the gala. But I always keep my promises." His voice was low and filled with intent. "You know that, right?"

I managed a slight nod.

"I told you I couldn't be held responsible for my actions if you didn't wear a turtleneck." The sexy, sly grin he'd worn while naked in the spa crept across his handsome face. Excitement and expectation zipped through me, collecting between my legs. "Lucky for you, I have a meeting tonight and can't be late."

Disappointment slammed into my chest and knocked the breath from my lungs. I forced myself to breathe, determined to be as bold as I felt inside. "Maybe—" I swallowed. "Maybe I don't want to be lucky."

"Hmm," he purred, a satisfied rumble as he wrapped his arms around my waist. He brushed his lips in featherlight kisses down my temple until he reached my ear. I tilted my head to the side, offering more. "This is going to be the longest week of my life."

"I feel special. That's a lot of weeks, old man." I squeezed his bicep.

He hugged me closer. "You have no idea."

I pulled back so I could look into his obsidian eyes and he

could kiss me. More than anything in the world, I was desperate for him to kiss me. His gaze dipped to my lips, and they parted for him in silent invitation.

"I'd kiss you in earnest, but I can't. I won't be able to stop. Not till I possess every inch of your body. For now, this—" He took my top lip between his, and the light touch of his soft lips stirred my desire. Currents of sensation tingled up my legs, and my eyes fluttered closed as I relaxed into his embrace. He touched my mouth with the tip of his tongue before moving to take my bottom lip in another tender kiss. The gentle pressure made me shiver, and he hugged me close while lingering there for several heartbeats. He pulled back. "—will have to do."

He released me, and his absence tugged on my heart. "I'll see you next Saturday, mia bellissima Anna." He brushed his thumb across my cheek and spun away, taking long, quick strides across the courtyard to his Range Rover. He climbed into the backseat, and the black SUV sped away.

In a daze, I opened my front door and went through the motions of taking off my shoes, hanging up my coat, and setting my purse on the dining room table. I wandered upstairs to my room and sat on the edge of my bed. Sophie jumped up next to me and bumped her head into my arm until I relented and gave her the attention she thought she deserved.

My lips still tingled from Marco's gentle caress, and my body floated on a cloud of affection and desire. Yes, he was overbearing and demanding, but he was also caring and generous, tender and passionate. My misgivings dissolved in the wake of his kiss, and I lay back on the bed, letting my trust and belief in his virtue take control. I closed my eyes and placed my hands over my heart, relishing the warmth he'd placed there and allowing myself to tumble headfirst into a romance I could no longer deny.

Chapter Eighteen

Marco

"Marco." Gina looked up from where she sat in Mamma's rocking chair. A small fire rippled in the fireplace, and a glass of wine sat on the end table. She held a pen poised over the open notebook in her lap. "What are you doing here?"

"What? I can't drop in on my little sister?"

"Of course you can." She placed the pen in the middle of her notebook and closed it. "I was just going over my speech for the gala next weekend."

"Making sure to sneak in a few political jabs?" My sister was nothing if not opinionated, especially when it came to politics.

"Absolutely."

I unbuttoned my suit jacket and sank into Papà's chair. The fire flickered under the mantle. What a fucking day. And it wasn't over yet.

"Want some wine?"

"No. Grazie. I had some with dinner. I just need to sit."

She narrowed her eyes. "What's got you in a mood?"

I snorted. "That obvious, huh?"

"You look like you're about to strangle someone."

I waved a hand. "I'm worried about Luca."

She sat upright, feet flat on the floor, and red streaked into her eyes. "What's wrong with Luca? What happened?"

"Calm down. Nothing happened."

"Dannazione. Don't scare me like that!" She eased back in her chair, and her eyes slowly cleared. "What's wrong then?"

This wasn't going to be an easy conversation. Gina took her role as Luca's foster mother seriously. "He's so angry. I thought we'd gotten him past all that." I looked into the flames, unable to maintain eye contact, the pain in her expression too much to stomach.

She thought it was her fault, like she should have done more, been a better mother. But Gina wasn't to blame. Neither was I. That poison had started and needed to end with Luca.

"He thinks the answer is getting involved with Vinnie, seeking vengeance against the Shaughnessys. He won't listen to me." I turned back to meet her eyes. "But he'll listen to you."

She scoffed. "What makes you think he'll listen to me? He's a grown man." She lifted her wine glass. "He's going to do what he wants," she said and took a drink.

I ground my teeth. "You could at least try. Before he does something stupid and gets himself killed." My tone was more biting than I intended.

My sister arched an eyebrow. "Non usare quel tono con me, Marco Luciano." God, she sounded like Mamma. "You may get away with talking like that to Vito and Carmine and Angelo, but it won't fly in this house."

I sighed and swiped my hand down my face.

She set her glass on the end table and rested her elbows on her knees. Her mouth formed a stern line under eyes that told me I was in for a lecture. A lecture that would most likely piss me off. What was with everyone lately?

"You don't have to protect him anymore. You know that, right? You don't have to protect me either." She said the words slowly, her voice quiet. I opened my mouth to protest, but her withering stare made me think twice. I pressed my lips together and held my tongue. "Or Mamma and Papà. Or this neighborhood. Or every single blood demon in the state of Massachusetts. I know you think it's your responsibility, that it's your cross to bear, but it isn't. And it hasn't been. Not for a long time.

"You've spent your entire life making up for our childhood, but the thing is, we're fine. You don't have to keep fighting. You don't have to keep living like if you don't control the outcome, we won't make it. It's no way to live, and one of these days I hope you'll see that."

She retrieved her glass from the end table and held it loosely in her hands. Hands that had begged for food when Mamma and Papà had nothing left to give. Hands that had known hard work at too young an age. Hands that had shaken with grief after losing her baby. Everything I'd tried to protect her from, and failed.

"You can't save everyone, Marco. No matter how hard you try."

I thought about Anna, about how she'd upended her career to find the piece of her life that was missing. She'd been so brave to just walk away.

Maybe Gina was right. Maybe this was no way to live. Maybe it was time to allow myself that missing piece.

I thought about Anna again, this time walking down the steps of the Arlington Station T stop alone at night, and apprehension seized my body. Even if I wanted to, I didn't know how to stop my need to protect, to control. It was a part of me, down to my marrow.

"What else is bothering you?"

I gave my sister side-eye. "What, are you my shrink now?"

She lifted her eyebrows. "Conosco il mio fratellone."

"Non è niente." I dismissed her with a wave of my hand, but I knew she'd keep at it till I came clean. "I kinda had a date tonight."

There was no dramatic exclamation, so I chanced a look at my sister. She searched the living room as if someone else might be there. "Am I on camera?"

I groaned and rolled my eyes.

She laughed. "You. Were on a date. Kinda."

I shrugged a shoulder.

"You haven't been on a date since—"

"I'm aware the last time I dated, Gina."

"She must be pretty special if she was able to break the forty-year drought."

I glowered at her.

"Hey. Scusa." The depth of pity in her voice made me uncomfortable. I didn't want to talk about the past. "Losing Lucia was tough on everyone, but she chose not to drink from Tony. Even knowing the risk it posed to herself and to Luca."

Tony'd done everything he could to convince Lucia to bond and drink his blood. But the shock of learning blood demons existed and that her unborn child's father was one of them had been too much for her fragile human mind to accept. It had been a miracle Luca survived.

"She didn't choose. She couldn't. Finding out broke her. And losing her broke Tony."

"There's always the chance a human might react like that, but what happened to Lucia is not the norm. She's the only one I know of, and I've been alive for eighty-three years." She leveled me with a knowing stare. "And it's not like you've dated any blood demons either."

I sighed. Loudly.

"Your problem is you worry too much. You think if you take time for yourself or, Heaven forbid, go on a date, the world will collapse without you to hold it up."

My irritated glower returned with a vengeance.

"Am I wrong?"

"I don't need you to tell me what my problems are," I grumbled.

"I think you do."

I snorted and shook my head. "Aren't you supposed to be the *little* sister?"

"Someone's gotta tell the big bad Mafia Don how it is. Adesso." She got up, walked into the kitchen, came back with a wine bottle, and emptied its remains into her glass. "I want to hear about the woman who put a dent in the wall around my big brother's heart."

IT WAS a ten-minute walk to Vesuvio from my family home. I entered my club through the back door shortly after eleven. Vinnie was already there, sitting at the bar with a glass of scotch. His driver leaned against the far wall next to Matteo, two soldiers standing guard. A couple of poker games were underway. One waitress served the two card tables. Another was giving a lap dance to one of the regular track betters in the corner booth. Slow night.

I pulled out a stool next to Vinnie and lifted my chin at Enzo. Before Vinnie or I said a word, he returned with a glass of whiskey, neat, and set it on the bar in front of me.

"You reconsider my offer?" Vinnie asked and continued to stare into this drink.

"I have questions."

I spun my glass on the bar. I'd smoked my last cigar to

calm my nerves after dropping off Anna and needed an outlet for all my pent-up stress. And sexual frustration.

Vinnie eyed my glass. "You're gonna irritate the shit outta me with that. You need a smoke?"

"Yeah."

He reached into his suit jacket, pulled out a cigar case, and opened it with a flick of his wrist. "Honduran. I like the kick."

I took one from the case and ran it under my nose. Dark and earthy. I pulled out my cutter and got to work. "Luca says the Irish are expanding. More than I thought. He's worried about the cops. I don't know if he has information I don't, or if it's just the chip on his shoulder talking."

"I thought you didn't want to get involved."

"I don't."

"Sounds like getting involved to me."

I glared at him sideways and lit the cigar, puffing till the cherry blazed.

"You're not wrong questioning Luca's motives. That kid's got some vendetta."

"Gina reminded me a couple hours ago—he's not a kid anymore."

"Coulda fooled me." Vinnie shook his head and sipped his scotch. "Shaughnessy's been expanding his gambling rackets. That's true. Encroaching on our territory?" He rocked his head side to side. "You tell me. That's your game in the city. They don't come near the North Shore."

"I'm opening a new club in the financial district. Had a hell of a time securing the property. The Shaughnessys were asking questions."

He shrugged. "They can't make any big moves without starting a war, but they're growing. Doesn't help they have law enforcement in their pockets."

"Irish cops in Southie have always been crooked."

"I'm not talking about Southie, Marco, and I'm not talking about cops."

I swiveled my barstool and narrowed my eyes through the cloud of smoke.

"The feds. They put a major dent in our operations back in the eighties if you remember. Even started that witch hunt to investigate *cult accusations*?" He raised an eyebrow.

I remembered. I was living in Italy at the time. The damage they'd done to our earnings by shutting down key rackets was bad enough. The constant badgering and questioning of Sources? I'd run my lawyers ragged and spent a fortune keeping our secret under wraps.

"Rumor has it, Ciarán is following in papa Paddy's footsteps. Allying with the feds to dismantle *what's left of the Boston Italian Mafia*." He shook his head in disgust.

"How good's the intel?"

"Good as Mayor Kelson."

"Cazzo."

The Italians and the Irish in Boston divided bureaucracy like they divided neighborhoods. The Irish had law enforcement, and we had the law itself. But things got murky when the feds got involved.

He wrinkled his brow. "I thought you knew. That's why I didn't mention it at Terme. I thought you knew what was at stake."

I downed the rest of my whiskey, pissed at myself for not keeping up with the mayor. I tapped two fingers on the bar.

The last thing either of us needed were the feds poking around more than usual. Hiding in plain sight only got you so far. We did a pretty good job of combing the internet and covering our tracks, but all it would take was a little digging before our house of cards came tumbling down.

If the Irish were in league with the feds, that changed everything.

"Listen, Marco, I know you don't want to get involved, but you're a made man. You run your own crew, you have this place, and you're Italian. If Ciarán Shaughnessy decides to make a move, he's not going to give a single fuck you're not a part of my organization. As far as he's concerned, you're Cosa Nostra, just like me." He turned his stool to face mine, and it creaked under his weight. He gripped my forearm with his thick paw. "You want to protect our secret? You want to protect our Sources? You want to protect your family?"

Smoke and silence hung in the air between us, the answers to his questions a train wreck I couldn't avoid. We studied each other, neither of us wanting to give an inch, but both of us knowing we had no choice.

"I have conditions." The unwanted promise left my lips with a puff of smoke before I could stop it.

Vinnie Valenzano showed me his teeth, his face transformed by the victory held in his wolfish smile.

Chapter Nineteen

Anna

The numbers on the screen couldn't be right. I didn't want them to be right. I'd willed them to change before running the model for the third time, but they didn't. I'd wanted absolute certainty I hadn't made a mistake, so I'd kicked off the third simulation on the same data set before I'd left the office and let it run overnight.

But I hadn't made a mistake; the model returned the same unfortunate results. A third time.

It was Friday morning, and without all the distractions of permits, breakfast runs, and unexpected visitors, I'd finished my model late Wednesday evening, staying well past the end of the workday, consumed by my progress and the prospect of finally getting answers. I'd not realized how late it was until my phone buzzed with a text message. 9:00 p.m.

What did you wear to the office today?

I'm still at the office.

What!

I lost track of time.

I'm sending someone to take you home.

Tyrant.

When it comes to your safety? Absolutely.
Now, what are you wearing?

That red sweater you like.

Are you trying to torture me, woman?

You asked!

Cruel. Three more days. xo

I'd kicked off the simulation, unsure it would even complete. When I'd arrived at the office Thursday morning, my stomach turned over. It had completed all right.

I reached for my water bottle and drank, but it did nothing to combat the hit of adrenaline speeding my heartrate.

I'd hoped the results were an error on my part. A wrong parameter setting. A botched assumption. Something. Anything. But I'd double-checked my work and couldn't find a mistake. And if there was one thing I knew, I knew my algorithms. The math and the modeling approach represented my life's work. They were rock solid. So, I'd run the simulation again. And again.

Marco was right; someone was stealing from him. He'd told me multiple times he'd doubted it was the economy, and I realized then I'd never really believed him. I did now. The facts stared back at me as clear as the bright winter sky shining above the Commons. I sat back in my chair, looked out the window, and chewed the side of my fingernail.

Funny thing about the real world—events in the real world came with real consequences. Inside the confines of my old office, I'd churned over data sent in by a third party with whom I had no connection, no vested interest. My attachment to the results approached mild fascination at best. *This might make a good paper.* I was a distant observer, detached from the work and focused on one thing—publishing my next breakthrough in financial modeling.

But these results? These results had meaning. These results impacted lives. These results were personal.

Marco would be furious, and the pain of betrayal would fan his fiery anger into a blazing inferno. My heart broke for him, but I knew what I had to do. I slugged down more water and picked up my phone.

> I have the preliminary modeling results.

> Nothing over phone or email. I'll send
> someone to pick you up.

I printed the report, grabbed my things, and headed downstairs to wait for my ride. The hurt and anger I was about to cause tied my stomach in knots. But I had wanted to experience the real world, and in the real world, results had consequences.

A MAN in a gray suit and tan trench coat leaned against the lamppost outside the entrance of Terme di Boston. I tried to ignore him, but his eyes were fixed on me; I felt his unrelenting stare as keenly as the bracing cold.

"Dr. Barone," he said.

"Yes?" I narrowed my eyes, confused as to who he was and how he knew my name.

His dirty-blond hair shifted wildly under a gust of wind. He reached into his suit jacket, pulled out a leather wallet, and flipped it open, holding it next to his face. The letters FBI blared a silent warning. My coat and gloves were suddenly too hot despite the winter wind.

"My name is Agent Johnson. Do you have a moment?" he asked and flipped the ID closed, filing it away in his suit jacket.

"I..." I swallowed, trying to jumpstart the connection between my brain and my mouth, but I'd gone full deer in the headlights. I stood there stunned and silent.

"You have quite the resume, Dr. Barone."

My eyes darted to the entrance of Terme and one of Marco's security guards. He watched us from behind sunglasses, his face impassive.

"Uh... Thank you?"

"Must have been a big adjustment coming to work for DEI after being in academia for so long."

He smiled the kind of smile you'd expect from someone who wants you to think they're on your side. Someone who wants you to feel comfortable sharing war stories. Someone who wants you to admit something you don't want to admit.

My brain snapped into gear. *Do Not Name DEI as Your Current Employer.* Marco's NDA rescued me from paralysis.

"I'm sorry. I'm not at liberty to discuss my employment status." The words came out more stilted than they'd sounded in my head, but I was damn proud of myself for saying anything at all.

Agent Johnson's mouth quirked as if he was trying to force his sneer into a smile. "There's no harm in discussing your employment, but there is harm in obstructing justice."

My temper stirred. I stepped forward and lifted my chin. "That sounded a lot like a threat, Agent Johnson. You're fishing, but I'm not taking your bait. Now, kindly get lost."

The black Range Rover pulled up to the curb. Paulie jumped out and met us where we stared each other down. He offered his arm to me and a death glare to Agent Johnson. I wrapped my shaking fingers around his arm, and he led me to the car.

"We'll talk soon, Dr. Barone," Agent Johnson called after us.

I ignored him, climbed into the backseat, and stared out the window in silent shock as we made our way to the North End.

VESUVIO LOOKED different in the late afternoon. No inviting glow from behind tinted windows. No sexy, erupting sign. Just muted black trim outlining the windows and door of an old brick building topped by a dull, red marquee. Austere and functional instead of flashy and glamorous.

Paulie led me to the back of the building and up a set of wooden stairs to a second story landing where one of Marco's sunglassed sentinels stood guard. He punched a code into a panel on the left of the steel door. It beeped, turned the panel light green, and with a click and a buzz, the door unlocked. He opened it and ushered us inside.

The upstairs of Vesuvio looked like what I imagined the downstairs looked like during the day. The mahogany floors that had appeared so sleek and black at night were scratched and dented, and the wine-colored leather of the booths was cracked and worn. A carbon copy of the downstairs bar sat directly above its partner, stacked with the same top-shelf wine and liquor.

The difference? Six card tables occupied the space between the bar and the booths, and two pool tables replaced the high tops around the fireplace. Televisions were strategically placed in every corner of the room and at each end of the bar, and a stripper pole was centered in front of the benches along the back wall.

I was so out of my element.

A bartender leaned against the counter watching soccer. Two more security guards stood on either side of the front wall behind the pool tables. And in the center of the room, Marco, Vito, Luca, and two men I recognized from the last time I'd been to Vesuvio played poker. Marco and Luca smoked cigars, and a bottle of whiskey sat among a chaos of cards, chips, and stacks of cash.

Vito's head snapped up when we walked past the top of the spiral staircase. He lifted his chin, and each man at the table trained their dark eyes on where I stood clutching my printout in a shaking hand.

I waved awkwardly, shifting my weight between my feet. Understanding and compassion tugged at the corner of Marco's lips. He stood, walked over to me, and placed a hand on my hip and a kiss on my forehead.

"I missed you," he whispered, and my heart melted along with my nerves.

He introduced me to Angelo and Carmine, then led me down a short hallway beyond the pool tables. He rapped twice on the door before opening it. A woman with bleach blonde hair in sweats and a tank top looked up from where she sat on a couch watching a big screen TV. Marco jerked his head toward the door, and she turned off the TV and scooted out of the room giving me a warm smile as she passed.

"We can talk in here," he said and shut the door.

Even though I knew no one else was in there, my eyes darted around the room. We were talking about corporate larceny, and I'd achieved new levels of paranoia after my encounter with Agent Johnson.

"It's okay," he said and twirled a finger. "It's sound-proofed. And swept for bugs every week."

My eyebrows reached for my hairline, and I shook my head in disbelief.

"An FBI agent stopped me outside Terme while I was waiting for Paulie." The words flew from my lungs, and my voice trembled in their wake. An ache formed in my throat, emotion threatening to spill out, a delayed reaction to an encounter that had left me rattled and confused.

"Cazzo," Marco swore and ran a hand down his face. "I could strangle Vinnie right now," he growled.

I opened my mouth to say something, but nothing came out.

"Vieni qui," he said and opened his arms.

I went to him, and he wrapped his arms around me and kissed the top of my head.

"That's why he was there," I whispered, more to myself than Marco. "Because of Vinnie." I didn't want to entertain another explanation.

He ran his hand up and down my back. "You okay?" he asked, voice gentle and concerned.

I let out a tremendous, shuddering breath, rested my head on his chest, and relaxed into his arms. "Yeah, I'm fine. Now."

The irony that I was taking comfort in the arms of the man who was the reason for the FBI agent was not lost on me. I didn't care. I nuzzled my face into his chest and breathed in the safety of his scent.

"He didn't harass you, did he?" Marco grumbled.

"No."

"Good."

"He was fishing for information."

"That's what he does."

"I think he was trying to intimidate me."

He squeezed me closer. "That's also what he does."

"I told him to get lost."

His chest rumbled with laughter. "Mia bellissima Anna. Good girl."

I indulged myself a moment longer, taking comfort in his

closeness and letting it calm my nerves. But I'd come there for a reason, and it was time to rip off the Band-Aid.

I pulled back and held up my printout. "It's here," I said and turned the first page toward him so he could see the chart. "Proof."

His eyes darkened. "Proof of what? What am I looking at?"

I pointed at the chart. "This graph distills the results of the first Monte Carlo analysis I ran on the model of your European office. The black points represent expected profits under various scenarios, and the red line represents your actual profits." I glanced up at him.

"For the past... year, the black points are all above the red line."

"Exactly. The model predicts are consistently higher than your actuals. The previous year, the points *surround* the line, see? Those are normal variations—stochastic noise—deviations you'd expect in this type of simulation. But then about a year ago, the red line started to move away from the point cloud in a meaningful way. Slowly at first, but uniform behavior like that isn't noise. That's true financial movement." I dropped the papers and looked up. "Someone is stealing from you, Marco."

He tensed, taut as a bowstring. An ominous energy surrounded him, made worse by a trick of the light. It highlighted his eyes, and for a moment, made them look like they glowed a devilish crimson. "You're sure," he ground out through clenched teeth.

I nodded and lifted the papers. "Look here. The movement is even more pronounced now. There's been a serious gap for the past six months."

"Why the growth?"

"No idea." I dropped my arm and the papers to my side. "My guess? Whoever's doing this figured you hadn't noticed.

Thought they could get away with more. Or..." I chewed my lip, not wanting to vocalize my rampant paranoia.

"Or what?"

"Or they wanted to expedite an endgame. Whatever that is."

The fury in his eyes and the pain contorting his handsome face punched me in my chest and bruised my heart. Despite his conviction that it hadn't been the economy, Marco hadn't believed someone he trusted was stealing from him. Not really. And the truth was devastating.

"The model output a lot of data. I haven't gone through it all yet, not in detail. Once I do, I can run additional simulations to characterize the drain. I'll start on Monday, but it'll take time before I can nail down exactly how this is happening. But I—I thought you'd want to know."

He turned away and rested his hands on his hips. "Thank you," he said quietly.

"I'm sorry, Marco."

He looked over his shoulder and gave me a terse nod.

I waited in the strained silence, unable to imagine the thoughts and emotions racing through his head. Over the past few weeks, I'd come to understand how important his business and his staff were to him. He treated DEI like an extension of his family, and I'd just given him proof that one or more of his family members had stabbed him in the back. Right under the nose of someone he considered a son.

When he finally turned back to face me, he exercised his exacting control; he dropped his arms, rolled his shoulders, and relaxed his jaw and forehead.

The impenetrable Marco DeVita stood before me once again. He'd walk out of this room and join his COOs like nothing happened. But I knew the extent of anger and hurt he'd just caged. He was a powder keg, ready to blow, and I hoped for his sake, and theirs, none of them were the fuse.

Chapter Twenty

Anna

The Range Rover pulled up to the curb behind a line of town cars, limousines, and cabs waiting for their turn to stop in front of Terme di Boston. There wasn't a huge crowd outside the velvet ropes, but photographers, the local news, and a few passing tourists looked on and snapped pictures as the Who's Who of Boston, decked to the nines in formal attire and equally dazzling smiles, were ushered inside.

My dress roused a healthy measure of exasperation and excitement, but more than anything, a warm flutter in my chest.

I shouldn't have been surprised when my morning coffee was interrupted by a delivery man carrying a massive box from Nieman Marcus topped with a glittering gold bow. I'd stared at the box in confusion as I set it on my dining room table. Sophie had attacked the bow while I'd opened the unmarked envelope.

Your dress for tonight.
M

Of all the arrogant presumption…

I shook my head and smiled remembering the burst of indignation I'd had reading the card that morning. And how quickly it had vanished as soon as I'd peeled back the tissue paper.

My hand had flown to my mouth in a move reminiscent of an over-acted period drama. Blood-red material was buried within gold paper, and a Givenchy label announced the extent of my buried treasure. With shaking hands, I ran my fingers over the dress like it was a dream that might vanish under the reality of my touch. I pinched the thin straps, pulled the evening gown out of its box, and giggled, literally giggled, at the plunging neckline of the narrow bodice.

The gown was a work of art. The bodice tapered following the deep *V* of the neckline, and the soft, springy material was ruched from its bottom to the slit that travelled from the floor to mid-thigh. Equally daring, the back of the dress was missing, for lack of a better word. Instead, a short train of material pooled at the floor.

The dress was beautiful. I'd never worn anything so exquisite, and gooseflesh pebbled my skin in anticipation of wearing it for Marco.

I was beautiful. Anna Barone, a modern-day Cinderella decked out in Givenchy and arriving in her Range Rover carriage to meet her Prince Charming.

Well, maybe not that last part. Marco was about as charming as a lion in heat. But I couldn't deny my life had changed since he'd been in it.

The wallflower professor would never have worn anything so daring and attention-grabbing, much less walk a red carpet lined with cameras. He knew that. The dress was a nudge, however presumptuous, and his encouragement tugged at my heartstrings. I was nervous as hell, but armed with Marco's support and the confidence I'd gained over the past few weeks, I was ready to enter the gala with my head held high.

Vito inched us forward the final car length, and my palms started to sweat. Great. Classic Anna. I wiped them on my coat and wondered what I was going to do inside sans coat when my nerves kicked into high gear. I grabbed my clutch and took several deep breaths while Vito walked around the outside of the car to open my door.

"You've met the Don of Boston," I mumbled to myself, "witnessed a shakedown at city hall, fended off an FBI agent, and interrupted a mafioso poker game in an illegal gambling club. You can handle a few cameras, Anna."

The door opened and bright lights lit up the night, a bewildering blitzkrieg of flashes and brilliance. Vito offered me his hand, and I climbed out, teetering on the strappy heels I'd bought as soon as I'd seen the dress. The sea of lights and people and noise overwhelmed me, and I squeezed Vito's hand worried if I let go, I might drown.

"You know boxing?"

I glanced at Vito, confused. "A little."

"Get your guard up. It'll protect you no matter what punches they throw."

The sage advice in Vito's gruff, familiar voice buoyed me like a life preserver. I nodded, released his hand, and lifted my chin with an air of bravado I didn't have but did my dress justice. No one had to know my palms were sweating or that I was silently thanking God none of the cameras were pointed at me. I strutted toward the entrance, my feigned confidence my guard.

Out of the corner of my, I caught a glimpse of dirty-blond hair and a tan trench coat. Agent Johnson tracked me from behind the small group of photographers. I kept my eyes focused on the entrance, blocking the punch while maintaining my balance.

But my dream of flying under the radar was dashed halfway down the red carpet with a firm hand on my lower back. "Right on time." Marco's deep voice and the intoxicating scent of expensive aftershave and cigar smoke flooded my awareness.

Someone must have caught sight of my elusive boss before I did; one click and flash later and all the cameras were trained on us in a blinding array of attention. Marco stepped next to me, ignoring them all, and offered me his arm.

God, he was gorgeous. The silver streaks in his slicked-back hair glinted beneath the flashing cameras, and his black eyes smoldered above the harsh angles of his cleanly shaved jaw. The tuxedo's sleek lines hugged his powerful frame, the designer cut made sexier knowing the hard body hidden underneath.

"I'm so glad you're here," I said as he led us down the red carpet.

"This is my charity event."

"I meant out here. Outside." Everyone was staring at us, but I followed Marco's lead and tried to ignore them, focusing on the steadiness of his arm.

"I didn't want anyone to wonder who you were with tonight." We stepped through the doors into the foyer, and he lowered his lips to my ear. "You're mine."

I shivered, but before I could respond, an attendant ushered us out of the way of incoming guests.

"May I take your coat, madam?"

The abrupt warmth of the lobby and Marco's declaration had me overheating. I blinked a couple of times before I nodded and handed my clutch to Marco. I unbuttoned my coat, and the attendant eased it off my shoulders. I thanked him, and he hurried off to the coat check.

I turned to Marco, and he stared at me with such unmasked desire, my sex tingled with anticipation. His obsidian eyes travelled the length of my body and lingered where the neckline plunged past my breasts.

His eyes returned to mine, and they burned with sinful intent, napalm on the flames of my desire. Every day we'd spent apart, the wildfire had expanded, and now it consumed me.

"Thank you for the dress," I said and reached for his hand. He interlaced his fingers with mine, but their steady strength provided only a fraction of the touch I craved. "It's beautiful."

"It's only beautiful because you're wearing it." He pulled me into him and slid his hand around my waist to the bare skin of my back. It prickled with goosebumps from the glide of his fingertips along my spine. "And I can't wait to get you out of it." He breathed in my hair, and when he exhaled, his chest rumbled with satisfaction. He released me and pressed us forward into the milling crowd.

Flowers, tuxedos, and satin transformed the lobby into a five-star gala. Flutes of champagne, crystal tumblers of whiskey, and fat red wine glasses sparkled under the chandeliers. A jazz quartet floated smooth notes across the space, background to the chatter and laughter of the lively crowd. The scene was a spectacle of wealth, power, and class.

Marco stopped when we reached the center of the lobby, turning more than a few heads and making me self-conscious. He scanned the room, his cold survey calculating, but I was sinking under the weight of whispers and glances. I wanted to escape, fade into the background, be one of the spectators, not the spectacle. I kept my eyes down and stepped forward, hoping to pull him along, but he held me in place.

"Wait, mia cara."

"Why? Everyone's watching us."

"I know."

Confused, I looked up.

His eyes captured mine, and they were filled with so much

affection and pride, I thought my heart might explode. "You're brilliant and beautiful, and I want everyone to see how brightly you shine." He lowered his lips to my ear, and they brushed against its ridge sending a shiver down my spine. "And I want everyone to know, later tonight, I'll be fucking the most beautiful woman here."

His whispered promise and the brush of his lips sent a shockwave of sensation through my body. It made me tremble, and the slick evidence of my desire moistened my thong.

He pulled back, his touch replaced by a cold emptiness I couldn't wait for him to refill, and we resumed our journey toward the bar. He nodded to several people along the way, none of whom I recognized, until a short, round man with gray hair and an artificial smile stepped into our path.

Holy shit. The mayor of Boston.

I flexed my fingers, cursing their clamminess. In a moment of frantic clarity, I wrapped my right arm around Marco's waist knowing there was an inevitable handshake in my future and refusing to use a dress that cost more than my mortgage payment as a towel.

"Marco!" Mayor Kelson's familiar voice rang across the closing distance. "Good to see you. Excellent turnout."

"Rich." Marco took the mayor's outstretched hand and gave it a single pump. "Glad you could make it."

"Wouldn't miss it. Important cause and equally important guests. It's an election year, you know," the mayor finished with a chuckle. His pale blue eyes darted to me and back to Marco. "And who's this?"

"This is Dr. Anna Barone. Anna is a professor of international finance at Sloan."

The mayor's head jerked back enough for me to notice, and his eyes traveled down my body.

I bit the inside of my cheek and forced myself not to roll my eyes. This wasn't the first time I'd experienced that reaction. An academic with curves? Impossible! I bit my cheek harder.

He held out his hand. "A pleasure to meet you, Dr. Barone. And thank you for contributing to the educational excellence of Boston. This city wouldn't be the same without MIT."

I dragged my palm down Marco's back, then took the mayor's hand in as confident a grip as I could manage. "The pleasure is mine, Mayor Kelson. I'm impressed by what you've accomplished this term, increasing funding for public education. It's an important investment in our future. Thank you."

"There's a lot of work left to do, so don't forget to vote." He wagged his finger. "Marco, I have rounds to make. Thanks again."

"There's something I'd like to discuss with you tonight, if you can spare a few minutes from your canvassing?"

The mayor's lips twitched, and he eyed Marco warily. "For you, Marco? Anything."

"Excellent. I'll find you after we get drinks. Ciao."

The mayor walked off to greet the next group of wealthy socialites, and the weight of Marco's heavy regard tugged at my attention. I looked up, and the usual slash of his severe mouth had turned into a gleaming halfmoon of amusement.

"Did you just wipe your sweaty palm down the back of my Armani?"

"It was either Armani or Givenchy!" I whined and grimaced.

The deep boom of his laughter filled the space around us and transformed him from a serious executive with an impenetrable poker-face into a warm, carefree soul who made my heart leap with affection.

"You're so goddamn sexy," he said with a shake of his head and lowered his lips to my forehead.

The smile on my face threatened to split me in two. Marco

had me tied around his finger in a neat little bow, and it didn't bother me at all.

He scanned the room, and as if on cue, Vinnie Valenzano and his entourage walked on set. They sauntered across the lobby with all the swagger and thinly veiled menace of an old Western posse, but instead of cowboy hats, chaps, and spurs, they wore slicked-back hair, custom tuxedos, and Italian-leather Oxfords.

My body stiffened. "What—What is he doing here?"

"Relax. I told you. Vinnie is an important part of the Italian-American community." Marco's tone suggested I should understand why he was there, but I couldn't get past who he was.

Mayor Kelson didn't miss his entrance, either. He made a beeline for Vinnie, his hand held out in eager obeisance.

"Why don't you get a drink. I need to go over there, and it'll just make your palms sweat."

I slugged him in the arm, and he chuckled.

"Go. Mingle. Introduce yourself to people."

I raised an eyebrow.

He laughed in earnest and held up his hands in defeat. "All right. Well, at least get yourself a drink. Maybe some appetizers?" He glanced around. "Siobhán is around here somewhere."

His hand moved from my lower back to my face, and he brushed his thumb over the two birthmarks on my cheek. A kiss to my forehead and a reassuring smile, and he left to join two of the most powerful men in Boston.

I took a deep breath and continued the journey we'd started toward the bar. I needed something to take the edge off. I needed champagne.

"Anna! Anna Barone!"

The familiar voice made me stop in my tracks and groan under my breath. I just wanted a drink but reluctantly turned to its source and what was sure to be an uncomfortable conversation.

"Tim," I said and plastered a smile on my face.

"Anna!" He held out his hand, and I shook it. "I saw you come in but couldn't believe that was you. You look so..."

I tilted my head after an awkward pause.

"So different," he finished and ran a hand through his unkempt hair. "I didn't recognize you at first."

"Must be the dress," I said with an embarrassed smile and a shrug. "But it's still me."

"No. It's not just the dress, although you do look stunning. Something's different." He narrowed his eyes.

"What are you doing here?" I asked, eager to change the subject.

"My wife volunteers for the DeVita Foundation. Teaches English as a Second Language. Very good cause. In fact..." He glanced around the lobby. "Wasn't that Mr. DeVita you came in with?"

"Yes."

He stared at me, waiting for more explanation than my one-word answer. I really needed that champagne.

"I'm working for Mr. DeVita as a consultant. Unfortunately, I can't share more details than that. NDA."

"Ah."

I nodded.

He rocked onto the balls of his feet and back down.

Someone, anyone, please, beam me up.

He leaned forward. "I didn't think you'd actually take an industry job. I figured you just needed a break to recharge your batteries before the fall semester."

I bit the inside of my cheek for the second time that night and gave myself the moment I needed to remove the edge from my voice. "You figured wrong. I meant what I said in your office, and so far, the experience has been everything I hoped it would be."

He grunted, his expression landing somewhere between skepticism and scorn. "No, something is definitely different."

"Well." I looked down at my hands, clasped in front of me, and nodded. Maybe it was time to throw a punch instead of just keeping my guard up. I met and held his eyes. "Turns out, I do have the temperament to work in corporate finance, and you may have gotten the chance to see that if you hadn't passed me up for the Deloitte partnership."

His jaw dropped, and my fake smile turned genuine with my small victory. "Have a wonderful night, Tim," I said and resumed my quest for champagne, leaving a stunned Dean of Finance in my wake.

The bartender handed me a glass of champagne, and I downed half in one long drink. Not the most elegant move, but better than throwing back a shot. With my empty stomach, the bubbles immediately went to work. Perfect. Now to find somewhere I could fade into the background for a long minute.

"Hey, stranger." Siobhán's sultry voice cut through the din of the lobby, and my shoulders relaxed. I spun to face her, and my mouth hung open like it was on a broken hinge.

Her short blonde hair was smoothed into perfect pin-curl waves and cinched by a silver bandeau around her forehead that highlighted her sharp cheekbones. The silver threads of her fringed flapper dress and long strands of white pearls shimmered beneath the lights and hung on her body in a way that accentuated her lithe frame. *God, what I wouldn't give for legs like hers.* They went on forever before ending in a pair of spike heels with t-straps, the past meeting the present in a style quintessentially Siobhán.

Heads turned as she sashayed to meet me, several men

ogling her so obviously they might as well have had tongues lolling out of their mouths like cartoon wolves.

Her teeth gleamed white behind bright red lipstick, and she held out her hand. The other carried a half-full martini chock-full of olives.

"Anna!" She took my hand and gave me air kisses. "That dress! Girl, you look absolutely fabulous!"

"Thank you. But not as fabulous as you. Jesus, Siobhán."

Her lilting laughter danced above the music and chatter. "Come on, now. What I wouldn't give for curves like yours. Gorgeous! I, on the other hand, look like someone bombed a beanpole with glitter."

I shook my head, laughing at her ridiculous assessment of herself. "The 1920s vibe really does suit you. You look like an Old Hollywood movie star."

She waved a hand at me and sipped her martini. I followed suit with my champagne. We found an empty high top, set our clutches and drinks on the table, and stood facing the crowd.

"So," she said in a low voice. My eyes darted to her. She wore a wicked smile, and one of her eyebrows was cocked in gentle judgment. "I saw you and Marco come in."

Across the lobby, Marco stood with Vinnie and Mayor Kelson, his laughter and smile a mask of public persona. He glanced in our direction, and his dark eyes held mine for a moment before turning back to the formidable group.

"Have you slept with him yet?"

My head snapped to face her, and my neck and cheeks burned so hot, they probably matched my dress. "What? No!"

She laughed. "Could've fooled me the way he paraded you around like a trophy. That man was sending a message."

"Ugh." My shoulders sank like that might help me fade into the background. "He can be such a caveman."

"I told you to be careful," she said with reproach. "Too late now, though. That man has made up his mind."

I huffed. "I'd like to think I have some say in the matter."

"Good luck with that," she said dryly and turned back to the crowd, sipping her martini. "They're all the same." The tenor of her changed to something distant. "The whole lot of 'em."

I followed Siobhán's eyes across the room.

Luca.

He looked as though he'd stepped off the red carpet at the Met instead of Terme di Boston. His fitted white tuxedo with black lapels was a stark contrast to the uniform black worn by the rest of the men. With his matching white smile, slicked-back hair, and *GQ* cheekbones, he pulled off the daring fashion statement with effortless insouciance.

He chatted with Carmine and Angelo, and a blonde woman in a skintight, strapless cocktail dress clung to his side, hands resting atop his shoulder. She whispered something in his ear, but he barely acknowledged her—a distracted glance, a quick nod—never breaking conversation with the two men. She turned away, and I nearly choked on my champagne when I saw the size of her breasts; her dress defied the laws of physics. She walked away with short, dainty steps on platform heels toward the restroom.

Siobhán's eyes never left Luca, like she was torturing herself with his presence. Before I could warn her to stop staring, Luca's attention drifted across the room. He frowned for a fraction of a heartbeat, then his mouth twisted into a sexy sneer.

One hand in his pocket, the other holding a crystal tumbler, he said something to Carmine and Angelo, and started a casual saunter toward us, eyes fixed on Siobhán.

Siobhán threw back the rest of her martini.

"Okay," I said. "I know you two don't get along, but..." She met my eyes, and hers were filled with defiance and sadness. "There has to be more to the story."

"Unfortunately," she mumbled.

Luca rested the heel of his hand on the high top and drummed his fingers. "Good evening, ladies," he said with a roguish smile. "Anna, you look ravishing. Rumor has it you're a touch over-qualified for your administrative assistant position. Brilliance and beauty. Marco's a lucky man."

Unease shot through me like an arrow. "Oh. Uh... Thank you, but I... That is..."

"What is it, Luca?" Siobhán's confident voice sliced through my nervous stammer. She lifted a toothpick lined with olives and touched the last of the green orbs to the bottom of her parted red lips. Luca's eyes landed on her mouth, mesmerized by the olive. "Jealous Marco found a woman with more than two brain cells to rub together?"

She ran the olive along her lower lip and poked her tongue out just enough to touch it before she slipped it into her mouth. She closed her lips around the olive with a pucker and pulled it off the toothpick.

Luca's throat bobbed through a slow swallow. "I think we both know I'm not the one who's jealous, Shamrock." The bravado had left his voice, and his taunt came out choppy and strained as he continued to stare at Siobhán's mouth.

"Please," she scoffed and quirked a wicked smile. "I'm just concerned your date might not find her way back from the bathroom. It's a terribly large hotel, and I worry she can't count high enough to remember all the left turns."

She trailed a red fingernail down his shirt from just below his chest to where his tuxedo jacket buttoned at his waist. She let her finger dally there, tracing it in circles. Luca tensed. His hand atop the table balled into a fist, and his nostrils flared with effort.

"Did you let her know if she takes too long, you'll move on to the next set of big breasts stupid enough to fall for your BS?"

Luca's pouty lips thinned into an unhappy line, and he snatched Siobhán's hand away from his waist, holding it between them by her wrist. "Tsk, tsk." Luca shifted his weight and closed the gap. "Jealousy is not a good look on you, Shamrock, even if green is your color."

She jutted her chin toward him. "I told you not to call me that," she hissed, each word slow and hot.

Luca leaned in, animosity and sexual tension crackling in the few inches of air left between them. "There's that Irish temper. You can pretend all you want you're not from Southie, but that accent always comes out when you lose your temper. Or, if I remember correctly, when you've had too much booze."

"Why you—"

"You two behaving yourselves?" Marco's deep voice ended the standoff.

"Always," Luca said and released Siobhán's wrist. He rolled his shoulders and eased himself back, schooling his expression and clearing his throat. "Marco."

"Luca."

"Well." Luca downed the rest of his scotch and set the empty tumbler on the table. "I better go find my date. Wouldn't want her to get lost." He turned toward the center of the lobby and took a few steps before tossing one final barb over his shoulder. "Right, *Shamrock*?"

Siobhán's lips pinched into a tight pucker, and she gripped the stem of her martini glass so hard I thought she was going to fling it at the back of Luca's head. "I need a drink," she grumbled and stormed off.

Marco puffed his cheeks and blew out a slow breath.

"What was that?" I asked, astonished.

"Damned if I know. They've acted like that for..." He waved his drink before bringing it to his lips.

I joined him and finished my champagne. "Why?"

"I have no idea, and I have a feeling I don't want to find out." He swirled the last vestiges of his whiskey among the melting ice cubes. "You ready for another?"

"After that? Absolutely."

For the next half hour, Marco introduced me to some of the most wealthy and influential people in Boston, and fortified with bubbles, I said more hellos and shook more hands than I'd probably done in the past ten years. Guests started migrating to the ballroom, but I needed a moment away from all the noise and bodies and attention before another round of socializing.

I squeezed Marco's forearm and handed him my empty champagne flute. "I'm going to the restroom."

"Our table is at the front of the ballroom near the stage. I'll meet you there." He kissed my forehead, and my stomach danced with butterflies. I could get used to those kisses.

Past the front desk and toward the back patio, I was betting no one would venture that far for a restroom. I veered left but slowed when a woman's flighty gasp and a man's deep groan echoed down the short hallway. Deterred by the sounds but motivated by my need to pee, I stopped and peeked around the corner.

Luca's white tuxedo jacket and his date's platform heels were instantly recognizable. His large frame crushed her into the wall, and his hands pinned her wrists at her sides. Her head was tilted back and toward me. It rested on the wall and gave Luca access to her neck. His mouth was pressed there, and his throat worked as if he was swallowing.

She released short gasps and mewls, her face relaxed in pure bliss, the rest of her motionless behind the cage of his body.

Luca released one of her wrists and slid his hand up her skirt. She writhed under his touch, tilting her head further to the side like the source of her pleasure wasn't coming from his hand but whatever he was doing with his mouth.

What *was* he doing with his mouth?

Adrenaline pumped into my bloodstream and stunned me motionless with irrational panic. I didn't understand why I was having such a visceral reaction, but I knew what I was witnessing was somehow wrong.

The woman moaned through an orgasm, her erotic vocalizations high and breathy. Luca's movement at her neck slowed and with it her breathing. He lifted his head, swept his tongue twice over the length of her neck, and licked his lips. He backed away, straightening his suit jacket and bowtie.

The cool disinterest in his handsome face startled me into action, and I rounded the corner with quick, purposeful strides.

"Hi, Luca," I said with a high-pitched squeak and fake smile. "They're getting ready for dinner up there, so…" I eyed the restroom door.

He stalked toward me and wiped the corner of his mouth with the back of his hand. It came away with a deep red smear, which he cleaned off with another swipe of his tongue. He passed me with a smirk, and a long, sharp eyetooth dominated his smile.

My heart hammered against my ribs, and blood rushed in my ears. I pushed open the restroom door and escaped into a stall. I gathered my dress, pulled down my thong, and sunk onto the seat holding my head in my hands. I relieved myself while trying to bring my frantic breath under control.

Red lipstick. That's all it was. Red lipstick.

She'd been wearing bright red lipstick, right?

No. That was Siobhán.

But Luca's date had it on, too. Right?

No, Anna. That wasn't lipstick. That was blood.

I pressed my hands into the cold metal. I couldn't breathe.

I couldn't get air into my lungs. I straightened my spine, extended my torso, and tipped my head back, trying to give my lungs enough space to expand. I needed oxygen; I was suffocating.

The restroom door opened, and the click of heels echoed off the tiled floor.

The presence of another person snapped me back into my breath. I sucked in as much air as I could—once, deeper, twice —and tamed my runaway panic.

I righted my dress, gathered my courage, and walked out of the stall. I joined Luca's date at the sinks and turned on the water, pretending like I hadn't seen them in the hallway or was having a panic attack.

She angled her neck toward the mirror and brushed her fingertips across an angry, swollen patch of skin surrounding two red welts.

My vision swam before me, and it included a pointed eyetooth. I blinked hard and tried to focus on washing my hands. Maybe I could wash away the memory.

"You're Marco's new Source, right?" She'd taken a compact out of her purse and was smoothing concealer over what I decided was a hickey. It had to be a hickey. It couldn't be anything else.

No idea what she was talking about, I played along, wanting to get out of there as fast as possible. "Yes, I'm here with Marco," I said to her reflection.

She turned her head back and forth, and satisfied with her cover up job, rummaged through her purse and pulled out a tube of lipstick. "I've never heard of him cozying up to a Source. You must be doing something right." She pulled off the cap and smoothed the hot pink lipstick over her lips.

Pink. Not red.

Her image in the mirror became fuzzy.

She pressed her lips together and puckered. "You are one

lucky girl." She replaced the cap, tossed the lipstick back in her bag, and started a new search.

I smiled awkwardly.

She pulled out a short fat vial and unscrewed its cap. I turned off the water and grabbed a towel from the counter. The cap came out followed by a flat stick. She dipped the stick back into the vial before holding it to her nose and snorting the white powder at its end with a sharp inhale. I dried my hands while she stretched her nose and sniffed. She held the tiny stick toward me, and I shook my head. She shrugged, dipped the stick back in the vial, and took the bump up her other nostril.

"You shouldn't be embarrassed, you know," she offered between sniffs. She screwed the cap back on her stash and tossed it in her bag.

She turned to me and smiled, a comforting, reassuring expression you'd expect from a best girlfriend. Her pupils were dilated, lips and nose twitchy from the blow, but she clearly wanted to have a moment.

"I saw you blush, but you shouldn't be embarrassed. If Luca gave me half the attention Marco gives you, I'd be strutting around here like I owned the place. He barely notices me unless he wants to feed. But the way Marco looks at you?" She sighed like a lovestruck fool. "It's like he's hungry for more than your blood. He wants you. All of you. Like I said, you are one lucky girl." She winked and slung the chain-link strap of her purse over her shoulder. "Own it, sister!" She reached out, squeezed my hand, then turned on her platform heels and walked out the door.

Chapter Twenty-One

Anna

Sources.

Wanting to feed.

Hungry for my blood.

I wobbled on my heels and leaned against the counter, words and images flashing and crashing, a pandemonium that blurred my vision and constricted my lungs. I started hyperventilating, and my desperate gasps for air and the blood rushing in my ears created a cacophony of panic.

Luca had been feeding on that woman's neck.

I braced myself on the outside of the stall and the edge of the counter. My sweaty palm slid down the metal, but I splayed my fingers to regain traction.

The cold, hard surface grounded me, and I slowed my breathing. The last thing I needed was to black out in a hotel with vampires.

Hysterical laughter broke through the gasps of my shallow breathing. My logical brain rejected the ridiculous idea. *Vampires? Yeah, right!* The denial allowed me to bring my breathing back under control. I faced the mirror and leaned on the counter, pressing the heels of my hands into its cool, marble edge.

The world had shifted on its axis, but aside from the bright flush of my cheeks, Anna stared back at me. Same, mundane, forty-five-year-old Anna Barone. The world was exactly the same as it had been twenty minutes ago. The difference? Knowledge that my understanding of the world was limited. But I was an academic; I already knew that.

So, what did I know for sure?

I knew a woman doing blow used an odd word to describe herself—Source. Maybe it was Mafia lingo I'd never heard before.

I knew she talked about feeding and blood, but talk was cheap. Maybe she was into some sort of vampire cosplay kink. People were into that stuff, right?

As for Luca's eyetooth? I'd never spent more than ten minutes with the man. I probably hadn't noticed it before. Different people had different shaped teeth. And if he was into the same kink, maybe he sharpened them on purpose.

My nerves calmed, and my vision cleared, my body settling back into its natural rhythms. There was a rational explanation for all of this. I'd just jumped to irrational conclusions because of frayed nerves and champagne.

Determined not to let the incident ruin my night, I walked out of the restroom on shaky legs, down the hallway to the lobby, and straight to the bar. The bartender handed me a glass of champagne, and I took a long, deep drink. Braced with liquid courage, I headed for the ballroom.

Marco waited at the entrance, and my unhinged suspicions made his familiar black eyes take on a menacing quality. He watched my approach, a curious tilt to his head, and with each step, my heart pounded faster against my chest. I reached for my necklace, the one my father had given me on my sixteenth birthday, but my anchor wasn't there. I'd foregone my jewelry in deference to the dress, and my fingers opened and closed around air.

He frowned, his gaze focused on my fingers, and reached for me. He wrapped his arm tight around my waist and placed his hand on my hip. Still jumpy from the restroom, I stiffened beneath his touch before relaxing into his arms.

"You okay?" he asked, concern evident in the softness of his voice. "What took so long?"

"Nothing," I mumbled. "I—"

His powerful body dominated the space around me, and his handsome face filled my vision. I imagined him pushing me up against the wall and sinking his teeth into my neck.

Adrenaline surged into my blood, and desire shot up my thighs and down my spine. Fear gripped my chest, and heat and wetness pooled between my legs. Dizzy with conflict, I blinked rapidly and shook my head.

Marco searched my face, worry etched into lines across his brow and around the corners of his mouth.

"I'm fine." I laid a hand on his lapel and gave him a reassuring smile, overcome with the guilt of my ridiculous and unfair panic. "I needed some quiet. That's all. This is a lot for me."

He squeezed my hip, the pressure of his large hand a warning and a comfort. "I know." He led us toward the front of the ballroom. "But you're doing great." He lowered his lips to my ear. "And you look delicious. Good enough to eat."

My knees buckled.

"Whoa." Marco tightened his hold around my waist, keeping me upright, and we continued seamlessly toward the table. "You sure you're okay?"

"Yes, I—I'm just hungry." I smiled again, hoping to ease his worry.

"Let's get you something to eat." He kissed my forehead

and rubbed his thumb across my hip, and the tension and panic holding my body hostage started to release.

Faces and raised glasses went by in a blur. Most guests had taken their seats and were chatting with their neighbors, while others like Angelo and Carmine stood behind their chairs, drinking and laughing. Two women I assumed were their wives or girlfriends sat at our table, engrossed in conversation.

Marco pulled out a chair for me, and I gladly sat down. He squeezed my shoulder, then stepped to meet Luca, who'd appeared in front of our table and lifted his chin to grab Marco's attention.

Servers wearing white gloves and carrying four plates a piece filed into the ballroom. I placed my hands on top of my silverware, anchoring myself, thankful the food was arriving. I really did need something in my stomach. Hopefully the quiet of dinner conversation with Marco would finally settle my nerves.

"Mamma Gina!"

Luca's enthusiastic voice boomed over the din of the ballroom. A woman who bore a striking resemblance to Marco met the two men in front of our table.

Curls the same color as Marco's hair were piled atop her head, loose tendrils spilling over to brush her collarbone. Her evening gown was a deep green, and it complemented the tanned tone of her flawless skin. Her eyes and nose were a carbon copy of Marco's, and déjà vu swept over me like a tsunami. She was clearly Marco's sister but where had I seen her before?

Marco glanced over his shoulder, and the woman followed his gaze, her wide smile brightening when her eyes landed on me. The woman, Luca, and Marco turned to face me and standing like that, together in a row...

A black-and-white photograph in a newspaper article from 1988. A funeral. Little Luca Moretti staring at a casket, standing in between a man who looked exactly like Marco and a woman who looked exactly like his sister.

My stomach dropped, the shock of the connection making my vision swim. I hung my head and stared at my hands, clasped and sweating in my lap, and breathed through the nausea. I'd convinced myself the man in the picture had been Marco's father, that he and Marco shared an uncanny resemblance. But his sister, too? Looking identical to their mother? There was only so much coincidence I was willing to accept. I inhaled a shuddering breath and raised my head.

Luca took the woman's hand, kissed her on the cheek, and left for his table. Marco and Gina walked toward me.

Stay calm. This is Marco's sister. You need to make a good first impression.

The reflex to mind my manners was so outrageous given the circumstances, it jarred me into action. I braced myself on the table and the back of my chair and stood.

"Anna. This is my sister, Gina."

She held out both hands, her warm smile and inviting demeanor oddly comforting. "Bellissima," she said and squeezed my fingers, air kissing me on both cheeks. She muttered something to Marco in Italian, and he grunted behind a wry smile. "Marco has told me so much about you. I hope we get a chance to chat before the night is over."

The sincerity in her voice helped take the edge off the fear and panic tying my stomach in knots. "I hope so, too."

A server interrupted us, placing salads on the table.

"That's our cue," she said and took the seat to her brother's left.

Marco squeezed my elbow and leaned in. "I think she likes you."

My lips quirked in a nervous approximation of a smile, and I was thankful he immediately turned to talk to his sister.

I forced myself to eat, knowing I needed something in my

stomach, but old newspaper articles and their pictures played back like a movie reel.

Vinnie Jr. had looked exactly like his father. Maybe he wasn't a junior at all. Maybe junior and senior were one and the same.

And what about Tony Moretti? Luca's father. Marco's best friend. Was he *the* Antonio Moretti? Had Luca's father and Marco worked together for Big Frankie Valenzano as far back as the 1950s?

My head spun with wild theories and connections, the puzzle pieces fitting together too seamlessly to dismiss. But I shoved them away, unwilling to accept any explanation, however convenient, that involved vampires.

Carmine's wife sat to my right and, halfway through the main course, started regaling me with stories about her kids. I couldn't get a word in edgewise, which was perfectly fine with me. I was grateful for the mundane; it helped take my mind off the supernatural.

By the end of the meal, I'd finished another glass of champagne and was solidly buzzed, bordering on drunk. Gina gave a speech about the importance of immigrant services and our government's duty to protect their chance at a new life. Guests sipped their espressos, ate cannoli, and nodded in agreement. She finished, and the mayor thanked her and Marco for their service to the city.

The ballroom started to clear. Marco was talking to Mayor Kelson, so I quietly excused myself from the table and followed the first wave of guests into the lobby, my limbs liquid and mind numb from the bubbles.

No destination, no direction, no resolution, I drifted past the front desk and realized the source of my numbness wasn't the champagne. It was shock.

No matter how much I didn't want to believe in the supernatural, my analytical brain, trained for over twenty-five years in academia, couldn't ignore the preponderance of evidence, even if it was circumstantial.

So, I sat at my desk on the penthouse floor and waited for the man who could give me definitive proof, wondering what I'd do if he gave it to me.

The elevator dinged, and the doors opened. I stood and stepped out from behind the desk.

"Anna." Marco walked off the elevator with open arms, worried confusion creasing his brow. "I couldn't find you. Siobhán said she saw you get on the elevator."

My heart raced, driving my breath. Sweat beaded my forehead and pooled beneath my arms. I wiped my clammy hands down the sides of my dress and clasped them in front of me to stop them from shaking. I opened my mouth to say something, but nothing came out.

"Anna," he said with more urgency, his voice firm and unyielding as he moved toward me. "What's wrong?"

The familiar scent of cigar smoke and aftershave had a soothing effect, enough for me to blurt out the question hammering my lungs for escape.

"Are you a vampire?" The question tore through the foyer like a cannonball.

He tilted his head, regarding me as if I were a curious specimen. "No. Of course not," he said in a tone indicating how ridiculous he found the idea. "Vampires aren't real."

My body relaxed, and I closed my eyes.

See, Anna? Vampires aren't real. What a ridiculous idea. There was a rational explanation after all. Of course there was. I nodded my head, agreeing with myself, and let out a long, tremulous exhale. Then, I opened my eyes.

Flecks of red interrupted the solid field of Marco's obsidian gaze. They danced around his pupils, expanding and spreading in swirling eddies of color until the entirety of his irises blazed like fire.

My hand flew to where my necklace should have been, and I gasped for air. I stumbled back, arm outstretched, searching for something to hold on to as the world I understood crumbled around me.

No necklace. Nothing to hold. No one else but a man with glowing red eyes.

Panic overtook rational control, and my primal instincts fueled a mad rush for the elevator. But Marco stood between me and my escape. He grabbed my wrist, pulled me into his arms, and held me tight against his hard, unyielding body.

My legs and shoulders shook uncontrollably, but through the darkness clouding my vision, the blazing inferno of his eyes held me in place.

"What—What are you?" I asked in a stunned whisper.

"I'm a blood demon." Marco's answer was low, gravelly, and filled with remorse, his crimson eyes a window into worry and pain.

I lifted my hand and tried to brush away their demonic glow, but blackness ate at the remaining smears of light until there was nothing left. I tumbled out of consciousness and into the blood demon's waiting arms.

Chapter Twenty-Two

Anna

The pillow's satiny finish was cool against my cheek. I extended my arms overhead, pointed my toes beneath the linen sheets, and pressed my legs into the soft feather bed for a full body stretch.

This is the most comfortable bed I've ever slept in.

Awareness doused my sleepy mind like a bucket of ice water, and my eyes snapped open. I pushed the comforter down, propped myself up onto my elbows, and brushed the hair out of my face. A wide sleeve slid down my arm. I fingered the white fabric crossing my heart. A robe, cinched at the waist, the weave of the cotton so fine it caressed my skin like silk.

The black of night enveloped the room, the only source of illumination the lights of distant buildings and the soft glow of streetlamps visible through a wall of windows. Until the flick of a match.

A flame sparked to life at the hands of a man who sat on a leather sofa facing the windows. He lifted it to light the stub of cigar he held between his teeth, and it highlighted the angular cut of his jaw.

Marco puffed until the cherry burned hot. He shook out the match, tossed it into the ashtray next to him, and rested his arm on the back of the couch. He stared out the window into the dark Boston night, and tendrils of smoke, backlit by the cigar's muted glow, trailed toward the ceiling.

I was in Marco's suite. Or was it a cage? Was I prey trapped by a deadly predator?

I'd fainted the night before. That I remembered. The transformation of his obsidian eyes into crimson fire had pushed me over the edge into darkness. But he'd caught me. Taken care of me. Undressed me, wrapped me in a robe, and tucked me into bed.

Was I making excuses? No. Marco would never hurt me. Of that, I was sure. Wasn't I?

I swung my legs out from under the comforter and over the side of the bed, testing them on the cold slate floor. My cheeks burned at my near nakedness. The robe so thin it was almost transparent, so short it barely covered my ass. Curiosity restrained by fear, I took tentative steps toward the sofa, stopping at its end, and gathered my hair over my shoulder.

Marco still wore his tuxedo pants, but his coat and bowtie were gone along with his socks and shoes. He'd lost his button-down in favor of a sleeveless undershirt, and the glow of his cigar accentuated the bulges of his muscled arms. He took a long drag, eyes still fixed on the window.

I twisted my hair into a tail, needing something to fidget in place of my necklace, an anchor to help me muster the courage to finish what I'd started.

He glanced at me sidelong and tapped his cigar into the ashtray on the end table. "Good morning," he said, his voice deep and rough.

"What time is it?"

He flipped his wrist to look at his watch, and the snake on

his arm twitched with the flex of his muscles. "A little after three."

My eyes dropped to my feet. I wiggled my toes into the shag of the area rug covering the space around the sofa.

"Your dress and shoes are in the closet. Siobhán put you to bed last night."

I pressed my lips together, arresting a sigh of relief. "Thank you."

I could have left. Gone to the closet, gathered my things, and left. Instead, I rounded the corner of the sofa and sat, holding the bottom of my robe closed as I reclined into the sofa back.

He took another drag off his cigar, blew a smoke ring, and angled it to study the burning ember at its end. "What made you suspect?"

"Luca." I picked at the ends of my hair. "I saw him feeding on his date outside the restroom before dinner."

He chuffed out a breath and looked askance. "Fucking Luca," he muttered under his breath.

"It wasn't just Luca. I ran into his date in the restroom, and she asked me if I was..." I stumbled over the word she'd used. What had she called me?

He side-eyed me. "Asked if you were..."

"Your—your Source?"

He shook his head, annoyed, and brought the cigar to his lips.

He smoked. I watched.

After a time, he turned and studied me. "You could've taken a cab home. Locked your door. But you came up here. Why?"

My stomach flipped. I couldn't answer with the truth, at least, not the entire truth. Yes, I'd wanted to know if the conclusions I'd drawn were reality. But what I didn't want to admit was the darker reason I'd ventured to the penthouse.

I burned for Marco. Still. The danger of what he might be had done nothing to dissuade my body from aching for his touch. If anything, it had made it burn hotter. And after all the champagne, curiosity and excitement combined with lust to eclipse fear.

I cleared my throat and shrugged a shoulder. "I thought there was another explanation."

He regarded the stub of his cigar with a smirk, took a puff, and set it in the ashtray. "I told you before." He swiveled his torso to face me, drawing my attention to his eyes. "You're a terrible liar."

My mouth opened and closed like a fish out of water. I tugged at my hair and focused on the cracks in the aged leather even as the interplay between danger and seduction drove my body wild.

He shifted his weight and bent a knee to rest his leg on the couch between us. His arm extended along the back of the sofa, and he drummed his blunt fingers against its wooden frame.

"Do you want to know what I think?" His voice dropped, its timbre a sinful taunt. "I think you came up here because you wanted me to fuck you. You want to know what it feels like to have me inside you, dominating you."

My lips parted, my breath quickening. I squirmed under the intensity of his attention and the danger of his presence, desire throbbing between my legs.

He picked up a lock of my hair and ran it between his fingers. "And after last night—" The corner of his mouth twitched, and his eyes illuminated with specks of glowing crimson. "You want to know what it feels like to have me bite you."

My breath hitched on a sharp intake, and I launched off the sofa. I aimed myself at the door, terrified he would catch me, but just as terrified he might let me escape.

His fingers closed around my biceps in a punishing grip. He spun me to face him, caught my shoulder, and pushed me until my back hit cold glass. I scrambled to break free, but he hauled my arms above my head and pinned me to the window by my wrists.

I struggled in vain to break free of his iron-clad grip, my frantic breath as loud as the blood rushing in my ears. He pressed his body flush against mine to still me, and the cold at my back heightened the sensation of his hard heat. He lowered his head, and I twisted my face away. Soft lips brushed the space below my ear, and his warm breath sent tingles down the length of my spine. He dipped his head lower, and I felt his smile against my shoulder.

Something sharp and pointed dragged along the length of my neck, from its base to where my pulse beat against the skin of my throat like a drum. Gooseflesh pebbled my arms, and desire surged between my legs. Until I realized the source of the delicious sensation. A fang.

I thrust my elbows forward and arched my shoulders off the glass in a desperate attempt at escape. I thrashed violently against the immovable cage of his body, my heart and breath racing. I squirmed my torso and lifted a knee, but he pressed his hips into mine forcing me flat against the window. The hard length of his erection jutted into my belly, and I froze, the unexpected torrent of desire shocking me into stillness.

The glow of Marco's eyes drew my attention, and I lifted my gaze to stare at the blood demon in fascinated horror. His fangs were extended in a feral baring of teeth, their razor-sharp points reaching just past his bottom lip. His nostrils flared with exertion, and his eyes shone the same burning crimson I'd seen the night before.

The air between us was thick with the impending outcome of our sexual standoff. Danger and need fed off each other and drove me to a reckless peak of frenzied lust.

"Fuck me," I ordered. "Now."

His mouth crashed into mine, a violent thunderclap of passion, the softness of his lips a delicious contrast to the harshness of his kiss. His tongue swept into my mouth with animalistic ferocity demanding submission, and I met his hunger stroke for stroke.

My tongue slid across a fang, and he groaned, a deep rumble of pleasure that reverberated through his chest and made my nipples tingle. He released my hands and wrapped his thick fingers around my neck just below my chin, squeezing hard enough to let me know he was in control. I grabbed the back of his head and ran my nails through his hair and along his scalp, pressing him closer. He ground his erection into my belly, and my pussy turned slick, ravenous for his cock.

His hand slipped between us, and the sharp hiss of a zipper made my sex throb. His hips shifted, and the tuxedo pants fell to the floor.

He broke our kiss but didn't pull back. His lips teased mine, light brushes and touches amid the warmth of our shared breath, driving my arousal to a peak.

He released my neck, wrapped his hands under my thighs, and lifted me off the floor. The robe slipped as he pushed me up the glass, falling open to reveal one of my breasts.

His eyes flared in the darkness. "Those fucking tits," he growled and sucked my nipple into his mouth. He dragged it between his teeth, and I groaned at the harsh sensation, pressing my heels into his ass.

He shifted again, and the thick head of his cock glided through my wetness until he found my entrance. He slammed his full length into me in a single punishing thrust and ground the base into my clit. He stretched and filled me, and the sting of his size spiked my pleasure.

"Finally," I breathed, and rested my arms on his shoulders.

His mouth hovered before mine in open invitation, and he circled his hips, grinding himself harder against my throbbing sex.

"Unh!" The low husky sound that escaped me matched the wild intensity of his inhuman eyes. He pulled out until the thick bulb of his head teased my entrance, then slammed back into me, tearing another low groan from my lungs.

He ran his tongue over my top lip and eased himself out before feeding my hungry folds with the full length of his cock. He repeated the sensual torture again and again, slowly picking up the pace until he was fucking me against the glass.

Each stroke and press of his hips brought me closer to release. I ground my swollen, needy clit into him, matching the beat of his rhythmic strokes, given over to the exhilarating blend of danger, pleasure, and pain.

He growled from deep within his chest, fucking me harder and faster as he destroyed my mouth with another savage kiss. The walls of my pussy clenched from unrelenting sensation, and my orgasm exploded into being to take ownership of my body.

My head fell back against the glass, and I moaned, throaty sounds wrenched from my core with each wave of pleasure Marco wrung from my body. My toes curled, and I dug my fingernails into his shoulders, every muscle clenching in response to the orgasm claiming me. My cries filled the room in debauched harmony with the wet slap of his hips between my legs and the guttural sounds of his impending release.

The tendons in his neck and the veins at his temples strained, and with a final punishing thrust, Marco surrendered. He grunted, and his powerful body stilled for a moment before he pushed his hips into mine. My walls tightened around his pulsing member, and his chest rumbled with each stream of cum he released into my body.

He relaxed, chest heaving, and rested his forehead against my collarbone. We held each other and breathed, slowly descending back to Earth from the heights of shared ecstasy.

Chapter Twenty-Three

Marco

"I'm not finished with you," I told her, my voice a growl over our combined panting.

I stepped out of the tuxedo pants bunched around my ankles, still sheathed in the warmth of Anna's perfect cunt, and backed us away from the window. She tightened her arms around my neck, legs around my waist, and rested her head against mine. Her silky hair brushed my arm, sending a shiver down my spine. I pulled out to lay her on the bed, and my body rebelled, hardening again, straining to bury itself in her luscious heat.

Her hair splayed in a dark halo around her luminous face, lips swollen from my hungry kisses. Her robe had come undone, and I drank in the beauty of her full breasts, completely bared to me for the first time. The dark rose of her taut nipples begged for my mouth.

"You look like an angel," I whispered, awed by the blessing laid out before me.

A sly smile claimed her lips. "Are you my devil?" Her chest and neck were already flushed from sex, but her playful taunt added redness to her cheeks. She reached for me.

I peeled off my undershirt and climbed onto the bed, knees on either side of the inviting swell of her hips. I stroked my cock back to its full length and hardness, and her pupils dilated watching me fuck my hand.

I squeezed one of her tits, pinching the nipple till she gasped and arched her back in a wordless plea for more. "Christ, I love your tits. I want to shove my cock between them and fuck them till I come all over your chest."

She groaned, deep and rough, and squirmed atop the sheets. "Yes, Marco! Please!"

I laughed darkly. There'd be time for dirty fucking later. Right then I needed to take her slowly, enjoy each stroke after the frantic pounding I'd given her against the window.

Rock hard and dripping with need, I pushed her legs open with my knee, pressed my body against hers, and devoured her mouth. I propped myself up enough to feel the firm peaks of her nipples brush my chest. Our tongues danced, and she rocked her hips against my leg, sliding her wetness up and down my thigh.

She broke our kiss and tilted her head back and to the side, inviting me to feed. I wanted nothing more than to press my fangs into the warmth and resistance of her flesh; they ached to experience that pleasure. But it was a step too far, a line I wasn't ready or willing to cross no matter how fierce the temptation.

I rolled onto my back, pulling her with me till she was on her knees astride my hips. The robe fell from her shoulders, and finally, we were both naked.

I pinched her nipples. She sighed contentedly, and her eyes fluttered closed. She arched into my touch and lifted the hair off her back in a move so sexy I thought I might come just from watching her. I slid my hands over her breasts and the curve of her tapered waist to the flare of her hips. My fingers dug into their soft swell in a punishing grip, holding her still as I struggled to maintain control.

She opened her eyes and rested her hands on my abs. "You want me on top?"

The huskiness in her voice made my cock twitch, and cum dripped from its tip onto my stomach. "Are you kidding? I've been waiting to see those tits for weeks. I want to watch them bounce while you ride my cock."

Her laughter was deep and sensual. I dominated her pleasure, but she was enjoying her moment of control. And it was so fucking hot, I gave biting her a second thought.

She shifted her hips till she found me with the wet lips of her swollen cunt. She slid her folds up and down its length, releasing sighs of pleasure with each stroke. Then she smiled mischievously and took her nipples between her thumbs and forefingers and pinched them till she screamed my name.

I fucking lost it. I lifted her onto her knees, lined myself up with her entrance, and slammed her down.

She cried out. I wasn't a small man, not by any means, and I was so engorged for a moment I thought I'd hurt her. But then she leaned forward, a wicked smile on her face, and rested her palms on my pecs. She rocked her hips up and down my length, her warm, wet cunt gripping me tight, the slow movements torture. I fought the urge to thrust my hips and force her to move; I sure as shit wasn't about to interrupt the show.

She was using my cock like a fucking toy, moving to maximize her pleasure, dragging her clit through the hair at its base and working herself into a frenzy. Her body moved like a wave, full breasts swaying with every sultry motion, and each time she stroked her clit against me, she rode me harder and faster.

Her hair fell on either side of her flushed face, a gentle caress against my skin even as she dug her nails into my pecs. The contrast between pleasure and pain drove me wild. I squeezed my fingers into her fleshy hips, forcing her upright so

I could fuck her in earnest, and she clawed her nails down my torso so deeply I knew she'd drawn blood.

I lifted her enough to slam her back down, forcing myself deep and setting the rhythm I needed. She didn't hesitate; she knew what I wanted to see. She lifted her hair off her body, elbows out to the sides, and rode me, tits bouncing with every thrust.

"Fuck," I growled. I wasn't going to last long watching that display. I pressed her clit with two fingers and rubbed furiously. The walls of her cunt squeezed me so hard, the beginnings of my release formed deep in my balls. I pressed my fingers harder and tipped her over the edge.

Her body arched, her tight cunt clenching with each wave of her orgasm, making her cry out with high-pitched sighs.

Her pulsing muscles ripped the orgasm out of me, pulling sensation down my spine. My nuts constricted, and hot cum shot through my cock into her hungry warmth. I held her in place, emptying myself into her, coming so hard I saw stars.

My vision cleared, my cock softened, and Anna's smiling face stared down at me. Christ, she was beautiful, flushed and happy from sex. And not just need-to-get-my-rocks-off sex. Life-changing sex. Real passion.

"Vieni qui," I demanded and held my arms open.

She lifted herself off me, and our combined cum dripped onto my stomach and down her leg. She lay on her side next to me, head on my shoulder, thigh draped across my hips, and placed her hand over my heart. It added a warmth there I hadn't felt in decades. I brushed the hair from her forehead and kissed her, letting my lips linger, and drank in the combined scent of roses and our passion.

She brushed her fingers across my chest and the tracks she'd left when she'd raked her nails down my torso. "That was remarkable," she breathed.

I ran my fingers up and down her spine. "Remarkable, huh?"

"Two orgasms? I'd call that remarkable."

I frowned. "Like I said, you've been dating the wrong men."

She laughed. "No kidding."

She tickled my chest with a light brush of her fingertips. It made me shiver. My body relaxed. My breathing slowed. Peace and contentment were the center of my world.

"You're so calm," she said.

She was right. The tension that normally gripped my insides and kept me alert, that maintained the cold calculation I needed to run my empire, it melted in Anna's arms.

"It's you," I whispered. "You do this to me."

She nuzzled her face into my shoulder, and my fingers continued their soothing journey up and down her back.

"We were irresponsible," she said quietly.

"How so?"

"We didn't use protection."

I looked down at her, surprised. "Do you need to get a morning after pill?"

"No." She lifted her head, and her lips curved into a sad, resigned smile. "I'm not worried about that."

"You're on the pill?"

"No. I—I can't get pregnant." The words were quiet, but matter-of-fact.

"I'm sorry," I said, no idea what I'd walked into. After what my sister went through, I knew the subject of children and pregnancy had the potential to carry a lot of baggage.

"It's okay. I mean... It wasn't. For years, it wasn't. But I came to terms with it a long time ago."

Her strength never ceased to amaze me. I kissed her forehead. "Then, what are you worried about?"

She widened her eyes and lifted her eyebrows.

I searched her face for an answer. Realization dawned, and I snorted. "I'm immortal, Anna. I don't get diseases."

"Ahh," she sighed, and laid her head back down on my shoulder. She traced the fading scratches on my chest. "I scratched you."

"You did. It was hot as hell."

"They're almost gone. Same thing, I suppose."

"Yes. Same thing."

"And aging?"

"Yes. That too."

"What I wouldn't give to have my butt and stomach from ten years ago."

"What's wrong with your butt and stomach?" I asked, dumbfounded.

"My butt is nowhere near as perky as it used to be. It's... kinda saggy." She squirmed with each defeated word. "So is the skin on my stomach. Saggy and crepey."

I took her chin between my thumb and forefinger and tipped her head up to level her with a stern look. "First of all, don't you dare say anything bad about your ass. I love your ass. It's fantastic. It's plump and ripe. The perfect size for me to grab onto while I'm fucking you." She laughed, and her eyes sparkled with gratitude and pride. "Second, at what point this morning did I give you any indication I didn't adore every inch of your body? Hm?"

She craned her neck, straining for a kiss. I obliged, planting one firmly on her lips.

"Charmer," she said and laid back down, nestling into my shoulder. "I googled you, you know."

"Oh yeah? What did you find?" I already knew the answer. My cybersecurity was rock solid courtesy of Cambridge Management Group.

"A couple of pictures. Only one where I could see your face."

I knew the picture. I approved every picture I wanted to remain on the internet.

"I suppose that's important in your position," she continued.

I trailed my fingers down her arm, and she shivered. "And what's my position?"

"An immortal with connections that..." She scrunched her face the way she did when she was searching for the right words. "That have a tendency to make the news."

I chuckled and shook my head. The way she put things.

She laid her head back down and resumed stroking my chest. "I did find more pictures. At the library."

"Hmm." Running my fingertips up and down her arm soothed me. I could do it for eternity.

"Microfiche."

Clever woman. In all my years covering up my immortality, no one else had managed to piece together the trail of evidence I couldn't eliminate.

"How do you do it? People must recognize you. I can't be the only one who's figured it out."

"My little researcher," I said with a smile and kissed her hair. "So brilliant. I should have known you'd figure it out." I bent my arm behind my head and stared up at the ceiling. "You'd think more people would figure it out, but I—we— have been doing this for a long time, and the reality is people don't want to believe."

"I get that. I didn't. I made up every excuse I could. Until I couldn't."

"It became harder with the internet."

We'd scrambled in those early years figuring out how to maintain our anonymity. The technology and personnel and skills we needed were all so new and changed so rapidly.

"I started spending a small fortune on cybersecurity. More than I ever spent paying off reporters and newspapers. They scrub the internet, news outlets, and paparazzi channels for pictures and information. I'll never be able to get rid of those old print articles, but"—I shrugged—"these days if it's not online, the chances of someone making the effort to find anything is pretty slim."

"What about your employees? Acquaintances?"

"We move. My parents live in Italy right now for that very reason. Local memory is short. Every thirty years or so, I change my primary residence. The locals don't recognize me, and if anyone does, they think I'm my own son. I can run my business from anywhere. Especially now. Like I said, it's not as difficult as you'd think."

"Aren't you scared I'll say something?"

"No."

"Why not?"

"Because if you tell someone I'm a century-old blood demon..."

"They'll think I'm crazy."

"Exactly."

"There have to be downsides."

"Like what?"

"I don't know. Like being burned by holy water or not being able to see yourself in the mirror or—"

I laughed out loud, and my shaking chest jostled her head.

"What?" she asked.

"I already told you. I'm not a vampire. Vampires don't exist. You've seen me walk outside during the day, right?" She nodded against my shoulder. "I was raised Roman Catholic. Went to church every Sunday with my family. Never once spontaneously combusted. Not to mention, I'm Italian. If garlic was going to kill me, I'd be dead a million times over."

She buried her face in my shoulder, and her body shook with laughter. "I'm sorry!"

I laughed with her and hugged her close. "Don't be sorry. I

wouldn't expect you to know what makes blood demons different. Especially with all the vampire nonsense in books and in the movies. It's been going on for centuries.

"Thing is, we're not that different from humans. Yes, we're immortal and our blood has restorative properties. It heals us and prevents us from aging. And yes, we need to feed on blood. It strengthens our bodies and abilities. But other than that..."

"What about—what about being bit?"

"What about it?"

"Does it turn a human into a blood demon?"

"No." I shook my head. "Total bullshit."

"I figured, given Luca's date didn't—"

"Die outside a bathroom in my hotel only to come back with red eyes and fangs?" I finished for her with no small amount of sarcasm.

She chuckled. "It does sound ridiculous when you say it that way. Although yesterday I would have said the existence of blood demons sounded ridiculous."

"Fair."

"How do you become a blood demon?"

"We're a different species, Anna. I was born a blood demon."

"Oh," she said softly.

I detected confusion behind her short response and suspected I knew why. "You're wondering what happens when a human and a blood demon get together."

She nodded and buried her face deeper into my shoulder.

I wasn't ready to talk about this, but she needed to know. "Humans can't turn into blood demons. You're either born a blood demon or you're not. But we can prolong a human's life. When a blood demon bonds with a human, they feed from the human, injecting them with their venom, and the human regularly consumes their mate's blood. That's where the vampire myth came from. Humans weren't being turned. The combination of venom and blood from the same Source just made it seem that way.

"We don't share our blood lightly, though. It's only done as part of our sacred vow to bond. It requires understanding and agreement from both parties because it's a commitment that lasts eternity. Anything less than full consent is a violation of a person's body and autonomy. It's an egregious sin. Same with our venom. It's why Sources are so important."

"I understand," she said and nuzzled my shoulder.

Our combined breath and heartbeats filled the silence. I stroked her back and let her digest all the truths I'd just dropped while trying to figure out what the hell I was going to do with this woman. She'd managed the impossible and crumbled the walls I'd erected around my heart, but was I ready for what came next?

Her energy shifted, and she squirmed. Something else was bothering her. "What?"

Her hand stilled atop my chest, and she tilted her face up. I turned mine down to meet the curious look in her eyes. "Are you in the Mafia?"

A bark of laughter escaped me, and I wrapped both arms around her, squeezing her tight. "That's what you're worried about? You just had sex with a blood demon, and you're worried I'm in the Mafia?"

"Well, are you?"

I laughed again and released her, relaxing back onto my forearm. "No. I'm not in the Mafia."

The statement didn't taste right on my tongue. It tasted like a lie. There was a difference between wanting something to be true and it being true. I'd wanted it to be true for so long, I'd started believing my own bullshit. Fact was, my situation warranted far more nuance than a firm denial, and I couldn't lie to this woman any more than I could lie to myself. Not anymore.

"Okay," I sighed. "Not true. Look, I want to be honest with you, but it's not a pretty story."

"Life isn't always pretty. Even I know that."

I snorted.

"And I want the truth."

She might regret that decision after this conversation.

"I was in the Mafia. For a long time. Then, I got out. Or, at least, I told myself I got out. But you never really leave. Not when you're made, and not when it's all you've ever known. So..." I looked down at her, and she shifted to meet my eyes. "The real answer? It's complicated."

"I want to understand." Her words didn't hold any judgment or fear, and I believed her. "You were part of Big Frankie Valenzano's crew with Luca's father, weren't you?"

"He was my best friend."

"And a blood demon?"

"Mm-hm."

Memories surfaced, highlights I cherished and those I wished to forget. She was quiet, wanting a story, but didn't know the questions to ask. Nostalgia and my need for a connection with her got the better of me. I stared at the ceiling, and my lips parted before I could stop them.

"Big Frankie was Don when me and Tony joined. We were lucky; he knew us for what we were. He'd fallen in love with a blood demon—Vinnie's mother. Spotted the signs right away. Welcomed us into the family. Said he needed a couple reliable runners, ones he could use with his outfit of blood demons."

"Are there a lot of blood demons in Boston?"

"More than anywhere else in North America. We emigrated from Italy around the same time as the other European immigrants looking for a better life. Classic tale... Someone moves to a city, you follow, knowing there will be at least one other person who speaks your language and understands your struggles. Then more people follow..."

"You or your parents?"

"My parents. They had nothing. Decided life couldn't be any worse in America. Especially with all the stories making their way back to the villages from those who'd made it, who'd found work, or so my papà tells me. Turns out, there were only so many jobs to go around. Papà struggled with English. At first, he couldn't find work for more than one, two days at a time."

"So, you became a runner for Big Frankie," she whispered.

"It was better than the alternative. Watching my parents and little sister go hungry. Living in a rat-infested basement." *Walking in on Mamma selling herself.* I swallowed the words. "We needed the money."

I'd never shared those memories with anyone, never even had the inclination to try. But Anna understood me. She saw me. And the partnership I was missing, the partnership I'd grown to crave, deepened with every word.

"How old were you?"

"I was twelve."

"Twelve?!" She sprang off my shoulder and sat upright, a horrified expression on her face. She gripped the sheet covering her chest like a life vest, like if she held on tightly enough it would save her from my truth. It wouldn't.

I reached for the spare smoke I kept stashed in the drawer of the nightstand. I lit the cigar and held it between my teeth, puffing it to life as I shifted myself back against the headboard. "Vieni qui," I commanded around the cigar and urged her toward me with the curl of my fingers.

She eyed me like she might eye a wounded puppy. I needed to disavow her of that notion entirely. If anything, I'd been the one wounding the puppies.

I grabbed her around the waist, spun her back to my front,

and pulled her between my legs, settling her against my chest. I wrapped a forefinger around my cigar and took a deep pull before removing it from between my teeth. "That was a long time ago," I said. "Multiple lifetimes ago. The world was a different place back then. My family needed help. I had an opportunity to help them. I took it."

"But you were so young."

I shrugged and dragged on my cigar. "Maybe by today's standards, but back then?" I blew smoke rings, and she followed them as they expanded upward and disappeared into the darkness. "Big Frankie was good to us. Treated me and Tony like part of the family. From his perspective we were. We were Italians and we were blood demons. We ran messages between his made guys. We were their eyes and ears on the streets. Most of them used restaurants and bakeries as fronts. We got paid in bread and pasta and a little cash. Back then, that's all we needed. That and Sources."

I took another drag. She wouldn't want to hear the next part of the story. The part where Tony and I grew up and realized we could have more than the bare minimum we needed to survive. The part where we became two of the most ruthless men in Boston. The part where we pulled ourselves out of poverty with other men's blood.

"Sources." She rested her head on my chest and turned her face up. "That's what Luca's date called herself. She asked me if I was your Source."

"I'm not surprised. Luca uses his Sources like escorts. If she's only ever sourced for Luca, she might think that's par for the course, but it's not."

"It's not?"

"No. Not for me. Blood is a necessity. Like air or water. I can live without sex—not that I'd want to—but I can't live without blood. And anytime you add sex to the equation, shit gets complicated."

"I'm confused. What I saw looked and sounded sexual."

"It is, to an extent. Our fangs inject venom when we bite, and it hits the bloodstream like a drug. The Source relaxes, starts feeling the same sensations they feel during sex. The more venom, the stronger the sensation. It's one of the reasons humans agree to become Sources. But they do get paid for their blood, and most Sources leave it at that. Some don't. Some want more."

"Then why use a Source at all? Why not go to a blood bank or something and avoid all the complications?"

I chuckled. "So logical," I teased and kissed her head. "Blood demons weren't meant to drink blood through a straw. We're predators even if we've evolved past victimizing our prey. My fangs ache when I don't feed. They need to press into flesh to release venom. A blood bank works in a pinch, but it's not a long-term solution."

"Luca looked like he was enjoying himself almost as much as his date."

I shrugged and dragged on my cigar. "It feels good."

"Like sex?"

I considered the question while blowing out another trail of smoke. "Similar, but different."

She ran a fingernail along my forearm, tracing the outline of the tattoo I'd gotten with Tony over a half-century ago when we got made.

"You didn't bite me."

Her disappointment made me flinch. I really didn't want to have that conversation. "I didn't."

"Why?"

"I don't mix feeding and fucking."

"But you could."

"I could."

"Have you?"

"No."

"Not ever?"

"Not ever."

"Hmm." She outlined its scales as if that was her focus and her line of questioning an afterthought. "What about girlfriends?"

"What about them?"

"Don't they—" She swallowed. "Don't they get jealous of your—your Sources?"

Nervous Anna resurfaced with that question, the hesitation in her voice telling me everything I needed to know. This had meant more to her than a simple fuck, and she was worried I didn't share the sentiment.

I stubbed out my cigar. I lifted her up enough to move her out from between my legs, rolled on top of her, and slid us down the mattress till her head rested on the pillow. I covered her with my body and kissed the tip of her nose. "Jealous already?" I kissed her collarbone from her shoulder to the hollow of her neck.

"I—I thought you were going to bite me."

I continued the kisses till I reached her ear. "You didn't seem to mind when I was fucking you." I dragged her earlobe between my teeth. She gasped and turned her face, tempting my mouth away from her ear with an invitation of parted lips. I kissed her, passionately, and pressed my hardening cock into her mound, distracting her from questions about my bite and a future together I wasn't ready to answer.

Chapter Twenty-Four

Anna

The Charles River bent just before the Boston University bridge where it widened to separate MIT from the Back Bay and let me know I was halfway through my run. It was mid-morning Thursday, and Marco had come to my condo the night before, staying later than either of us anticipated. Not that I minded. But before he left, and in typical Marco fashion, he'd ordered me to sleep in and, with a wicked smile, not to worry about his breakfast.

I'd spent the early part of the week refining and running simulations, working late nights only to hit brick wall after brick wall. I was missing something. I was sure of it. I'd successfully characterized the leak but couldn't figure out where it was coming from or, in turn, who was responsible.

The rhythmic pounding of the pavement and the cadence of my breath cleared my mind, more so than at any time over the past few weeks. It wandered from images of Marco hovering over me and the pleasure he'd so easily wrung from my body to the demonic glow of his eyes and the anticipation of his fangs in my neck. Surprising given that less than a week ago I hadn't even known supernatural beings existed. But acceptance had quickly replaced shock and fear, my scientific brain recognizing the facts for what they were—facts. Once that happened, curiosity took over, and I wanted to understand more of his world. And experience the extraordinary pleasure only Marco could provide.

He still hadn't bitten me, and I could tell he didn't want to talk about it. I understood his reasons, but that didn't mean I wasn't disappointed. Not all blood demons put restrictions on their feeding like Marco. Luca certainly didn't. And although I respected his boundary, I did wonder where it came from.

We hadn't known each other very long, but the urgency propelling me to live my life was no less pressing now than when I'd taken the leap and gone on sabbatical. Marco and I had a connection, a magnetic, exhilarating, sensuous connection, and I didn't want to wait to explore its potential.

Everything about him excited me. His Italian heritage and immigrant upbringing; his sharp, calculating mind, and even sharper tongue; his gorgeous eyes and stern mouth; the danger inherent in his less-than-legal businesses; even the knowledge he was a blood demon.

I'd never met someone who could drive me so wild with need and hold their own with me in a conversation about finance. And he was so charmingly brazen. The man had commented on my tits in the same email he'd explained his company's foreign tax journaling, and—

Puzzle pieces crashed into place, and adrenaline rushed my system with the force of their fall. It made me woozy, and I stumbled to the side of the path, bent over, ready to hurl my breakfast into the dirty snow. How had I missed the connection?

I took my phone out of my running belt with shaking hands.

I know how he did it.

I'm in my office.

I'd already made it to East Cambridge and the Longfellow Bridge; at this point, it would be faster to run. My heart hammered in my chest as I picked up the pace. I didn't want to tell him. He was going to be furious, but more than that, the news would break his heart.

"Anna!" Siobhán's voice rang out across the lobby.

"Hey!" I glanced over my shoulder, only slowing for a moment in my speed-walk toward the elevators. "I'll call you later!"

She gave me a confused once-over and frowned. Sweat dripped down my face and soaked through my long-sleeve thermal, but I didn't have time to explain.

On the elevator, endorphins and adrenaline joined forces and had me bouncing on the balls of my feet. My brain cycled through a million different scenarios searching, reaching for any other explanation than the one I knew to be true.

Nothing.

The elevator dinged and the doors slid open. Marco's office door was ajar. He was on the phone and waved me in. I closed the door behind me.

"Look, I'll have to call you back later. Yes. That's fine. Ciao." He placed the phone on his desk and eyed my feet.

Melted snow and dirt covered my running shoes. I grimaced. "Sorry."

He waved his hand. "Must not be very good news if it couldn't wait till after your run." He eyed my thermal. "Or a clean set of clothes." There was an edge to his voice that matched the stern lines of his face.

"I know how he did it."

His obsidian eyes became impossibly darker. "How *who* did *what*?" The sharp *t* cut like a knife.

There was no way to break the news but to break his heart. "I know how—how Luca stole the money."

"How *Luca* stole the money?" he growled.

"It had to be Luca." I walked up to his desk. "He's the only one that could have pulled it off."

"Pulled what off, Anna?" Marco asked, loud, demanding, impatient. Red sparks appeared across the midnight field of his eyes.

"Changing the taxes. That's how he did it. That's why I didn't see it at first. I—I was on my run and..." I paced back to the center of the room, and my hands flew through the air as fast as the thoughts streamed from my brain to my mouth. "And I was thinking about us and how you'd harassed me and called it flirting. And that email. The—the one about my tits." Marco blinked and looked at me like I was a mad woman. "And then I remembered what started that email chain. The missing years. The missing taxes."

I stopped waving my hands, rested them on the edge of his desk, and took two deep breaths, needing to slow down so Marco would understand. "I couldn't find any record of state and local taxes in the expense reports, remember? You had to email them to me. Because they are journaled separately. Remember?" I swallowed. "And—and that's how he did it. That's how he hid it."

I'd almost tripped over my own feet when I'd connected the dots, it was so glaringly obvious. Had I not wanted to see the truth?

"He changed the chargeback of the state and local taxes in

the expense reports only on the accounting side. Since taxes are uniform across all income sources, the operating and net profits looked totally normal. That's why no one in the accounting department picked up on the discrepancy.

"But the model did. It's comprehensive of both streams as well as tax, inflation, and exchange rates. You saw the uniform drain yourself. He must have funneled the chargeback difference into a separate account before paying the actual taxes. It's quite ingenious when you—" My voice hitched, and I winced. "Think about it," I finished quietly. God, what a jerk. "I'm sorry, Marco. I'm so sorry."

Marco's hands fisted, and his nostrils flared with angry breath. The muscle in his jaw twitched, and the crimson sparks in his eyes solidified into a steady fire.

I shifted, alternating my weight between my feet, unsure what to say or what came next.

He rose, picked up his phone, and sent a text, all the while vibrating with rage. He came around the end of his desk, pulled me into him with a firm hand splayed across my sweaty lower back, and kissed my forehead.

"Thank you," he said, but the words were heavy and terse. He looked into my eyes. "Don't mention this to anyone. Capisce?"

I nodded.

"I'll text you later."

He kissed me, hard and fast, then released me and headed for the door. He pulled on his coat. "Lock it on your way out," he commanded and walked out of his office. The elevator dinged like a scene break, starting the next act in this surreal movie.

I exhaled, and my shoulders descended out of my ears. What a mess. Luca Moretti, the man Marco raised and loved like a son, had stolen enough money from his foster father to jeopardize his business. I had no idea where Marco was going or what he was planning to do, but I had a feeling I didn't want to know.

Chapter Twenty-Five

Marco

My right fist connected with the thick leather—*Smack! Smack! Smack!*—till my shoulder burned. Vito glared at me from behind the hanging bag.

"Cazzo!" I raged at no one. At everyone. At myself.

I pivoted and took long strides away from the bag. I flexed my hand and inspected my red knuckles. I should've wrapped them better. They'd be a bloody mess by the time I was done. I didn't care. I needed to pound something, and better the bag than Luca's face.

Sweat stung my eyes. I grabbed a towel off the ropes and wiped it from my face. "Not a fucking word. Nothing. Not till we know whether Vinnie is involved." I locked eyes with Carmine, then Angelo. They were in their shirtsleeves, leaning back against the ropes, watching me unleash my rage. I pointed at each of them with the sweaty towel. "Capisce?"

Angelo nodded.

"Not a word," Carmine said.

I spun around and pointed the towel at Vito.

"Got it, boss."

"I doubt Vinnie knows," Angelo said and shook his head.

"You're not gonna like this, Marco, but it needs to be said. That kid's volatile. Always has been. He's a blind spot for you, and you know it."

Rage swelled and made my head feel like it was going to explode. I let out a roar that would've made a wild animal jealous and lost control. My fangs descended and so much power surged through my blood, my eyes must have lit up like a goddamn satanic lighthouse.

Over the rush of blood in my ears, Carmine shouted, "Grab that bag, Vito!" right before I unleashed my fists in a flurry of hooks and swings. My power flowed freely, and I channeled all my unbridled anger, frustration, and pain over Luca's betrayal into that bag. I drained myself before taking one final swing. I slammed my left fist into the bag with everything I had left. Vito grunted, and the cracked leather split, fraying at the edges of a fist-sized tear.

"Goddammit, Marco!" Vito's eyes glowed red with effort and irritation.

I shoved my hands into my hair, panting with effort. They throbbed with the beat of my pulse. Blood soaked through the wrap around my left hand and dripped onto the floor.

Vito came up behind me and handed me a towel. "You owe me another heavy bag."

"Send me the bill," I growled and glared at him.

"Don't be a dick," he snapped.

I hauled back to punch him, but Vito was quick, and I was exhausted. He blocked my swing and pushed me away, eyes a dim crimson.

"You need to cool off, boss." He pointed a finger in my face. "Get that rage under control. I know Luca is like a son to you, and I know this is bringing up all sorts of shit with Tony, but you need to get it together unless you want to tip him off."

I wiped the dripping sweat from my face with bloody fingers. Vito was right, as usual. But fuck if Angelo wasn't right, too. Luca was volatile, and I had always looked the other way. How was a father supposed to find fault with his son?

The rage coursing through my veins was directed at myself as much as Luca. I'd failed him. I'd failed Tony. And once again I'd failed Gina; this shit was going to kill her.

Vito's eyes dimmed, and he joined Carmine and Angelo against the ropes, arms crossed.

I unwound the bloody tape from my knuckles and tossed it in the trash. "I take full responsibility for this mess. Not just Luca, but the other shit with the Irish and the feds."

I'd told them about the conversation with Vinnie during my first round of pummeling the bag. They'd been a part of my crew since I broke with the Valenzanos, and it was time to stop pretending we were anything but what we were—a family in Cosa Nostra. It was all or nothing. Anything in between would get us killed.

"This half-assed shit stops today. Two weeks," I said and pointed at each of them. "You have two weeks to figure out who else is involved." I shifted my gaze between Angelo and Carmine. "I need the two of you to stick around till this is sorted. Ears to the ground. Call in favors but keep it discreet. I want to know what we're up against before I decide what to do about Luca and how we move forward with Vinnie."

"All you had to do was say the word," Carmine said.

I looked between the three men—my capi, my brothers. They each gave me a short nod.

Spent from the bag, I ran a hand through my sweaty hair and turned for the locker room, but a shower and food would only do so much. I needed to feed. I also needed to see Anna. I hungered to see Anna, but there was no way I could control myself around her in this state.

Guilt punched me in the chest thinking of visiting one of my Sources. Anna's voice when she'd asked about feeding and why I didn't bite her... It had sounded so small, so hesitant.

But for me, feeding for pleasure was a bond that would last eternity. I wasn't ready to make that commitment. Especially when she was better off without me. I hated myself for letting things progress this far.

"Vito." I leaned a hand against the entrance to the locker room and glanced over my shoulder. "Get one of the emergency blood bags out of the freezer."

He lifted an eyebrow, and Angelo and Carmine cast suspicious glances at each other.

"Just fucking do it," I snarled, and walked into the showers.

Anna opened her front door, and the tension in my chest eased. She wore black leggings and an oversized Harvard Hockey sweatshirt, so worn the lettering was faded and the cuffs were frayed. Between the messy bun on top of her head and the pair of round glasses that covered half her face, she'd never looked more beautiful.

I lifted the box I carried, wrapped my other arm around her waist, and picked her up.

"You brought Mike's Pastry," she cooed through a giant smile and held my face between her hands. I kissed her gently and walked us into the foyer, kicking the door shut behind me. I set her down, and she clasped her hands behind my neck.

"Ricotta pie." I kissed her nose. "I didn't know you wore glasses."

"I don't. I was reading. My eyes aren't what they used to be."

"Readers?"

"Yup." She dropped her arms and took the box by its strings. "I suppose blood demons don't have to worry about that when they reach their mid-forties." She put the box on the island between the kitchen and her living room.

I quirked the corner of my mouth. It was as close to a smile as I could manage given the day I'd had and the dread pooling in my stomach at the reminder of her humanity and my immortality.

She tilted her head and scanned my face. "You look like you could use a drink."

"That good, huh?"

She stood on her toes and pressed a kiss to my lips. "Handsome as ever. Why don't you have a seat. Relax. I'll pour you a glass of wine."

She hurried off to the kitchen, and I stared after her in awe. The reassuring warmth of her presence. Having someone take care of me that wasn't Gina. Quiet companionship on her couch. It was nice. Complicated and unnerving, but nice.

I hung my coat and suit jacket on the hook near the door, unfastened my cufflinks, and rolled up my shirtsleeves while I glanced around the condo. It had been dark the other night when I'd visited, and we'd gone straight to her bedroom.

The entryway and living room were decorated in muted blues and toasted browns. She had one of those fake fireplaces across from her plush, suede sofa, and it blazed and crackled like it was real. A big area rug covered the hardwood between the couch and the faux fireplace along with a square coffee table. Atop the distressed wood sat a neat arrangement of cream-colored candles, a bowl of fresh-cut flowers, and a coffee table book about the history of Boston. A paperback romance novel sat next to it, and the top of a glittery pink bookmark peeked out from between its pages.

Warm, inviting, and cozy, the space screamed Anna, and it was about a million light years away from the world I'd just left. A world of embezzling nephews, rival gangs, and federal surveillance. In her space, there was peace.

I sat at the end of the couch, and Anna's cat appeared out of nowhere and climbed into my lap. "Hello," I said and petted its gray and white fur. It started purring and kneading its claws into my custom-tailored slacks.

"Sophie!" Anna exclaimed and handed a big glass of red to me over my shoulder.

"It's okay. I think she likes me."

"She likes anyone who pets her. She's an absolute attention whore." Sophie intensified her kneading. "Sorry about your pants."

I waved it off. "I like cats. They like me. Always have. There was a stray who used to come around our apartment when Gina and I were kids."

The wine was more acidic than I preferred but the alcohol had an immediate soothing effect. Especially with the cat on my lap and Anna's warmth at my back. They all conspired to create a sense of comfort and home.

"The wine isn't nearly as good as the ones I've had with you." She rested her hands on my shoulders and started massaging my stiff muscles. "But I like it. Gets the job done."

"It's perfect." I tipped my head back. "This is perfect."

She bent over and kissed my forehead. "I'm glad you came over. I thought you might—" Her hands froze. "Marco?"

"Hm?"

"You have... There's blood on your shirt."

I glanced down to where Anna fingered my collar. "Huh. Don't worry. It's not mine."

As soon as the words left my mouth, I knew I'd fucked up.

She came around the end of the couch and sat facing me, folding her hands in her lap. Knowing Anna, they'd probably started shaking. "Whose is it?" Her question was small and tentative, and it squeezed my heart.

I'd promised myself I wouldn't lie to her, and I planned on

keeping that promise. "Someone's. I don't know. I needed to feed."

Her face fell as if she suspected as much, but hoped I'd come back with a different answer. "Oh."

That "oh" stabbed me through the heart and nearly killed me. She wasn't angry or raging or throwing a fit. She just sat there, her hurt and disappointment wrapped up in a sad little "oh."

I was the biggest fucking asshole on the planet.

"Who—Who is she?"

"It's not important."

"It's important to me."

"I really don't know. I didn't use a Source. It came from a bag."

She lifted her eyes, and they were glassy with unshed tears. My heart broke, the look on her face twisting the knife.

"You didn't have to do that," she said softly. "You could have fed from me. I would have let you."

Goddammit. I ran a hand down my face. The day was already fucked. Might as well finish it off. "No, Anna. No, I couldn't."

Her eyebrows drew together. "I don't understand. I gave you permission."

"I already told you. I don't feed from people I'm fucking."

She blinked and gave her head a quick shake, a flash of anger visible through the hurt in her eyes. "Is that what we're doing? Fucking?"

I winced. "No. I mean, yes, but that came out wrong. I didn't mean it like that."

"How did you mean it?"

What a nightmare. My capacity to deal was already hanging by a thread after watching my tightly controlled world unravel. This conversation was sure to make it snap.

"You're human," I said.

"Last time I checked."

"I'm a blood demon. An immortal blood demon. An immortal blood demon connected to the Mafia."

"And?"

I ground my teeth. "I don't feed for pleasure."

"Why not?"

"Why not? Because it's one or the other for me. Always has been."

Because I'd never been able to get the image of a stranger drinking from Mamma's neck out of my head. Because separating feeding from pleasure was the only way I'd been able to live with the guilt of her sacrifice. Because tearing down that wall meant committing to Anna, and committing Anna to risking her life. For me. I couldn't allow her to make that sacrifice.

"If I start feeding from you, I won't want to stop. I won't want to feed from anyone else, and I can't depend on you for blood. You don't belong in this world."

"What's that supposed to mean?" A sharp edge entered her voice, but there was no stopping this avalanche. It was barreling down the mountain at full speed.

I rested my elbows on my knees, shoved my hands into my hair, and stared at the carpet. "My life is dangerous. The only way I can protect you is to keep my distance, and I've already fucked that up. I was reckless at the gala. I risked your safety parading you around. Put a target on your back. The feds went after you for information even before the gala. They'll be more aggressive now. I seized all the pictures of us, but I can't erase people's memories. People talk, and I have enemies."

I shook my head in my hands. "You don't want a future with me. You don't want to give up your life as a human and bind yourself to a blood demon. You don't want to be a pawn in this game, leverage the feds or the Irish can use to get to me.

You deserve better than that. You deserve safety and security. If I failed you, if I failed to protect you…"

My voice broke saying those words out loud, and I didn't have the strength to finish the thought. I'd failed so many people. If I failed her, it would kill me.

"You're too precious to be a part of my world, Anna. I can't allow it."

I turned my head in my hands, finally able to face her.

All traces of sadness were gone. Red splotches of fury crept up her neck and her eyes flashed with anger. "You won't *allow* it?"

Her heated tone snapped the final thread of my control. "No," I clapped back. "I won't allow it!"

She stood and shoved a finger in my face. "Fuck you, Marco DeVita!" Her face turned a fiery red. "You've got a lot of goddamned nerve." She stalked to the other side of the room, fuming.

Before I could explain all the reasons she was better off without me, she threw her hands in the air and laughed hysterically at the ceiling. "What is it with people telling me what I can and can't handle?"

She planted her hands on her hips and leveled me with a heated stare, tears spilling down her flushed cheeks. "Guess what, Marco? You do not get to make my decisions for me. In one day"—she held up a finger and started counting—"I found out supernatural beings existed, the man I'm falling in love with is one of them, and he's in the Mafia! In one day! Barring the fainting spell, I think I handled it pretty fucking well." Her chest heaved with the ferocity of her temper.

I got off the couch and gave her a slice of my own. "This isn't a game," I roared. "I'm looking out for you. Be reasonable. You could get hurt."

"Don't tell me to be reasonable! Don't tell me what to do or how to feel or what I want! Don't tell me what I can't handle!" Her voice went shrill, shaking through each declaration. Hot, angry tears streamed down her face.

God, I'd fucked up. Pressed the worst possible button. And I was too exhausted from the ring and Luca and the shitstorm that was my life to figure out what to do about it. I opened my arms, needing to hold her, but she held up her hands.

"Why did you come here tonight?" Her voice went quiet. "If you never saw a future for us, why did you come here?"

"I wanted to see you. I need you."

She nodded. "But not enough to bite me." She canted her head. "Right?"

"That's not fair," I ground out through gritted teeth.

She hiccupped on a sob and swiped the tears from beneath her glasses. "You don't get to come in here and dictate the terms of our relationship. There are two people standing here, and we both get a say." She sucked in a deep breath, closed her eyes, and let out a shaky exhale. "Well, here's mine.

"It's taken me years to figure this out, but now that I have, there's no going back. I'm done compromising what I want. I'm done short-changing myself because I've bought into someone else's rhetoric. I know what I want, Marco. I want this." She waved a finger between us. "I want you. And you might not feel the clock ticking, because you're immortal, but I sure as hell do. My life's too short to waste a single precious moment on something that's not going anywhere.

"You need to decide what you want. Do you want to continue playing the martyr? The noble hero who sacrifices his own happiness for the sake of others? Or are you ready to start living your life for a reason other than making up for past wrongs?"

My jaw clenched and so did my fists, my temper rising to a vicious peak. I needed to get out of there before I exploded and made the entire fucked-up situation even worse. I grabbed my suit jacket and coat off the hook. "This conversation isn't over," I growled and put on my coat.

She wrapped her arms around her middle, and her face fell, the hurt and disappointment returning to drive the knife deeper into my heart. "Isn't it? What's left to say? You want this to end. I don't."

I pressed my lips together and shook my head. "I don't want this to end. Not at all." I opened the door. "But what I want will change your life and put you in danger. And more than anything, I want to protect you."

Tears fell and her lip quivered, and I couldn't handle her pain on top of my broken heart. I walked out the door before I lost my resolve and put the life of one more person I loved in jeopardy.

Chapter Twenty-Six

Anna

My Saturday night was going about as well as expected given Marco's latest and most infuriating foray into tyranny. It took nearly an hour for me to finish my slice of reheated pizza and Caesar salad between sporadic bouts of crying, the latest spell triggered by the Mike's Pastry box still sitting on the counter. That one dragged every last tear out of me. Deflated, I poured myself a glass of Chianti and sank into the corner of my couch to watch my fake fireplace dance to Dean Martin and stroke Sophie's long, soft fur.

More than sadness or even frustration, I was disappointed, in the situation and in Marco. As much as I wanted to diminish my feelings and relegate them to lust, I couldn't lie to myself. I'd finished lying to myself when I'd gone on sabbatical, and I wasn't going to start up again now. We were good together. We had the chemistry and the connection to build a solid, fulfilling future, and he'd ruined it with his over-protective, caveman bullshit.

My phone vibrated on the coffee table, a short, intense earthquake that made me jump and spill wine on my sweatshirt. "Shit!" The screen lit up, and I craned my neck to see the number, hoping it was Marco and hoping it wasn't.

I sighed, heavy with disappointment and relief. I set my wine down and picked up the phone. "Hey, Siobhán. What's up?"

"What are you doing?"

"Not thinking about Marco."

She snorted. "Right. And I'm not thinking about Luca."

I chewed the side of my fingernail. Siobhán didn't have a clue about the whole Luca debacle yet. What a mess.

"Wanna go out? Not think about them together?"

"Sure. I could use a girl's night. Where to?"

"Duh. Vesuvio."

I groaned.

"Don't worry. Marco won't be there. He's at Terme hosting a dinner for some big muckety-mucks. Come *ooon*." The long whine of her *on* made me laugh. "I don't want to pay for drinks."

"All right, all right. Vesuvio it is. Gimme like thirty minutes to get dressed." I fingered the messy pile of hair on top of my head. "And do something with this mop."

"Yes! Thank you! I'll grab a cab and pick you up."

"See you soon."

I curled my hair and brushed mascara onto my eyelashes, but it failed to hide the puffiness from crying. I decided on the low-cut red sweater that always drew Marco's eye, a new pair of faux leather leggings, and heels high enough even Siobhán would raise her eyebrows, determined to feel fabulous regardless of how miserable I felt. Thirty minutes later, I walked out of my condo on a mission to have fun and stop brooding over unapproachable blood demons with a foot in the Italian Mafia.

I scooted into the back seat of the cab, and Siobhán, effortlessly stunning as usual, scanned my ensemble. "Damn, girl! Let's do this!"

The line to enter Vesuvio extended the entire city block. We climbed out of the cab, and Siobhán led us straight to the entrance, bypassing the velvet-roped line of patrons.

"Matteo," she purred and flashed her starlet smile at the bouncer, one of Marco's immovable centurions complete with sunglasses.

He nodded. "Ms. Connelly." He addressed me with an equally formal nod. "Ms. Barone."

I shouldn't have been surprised he knew my name. In fact, knowing Marco, every bouncer, chauffeur, and doorman on the DEI payroll probably knew my name, blood type, and shoe size.

He held the door open, and we crossed the threshold into a wall of bodies and heat.

A DJ spun house music from turntables in front of the empty fireplace. Men and women in cocktail attire sipped drinks as expensive as their clothes and gyrated to the hypnotic beat under a dizzying array of dancing lights.

Eric the bartender spotted us above the crowd in front of the bar. Siobhán flashed a ruby-red-manicured peace sign, and he lifted his chin and winked.

"Can't beat the service," I shouted over the music.

She smiled mischievously. "Now you know why I come here."

Eric raised two martini glasses filled with a hazy, clear liquid and garnished with fat olives. I licked my lips. Siobhán wedged her way through the crowd and reached between heads to grab our drinks. She handed one to me, and I almost groaned with my first sip of dirty martini. Salty, smooth, top-shelf perfection.

She led us to the back of the bar near the roped-off winding staircase. A bar top protruded from the wall in the tucked away corner where the speakers faced away from us and gave us a reprieve from the heavy bass.

Siobhán swigged her martini and set it on the counter. "Talk to me. What's going on with Marco? That's an all-men-can-fuck-right-off outfit if I've ever seen one."

I rolled my eyes. "I wanted to look fabulous, that's all."

"Mission accomplished," she said dryly.

"As for Marco? He's just being Marco, I suppose."

"Lemme guess—over-protective, over-bearing, and unreasonable?" She raised an eyebrow and bent her mouth in a look that said, "I told you so."

I avoided her eyes and sipped my drink.

"Well, the damage is done. But..." She sighed. "It's cause he's into you, Anna. Really into you. And..." She looked askance, as if weighing her words.

"And what?"

"And men like Marco don't do dating lightly."

I snorted. "Understatement. I don't think he does anything lightly."

She tipped her martini glass toward me before taking another sip.

"He doesn't..." Siobhán knew about Marco and Luca's Mafia connections. That much was clear. But the existence of blood demons? Doubtful. "He doesn't want to pursue a long-term relationship."

"Did he say that?"

"Not in so many words, but he thinks his life is too dangerous for me."

"Uh..." Siobhán looked around as if she was missing something. "Isn't that up to you to decide?"

I threw my arms in the air. "Thank you!"

"Made men. They're all the same. They think because they run their little empires, they get to run our lives, too." She scoffed and slammed back half of her drink.

"How do you know so much about this?"

"Let's just say I wasn't always the refined businesswoman you see standing in front of you. Luca may be an asshole, but he's right about one thing. There's a lot of truth and history wrapped up in this accent." She let her guard down with that last statement, and the harsh vowels of Southie emerged from beneath their polished, vaguely British veneer.

She hid it well, but Siobhán had the hard accent that came along with a hard upbringing in a hard neighborhood. Knowing the tension between the Italians and the Irish, I wondered how much that had played a role in Luca and Siobhán's volatile relationship.

"Was that the problem with you and Luca?"

"Him being over-protective and wanting to run my life?" She scoffed. "No. It was never like that with us," she said, and a sad smile took over her face.

She stared into her drink for a moment before pulling one of the olives off the toothpick with her teeth, careful not to mar her bright red lipstick.

"I thought he was someone different. He thought the same about me. I flew off the handle. So did he." She shrugged. "And now we have a completely dysfunctional relationship." She lifted her glass in a mock toast before taking a hefty swig.

I took another drink myself, and the vodka burned as it trailed down my throat and settled in my stomach. The martini was going down way too fast and way too easy.

"It's okay you have a thing for him, Siobhán."

"No, it's not. Who has a thing for players?" She took the toothpick and remaining olive out of her drink and pointed it at me. "Players who don't even like you. Players who actively dislike everything about you." She ate the olive and drained her drink. "That's messed up."

"Consider you're talking to someone pining after a man

who told her they had no future together." God, that hurt to say out loud. Siobhán winced, and I finished my martini. "You know what's the worst part about the whole thing?"

"What?"

I leaned in conspiratorially. "I'll have to go back to having boring sex."

"Oh God." She grabbed my arm, and a horrified expression crossed her face. "Was that what you were doing before Marco? Having boring sex?"

"Terrible! I can't go back to that any more than I can go back to teaching. I can't." I shook my head. "I won't!"

Her eyes widened. "This requires more alcohol."

The second martini went down as easily as the first, and responsible middle-aged adults that we were, we slowed our roll with the third. I had enough trouble standing in high heels, I didn't need any added challenges.

We danced in our corner to the music, free of troublesome men and inhibitions, and in a blur of vodka, dancing, and laughter, 12:30 a.m. and last call came out of nowhere.

"You're not done, are you?" Siobhán asked, eyes sleepy with alcohol. "Do you want to go home?"

"Nope." I glared at my martini glass, its emptiness a personal affront.

She cocked her head toward the winding staircase, which now had a bouncer standing in front of its velvet rope.

"Really? We can go up there?"

"Hell yeah, we can go up there."

"Awesome."

Siobhán grabbed my empty, put both glasses on the bar, and with an off-kilter twirl, pointed at the bouncer. "Upstairs!"

I laughed and half-danced, half-stumbled up the winding steps.

Cigar smoke stung my nostrils. The vents were working

overtime to pull the thick smoke into the chimneys, but in the presence of a full gambling house, it was a losing battle.

All six card tables worked in earnest, hundred-dollar-bills stacked in piles next to each seat. Waitresses hurried between tables and booths, and a topless dancer spun suggestively on the pole in front of a few men chatting and placing bets with one of the servers. Marco's men dotted the periphery, all muscles and sunglasses and intimidation.

Siobhán and I grabbed the last two seats at the bar and ordered another round of drinks. The smell of cigar smoke and leather combined with the dim lighting and soft music reminded me of Marco and the first time Siobhán and I had gone to Vesuvio for drinks. I'd already been smitten. I was still smitten.

No more lying to yourself, Anna.

All right. I'd fallen in love with Marco sometime between our first dinner and the night he showed me off in front of Boston's high-society, pride and adoration beaming through his million-dollar smile. I couldn't pinpoint the exact moment, but I was sure it had happened, because every time I thought of a future without him, the space he occupied in my heart ached with emptiness.

I sighed and spun on my stool to face the card tables. Whatever. I didn't need one more person telling me what I should and shouldn't want from my future. That part of my life was over. Marco needed to come correct. And if he refused? Good riddance. I wasn't about to try and make something work with a man who thought he could make my decisions.

A loud thump drew my attention to the back door. Two muffled thuds. The guards closest to the back straightened and signaled to the guards at the front.

The door swung open and slammed into the opposite wall with a bang. It startled me so severely I slid off my chair and landed on my knees. I scrambled, pushing the hair out of my face, and gripped the barstool.

Men dressed in black and wearing ski masks charged through the door pointing handguns and shouting.

Some of the poker players shot up from their seats and lifted their hands in the air. Others sat back, mouths agape, palms flat on the playing surface. The dealers spun around, eyes darting to where Marco's men froze in place. The dancer pressed herself against the wall and covered her breasts with shaking arms.

Siobhán stood in front of me. The pale fingers of her left hand quivered even as her right hand reached behind her back, took the cell phone out of her jeans pocket, and handed it to me. My hand shook so violently I almost dropped it, but I managed to hold on, hiding it beneath my palm against the top of the barstool.

"Don't fuckin' move and don't even think about going for your weapon or I'll put a bullet through your fuckin' head." The masked man's voice was thick with the Boston accent.

I couldn't see much from my crouched position behind the barstool, but on my right, two men shoved stacks of bills into duffel bags.

Behind her back and out of anyone's sight, Siobhán's fingers formed a two, a three, a one, a five. I activated the screen and typed in the numbers.

Glass shattered behind the bar to my left, and I instinctively covered my head. The harsh clash of glass on glass continued, but I lifted my eyes to Siobhán's glowing home screen.

"This is a message from Ciarán Shaughnessy." The same accented voice boomed above the smashing and crashing of bottles. "There's no gaming in this city the Irish don't run, and we're here to make sure the DeVitas get the message. Capisce?" He spat the Italian word like it tasted foul, and the rattle and hiss of spray paint replaced the sounds of breaking glass.

The first two attempts to dial Marco's number failed. I rose from my crouch needing to brace myself on the stool so I could get it right. His name appeared after my third attempt, and the call tried to connect.

"I thought I said, don't move."

The man backhanded me before I even saw him approach. I reeled from the shock of the blow, and the phone clattered to the ground. I'd never been hit before in my life, and the impact combined with three dirty martinis made my knees buckle and vision blur. His hand clamped around my biceps to keep me upright, and he squeezed so hard I was sure it would bruise. Tears stung my eyes, and the metallic taste of blood coated my tongue.

He tugged on my arm until my body was pressed into his and lifted his gun between us, turning it over like I hadn't seen it. He leered at me, but I couldn't peel my eyes away from the glint of metal under the broken bar lights.

"Listen," he shouted, loud enough for everyone to hear, and I flinched. "When I fuckin' talk, *listen*, or she'll get more than a hand across her face."

The room came back into focus around the gun, a fucked-up backdrop to the weapon my captor used like a classroom talking aid. The men who'd been cleaning off the card tables emptied the register while another finished spraying "Shaughnessy" in neon yellow paint across the wall opposite the bar. Three masked men held Marco's security at bay, pointing pieces at their heads. Siobhán stared at me in horror, pupils dilated, but her lips pressed into a thin line as if an inner turmoil and untapped rage boiled just below the surface waiting for the right moment to explode.

A flash of movement caught the corner of my eye and a loud *crack* ripped through the space—a gun discharged.

Chaos.

One of Marco's men moved so quickly, he couldn't have been human. He shoved a gunman's arm up and another *crack* rang out through the bar, the gun firing into the ceiling. A waitress screamed even as Marco's man snapped the gunman's neck.

Siobhán spun around and kicked the man holding me between his legs so hard he dropped his gun with a pained grunt and doubled over clutching his crotch.

The rest of Marco's men moved like lightning, their unnatural speed and strength finally cluing me in to the reason they all wore sunglasses—blood demons.

Matteo's voice hollered at us from the top of the stairs. "Siobhán! Anna!"

We spun around to the front of the room.

"Run!" He bent another attacker's arm at an unnatural angle. The man cried out and released the gun from his limp, broken arm. "Get out of here! Both of you! Run!"

Siobhán and I didn't need another reminder. We high-tailed it to the twisting stairwell, suddenly sober despite all the vodka, and hurried down the stairs. We skidded to a halt once we reached the front, our escape thwarted by the locked door.

"Shit!" I cried.

Heavy steps landed behind us on the metal stairs. "Come here, you fuckin' bitch!"

"I don't think he liked you kicking him!"

I fumbled with the deadbolt, finally twisting it enough times to unlock the door. I pushed it open, and we spilled out of Vesuvio into the cold, dark night. I glanced over my shoulder, and my attacker stalked toward us, mask forgotten, cold fury in his blue eyes.

Siobhán bolted across the street. "Anna!"

I couldn't pull my attention away from the man coming for us. I stared at him, frozen.

"Anna!" she called again, and the shrill in her voice snapped me out of my shock and back into the reality of survival.

I darted into the street, eyes still locked on the man stalking toward us.

The squeal of tires and a car's horn blared. My head snapped around. I stopped for no more than a heartbeat before a flash of white metal slammed into my hips and threw me into the air.

"Anna!" Marco's voice pierced the night with terror and rage. It carried over the sounds of my body tumbling across the hood of the car and was the last thing I heard before my back and head hit the pavement and my world fell into darkness.

Chapter Twenty-Seven

Marco

My phone buzzed. I pulled it out and glanced at the screen. Matteo. "Yes."

"Ms. Connelly and Ms. Barone are here."

Tightness pinched my chest. I'd fucked things up Thursday night but hadn't had the balls to do anything about it. Now she was at my club?

"And?"

"They seem—" He coughed and cleared his throat. "They seem determined to put a dent in your vodka supply. Thought you'd wanna know."

Anna drunk at Vesuvio. My teeth clenched. I knew what happened there; it was my club, for Chrissake. Matteo wouldn't have called unless those two were really tying one on. Which they probably were. *Girls' night*, or some such nonsense, caused by yours truly.

"Understood." I glanced sidelong at Vito in the driver's seat. We'd just left Terme and were heading west out of the city to a high-stakes poker game. "I'll be there shortly. Keep an eye."

"Yes, sir."

Vito took the next exit. "Where?" he asked.

"Vesuvio. Siobhán and Anna are upstairs."

"Christ."

"We'll only miss a hand or two."

He gave me withering side-eye.

I shrugged. "I want to see them home safely."

What a crock of shit. I wanted to see her, period. I should have stayed away. I knew that. But for the first time in my life my willpower wasn't enough. Somewhere along the line, sometime after I'd met Anna, my need for comfort and partnership had overtaken my need to control and protect. Her accusation had cut, but she wasn't wrong. And being with her had become as necessary as oxygen. As necessary as blood.

Vito turned the car around and headed east. Streetlights glinted on the drive to the North End amplified by the humidity in the crisp midnight air. My phone vibrated again in my pocket.

I took the phone out and frowned at the screen. "Siobhán?" Silence. "Siobhán? Are you there?" Nothing. My stomach turned over.

Muffled grunts. Shuffling. The unmistakable *crack* of a gun.

My heart leapt into my throat. "Something's wrong. Move!"

Vito slammed on the gas, and the car lurched forward. He blew through a stoplight and took the next corner on a dime. I pressed the phone to my ear, trying to make sense of the muted sounds coming across the open line over the harried rush of blood in my ears.

Another gunshot.

"Cazzo!"

We were almost there, but what if it was too late? Panic tightened my insides.

"Come on!"

More indistinct shouting.

The Range Rover screeched to a halt in front of Vesuvio. I threw open the door.

Siobhán darted across the street. "Anna!" she cried.

Anna stood on the far side of the street staring back into the club.

Siobhán shrieked her name again.

Anna spun around, her face contorted in shock and confusion. She staggered forward, unsteady, but swiveled her head to watch the door as she ran into the street, completely oblivious to the oncoming car.

A horn blared. It combined with the car's screeching tires to announce my worst nightmare.

The driver tried to veer from where Anna stood frozen in the middle of the street, arms lifted as if she could block the oncoming impact.

"Anna!" I shouted into the night.

The corner of the bumper slammed into her middle and tossed her into the air. Her tiny body tumbled over the hood and fell limp onto the street. The back of her head bounced off the frozen pavement, and she went completely still, arms and legs strewn at unnatural angles.

"Call an ambulance!" Panic and helplessness fueled each movement. I ran to her, reached for her, desperate to gather her into my arms and protect her.

I pulled back. What if her neck was broken? My stomach heaved. I pressed my fingers to her wrist instead. She had a pulse, and her chest rose and fell with her breath.

"Grazie a Dio," I mumbled. "Anna." My voice shook as badly as my hands. "Anna. Please."

Blood trickled from her mouth. A bruise purpled the side of her face. I frowned. That wasn't from the car.

I looked up, trying to piece together what the hell had happened. A man stood on the sidewalk outside Vesuvio. He was dressed in all black, a gun held loosely in his hand. He stared at me, crouched over my Anna's broken body.

Rage launched me off the pavement and across the street, and its heat blazed through my eyes. The man paled and ran back through the entrance.

The club was dark except for the neon exit sign at the rear. It backlit another man standing in the middle of the room. He lifted his gun and shot me twice in the stomach.

The bullets tore through my abdomen and out my back, a searing path that ripped a howl from my lungs. I stumbled, and my hands flew to the bloody wounds.

I'd been shot before; nothing prepares you for the impact or the burning pain. But I caught my breath after only a heartbeat, my blood and adrenaline fueling my body's accelerated healing. It surged with the unnatural strength released by the rage coursing through my veins.

Hot, manic fury took control, and my fangs descended in an unholy promise. "You're a fucking dead man!"

I sprang across the distance like a feral animal and knocked the gun from his grip. I held his head with my right hand and drove my left fist into the side of his stunned face. It crushed his skull at his temple, and he fell to the floor, dead.

The man I'd followed into the club looked on in horror. I fixed my attention on him, and he lunged for the emergency exit at the back. I reached him in no more than a heartbeat, grabbed his arm, and spun him around to face me. I gripped him by the throat and clamped down on his windpipe. His fingers tore at mine, clawing for air, and I squeezed.

"Who sent you?" I snarled.

His eyes went wide, bulging out of his face.

I pulled back. I needed to find out who'd hurt my Anna. "Who! Sent! You!" I bared my fangs.

Tears slid down his cheeks as he clawed at my hand. The

sharp smell of urine pierced my nostrils. He opened his mouth and tapped my hand. I loosened my grip.

"Sh—Shaughnessy," he croaked.

Rage spilled over, and I howled a barbaric scream containing all the anger that had been building since I'd found out about Luca and my absolute terror at the thought of losing Anna.

"Did you touch her?" I bellowed, and my unrelenting grip turned deadly.

He opened his mouth but couldn't answer; I'd crushed his windpipe. It didn't matter; I saw the answer in his eyes.

My fingers dug into his neck, burrowing into flesh till I clenched my fist around its insides. Blood oozed between my fingers and streamed down my forearm. With a jerk, I ripped out his throat. His body crumpled to the floor. My breath came hot and fast, and I tossed the man's throat onto the bloody mess of his corpse.

"Marco."

Blood dripped from my fingers, but it was nothing compared to the river of blood that would flow in the wake of my vengeance against the Shaughnessys.

"Marco!"

"What?" I snapped and spun around.

Vito stood in the doorway, but I didn't wait for an answer. I pushed past him and ran to where my Anna lay in the street.

Siobhán hovered over her still form, softly weeping against the back of her hand. I nudged her out of the way.

"Vito!"

He crouched on her other side and lowered his voice. "One alive. You killed the two that got away. The rest are dead."

"I want answers," I growled.

Anna's breath was shallower than when I'd left her. I

grabbed her wrist. Her heartbeat was fading. Where was the fucking ambulance? I started to panic; I couldn't lose her.

Siobhán watched us, tears streaking through her makeup. The driver of the car that hit Anna paced nervously behind her, his hands tugging at his hair.

I shot Vito a look. "Get them out of here. And get me a clean shirt."

He nodded, and I gave him a moment to clear the area before I turned my attention back to Anna.

I had to save her. I couldn't let her die.

Faced with a life without Anna, faced with losing the only woman I'd ever loved, I realized how stupid I was to deny us a future. She'd wanted me to bite her. She'd been furious with me for denying her the right to choose, because she'd already chosen us. She'd accepted this life, accepted me, and that was all the permission I needed.

I tapped her lightly on the cheek, careful not to jostle her, but I had to coax her back to consciousness. I shouted her name and struck her cheek harder. I needed her awake for this dammit!

She groaned.

"Grazie a Dio."

I shrugged out of my suit jacket, furiously wiping the gunman's blood from my hands. I tore off the remains of my bloodied shirt, and my fangs descended for the second time that night.

I pierced the skin at my wrist, deeply to make sure the blood would flow. It ran down my arm. I pried her lips and teeth open, held my wrist over her mouth, and my blood streamed onto her tongue.

"Come on, amore mio. Swallow for me."

She grunted and groaned, but instinct prevailed, and she swallowed before she choked. Once. Twice. Her head jerked back and forth, face contorting, and she slammed her mouth shut.

The wail of an ambulance sounded in the distance.

I squeezed her cheeks, forcing her mouth open. "One more, Anna. One more mouthful, amore."

Blood drained out of my wrist into her mouth. When it was full, I held her lips shut, forcing her to swallow instead of cough. Her body lurched like she was going to throw up. I smoothed the hair off her forehead and held her in place. "Ti prego, amore mio. Ti prego."

Finally, her body relaxed, and she swallowed.

The wail of the siren grew louder.

Anna's body slackened, and her head rolled to the side. Unconscious again, but at least with three mouthfuls of my blood inside her. "God, I hope it's enough."

Vito shoved a fresh shirt in front of my face. I lost the undershirt full of bullet holes and blood and pulled the long-sleeved polo over my head just in time.

The medics arrived in a flurry and pushed me out of the way. I stepped back and shoved a hand into my hair. A drop of blood hit my face. I wiped it from my cheek and licked my wrist to staunch the bleeding. I stood helpless while the medics took Anna's vitals.

Thin fingers landed on my arm. I didn't need to turn to know it was Siobhán. I scented her perfume and felt the worry in her shaking touch.

"Marco." Her voice was small, barely above a whisper. "She's going to be okay. She's so strong."

They strapped a brace around her neck and placed an oxygen mask over her face, and my chest constricted, making it hard to breathe. They transferred her onto the spinal board, and I ground my teeth to prevent myself from shouting at them to be careful.

"Who are you trying to convince, Siobhán?"

She sniffled.

I turned to her, unable to watch the paramedics lift Anna onto the stretcher.

Siobhán's face was wet with tears, her black eye makeup smeared in their wake. Her pale blue eyes were red and puffy, but they bored into mine with all the determination of one of my fiercest men. "It wasn't the Shaughnessys." Her voice dropped an octave, and there was steel in her accented words, so hard and so final, I didn't dare question them.

I searched her face for the source of her conviction.

"They'd never come this far north. And never into your territory. Just like you and Vinnie would never set foot in Southie. It's not done." She'd dropped the affected accent I knew she used, and her harsh South Boston pronunciation made the words land with unquestionable impact.

My mouth snapped shut, and I narrowed my eyes.

She smiled sheepishly like a child caught with her hand in the cookie jar and brushed an errant hair off her face. She edged closer and lowered her voice. "Before I tell you this, know that my loyalty lies with you." She stared up at me, eyes wide and waiting for acknowledgement. I nodded. "My mother's name was Shaughnessy, but I never wanted that life."

I grabbed her arm, hauled her forward, and shoved my face into hers. "What the fuck, Siobhán?" I growled, teeth bared, control hanging by a thread.

She opened her mouth to say something, but the clatter of the stretcher screamed for my attention. I looked over my shoulder. The medics hoisted Anna into the back of the ambulance.

I faced Siobhán, furious, but I didn't have time to deal with her shit. "We'll talk about this later," I snarled, a promise I intended to keep.

She nodded, and tears spilled down her pale cheeks.

"I'm with her," I called and jogged to the back of the

ambulance, a don't-fuck-with-me look plastered on my face. The medic lifted both hands in surrender. I climbed in after him, sat on the bench, and took Anna's limp hand in mine.

Sirens blared and rounded the corner. Two black-and-whites.

"Vito!" He looked up. "Deal with it." He nodded, and the driver closed the ambulance doors. Seconds later, we sped off to Mass General.

THE SURGEON SAT NEXT to me in the waiting room at seven in the morning.

"I'm not going to sugar coat it," he said. "There was a lot of damage. She was bleeding internally. Her spleen ruptured. Five broken ribs and a punctured lung. On top of that, she has a concussion, probably from hitting the ground. She made it through surgery—she's tough, I'll give her that—but the next twenty-four hours are critical."

His clinical explanation made me want to strangle him. I focused on caging my anger, knowing he'd probably saved her life.

"Can I see her?"

"Yes. She's sedated, and you're only allowed fifteen minutes in the ICU, but you can see her."

"Where is she?"

"Down the hall." He turned and pointed. "Room two fifty-one."

Without another word, I left him for Anna's room. The heart monitor beeped and blinked, the glowing display of signals and numbers bright against the room's low light. She looked so fragile lying there, tubes coming out of her nose, the side of her face black and purple with bruising, IVs taped to each arm leading back to bags of fluids and sedatives. I sank into the chair next to her bed and rested my elbows on my knees, my chin in my hands.

How the fuck had I let this happen? My carefully controlled world was crumbling around me. Luca stealing from his own family. The Source racket at risk from the feds. The Irish starting a turf war. And now this...

I pressed the heels of my hands into my eyes. I'd wanted to shelter her, keep her light away from my darkness. Instead, she'd been caught in its relentless undertow.

You can't save everyone, Marco. No matter how hard you try.

And the Lord knew I'd tried. I'd done everything I could to keep Anna safe—had her tailed, forced her to use a driver, even told her we couldn't have a future—and it still wasn't enough.

I'd failed her. Just like I'd failed Tony and Gina. Like I'd failed Luca. Like I'd failed myself.

I sat back in the chair and closed my eyes. Gina was right. The tight rein I held over my empire was a charade, a way to convince myself I had control when in reality, I had none. All I had to do was open my eyes to see the evidence of my hubris lying before me, unconscious, bruised, and broken.

"Mr. DeVita," a nurse said from the door. "Your time is up."

I stood, humbled, hurting, and hoping I'd get another chance. I brushed Anna's hair off her forehead and placed a kiss there. She was the love of my immortal life, and I'd never forgive myself for pushing her away.

The fluorescent lights outside the ICU had my eyes straining to adjust, and a dull headache formed behind them, exhaustion, worry, and the fallout from my prior rage all needling my skull. I needed to feed. I'd drained myself at Vesuvio, and my hunger for blood pressed down atop every other burden like a dead weight.

I didn't want to leave her, but there was nothing to do but wait. I should call Vito for a bag of blood. I should call Jeff, let him know what happened. He could call her parents.

The waiting room had one of those espresso vending machines that had popped up in Europe a decade ago and finally made its way to the States. I punched in my order for a double espresso and leaned my forehead against the cool glass while the machine ground and whirred my liquid energy into reality.

"Marco?"

I sighed, long and slow. "Go home, Siobhán. This is not the time." My voice was raspy and exasperated.

"I need to know how Anna is doing, how you're doing."

The machine stopped gurgling. I raised my head and lifted the plastic guard to retrieve my coffee.

Siobhán had changed into track pants, sneakers, and an oversized sweatshirt. Her hair was tied back in a short ponytail, and without makeup, her wrinkles were more pronounced, the smattering of freckles across her nose visible. Her complexion was paler than usual, her face drawn and worn.

I brought the paper cup to my lips. The coffee scalded my tongue, and I welcomed its bitter burn. "She's out of surgery. Stable in the ICU."

"Thank God." Her shoulders relaxed, but the rest of her vibrated with tension. A tear slid down her face, and she wiped it away. Her bottom lip trembled, and she hugged her arms around her waist like she was trying to comfort herself.

She was in bad shape, but I'd had enough of betrayal. Siobhán was a member of the family who'd hurt Anna, an inconvenient truth she'd managed to hide from me for years. I ground my teeth, my exhaustion the only thing caging my temper.

"I thought I'd gotten away from this shit. I thought I'd put it behind me." She trembled and hiccupped a sob. "But it follows me wherever I go." Her thin frame shook, and she devolved into tears.

Goddammit.

A couple and an older man were the only other people in the waiting room, and they stared at us with concern and suspicion. There was a door halfway open across the hall. I placed a hand on her shoulder and pressed her forward.

The room was empty. I shoved her inside and closed the door. She leaned against the edge of the bed, wiped her nose with the back of her sleeve, and looked at me, sad, glassy eyes filled with remorse.

"My mother was Paddy Shaughnessy's youngest sister. Ciarán is my first cousin." Her eyes held mine without hesitation.

"Are you fucking kidding me?" I straightened from where I'd been leaning against the door and stepped forward. "The general manager of my flagship property is a first cousin to the boss of the Irish mob?" My jaw tightened under the strain of controlling my rage. "Are you *fucking kidding me*, Siobhán?"

"No. I—I meant to tell you, but—"

"But what? You forgot?" My voice dripped with bitter sarcasm, and I took another step forward. "I brought you into my family. I trusted you with my business. Seems like something you should have shared before now, don't you think?"

"No," she said, firm and clipped. "It's not. I want nothing to do with being a Shaughnessy. I spent my childhood in that shit, and I never want to live like that again. I moved to Ireland to get away from them. Took voice lessons. Did everything I could to distance myself from this shit exactly." Her voice rose through her rant, her pale face splotchy with emotion and wet with tears.

She reached for my hand, but I snatched it away, unable to reconcile how much she'd kept from me with how much I'd trusted her.

"Please," she said, her bottom lip trembling. "Please, Marco, you have to believe me. I didn't know who you were when I started working for you, and by the time I figured it out…" She tried for my hand again, and I was too tired and too stunned to care. She wrapped her thin, bony fingers around mine. "It's not like I could wander up to your office—Hey, Marco, you should probably know…" She shook her head and wiped the tears from either side of her face. "It doesn't matter. That part of my life is over."

"You and I both know it's never over for people like us. If you grew up like I did, you know that."

Her eyes locked with mine, and her lips pressed into a tight line. She didn't want to admit it any more than I did, but I was done pretending, and what I'd said was the honest-to-God truth.

"I may not be involved in my family's business, but I know how these things work. What happened last night? That is not how these things work. So…" She grimaced. "I called Ciarán."

"You did *what*?" The words burst out of me, my shock at the entire conversation reaching new levels. I pulled my hand away, but she grabbed it back.

"Please, Marco. Let me explain. I came here to tell you. I wouldn't have called him if I thought it would cause trouble, but I knew he didn't order that raid. And when I told him what happened…" She squeezed my hand tighter, eyes blazing with sincerity. "It wasn't Ciarán. Those men weren't Shaughnessys."

I seethed, nostrils flaring, jaw clenched trying to contain my rage so she wouldn't see me turn.

"We're the same age, Ciarán and I. Our parents raised us as brother and sister. Tried to pass us off as twins." Her face softened. "He would never lie to me." She shook her head. "Not me."

Through the fog of my exhaustion and worry, the survival

instincts I'd honed over decades working for Big Frankie kicked in. She was telling the truth; I could see it in her eyes. But could I trust her? And who would gain from attacking Vesuvio? My brain cycled through countless possibilities.

"Trust me on this, Marco. You can trust me. You took me into your family, and my loyalty has been with you ever since. It wasn't Ciarán, but someone wanted you to think it was."

The chain of events fell into place and told a story I didn't want to believe, but deep in my gut I knew who to blame. The white-hot flame of betrayal sped through my insides like wildfire. It burned away any remaining affection I had for my adopted son, leaving behind nothing but the scorched earth of our past.

A primal scream ripped free of my lungs. I spun away from Siobhán and hurled my coffee against the wall, black remnants splattered across beige paint. My chest heaved trying to control the rage, but I lost the battle. I turned my back to her, panting, devastated, and unable to hide the blazing fury in my eyes.

"Keep this to yourself," I growled over my shoulder, hand poised on the doorknob.

"Marco, I—"

I tilted my head enough to see her face out of the corner of my eye. More tears spilled onto her cheeks.

"I don't want to know what happens next." Her mouth twisted in a strained effort not to cry. "Please. I don't want to know what you do to him. Please don't tell me." Her voice wavered through the earnest plea, and her shoulders shook through silent sobs. She suspected the same man.

I nodded and walked back into the waiting room. It was time to call Vinnie.

Chapter Twenty-Eight

Marco

The door clattered open and a whoosh of late February air wafted across the club followed by the hard fall of Luca's footsteps. My *nephew* appeared, and the toothy smile he'd worn since he was a child punched me in the gut. He looked so much like Tony. It was like losing my best friend all over again.

No. Worse.

Luca was as close to a son as I might ever have, and his betrayal hurt worse than death.

"Marco." Luca shrugged out of his coat.

"Luca." I dug my fingers into the arm of the chair and tried to remain calm.

"You got rid of the keypad." He unbuttoned his suitcoat and sat across from me at the poker table. He reached inside his left breast pocket and retrieved the cigar case he kept there, a habit he'd learned from me. Like father, like son. Loss shrunk the space around my heart.

"Passcodes can be leaked. Better to have a man on either side of a deadbolt. Lesson learned."

He eased back into his chair, lit the cigar, and extended his long legs, crossing them at the ankles.

Enzo stood on a chair, scrubbing the last of the spray paint off the brick.

"Enzo."

He looked over his shoulder, and I nodded toward the door. He tossed the brush and rubber gloves on the floor, grabbed his coat, and walked out.

"You wanted to talk?" How I managed to keep the vitriol out of my voice, I had no idea, but I needed to hear what he had to say without tipping him off. He'd called the meeting before I'd had the chance. Saved me the trouble. Either way, the conversation would have the same ending.

His expression morphed into one filled with concern. I'd known Luca his entire life, knew how easily he masked his true feelings with bullshit, and that was his bullshit face.

"I heard what happened," he said. "Wanted to let you know, I'm ready to move on those Irish fucks. Just say the word."

And there it was. All the confirmation I needed.

I brought my cigar to my lips and let the slow burn temper my anger. I'd known, of course, but that didn't make the validation any easier to stomach.

A quiet calm settled over me, a kind of begrudging acceptance. I couldn't control everything, that much was clear, and it was time to let Luca lead his own life.

My shoulders relaxed, and my voice turned cool and conversational. "Did you know in over fifty years, the Irish have never once—not once—crossed over into the North End? Charlestown, yes. But never the North End." I flipped my cigar to stare at its burning red end. "And the Italians have never set foot in Southie."

Luca leaned back and licked his lips, a nervous tell I'd warned him about for years. He puffed on his cigar.

"There's a line that divides Boston. Invisible, but hard as steel. Strange how Ciarán Shaughnessy decided now would be a good time to cross it."

Luca shifted in his seat but nodded. "They're lawless thugs who want control of our city."

I drew on my cigar. "That's one explanation."

His eyebrows pulled together. "That's the only explanation." His bouncing knee told me he knew otherwise.

"Or..." I canted my head. "Someone wanted me to move against the Irish badly enough to make a very poor decision." The words came out slower and more suggestive than I'd intended, but I was barely holding on to control.

Luca scoffed and looked away, but his knee picked up speed. "You're grasping," he spat the bitter words. "Another excuse not to get involved. Un-fucking-believable."

How I'd been so willfully blind to Luca's lust for revenge was a disgrace. I'd wanted to do right by Tony, but the happy little boy I'd raised with Gina was gone, and the volatile adult who'd taken his place was no longer my responsibility.

"It was the Shaughnessys," he snapped.

I rested my cigar on the lip of the ashtray and folded my hands in my lap. "Ciarán Shaughnessy says otherwise."

He leaned forward as if to protest, but I cut him off.

"Anna was at Vesuvio. Did you know that? So was Siobhán." His face paled, and his lips parted, but I kept going, done with excuses. "Anna was hit by a car when they ran out. She's in the ICU at Mass General." Angry heat traveled up my neck and into my eyes at the thought of Anna's damaged body in that hospital bed. "Siobhán got lucky, but she's a fucking mess."

"Oh my God," he said in a horrified whisper. His throat bobbed, working through labored swallows. "Marco, I—"

"I know about the money."

"Wh—what..." He shook his head and blinked. "What money?"

"I thought maybe Vinnie put you up to it. Wanted you to help him force me into a deal. But after last night..." I picked up my cigar and took a deep pull trying to numb my rising anger. "You thought the money would be enough. You thought if you could put DEI at risk—put our family at risk—you could tip Vinnie off, tell him I'd be open to an arrangement. Isn't that right?"

Luca's jaw twitched under the strain of his clenched teeth.

"Answer the fucking question, Luca."

"I—"

"And when that didn't work?" I cut him off and stood, leaning forward, knuckles pressed into the poker table, unable to cage the fury in my blood. "When that *didn't fucking work?*" I shouted, and Luca scrambled to his feet. "You sent a group of thugs to threaten me and force my hand."

My eyes turned and fangs descended from the intensity of unleashing my pain on its source. I stepped around the table, and Luca's nostrils flared with short, rapid breaths. I gripped the back of his neck and squeezed to hold him in place. I wanted to look him in his red eyes when I laid out the truth of what he'd done. "You attacked a made man. Came in fucking heavy. And now the woman I love is fighting for her life."

Luca pushed back against my hand, his eyes glassy with awareness and regret, the color leeched from the hard lines of his conflicted face. "I was trying to protect us," he mumbled, his unwavering bravado finally shaken. "I was trying to get you to lead our family."

I pulled him closer. "Basta con le stronzate, Luca. You wanted revenge. This has nothing to do with family."

"Doesn't it?" Luca grabbed my forearm and threw my hand off his neck. He stepped back, and his face twisted into an angry sneer. "The noble DeVita family. Walking away from

Cosa Nostra. Adopting the poor, parentless child of a fallen capo, determined to lead him away from his father's despicable life and down the path of righteousness." He pointed a finger in my face. "This has everything to do with family!"

Luca's crimson eyes were filled with so much resentment, I knew I'd lost him.

"The DeVitas are built on as much blood as the Valenzanos and the Morettis. Or have you forgotten? The only difference is we fucking own it! And my father's blood—the Moretti family's blood—is a stain on the DeVitas and the Valenzanos that has never been wiped clean." His words were bitter poison that burned for all the truth they contained. He stepped forward, hands fisted at his sides. "This *is* about family, Marco. And if you, *mio zio*, aren't going to help me make this right, by God, I will do it alone."

I stared at Luca—mio nipote, my son—and shook my head in disbelief. "There are more important things at stake than this vendetta, Luca, and you put them in jeopardy with this stunt. You took an oath. You should have trusted me.

"Your father and I made a promise to each other the day we met. We were brothers, and we'd protect each other like brothers. Gina and I honored that promise by raising you a DeVita." My voice caught on our family name, my throat tightening around words that held all the love I had for my brother and his son. "And your actions—the money, the attack..." I shook my head. "They dishonor that promise. You have dishonored your father's legacy."

I showed him my back. The pain of his betrayal, the anger at his callous regard for the sanctity of our family and Anna's safety was too much to face.

"You made a mistake crossing a made man, and you will pay for that mistake. You want to be a part of this world so badly? Cosa Nostra has rules, and you violated more than one."

"You won't hurt me." His bravado returned, but I recognized the undercurrent of fear in his brash words.

I glanced over my shoulder. "If you were any other man, you'd already be dead."

Weariness grabbed hold of my body, as if all ninety-four years caught up to me in that one moment. I sat down and retrieved my cigar. It had burned an inch while we'd talked, and I tapped the ash from its glowing red end before bringing it to my lips.

Luca stood between me and the exit, between understanding how deeply he'd violated our laws and the righteousness he thought justified his actions.

"You took an oath when you got made in the DeVita family, and you broke that oath. It's well within my rights to kill you. But unlike you, I've never broken an oath in my life. Not to Cosa Nostra, not to the Valenzanos, and not to your father. I'm not going to start now." I released a mouthful of smoke and met his eyes one last time. "You're no longer part of the DeVita family. You're Vinnie's to deal with now, and I've never known Don Valenzano to suffer fools."

Luca stiffened and sweat beaded his forehead. Vinnie was old school, like me, and his tolerance for violating Cosa Nostra law was exactly zero. For all Luca knew, he'd walk out of Vesuvio and straight into a bullet through his head. Just like his father, but without honor.

I bit the end of my cigar. "Now get out of my sight."

Luca retrieved his coat, his motions slow and stiff. He reached the top of the spiral staircase and looked over his shoulder. "I'm sorry about Anna. I had no idea. But I'm not sorry for trying to get you involved or trying to avenge my father. The Shaughnessy's day is coming."

"Not before yours, Luca."

He stared at me a heartbeat longer, then walked out the

back door to where I knew Vinnie's enforcer waited in the alley. I pulled out my phone.

He's all yours.

Vinnie's reply appeared immediately.

I'll do right by Anna. And by Gina.

Grazie.

Gina had begged Vinnie to spare Luca's life, and I'd let her. Vinnie wouldn't kill him; he didn't have to. Luca was a blood demon, and knowing Vinnie, Luca'd wish he was dead by the time Vinnie was through with him. Immortality wasn't always a blessing. Some fates were far worse than death. Luca Moretti would reap what he'd sown.

How is she?

Stable.

Grazie a Dio.

We need a sit down. You and me. After this is over.

Let me know.

I tucked the phone back in my pocket and pushed myself to standing. I rubbed the back of my neck, stretching it, and walked behind the bar. I needed to get back to the hospital, but I needed a drink first, something to numb my nerves.

The silence in Vesuvio was deafening. I turned on the satellite radio. Frank Sinatra's voice floated through the empty interior. I poured a finger of whiskey, shot it back, and poured two more. I leaned against the bar, crossed my ankles, and closed my eyes.

For better or worse, I'd done it my way. Standing there after all those years, I recognized my truth—I'd never really gotten out. I'd admitted as much to Siobhán at the hospital. What I had done was forge my own path through Boston's underworld, one that I could live with. But going forward, I wouldn't live in the space between worlds. I'd embrace my truth.

A made man in Cosa Nostra. The boss—the Don—of the DeVita crime family.

Chapter Twenty-Nine

Anna

The buzz of fluorescent lights and the beep of a heart monitor were background music to Jeff's rhythmic snoring. I'd heard the thunderous rumble enough times in grad school to know it was him.

Light reflected off the glass of a generic flower print hanging on the beige wall in front of me. I stared at it, disoriented until I registered where I was—a hospital room. An IV ran from the inside of my right forearm to a bag of fluids hanging next to a heart monitor showing the steady beat of my pulse.

I turned my head toward the relentless snoring and winced at the ache it caused in my neck and shoulders. Jeff was slouched in a chair, arms crossed, head resting against the wall. His eyes were closed behind his glasses in what looked like an extremely uncomfortable sleep.

"Jeff." His name came out more like a croak than a word. I cleared my throat; it was sore and dry. "Jeff."

He started and sat up, blinking his eyes until they focused. "Anna. You're awake," he said, mystified and relieved. He pulled the chair over to my bedside and took my hand.

"Thank God, you're awake." Tears pooled in his eyes, and I squeezed his hand.

"I'm so thirsty."

He released a nervous chuckle, and tears spilled down his ashen cheeks. "I'll call the nurse." He opened the door, shouted down the hallway, and came right back to my side. "Marco would kill me if I left you. Even for a second." He smiled, his expression filled with so much relief, *I* wanted to comfort *him*.

"Marco was here?"

"Are you kidding? He came in with you in the ambulance. Stayed all night and yesterday. He didn't want to leave until you woke up, but he had some urgent business." Jeff's jaw twitched, and his eyes darted away. "He told me not to leave until he got back. And to call if anything changed."

"What—" I swallowed, desperate for water. "What happened?"

A nurse appeared carrying a Styrofoam cup with a bent straw. "Be careful," she said. "Small sips."

"Thank you." The cool liquid coated my mouth and slid down my throat like ambrosia.

"I'll let the on-shift doctor know you're awake. He'll be in shortly," she said and walked out.

I sipped the water, my head still resting on the pillow, and raised my eyebrows to get Jeff moving with the story.

"You were hit by a car."

I let the straw slip out of my mouth long enough to say, "I remember," and resumed my sipping.

"Marco was there when it happened. He called an ambulance. You were in surgery for five hours, the ICU for twenty-four. Then, they moved you here."

The straw fell out of my mouth. "Jesus."

"I know." He wrapped his hands around mine. "I was so scared, Anna. When Marco called, I..." Tears welled again, and he turned away, swallowing his emotions until they were back under control. "The doctors thought you might not make it, but I know"—he nodded to himself—"I know how strong you are. I knew you'd pull through."

He laughed then, a bit hysterical. "Your vitals were normal by lunchtime today. The doctors said they'd never seen anything like it. Called it unprecedented. A miracle."

Beyond Jeff's smiling face, Marco's imposing frame loomed in the doorway. He leaned against the jamb, arms crossed, his normally stoic features softened with relief and what looked a lot like exhaustion.

"Hi," I said.

Jeff followed my gaze over his shoulder.

"Hi," Marco said, the boom of his voice tempered into a low whisper.

Tears poured down my face.

Jeff stood and bent to kiss my forehead. "I'll let your parents know you're awake. They wanted to come down, but I told them to wait."

"Thank you."

"No problem. I'll call you soon." He squeezed my hand, grabbed his coat off the back of the chair, and made his way to the door.

"Grazie," Marco said and clasped Jeff's forearm. Jeff grabbed his in return and nodded. He looked back at me one last time and left.

"Don't disturb us," Marco barked over his shoulder.

I chuckled, but my amusement at Marco's demand quickly morphed into gentle sobs. He slowly and calmly shut the door behind him, removed his coat and suit jacket, and rolled up his shirtsleeves. He sat on the edge of the bed, took my face in his hands, and kissed the tears streaming down my cheeks.

I held on to his wrist, desperate to feel his skin against

mine, to hold on to him and never let him leave. He kissed my forehead and left his lips to linger there while I finished crying.

He trailed kisses down the side of my face until his head met the pillow, and his warm breath tickled my ear. "La mia bellissima Anna. Mi hai spaventato a morte. Non farlo più."

He kissed my ear and brought his face to hover inches above mine, and through my tears, I saw the unending depth of his love for me revealed through dark eyes.

"I am so sorry, Anna. This is why I didn't want you anywhere near this world. I could have lost you." His voice trembled through his confession.

I pushed my fingers into his silky hair and left them tangled amid the waves. His eyes lidded, and he shivered at my touch. "That was bad luck, Marco. The wrong place at the wrong time."

He winced, opening his eyes, and the set of his jaw hardened. "That's just it. I will always be the wrong place. Around me, you will always be at risk."

"No." I smiled and dragged my nails across his scalp. "No, Marco. You will always be the right place. A future with you is more than worth the risk. An accident like that could have happened anywhere, at any time. But you were there for me." Tears streamed down my face, and I tightened my fingers in his hair.

"Almost too late." He swallowed. "Anna, I..." He placed my arm on the bed, sat back, and swiped a hand down his face. "You looked so broken. Lying there." His lips trembled but from holding back tears or rage I couldn't tell. "Your pulse was weak. It was fading. I should have asked permission, but you were unconscious, and the fucking ambulance was taking so long."

"I don't understand. Permission for what?"

"I gave you my blood." He met my eyes, and his were haunted with shame. "Don't you see? You're safer without me, but I'm too fucking selfish to let you go. I know I said we couldn't have a future together, but I can't let you go." He clasped my hand with his own shaking fingers and kissed it over and over. His eyelashes fluttered closed, and a tear slid down his scruffy, drawn face. "I can't lose you. Please forgive me."

A miracle, Jeff had said. But it wasn't a miracle. It was Marco.

After that big argument and all the protesting, he'd given me his blood. He'd spoken about how intimate that was for a blood demon, how consent was a strict part of their moral code, and the guilt was plain in his plea for forgiveness. His integrity made my heart swell, and in that moment, I loved him impossibly more.

"Marco." He kissed my fingers again. "Marco, look at me." He lifted his eyes and squeezed my hand. "I wanted a future with you, remember? I asked you to bite me. I would have taken your blood eventually. You had my consent all along. You saved me, Marco." My quiet words filled the room with all the love and gratitude I felt for the man who'd been my salvation in more ways than one. I ran the back of my fingers along his cheekbone. "You saved my life."

He rested his head on the pillow next to mine and laid his arm across my waist. He kissed my cheek and nuzzled my neck. "No, amore mio," he whispered into my ear. "You saved mine."

Chapter Thirty

Anna

Twilight's shadowy fingers had spread across the Commons by the time Marco's key wiggled in the lock. I'd watched the encroaching darkness envelope the white blanket of midwinter snow. Lights flickered to life. Cars crawled down traffic-filled streets. And above it, I sat on the sofa inside the peaceful sanctuary of Marco's penthouse with Sophie purring in my lap.

My body ached. It hurt to breathe. But more than anything, I was emotionally raw. I'd had nightmares since I'd regained consciousness three days ago. The screech of tires and white metal... The flash of a gun and its loud *crack*... I'd woken up multiple times in a panic. But Marco had been there each time to hold me and wipe away the tears, his calm, comforting presence an anchor amid the turmoil of my trauma.

Keys clattered against the entry table followed by the rustling of clothes. He was removing his coat and suit jacket and rolling up his shirtsleeves, his nightly ritual. He crossed our living room to where I sat with Sophie.

Our living room. In classic Marco fashion, he'd refused to let me go back to my condo after the hospital discharged me.

When we arrived at Terme di Boston, my clothes were already in his closet, and Sophie was curled up on his bed.

Cigar smoke, leather, and the heat of his body surrounded me, an embrace of safety and belonging I'd forever tie to Marco. He laid his hands on my shoulders and kissed the top of my head. "Ciao, amore mio."

He dismantled the messy bun piled on top of my head, something he'd become fond of doing over the past couple days, and my hair fell past my shoulders. He ran his fingers through it, and I closed my eyes, relishing the tingle of the strands pulling on my scalp.

"How are you?" I asked, not daring to turn and risk twisting my broken ribs and causing myself more pain.

He bent down and whispered in my ear. "Now that I'm with you? È tutto perfetto."

Warmth spread across my neck and down my spine, and for a moment, I forgot about my broken ribs. I leaned back to look up at him and pain lanced my side. I winced, hissing on a sharp intake of breath. "Ow," I whined and resumed my safe position.

He walked around the end of the couch and sat next to me, concern breaking through the determined set to his brow and jaw. "You're hurting."

"Getting hit by a car will do that."

He grunted and narrowed his eyes. "You want to be with me."

"I do, but you already know that."

"Even knowing what it means. Outliving your family and friends, watching them fade. Moving every few decades. Living with a Mafia Don."

"At least you admit it, now." I gave him an arch look.

"I'm serious, Anna," he grumbled.

"Fine," I said, exasperated. "Yes. I want to be with you even knowing what it means."

"You're sure."

"Cross my heart, hope to die…"

"Don't joke like that," he warned, and his eyes sparkled red.

"So serious," I whined.

"This is serious."

"I know, but I already told you. I choose you. Which means I choose whatever life I need to choose to have you. I need you to believe—really believe—I'm strong enough to handle that choice."

The corner of his mouth twitched like it wanted to smile and he wouldn't let it. He picked up a section of my hair and spun it around his finger. "Of course, you're strong enough. I should have known better than to doubt you." He kissed my forehead, and the touch of his soft lips sent prickles of pleasure skittering across my skin. "I can ease your pain." The offer held a world of promise. Another kiss. "If you let me."

We stared into each other's eyes, finally at our crossroads. After this, our lives would be irrevocably changed. Our commitment to one another would start with me at his wrist and him at my neck, and there would be no turning back.

I didn't feel an ounce of anxiety. No sweaty palms. No doubt. No fear. Just unshakable certainty that this was right, that he was right. Life, even the short life of a human, wasn't worth living without Marco.

"I love you."

His eyelids fluttered closed as if he needed to give my words time to settle in his body, to let himself feel the weight of their truth. When he opened them, fire streaked through their obsidian depths.

He threaded his fingers into my hair and held my gaze with crimson intensity. "Ti amo, mia bellissima Anna. Sei il mio cuore. Sei la mia anima. I love you, my beautiful Anna. You are my heart. You are my soul."

Tendrils of fire spread to encompass his irises, and he lifted his wrist to his mouth. His lips parted, and his eye teeth descended, their tips elongating and sharpening until they extended an inch beyond his upper jaw. He slashed his wrist with the tip of one fang, and it cut like a razor. Blood pooled at the wound and trailed down his muscled forearm.

He held his wrist to my mouth, and my eyes followed the red stream down his arm. "Drink," he said, low and demanding.

Curious and alive with anticipation, I ran my tongue along the trail of blood, starting at his elbow and ending at the clean slash across his wrist. I lapped the thick liquid into my mouth, and it coated my tongue, its metallic bite unmistakable. I'd expected my instincts to rebel, to shiver with revulsion and gag, but his warm, sweet blood slid down my throat without issue or hesitation.

Marco stared at my mouth, transfixed, and his eyes glowed with unbridled need. He nodded, encouraging me, and I looked back down at his wrist. I ran my tongue over the wound, licking the blood pooled there before closing my lips over the slash.

I drank.

He groaned at the first pull, a primal, masculine sound heavy with satisfaction. More of his sweet nectar coated my mouth, and I relished its taste and the warmth of it traveling down my throat with each decadent swallow. I couldn't get enough. I pulled harder, filling my mouth with Marco's blood and holding his wrist in place, ravenous for more.

He squeezed his hand in my hair and pulled me off his wrist. "Enough," he growled.

I gasped for air.

Heightened awareness bombarded my senses. The room looked sharper, and Marco's breath roared like the ocean. The pain in my sides dulled with each heartbeat, and my muscles tingled with vitality.

Inside the blazing inferno of his eyes, Marco's dilated pupils held me in place. He lifted his wrist to his lips and swiped his tongue across the wound. The slash closed, leaving a faint red impression that faded as quickly as the pain in my ribs.

I licked the remains of his blood from my lips, over-whelmed by my senses and panting from the power surging through my veins. His breath came fast and heavy, and his eyes trailed down to my neck, his grip tightening in my hair.

Heat shot to the space between my legs in anticipation of his fangs sinking into my neck and fulfilling the fantasy I'd yearned for since the gala. He slid his hand around my back and pulled me close. His jaw muscle twitched, a silent struggle to contain his passion. He lowered his head, and I shoved my hands into his hair, urging him on his path to my blood. He traced my artery with his tongue, and his chest rumbled with satisfaction.

I sucked in a breath, my clit and breasts swelling with unknown need. He closed his mouth over my neck and sucked, drawing my artery and blood toward his mouth. He released me, his heavy breath hot in my ear. "Do you want this, Anna? Tell me you want this. I need to hear it one last time."

"Yes. Marco. I want this. I want you."

My throaty plea barely escaped my lips before Marco's fangs pierced my neck.

I gasped at the stab of pain, but the shock of his bite was immediately replaced by a rush of pleasure. Warmth radiated out from where his fangs penetrated my flesh. It spread down my neck and across my shoulders, following the path of his venom through my veins.

He closed his lips around the wound and drank, sucking

blood from my neck and wrenching a groan from my lungs. With each pull, the venom spread, and the remaining pain and tension in my body vanished, replaced by euphoria. He tightened his grip, holding my relaxed body in place, and I gave over to the sensation of his feeding.

Heat spread and surged through my body, and every nerve ending tingled, hypersensitive to even the slightest touch. His fingertips danced across my skin from my back to my front, and when he ran his thumb over my nipple, I gasped and arched my back begging for more.

"Marco," I sighed, dazed and dizzy. He'd barely touched me, and already I was on the verge of something spectacular. "Please. I need you inside me. I need you to love me."

He released my neck, his lips trailing lightly across my sensitive flesh. My chest heaved with panting breath, and my heart pounded with raging desire. He licked the wound and lifted me off the couch and into his arms. I ran my fingertips over his lips, swollen from feeding, and marveled at their beauty. He shivered and set me on my feet next to his bed.

"How do you feel?" He pulled my T-shirt over my head and brought my hair forward, laying it across my shoulders.

"Strong. Alive."

He ran his hands down my sides, hooked his thumbs around the waistband of my thong, and pulled it down to my ankles in one leisurely motion before trailing his hands along my legs on his way back up. He towered over my naked body, and I lifted my eyes to meet his hungry gaze.

"Unbelievably horny," I finished.

His chest rumbled with laughter and a rare smile blessed his handsome face.

"I waited almost a century to drink from a woman whose blood was destined for my lips and my lips alone. I want to spend my eternity tasting only you."

He pressed his lips to mine, kissing me softly, tenderly, in a way that conveyed all the love in his promise.

"Consuming only you."

He kissed me again, this time using his tongue to make love to my mouth with slow, gentle strokes.

"Loving only you."

He trailed his lips along my jaw to the other side of my neck.

"Worshipping every inch of your body. Here." One of his fangs glided across my skin. He didn't bite, but closed his mouth around where his tongue stroked my neck. Heat pooled between my legs.

The soft touch of his lips and the sharp edge of his fangs moved down my shoulder and past my chest until he reached my breasts.

"Here." He teased my nipple with his fang, pulled it into his mouth, and sucked. The shock of desire was so intense, I grabbed his shoulders to steady myself.

"Here." His kisses moved to the other nipple, and his fang broke skin when he dragged my sensitive peak between his teeth. Liquid fire sped through my breast, making it burn with need. I pinched and tugged on my other nipple wanting to mimic the feel of his teeth, and a deep, delicious ache traveled down my spine. I shifted my weight, my need to feel him inside me almost unbearable, and my arousal dripped onto the inside of my thigh.

He continued his sensual torment, trailing his lips, tongue, and fangs down my stomach until he knelt before me. He kissed me, just above my naked pussy, and my breath quickened. He looked up, eyes blazing demonic red, fangs extended just past his bottom lip.

"And here." He dipped his tongue between my folds and dragged it from my entrance to my clit. He closed his lips over my pulsing sex and pulled it into his mouth caressing it with his tongue.

"More," I breathed and shoved my hands into his thick, wavy hair. I pressed him closer. "More."

He released me, draped my leg over his shoulder, and kissed the inside of my thigh from my knee to where my wetness had spread onto my leg. He licked my pleasure from my thigh, and a slow rumble of contentment vibrated through his shoulder into my leg.

"You taste as good as your blood."

His hands closed around my hips, and he pulled me to his mouth. He swept the flat of his tongue up and down the length of my seam, moving in steady strokes until I was drenched. The venom leaking from his fangs tingled where it touched, intensifying the erotic sensations of his expert tongue. He covered my clit with his mouth and sucked in a slow, rhythmic way that made it feel like he was feeding, and I came apart.

My orgasm sent waves of pleasure crashing through my body, each pulse tearing long breathy sighs from my lungs. My fingers tightened in his hair, and my legs shook, nearly giving out, but he held me in place, hands squeezing my hips like a vise.

I descended to Earth from my physical nirvana, and he lifted my leg off his shoulder and stood. I staggered under my own weight, delirious with feeling, but he steadied me. He ran a hand down his face, swiping my wetness from his mouth, and unbuckled his pants.

I swayed as if drugged, lightheaded from the sweet aftermath of my first orgasm under the influence of his blood and his bite. With heavy-lidded eyes, I watched the most darkly beautiful man I'd even known undress.

He stood before me in boxer briefs, and I couldn't resist touching him. I ran my palms up his thick, muscled torso to his neatly trimmed chest hair, trailed my fingertips across his broad shoulders, and clasped my hands behind his neck, pulling him toward me as I stood on my toes to kiss him.

I tasted myself on his lips, and the flavor of my desire caused a swell of aching need. My breasts felt heavy. I pressed them into his torso wanting my nipples to brush against the planes of his abs, wanting his hardness against my belly. As if he read my mind, he wrapped his arms around my waist and lifted me off the floor. He kissed me savagely, devouring my mouth with a hunger that had only grown more rabid since nearly losing our future.

He inched us back until my legs brushed against the edge of the bed. I broke the kiss and scooted myself back. Extending my arms overhead, I laid down, writhing in sensual bliss atop the cloud of cool linens, presenting myself like a sexual gift fit for a king.

He shoved his thumbs into the tops of his boxer briefs and pushed them down. The swollen length of his cock sprang free, hard, proud, and ready to dominate. I opened my legs in wanton invitation.

He climbed onto the bed, on his knees between my legs, eyes red and hungry with blood lust. He held his cock at its base and ran the tip through my folds, coating it with my desire and teasing my clit with its broad head. But I wanted him inside me, wanted his thickness to fill me. I turned my head to the side, brushing my hair away to expose my neck, and spread my knees wider.

He descended, hovering over me on his forearms, and ran his tongue up the length of my neck, bringing his mouth to my ear. "I've never done this," he whispered and pinched my earlobe between his teeth. "In all my years, I've never fed while making love." He lifted his head, took my chin in his hand, and turned my face to look into my eyes. "You are the first. And the last. The only. La mia bellissima Anna."

The slow way he inched his thick cock into my wet heat was delicious agony. My walls gripped him, tightening, pulling, as hungry for him as he was for my neck. He pressed forward until he was fully seated, and his hard length stretched me to the exquisite edge of pain.

He turned my head to the side and licked me from collarbone to ear.

"I love you," he whispered and plunged his fangs into my neck.

A guttural sound emerged from deep within his body, a primal rumble that held almost a century's worth of longing and expectation. I gasped at the intensity of its rawness and the overwhelming sensation of him penetrating my body, my blood, and my soul. I twined my fingers behind his head and held him in place, just for a moment. A moment neither of us had shared or ever would share with another soul, a moment that was perfectly and singularly ours, a moment I never wanted to end.

He moved his hips, slowly and sensually, burying himself inside me and drinking my blood as he eased back. The feel of his cock in my pussy and his fangs in my neck brought me to heights of ecstasy I'd never imagined. Pleasure became my world, and I wanted to lose myself to its sultry embrace.

His hips stilled, and he lifted his head, licking my wounds and his lips. He propped himself up on his elbows and held my face between his hands, running his thumbs along my cheekbones, wonder and tears alive in his crimson gaze. "You taste divine." The rim around his dilated pupils flared like the sun, and his hips moved again, gently and lovingly, while he stared into my eyes.

His thrusts became more urgent, and he lifted himself to his hands. "I need to fuck you," he growled.

I laughed, threw my arms overhead, and arched my back, offering him my breasts. He pulled one of my nipples between his teeth and started pumping himself in and out of me in fast, steady strokes.

The beginnings of another orgasm danced along my spine, the venom in my veins fueling the sensation of Marco's thick cock moving inside me. He pressed up onto his knees and pulled my hips off the bed, pistoning his faster and harder.

My breasts bounced with each thrust. I took them in my hands, massaging them and squeezing my nipples. Marco groaned and shivered, his reaction spiking my pleasure. I repositioned my hands and pushed my breasts up and together, serving my nipples to him like a feast.

"Fuuuck," he groaned and dropped my hips to the bed. His mouth crashed into my left breast, and he sucked my nipple into his mouth. His hips slowed, and the base of his cock stroked the top of my pussy and tickled my clit, driving me to the edge.

A sharp pain stabbed my breast and sent hot, erotic fire straight to my nipple. Marco growled, a hum of animalistic pleasure. His venom spread fast and furious and drove me to physical ecstasy. My arms fell to my sides and the tension in my legs released as Marco drew my orgasm out with each rock of his hips. My breathy cries echoed through the penthouse, each pulse of pleasure amplified by the venom in my veins.

He freed my breast and propped himself up onto his forearms, the muscles in his neck taut with his imminent release. My blood smeared his bottom lip. He licked it away, and with that last drop, his orgasm took control. He grunted, loud and harsh, and his hips stilled, his cock jerking inside me. My walls clenched around him, greedy for every drop of his pleasure as we stared into each other's eyes, panting through the final pulses and twitches of our shared bliss.

He lowered his lips to mine and with passionate sweeps of his tongue told me more with a kiss than words could convey. He relaxed, pulling himself out of my body, and lay next to me, burying his face in my hair. I trailed my fingers down his sweaty spine, and he shivered.

Liberated-Anna was finally whole, her awakening complete, and she'd found her salvation in a man who'd been searching for his own.

"Amore mio." He kissed my neck. "La mia Anna." He kissed my forehead and looked into my eyes. "You were worth the wait."

Chapter Thirty-One

Anna

Two Weeks Later

Jeff sat at a table near the entrance of Scholar's Café staring at his phone in one hand and holding a cup of coffee in the other. It seemed like just yesterday we'd sat at that same table and he'd offered me the job with Cambridge Management Group to test the waters of working in the real world. A lot had changed since that fate-filled meeting.

"Hey, sweaty," he said.

I grabbed a napkin off the table and blew my runny nose. "Hey, yourself," I said and plopped into the chair across from him. I picked up one of the two glasses of ice water and drained it.

"Coffee?" he asked.

"Please."

He flagged down one of the waiters while I removed my hat and gloves and unzipped my windbreaker.

"How was your run?"

I'd followed the same course I always did, running along the Charles River from Harvard to East Cambridge. But when

I'd reached the domed and columned entrance to MIT at Killian Court, I'd stopped. That's where I'd stood on stage for commencement, adorned in my regalia and an ear-to-ear smile, my parents waving to me from the audience.

MIT had been the epicenter of my life and career for over twenty years—learning, studying, teaching, growing—and the debt of gratitude I owed it had made my throat constrict. But it was time to move on. Our marriage had come to an end, and the divorce was bittersweet.

"Good," I said with a resigned smile. "It was good."

"What can I get you?" A server appeared, holding a pot of coffee.

"A cappuccino for her—"

"Extra hot," I added.

"Extra hot," Jeff said with a smirk. "And a caprese sandwich for us to split."

"You got it," the waiter said and headed back behind the counter.

Funny. Amid all the revolution, there were some things I never wanted to change. Like caprese sandwiches at Scholar's with Jeff.

"Early lunch today," Jeff said.

"Yeah, sorry. Marco and I are leaving at one for Amherst."

"Meeting the parents?" He quirked a teasing smile.

"Sounds ridiculous, doesn't it? A middle-aged man going to ask his middle-aged girlfriend's parents for permission to marry?" I chuckled. "But you know Marco."

He laughed. "I do. And I think it's sweet. They'll appreciate it."

The waiter returned with my cappuccino, and I held the mug in both hands to steal its warmth.

"Is something wrong?" Jeff scrunched his eyebrows and examined me. "You seem a bit off."

I lifted the mug to my lips and took a tentative sip of the scalding brew. "A little maudlin, that's all."

"About…"

"I'm ready to leave MIT," I said, the closing of one chapter and the opening of another an emotional upheaval that tightened my chest. Tears prickled my eyes.

Jeff's mouth formed a tight smile. He folded his hands on the table. "You sure?"

The urge to cry burned the back of my throat. "More than I've been about anything in a long, long time."

His smile broke free of his restraint, and he reached across the table and grabbed my hand. "I am so happy for you, Anna. You deserve to feel fulfilled. You've worked too hard not to get up every morning and enjoy what you do." His voice cracked and lips quivered, and his unconditional love and support opened the floodgates.

Tears spilled down my face, and I laugh-cried for several breaths, a huge grin plastered across my face. "Thank you." I swiped the tears away. "Thank you for understanding. Thank you for getting this. For getting me."

He took off his glasses to wipe the tears from his scruffy cheeks. "I'd be a horrible best friend if I didn't."

I laughed nervously, struggling with all the emotion.

The server came back with our caprese sandwich, and Jeff didn't waste any time. He split it in half and lifted his portion to his wide-open mouth.

I chuckled. No, I didn't want this part of my life to change at all.

"So," he said through the mouthful. "What are you going to do instead?"

"Well…" I sunk my teeth into the sandwich and chewed thoughtfully. "I think I'd like to take a month off. Enjoy not working for a change. Marco wants to go to Italy for a couple weeks. Says we need the break. I tend to agree."

Jeff snorted. "No doubt. I wouldn't mind a break myself, and I didn't go through half of what you did." He popped a few chips in his mouth. "But then what? I know you. You're going to get real bored real fast."

"No kidding. One month is about all the vacation I can handle. So, I was hoping..." I picked at the edge of my sandwich. "When I get back..." I lifted my eyes. "I could come work for you?" Jeff stopped chewing, the tremendous bite held in his cheeks like a chipmunk. "I want to join your team. Get assigned to jobs like the one I just finished. Go to sites, work with clients, solve problems. I want to be a consultant."

His mouth arched into a smile that reached his eyes and wrinkled his crow's feet. He finished chewing, and his smile broadened, smug and eminently pleased. "Liked it, did you?"

Satisfaction and gratification swelled in my chest when I thought about the job I'd completed for DEI. It also left a sinking sensation in my gut, the reality of the truths I'd uncovered a painful reminder that not all stories had a happy ending. Regardless, I had made an impact, and however painful, it had helped DEI and Marco. I couldn't deny the depth of my newfound fulfillment.

"I did. I really did." It was time to start the next chapter of my career. Time to get uncomfortable and explore new spaces. Time to challenge myself and shatter the beliefs that had held me back from realizing my dreams. "So, do I have a job?"

"Hmm. I don't know." Jeff leaned back in his chair and stretched his arms overhead. "I'm not sure you have the qualifications. I mean, you did transfer to MIT for your doctorate instead of staying at HBS." His lips twitched through the barb.

I narrowed my eyes into a deathly glare, picked up a chip, and tossed it at his face. It bounced off his glasses and landed in his lap. He picked it up, popped it in his mouth, and chewed through a wicked grin.

"I love you," I said, laughing at antics that hadn't changed in twenty-five years.

"I know. I love you, too. And yes, of course, you have a job with CMG. Michael would divorce me if I turned you away." He winked and reached for the final bite of my sandwich. "Are you going to eat that?"

"Yes!" I swatted at his hand. "God, you're a bottomless pit! Michael is a saint."

"Don't tell him that. He already has a swollen head."

"You love it."

"I do."

Jeff's face lit up with affection, and for the first time in my life, I knew exactly how he felt. I finally had a deep, love-filled connection of my own.

BARREN TREES and melting snow sped past the passenger side window. The afternoon was overcast, gray clouds portending more snow, not uncommon for the second week of March. The turnpike was quiet, not a lot of traffic for a Saturday, and we drove in silence, enjoying the peace after the turmoil of the past month.

I glanced at Marco, and his handsome profile with its Roman nose and strong jaw sent a flutter through my chest. Months after our first meeting and he still evoked the same reaction, but now unconditional love accompanied lust.

I picked up his hand resting on the shifter between us. The big rock on my ring finger glinted in the afternoon light when he lifted my hand to his lips.

"I can't stop staring at it." I'd had the ring for all of two days, and I don't think my eyes had left the four-carat ruby for more than a few minutes at a time.

"It's a beautiful stone and given the amount of money I

paid for it, please, stare at it as much as possible." The corner of Marco's mouth ticked up in a wry grin.

I pulled my hand out from his and swatted his shoulder. "I told you it was too much."

"I'm joking, amore mio. It's not even a fraction of what you deserve." He glanced at me. "Or a fraction as beautiful." He retrieved my hand and brought my fingers to his lips for another kiss, then rested our joined hands on his thigh.

We'd promised ourselves to each other the night we'd bonded in blood, and our commitment was as sacred as any human ceremony. Blood demons signified their bond with rubies not diamonds, the red gemstones a symbol of the blood shared between partners. He'd surprised me after lunch on Thursday by taking me to a private appointment at one of Boston's most exclusive jewelers and telling me to pick out my bond ring.

I lifted my hand, holding it in front of me for the millionth time, and marveled at the simple setting around the beautiful stone. I couldn't think of a more appropriate token of our love. "My mom is going to squeal like a teenager when she sees this."

Marco chuckled. "I can't wait to meet her. And your father. I can't wait to thank them for bringing you into this world."

My cheeks heated. The things he said to me.

As far as blood demons were concerned, we were married, the only thing left a party with his family and friends to celebrate our bond. But I hadn't grown up in his world, and he knew how important it was to me to have a proper wedding with my parents and my small group of friends—Jeff, Michael, a few former coworkers from MIT, and now Siobhán. And Marco, being the traditional, over-the-top Mafia Don he was, insisted, "If we're going to do this, we're going to do it right."

"I can't wait to meet your parents, too," I said.

"And you'll get to. At the wedding." He gave me a quick glance and winked.

We'd decided to get married in Italy at the new property in Tuscany after renovations were complete. It wouldn't be ready for another nine months to a year, but we weren't in a hurry. We were already bonded, and that's all that mattered.

"And spend more time with Gina. She's lovely."

"As long as the two of you don't conspire against me, I'll allow it."

I snorted. I'd had lunch with Gina a few times over the past two weeks, and Marco and I had gone to his family home in the North End twice for dinner. She was a phenomenal cook, which after almost eighty years of practice, shouldn't have been a surprise.

There had been tension, though, between Marco and Gina. An unspoken heaviness weighed on their relationship. It showed in the brief moments when they reminisced about the past or talked about family, and I knew it was because of Luca.

I chewed the side of my fingernail. "Have you heard any news about Luca?"

"No." His reply was clipped and gruff.

"Have you—have you asked?"

"No. I told you. I'm done."

"Gina isn't."

Marco's jaw worked.

Despite his tough exterior, this thing with Luca was killing him. He'd never be able to walk away as easily as he wanted everyone to believe. Luca was his son.

He glanced at me and must have seen the concern in my face because he frowned. "Gina and Vinnie have known each other their whole lives. She'll check on Luca herself."

I didn't argue even though I knew cutting Luca out of his life wouldn't make him happy, not in the long run. Especially considering how it affected his relationship with his sister.

"I know you talk to Vinnie, now that you two have your…" I swallowed, still struggling to discuss Mafia matters with my husband. "Arrangement."

"With conditions," Marco interjected sharply.

"With conditions," I amended.

Marco had been clear when he outlined the details of his newly formed alliance with the Valenzanos. There were non-negotiable conditions—no drugs and no weapons the two lynchpins. Vinnie and his crew acknowledged him as Don DeVita, marking his official reentrance into Cosa Nostra and establishing him as the head of a second family in control of the Boston Italian Mafia. He assured me, and I believed him, that his intention was to protect blood demons and their Sources from the feds, nothing more. He and Vinnie still needed to work through the details, and the new arrangement would be an adjustment, but he was already more at ease than he'd been since we'd met.

"Now that you have this arrangement, I know you talk to him, and I know he's responsible for Luca's future. You could ask."

He placed his hand on my thigh and squeezed. He was quiet for several minutes, pensively staring down the long stretch of turnpike.

"I had to let Luca go, Anna." His voice cracked, and the muscles in his jaw twitched, the telltale sign he was trying to control his emotions. "I can't protect him anymore. I tried to raise him right, tried to do right by Tony, but that's all I could do. He needs to live his life and accept the consequences of his actions." He looked at me for a brief moment. "We all do."

He was right, of course, and I was proud of him for admitting it. The weight of responsibility Marco carried for those he loved was heavy. And he loved so passionately and thoroughly. He'd finally let go of the impossible burden, and as difficult as it was, he'd known it was the only path to peace and happiness.

Our comfortable silence returned as we followed the off-ramp north toward Amherst. Soon, we exited the interstate into my old neighborhood and turned onto my parents' street. Marco parked the Range Rover in front of my parents' little slice of suburbia and turned off the car.

He reached across the seat, shoved his hand into my hair, and wrapped his thick fingers around the nape of my neck, pulling me to him. His lips moved tenderly over mine, and he slid his tongue into my mouth telling me how much he loved me with a slow, passionate kiss.

He leaned his forehead against mine. "No more talk of Luca or the Mafia or the feds or any of it today, okay?"

"Okay."

"It'll all still be there when we get home. I know things are messy, and I will deal with it, but today is about you and me and your parents. I don't want the heaviness to ruin our time together."

"Thank you." I pulled away so I could look him in the eyes. I took his face between my hands. "I love you."

"Good, because I plan on loving you for eternity."

Epilogue

Luca

Fuzzy outlines and dull colors materialized under the glow of a single lightbulb hanging from the ceiling. My shoulders and head ached. They throbbed in time with my pulse, every beat fresh agony. I blinked, trying to clear my vision, and realized I was only seeing out of one eye. I moved to touch the other—was it missing or swollen shut?—but my arm wouldn't obey. My wrist snagged on rope, and the tight fibers stung my raw skin.

Awareness surfaced through the pain. My wrists were tied together, arms stretched overhead, and my body hung from the rope binding them. My vision solidified with each additional blink. I tipped my head to see the solid object beneath my feet, and a wave of nausea barreled through me. I dry-heaved until it passed.

A stool teetered under my slack legs. I pushed against it, trying to take the strain out of my shoulders. Rough wood scratched the soles of my bare feet. I pressed myself up, and pain radiated up my legs from my knees. I groaned.

Footsteps echoed through the warehouse that was taking

shape around me. The silhouette of a man approached from across the room. Another man sat at a table to my left.

The footsteps stopped, replaced by a familiar accented voice that echoed through the silence. "You're awake."

The statement held neither consternation nor applause, and I lifted my chin off my chest, swallowing through the dryness to make a smart remark, but no words escaped. At least, none I was willing to exchange for more torture.

"Not surprising given you haven't fed in..." Vinnie Valenzano looked at his watch like it counted weeks instead of hours. "Well, doesn't matter. Our kind wasn't meant to go without blood for this long, especially considering the number of times you had to heal."

I'd lost count of the beatings and maiming after the third or fourth session. He'd brought in a Source after the first one, allowed me to feed long enough to heal the worst of the damage. Damage that would have killed a human. Since then, he'd let me starve, my immortal body consuming itself to heal. The process took longer and longer with each session, drawing out my torment and emaciating my body. I couldn't endure any more. I needed to feed.

"I think you've learned your lesson, judging by your lack of commentary this time. Take him down."

The man at the table rose. Muted footsteps approached from behind. Something creaked. A short, muscled man wrapped his arms around my legs just above my knees and lifted me to slacken the rope. Hot, searing pain shot up my legs from my knees and ripped a scream from my lungs. The guard behind me unfastened the rope from whatever it was attached to, and my arms fell like overcooked noodles, limp, useless pieces of flesh hanging from shoulders on fire.

I collapsed onto the man holding my legs, and despite my height, he caught me and lowered me to the ground. I shivered, the hard surface cold and unyielding against my starved, naked body.

"Your knees are broken, so I wouldn't try to stand. And your right eye is missing."

The punishment came back to me in an avalanche of pain, violent struggles, and tortured screams, and I dry-heaved, reliving the excruciating horror.

"I'll bring in a Source shortly, after we discuss what's going to happen. Capisce?"

The man who'd caught me bent over my prone, broken body and slipped a knife through the ropes around my wrists. I opened my mouth to say yes, but all that came out was a grunt.

"Get him some water."

Muted footfalls retreated. I pressed my shaking hands into the concrete and tried to prop myself up, but I collapsed under my own weight, my body too weak to even raise itself off the ground.

Vinnie crouched next to me, resting his forearms on his knees, and lowered his head to stare into my remaining eye. "What am I going to do with you, Luca? Hm?" He shook his head. "So much potential, but so consumed by vendetta." He frowned. "It's made you sloppy," he said with disgust.

He leaned closer and grabbed my swollen cheeks, squeezing my jaw between thick fingers. I winced and tears spilled down my face, my eye watering from the entirety of my pain.

"You broke two of our most sacred laws. You attacked a made man without provocation and without sanction." He tightened his grip on my face. My breath quickened and made sickening sounds through the squeezed opening he made of my bloody mouth. "You attacked his girlfriend. What are you? Stunad? Anna Barone almost died because of you. And if Ciarán Shaughnessy's cousin hadn't been there with her, you'd have a fucking turf war on your head. Let me be clear, Luca. If Gina DeVita hadn't intervened on your behalf, if you weren't a blood demon, you'd be dead."

He released my chin and pushed me away as he stood. Bloody drool leaked out of the corner of my mouth and onto the floor.

The squat guard returned and shoved a glass of water at me. I struggled to raise my arm.

"Help him," Vinnie barked.

The guard lifted my head and poured water between my cracked, swollen lips. I drank as much as I could, nearly choking in my efforts to swallow. I coughed, sputtered, and turned my head away, but those few mouthfuls cleared the fog.

Ciarán Shaughnessy's cousin? With Anna?

"Lucky for you, I agreed to spare your life knowing I could bring you to death's door. Again, and again." He crouched to look me in the eye. "Your blood debt to Cosa Nostra is paid in full, Luca Moretti. Do you hear me? But if you *evah* pull a stunt like that again, if you *evah* break one of our laws again, there will be no mercy, no matter how much Gina begs. Capisce?"

"Capisce," I croaked.

"You can't go back to work for the DeVitas. Marco is done. But I don't think you want that, do you? I don't think you ever really wanted that. You always had a foot in the Valenzano door. You've certainly done your damnedest to lie, cheat, and steal your way into my organization, even if your efforts were ill-advised."

The click of heels echoed across the room, closing in on our location.

Anna was at Vesuvio last night. Did you know that? So was Siobhán.

Marco's voice echoed through my skull, and the connection snapped into place. I cried out from a new source of pain —the shattered remains of what was left of my heart crumbling into dust. My stomach lurched, and I vomited the water I'd just drank.

"Ah. Your Source. Pull him up."

The squat guard hoisted me up by my armpits. At that angle, all I could see were a pair of heels and stockinged legs. I slowly lifted my head off my chest and found Vinnie standing before me in a navy pin-stripe suit, the quintessential image of an Italian gangster.

He adjusted his cufflinks and stared down at me. "You work for me now, and unlike Marco, I didn't promise Tony shit. Pull yourself together and follow the rules, or I'll put a bullet through your head just like Paddy Shaughnessy did to your father."

He nodded to the guard escorting the Source, turned on the heels of his Italian leather Oxfords, and walked out of the warehouse.

The guard nudged the Source forward, and she sat on the ground next to me. She scooted closer until her breasts pressed against my limp body. Her hair was tied back, and she wrapped her arms around my shoulders taking my weight off the guard and onto her chest. She tilted her head and exposed her neck in front of my mouth.

I bit her, hard, greedily sucking the blood from her artery in deep, hungry pulls. She moaned, and her body slackened as mine strengthened.

And as I fed, as my mind sharpened with each mouthful of blood, the events leading up to my time in that Godforsaken hellhole came into focus.

The connection between Ciarán Shaughnessy's cousin and who'd been at Vesuvio that night no longer made me sick. It made me angry, and my fury rose knowing Marco had a fucking rat in his crew. He may have disowned me, and I fucking deserved it for hurting Anna, but I loved him, and Cosa Nostra didn't tolerate rats.

I released my bite and shoved the woman's slack body away from me. She was drained; one more pull and she would've died from blood loss. "Bring me another," I growled.

The squat guard picked her up and carried her out of the room.

My luck had run out, stolen from me by a devastating beauty who'd once stolen my heart. But the two-faced Shamrock had fooled me for the last time. There would be no end to my vendetta. My quest for vengeance was just beginning.

THE END

Thank you for reading!

Marco and Anna have their Happily Ever After, but the DeVita, Moretti, and Valenzano stories are far from over.

Find out what happens to Luca, Siobhán, and the rest of the crew in His Dark Vendetta, coming 2025.

For release updates, join my newsletter at www.katelynbrehm.com

Acknowledgments

This book was supposed to be the third novella in the Demons Among Us series. It had other plans. The concept started as two lines of dialogue that popped into my head over a year ago right in the middle of drafting *The Siren's Song*.

> "Are you a vampire?"
> "No. Vampires aren't real. I'm a blood
> demon."

Needless to say, the story avalanched from there. As I fleshed out the characters and the world, I quickly realized I couldn't do Marco and Anna justice in a novella, and I couldn't do their world justice in a single book. So, here we are, the end of Bonded in Blood Book One, and I couldn't be happier that *Her Dark Salvation* sent me tumbling down this mountain.

Once again, it took a village, and there were several individuals whose support gave me the courage I needed to take the plunge. Zoey Ellis, my critique partner and dear friend, I'm so grateful we found each other. No matter what happens, this is our year, and I can't wait to embark on the next chapter of our stories together. Nico Rosso, your insights into craft and Romance are invaluable. Without you, this book would be a shadow of itself. Thank you for getting real with me and challenging me at every turn. Margaret Curelas, my intrepid copyeditor, faced with the unenviable task of beating my grammar into submission, thank you for answering my never-ending stream of questions about the cursed language that is English.

To the (very) small group of readers who have been with me since *The Art Collector*, thank you for taking a chance on a nobody indie author. I can't put into words how grateful I am for you. If for no other reason, I will keep writing for you.

And last, but by no means least, Rhonda Parrish. You are my rock. I couldn't do this writing thing without you. Thank you for guiding me on this wild ride, for keeping me grounded in what's important, and for always being there when I'm freaking out. I couldn't have asked for a better mentor, and I'm lucky to have you in my corner.

About the Author

Katelyn Brehm is a second-generation German-American and native of Milwaukee, Wisconsin. She grew up watching far too much Star Trek, so much so, she decided to dedicate her education and career to space exploration. When she's not reading and writing fantasy and romance, Kat works as an aerospace engineer at NASA's Jet Propulsion Laboratory. She lives in Pasadena, California with her husband and two cats, Mini Wheat and Pepper.

Visit Kat
www.katelynbrehm.com

Also by Katelyn Brehm

Demons Among Us

The Art Collector

The Siren's Song

Bonded in Blood

Her Dark Salvation

His Dark Vendetta (Coming 2025)